BLOOD
ALLEGIANCE

BLOOD
ALLEGIANCE
ELIN BARNES

Other novels by Elin Barnes

Justification for Murder

Smoke Screen

This is a work of fiction. Names, characters, organizations, places, events, and incidents are either products of the author's imagination or are used fictitiously.

Text copyright © 2016 by Elin Barnes.

Published by Paperless Reads
www.elinbarnes.com

ISBN 978-0-9899880-5-6

Cover design by
CeKwaSa
www.behance.net/Cekwasa

Printed in the United States of America.

This book is dedicated to my dad and my grandma.
I miss you both every day.

CHAPTER 1

Monday

Oscar saw the gun on the counter, peeking out from under his folded coat. He pushed it in until it was completely hidden and wiped his tearing eyes with the back of his hand. He turned toward the cutting board and felt the knife slide in as he continued to chop the onion. His eyes stung and he felt another tear run down his cheek, but when his stomach rumbled at the smell of sizzling peppers, he forgot all about it.

The restaurant door opened, making the bells chime. He smiled and glanced over his shoulder. Carol weaved around the tables toward him. Her baggy coat hung over her frame, making her look even smaller. Her hair was pulled back in a ponytail that bounced as she walked.

"Smells great," she said, setting her purse down, bracelets dangling on both wrists.

"I'm making fish fajitas. You said you're watching your cholesterol."

He threw in the onions and pushed the peppers and mushrooms around on the flat grill. He checked the trout and flipped it over.

"With all the food you make me, cholesterol is the last thing I'm worried about." She laughed and sat on a tall stool across from him.

He liked the open kitchen. It was one of the appeals of the restaurant, because the smells of the various foods flooded the place when it was busy with patrons. He also liked it because he could grill while Carol rested her chin on her interlaced fingers and watched him cook for her.

He set the spatula off to the side and leaned over to kiss her on the cheek. She met him halfway and gave him a bear hug.

"Damn, woman, how can you squeeze so tight with those skinny arms?"

"It has nothing to do with muscles," she said, pointing at his biceps. "I just love you so much."

Oscar reached for her hand and squeezed it. She gripped his and looked away. He knew what she was thinking.

"You have to let it go," he said. "We're here now, and we have the rest of our lives to be together."

Fine lines framed her eyes when she forced a smile. He turned and checked the food, then drizzled a few drops of virgin olive oil on the grill.

"I've been looking forward to this all day," she said. "It's nice that Berto lets us use his restaurant when it's closed."

"He's a good man."

He slid the fish and vegetables onto a platter. The tortillas still needed a minute.

"I'm surprised he closes at all. This place is always packed," she said.

"Not bad for a hole in the wall in the worst part of San Jose, right?" He smiled at her over his shoulder.

The bells over the door jingled. His gut twisted, and this time it had nothing to do with hunger.

"We're closed," he said, and cursed under his breath, remembering that he'd removed the gun from the small of his back because Carol didn't like him being armed around her.

10

Chavo Buenavente trudged in, followed by two of his compadres. Oscar didn't recognize either, which surprised him, since he'd known Chavo for almost fifteen years.

"Holy shit, look who we have here."

Chavo's smirk almost looked like surprise. Oscar suspected his rival had anticipated finding him alone. He looked at Carol. Her arms were crossed, as if she were suddenly cold.

Oscar sized up the two unfamiliar men. One was skinny but wiry and had a red scar that wound like a worm from his left eye to the collar of his white T-shirt. The other was almost a foot shorter than Chavo but wide as an armoire. He was the one who locked the door.

Keeping the men in sight, Oscar grabbed the butcher knife he'd used for the onions, but it was no match for the guns his rivals were holding. Chavo and Scarface had four on him. Shorty pointed two at Carol. In all the fights he'd had with Chavo over the years, he'd never been so grossly underarmed.

"Put that down, *perro*," Chavo said. "Or things will get real ugly real fast."

Oscar fanned his fingers around the grip of the knife and fought to even out his breathing to control the spiking adrenaline.

Chavo took a step toward him, and Oscar knew he had to let it go. He lifted both hands over his head, surrendering. Then he slowly lowered the blade onto the counter.

"What do you want? Me and you have been square for a couple years."

Scarface moved toward the south wall. Shorty stepped around Chavo, picked up the knife, and walked behind Carol, blocking the back door. Even if Oscar managed to distract them, there was no way for her to escape.

"Let her go. The two of us can settle whatever brings you here," he said.

"This *pendeja's* not going anywhere." Chavo waved the Beretta toward Carol's head.

Oscar stared at the guns. The barrels looked like black holes sucking him in. *Can I take them?* There was no way. Even if he tackled Chavo, one of his homies would get him before he could wrestle a gun free.

Chavo aimed back at Oscar. "You know my reputation. I never miss a shot."

Why did Chavo want to mess with him? How did he even know he was here? Berto was the only person who knew where he was on Monday nights, and he would never rat on him.

"You don't want a war. Spell out why the hell you're here, and let's get this over with. My food's getting cold."

Oscar saw the darkness in Chavo's eyes and wondered if others had experienced the same emptiness when looking into his own seconds before he killed them. It didn't matter—he would never know.

Chavo tucked one gun into his belt but kept the other raised. "Climb over the counter real slow and come stand by your woman." He pointed toward her left.

Oscar started moving but scanned his surroundings for anything he could use as a weapon. There was nothing. The knives were out of reach, and his gun was hidden under his jacket on the other side of the grill. Not even a fork was in sight. Unless he was prepared to fight with a Valentina hot sauce bottle, he would have to use his fists.

When Oscar reached Carol, she leaned into him, and he felt her trembling.

"That's cute and all, but move over there." Chavo wagged the firearm away from her.

Oscar bent to the left, following Chavo's directions, but at the last second he sprang toward him instead.

He heard a shot.

A fire pierced through his skin and muscle, right below the left clavicle. The impact pushed him sideways, and he fell over on the table behind him, his elbow landing on the chair that had just tumbled onto the floor. He felt his chest burning but fought to push himself up. He lost focus for a second. He shut his eyes but forced them open when he heard the piercing scream of a woman in pain.

Scarface had lifted Carol from the stool and subdued her with a chokehold. She fought for air, grabbing his arms, trying to pull them away from her neck. Oscar tried to get up. He wanted to run to her, protect her, save her, but he felt the cold barrel of a gun pressed against the nape of his neck.

Shorty grabbed his left arm and forced it behind his back. Oscar managed the pain with a grunt expelled through clenched teeth. The punk yanked his right arm and cuffed him with a zip tie.

Oscar spun around and head-butted Shorty. His forehead hit the thug's cheekbone hard enough for the skin to split.

"Motherfucker!"

Shorty wiped the blood off with his T-shirt and punched Oscar in the liver. The pain made him buckle.

Chavo came behind Oscar and kicked the back of his right knee so hard he collapsed on the floor, slamming his nose on the table. Blood gushed into his mouth and down his throat, choking him. He coughed. Red phlegm smeared Shorty's sneakers.

"Fool, stop this shit and get him settled over there," Chavo ordered.

Shorty grabbed Oscar's forearm and yanked him up. He was shocked by the ease with which Shorty lifted him off the floor. Oscar had over a foot on him, but the guy was built.

13

The punk led him to a booth and jammed the gun into his ribs. Oscar didn't budge, but the thug shoved him, making him lose his balance and land sideways on the seat. Shorty struck his forehead with the grip of the Ruger, opening a gash. Blood seeped into his eyes, muddying his vision. The coppery smell made him gag.

"Enough!" Chavo yelled. "Wipe the blood off his face. I want him to see what I'm gonna do to his bitch."

Oscar pulled away when Shorty leaned in to touch him. His hands pressed hard against the back of the booth, and his left arm started to feel numb. He tried to wipe the blood with his shoulder but couldn't quite reach.

Chavo walked up to Carol. Sweat moistened her face and her eyes were wide open, but she didn't cry. Scarface still had her in a chokehold. Her feet were barely touching the floor. Chavo reached out to caress her face. She spat at him, but the spittle landed flat next to his boot.

Chavo laughed as if amused by her provocation. The sound echoed in the empty restaurant. He pressed the Beretta's barrel against her cheek and pushed. Her head turned, reminding Oscar of the girl from *The Exorcist*. He let go and said, "*Puta*, if you do that again, I'll hurt you so bad you'll wish you were dead."

"If you touch me again, I'll kick you in the balls." She puffed her chest toward him. The venom in her voice matched her defiance.

"*Mis huevos son de metal*, bitch." He cupped his crotch with his free hand.

He took a step closer, grabbed the top of her blouse, and ripped it open, exposing her white bra. Scarface tightened his grip as she fought to pull away.

Oscar sprung out of the seat, but Shorty punched him, forcing him back in the booth. In a quick move, the thug climbed

14

on the seat behind him and grabbed Oscar's hair, hitting his head hard against the back of the booth. A second later he felt the barrel of the Ruger pushed against his right temple and he stopped fighting.

"Enjoy this, *joto*," Chavo said.

He smiled at Oscar as he pulled a switchblade from his pocket, then turned and cut Carol's bra.

CHAPTER 2

Tuesday

Darcy Lynch heard the phone ring. He opened his eyes but couldn't see much. It was still dark outside, and the breeze from the open window made him shiver. He rolled on the bed to reach for his cell and answered by the third ring.

"Wake up, sleeping beauty," Sorensen said. "I've called you several times already."

The call log was empty. "No, you haven't."

"Just saying that for effect. Come on, we have a murder to solve."

"We don't work together anymore."

Darcy got up and headed for the bathroom.

"On this one we do, partner. Virago asked for you specifically."

"It's a joint task-force case?" Darcy asked.

"Fucking A, dude. Stop with the questions and get your ass over here. I'll text you the address and fill you in when you get on your way."

Darcy threw the phone on the bed and went to take a shower.

A joint task-force case could be interesting. He hadn't worked with his old team for over three months—not since

Captain Virago transferred from the Santa Clara Sheriff's Office to San Jose PD to lead CATCH, the Cross-Agency Tactical California Homicide Unit. Because San Jose PD was the agency behind the effort, they required Virago to switch organizations and gave her the option to bring three people with her. She'd taken Detective Erik Sorensen and Jon Evans, the intern who got promoted to a full-time gig as the unit's tech guru.

She had to leave Darcy behind, pending the Internal Affairs investigation for his shootings in the patent troll case. When he was cleared, he thought Commander Virago would expedite his transfer, but it didn't happen. The one time he brought it up she said, "Things have changed since we moved over. I don't have the only say on who comes into the task force. I have to wait until I get the sergeant position filled, and then he'll need to vote on your application."

So he'd waited. He heard that a sergeant he didn't know had joined them, and for the next couple of months he checked his email, but nothing came. And now he'd given up on the idea of making the move altogether.

This morning's call had piqued his interest and reignited a bit of hope. He hated himself a little for it.

Ten minutes later Darcy revved the engine of his candy-apple-red 1965 Cobra and roared out of the garage. He waited to call Sorensen until he reached Highway 280. Traffic was flowing freely, though there were more cars than he'd expected this early in the morning.

"What's the story?" he asked as soon as Sorensen answered.

"Carol Montes."

"The lab tech?"

"Yes. You know her?"

Sorensen sounded surprised.

"By name only. She works on gang-related cases, right?"

"Yes. She was found murdered in my favorite Mexican joint of all places."

"El Grullense?"

"No. That one's good, but Berto's burritos have no match."

"If it's that good, how come you've never taken me there?"

"You haven't deserved it."

Darcy smiled and merged onto Highway 101 South toward East San Jose. He'd almost forgotten how annoying Sorensen was, and yet he missed being partnered with him.

"Okay, I'm close. Tell me about the case."

"Wait, your gatekeeper just showed up. I'll fill you in when you get here. Hurry up."

Sorensen hung up before Darcy could protest. Gatekeeper?

A few minutes later he arrived at the scene. The street was cordoned off with orange tape, indicating SJPD jurisdiction. They were the only agency in Silicon Valley that didn't use the more common yellow crime scene tape. Maybe Virago decided to run it under the task force because Carol worked for the Santa Clara County Crime Laboratory. That would be a good joint case to solidify the partnership between the San Jose PD and the Sheriff's Office and set the stage for the CATCH unit.

Darcy decided to stop speculating about why Virago had brought him on and focus on the case. He parked by one of the patrol cars and walked toward the restaurant. Berto's stood in the middle of the block, on the east side of the street. Two large bay windows with the blinds drawn all the way down flanked the wrought-iron door. He took in the scene as he got closer. About a dozen police cars blocked the area. Several uniforms held off the media and spectators. A few cops were knocking on doors, canvasing for witnesses and video evidence. All businesses were still closed behind metal bar gates with large padlocks.

18

Darcy flashed his credentials, and the officer doing the intakes wrote down his name, badge number, and the current time: 6:47 a.m.

He spotted Sorensen, who started walking toward him and said, "It's ugly, man. The worst I've seen in a long time."

"Any suspects?"

"She's processed more gang evidence and testified in more cases than anybody I know, so the list is huge. But I've never heard of the Mob doing anything like this in California before." Sorensen shook his head, then leaned closer to Darcy, probably to avoid being overheard, and added, "But we got tags."

"We know which one, then?"

Darcy tried to recall what little he knew about gangs in San Jose and what graffiti was associated with which, but it was all mushed together in his brain.

"So it seems, but the MO is out of character."

Sorensen shook his head and led the way to the restaurant. Darcy stared at the sweat stain on Sorensen's back and wondered why he'd been called in. Even if it was a CATCH case, he had no expertise on gangs, so it didn't make sense that Virago wanted him there. He followed Sorensen, wishing that he'd stopped for coffee before getting to the crime scene.

Berto's door opened, and a man stepped out of the restaurant. He had a healthy salt-and-pepper mane and thick stubble framing a square jaw.

Sorensen stopped in front of him and said, "Sergeant Quinn, meet Detective Darcy Lynch."

Darcy's whole body tensed up. He was pissed at himself for not picking up on Sorensen's warning that Quinn, the very person who was stalling his move to CATCH, was there. But now he understood why Virago wanted him on the case. She was probably forcing Quinn to finally vote yes or no on his transfer.

Darcy took one step toward Quinn and they shook hands. He couldn't help but feel that now he would be scrutinized and graded, as if he'd just graduated from the academy and was on his first tour with the field training officer.

"Carol's one of our own," Quinn said. "The fucking Diablos are going to pay."

His voice was raw. Darcy had experienced the same rage on other occasions, but not knowing Quinn personally, he decided to keep any comforting comments to himself.

"I don't know much about San Jose gangs. Can you walk me through the scene?"

Quinn locked eyes with him and stared back long and hard, as if Darcy had said something in a foreign language. Then without breaking eye contact he asked, "Why the hell are you here, then?"

Instead of waiting for a response, Quinn turned and walked back toward the restaurant, opened the door, and let it close behind him.

Sorensen grabbed it before it shut. "I guess he just came out to greet us," he told Darcy, and shrugged before following Quinn inside.

Darcy stood outside for a second, long enough to notice that the ironwork on the door was shaped into leaves and flowers. He rubbed his left temple and hoped the nascent headache was from lack of caffeine and not from the tense situation that was building before him. He took a deep breath and walked inside.

The restaurant wasn't very big and smelled of burnt chicken. Eight tables were to his right, neatly spaced in a rectangular grid. In front of him was a long counter, lined with bar stools. A pathway about five feet wide separated the high chairs from the booths, which extended all the way to the back door, leading to the bathrooms. Darcy counted four CSIs collecting evidence. He spotted Madison, the ME, and his associate at the opposite corner, in the open kitchen by the burners, and assumed the body was behind them.

All the tables were empty. Everything was clean. Except for the people working, the only things out of place were a broken table and a fallen chair. Darcy wondered why Sorensen had described it as one of the worst crime scenes he'd ever seen.

"I recovered a bullet," a tech said by the back wall. He sealed it in an evidence bag, made a few notations, and set it on the counter.

Quinn picked up the projectile and inspected it against the portable lights CSU had installed.

"A 9 mm," he said. "Nothing special about it. I hope we can match the striations."

"I've never heard of this place being a gang hangout before," Sorensen said.

"It's frequented by everybody, including gangsters."

Quinn leaned forward, checking the hole in the wall where the bullet had been lodged.

"Who discovered the body?" Darcy asked.

"Berto." Sorensen and Quinn spoke at the same time.

"He's the owner," Sorensen added.

"He came in to open the place, like any normal day. He noticed the door wasn't locked, walked in, turned the lights on and saw..."

Quinn sounded choked up. He coughed, probably trying to mask it.

"Then he saw Carol," Quinn ended.

As if on cue Madison moved, and Darcy saw Carol too. The sight caused him to take a step back. The burnt chicken smell he'd noticed when he came in was not chicken. It was the smell of burnt human flesh.

21

CHAPTER 3

Darcy felt his stomach churn. He'd never had the urge to throw up from the sight of a crime scene before, not even when he was a rookie. He swallowed and breathed through his mouth as he took a closer look at Carol. Her body was dismembered on top of the grill, but only some parts were burnt. The biggest piece was her head, her eyes still open, staring back at them as if this were a macabre Halloween joke. He knew his brain would soon acclimate to the smell, so when he felt the saliva accumulating in his throat, he forced himself to swallow.

Sorensen looked at him. "I warned you." He patted Darcy on the shoulder and turned toward Quinn. "Did you ever see anything like this when you worked at the Gang Suppression Unit?"

"I still work at GSU," Quinn said, still focused on the wall with the bullet hole. "A couple mean *cholos* like using knives, but no, nothing like this."

Quinn turned, and his eyes settled on Carol's remains.

Madison and the other lab coat began to place Carol's remains in a black body bag. The smell intensified while they worked. Darcy looked away, but the gruesome sight was imprinted on his brain.

"Sergeant, Detectives." Madison met them by the tables, as if he didn't want to yell his findings across the restaurant. "I'm sorry to say that my initial assessment is that several mutilations were done perimortem."

"Son of a bitch!"

Quinn kicked the table next to him. It slithered until it crashed onto the next one, a couple of feet away, misplacing a few evidence markers.

"What are you doing?" Darcy yelled.

Quinn's look was a mixture of incomprehension and madness.

"You're disturbing the crime scene," Darcy said.

"Disturbing the crime scene?" He spun around, as if looking for something, then said, "Hey you, lab coat."

The tech who'd retrieved the bullet from the wall looked at him.

"You guys took pics of the scene when you came in, right?"

The man nodded.

Quinn turned to face Darcy. "See, asshole."

Photos were not good enough for Darcy. He liked to inspect the crime scene as it was found. He started to talk, but Sorensen interrupted him.

"Doctor, anything else?"

Darcy was pissed but let it go to listen to the ME.

Madison remained quiet for a few more moments, probably waiting for the situation to cool off.

"I will have more information as soon as I get to the morgue," he said. "I would really appreciate it if at least one of you came to the autopsy."

The three of them nodded, but none committed. Darcy noticed that the ME looked gloomier than normal and assumed it was because he knew the victim.

After Madison left, Quinn walked over to the counter, stepping around the scattered yellow evidence markers.

"Give me the light," Quinn said to one of the CSIs.

He aimed it at the turned-over table. Faint traces of blood were barely visible under the forensic light source. The floor had more, but somebody had washed both surfaces off with bleach. It would be impossible to get DNA or even a blood type, but it was obviously blood.

"My bet is that the bullet that got stuck in the wall went through somebody standing right here." Quinn walked backward about five feet toward the door and extended this arm, simulating a gun with his fingers. "The shot was fired from around here."

Sorensen added, "We haven't found any more bullets or casings, so either this was the only shot fired, or they picked up after themselves."

Darcy did a 360 and inspected the room. "Madison didn't say anything about Carol being shot. It also doesn't make any sense that they cleaned this mess but left Carol's body."

"And left plenty of blood behind the counter." Sorensen pointed with his index finger to where Madison had been.

Darcy looked at the dark smudges still visible under the special light. "I don't think the bullet was for her."

"Maybe she fired and hit the perp. That's why he washed it off—to destroy his own DNA." Sorensen made a wiping motion with his hand.

"She didn't own a gun, but she knew how to shoot. I taught her," Quinn said. His voice sounded heavy. "Maybe she wrestled one free during the struggle. She was stronger than she looked."

"There's no way she was collateral damage. The attack is too personal." Darcy pointed to the grill, still dirty with burnt human flesh.

Quinn walked deeper into the restaurant and waved for them to join him by the booths.

Flashing the forensic light on one of them, he said, "There was blood on the backrest too, also wiped."

"Two victims?" Sorensen asked.

Quinn kneeled down next to the seat. "This is a good spot for watching while they massacred Carol."

"Wait, you think a couple perps came here to get Carol, she fights and hurts one, who then sits, bleeding, to watch her being cut into pieces by someone else?" Sorensen asked. "Don Corleone in the eighties maybe, but a street gang today? Why?"

Darcy walked to the counter across from the grill. "This took a long time. If they just wanted to kill her, why not a drive-by? Or a stabbing?"

"Now you're suddenly the expert?" Quinn asked.

The retort surprised Darcy.

"No," he said. "But you said you haven't seen this kind of assault before, and so did Sorensen. I've investigated enough homicides to know that this took too long to be random. There's a message here the killer wanted to make sure we got."

Quinn wiped his face with both hands. "Okay, wonder boy, when you figure it out, make sure to tell me."

Sorensen walked between them and said, "Show him the graffiti."

Quinn turned and met Darcy by the counter. Pointing to the side of the burners, he said, "That's the Diablos' signature."

Darcy strained to see what he was pointing at. Finally, he spotted a "6" stain on the black marble surface.

"Los Diablos always leave a red six, tagged either with spray paint or with the victim's blood."

"Some sick fuckers," Sorensen said.

Darcy looked at the signature. "Why a six?"

"666?" Sorensen said.

Darcy wished he could dig a hole in the ground and hide. He shook off his feelings of inadequacy and hoped that the next thing that came out of his mouth was worth saying. He exhaled slowly and walked away from the counter.

He stared at the bloody six and thought about Carol's chopped body.

"It still feels too personal for a gangster," he said. "Could it be a ruse?"

"This may not look like a typical gang hit, but Carol has helped put away hundreds of mobsters," Quinn said. "It's totally possible that she was green-lighted, and some sadist decided to go beyond the call of duty."

Darcy considered it. "Maybe. But why clean the blood but leave the tag and the bullet?"

"It's typical for a gang to take responsibility for a hit, but unusual to leave us evidence to match to a particular perp." Quinn's voice sounded tense, as if he was losing patience.

"So might the bullet," Darcy pushed.

"I thought you didn't know anything about the San Jose mobs," Quinn said.

"I don't. But I know a whole lot about crime."

Sorensen stepped between them again, breaking their childish bout.

"How many guys do you think we're looking for?" he asked.

Darcy had nothing, and Quinn didn't respond.

CHAPTER 4

Oscar opened hiseyes but couldn't make sense of his surroundings. His entire left side had fallen asleep, and his arm rested, numb, on top of his stomach. It felt like a foreign object rather than his own limb. He massaged it until he felt a tingle, as if hundreds of ants crawled under his skin.

When sensation returned, he leaned to his side and groaned, feeling the excruciating pain shoot up from his shoulder. He rolled to his back and looked up, not understanding what he was seeing. He blinked several times. *A forest?* The tall trees, the sounds of birds chirping, and the sun warming his face convinced him that what he was experiencing was real.

He dug into the moist ground. As he pushed himself up, he felt dead leaves and small twigs press against his palm. His left arm wasn't responding. It wasn't asleep anymore, but it was dead weight. As soon as he sat, his head spun and he felt nauseous. *Did I get drunk last night?*

And then he remembered.

He touched his wound, and the pain made him dizzy. His shirt was soaked with blood, but it was brown and crusted. It looked like mud. He shut his eyes hard, trying to push them into his brain. But instead of making the horror go away, he relived it. Every second of it. He screamed until he had no breath left. The noise faded, slowly giving way to the singing birds, completely oblivious to his misery.

After a few minutes he managed to stand up. He walked a few feet and listened for cars. If he was in a park, he should be able to hear traffic. Maybe. He turned to his right and trudged another few feet, then pushed forward until he'd covered a couple of yards. More trees and birds but no sound of civilization. He checked his pockets and almost smiled when he found his phone.

It was off. He pushed the button to turn it on, but the screen remained black. He opened the back. The battery was gone.

Oscar leaned against the closest tree, his shirt catching on the bark as he slid down. The wood scratched his back, but he didn't care. In front of him, all he could see were brown trunks and green leaves. He had no idea where he was, but he was sure Chavo wouldn't have wasted his time driving him too far. He looked up at the sun, still shy between the trees. It felt like early morning.

He pushed himself up, turned, and with the sun on his back, started walking. If he wasn't in a park, he must be somewhere in the Santa Cruz Mountains. There were plenty of roads leading to summer homes, and if by any chance he missed all of them, he would end up by the ocean, where he could flag a car driving down Highway 1.

Oscar felt something wet on his chest. Thick blood dripped from his shoulder, filling with new stains the already brown and mucky shirt.

CHAPTER 5

Darcy stood in the middle of the restaurant and checked his watch. It was past 10:30 a.m. Quinn had left a while back to attend the autopsy, and Sorensen had gone outside to talk to potential witnesses. Darcy had combed the establishment inch by inch for hours, trying to get the feel for it rather than search for anything that CSU may have missed.

"I'm heading back to the PD," he said to the room full of techs, walking to the door.

"We'll be here for a while," Rachel said from behind the counter.

The lead lab tech had arrived an hour after Darcy and was already submerged in the crime scene.

"I'll start sending evidence to Mauricio so we can begin processing ASAP," she added.

"Will he be point on the case?"

Darcy was surprised. Mauricio was a great tech, but Rachel had the most seniority and took lead when Lou, the big boss, was out of the office.

"No. I will, but look at this place." Her shoulders visibly dropped. "We'll need all hands on deck."

"Understood." Darcy nodded and left.

The sun was bright, already warming the street. He filled his lungs with fresh air and felt as if he'd been holding his breath the entire time he was in the restaurant. When he didn't see his temporary partner, he got in his car and drove to the station.

The CATCH bullpen was deserted, and so was Virago's office. He headed to the basement to see if the witness interrogations had started. The intake officer pointed to Room 3, where Sorensen was questioning Berto, the owner of the restaurant. He sat and watched from the other side of the mirror.

The old man didn't have much to tell. His only day off was Monday, so he'd closed around eleven on Sunday night and didn't bother coming in until this morning. His wife and five kids could verify his whereabouts, as well as the next-door neighbor, who'd come for dinner and stayed well past the time of death.

Darcy would have pushed harder on some of Berto's answers, but it looked like his partner was content to leave the first round light. Occasionally, it was better to let some time pass so people could get over the shock of what they'd experienced.

After they escorted Berto out of the station, Darcy was stunned when Sorensen walked past the elevator and headed for the stairs, but he decided not to mention it.

"I'm pretty sure he has nothing to do with this," Sorensen said.

He puffed as he climbed the last flight to the third floor, where the CATCH unit was.

"There was no forced entry, and he said nobody else has keys," Darcy said.

"Like you've never used your fancy tool kit to break into places."

Sorensen stopped to catch his breath before walking down the long, gray hallway.

"There was cooked food on a platter, and something other than Carol's flesh was burnt on the flat grill. Somebody broke in to eat?"

"Maybe they were going to rob the place and got hungry?" Sorensen shrugged, but his tone made it obvious he didn't buy it either.

"Don't you think it's weird that Carol was at Berto's closed restaurant when he doesn't even know who she is?" Darcy pushed.

"Yes, why was Carol there?" Commander Virago asked, stepping behind them into the bullpen. "I just left a message for Lou. Carol was his prodigy."

She didn't need to say more.

"Where in Africa is he again?" Sorensen asked.

"Burundi. The international investigation he's leading is supposed to be a month long. I'm not sure he'll be able to cut it short."

"Didn't he leave last week?" Sorensen asked, and Virago nodded. "I never understood how he could get that much time off," he added.

"His lab is one of the most prestigious on the West Coast, probably in the country. And the international forensic work he does has had incredible success identifying victims in mass graves. I think he's allowed to do pretty much whatever he wants."

"I guess it's not as if he's drinking margaritas in Mexico," Sorensen said.

Virago turned to Darcy. "Nice to see you here."

She shook his hand.

"Good to see you too, Commander. I guess I should let Howard know I'm working this," he said to her.

"I've already talked to him." She winked.

"Did he complain?"

"Don't know. I wasn't listening," Virago waved her hand.

He laughed. "I've missed you. My new boss is a moron."

She met his eyes, but her expression was undecipherable.

Sorensen sat behind his desk. Darcy remained standing, dismissing the guest chair, as if taking it would seal his fate as the outsider.

Nobody spoke for a few seconds. Then Darcy addressed the commander.

"Can I talk to you for a sec?"

She nodded and walked to her office.

Before Darcy was out of range, Sorensen yelled, "Don't come to the SJPD. They don't have any junk food, and the elevator's always broken. Three flights of stairs—can you believe it? At this rate I'll end up losing weight and getting healthy and shit."

He put both palms on his belly. It wobbled like a water balloon.

"Shut up, Detective. You whine like a little girl," Virago said, holding the door for Darcy to go through. Once he did, she closed it.

He didn't sit. He wasn't sure how to say what he wanted to tell her. It was the first time they'd been alone since she'd left the Sheriff's.

"I would have appreciated a heads-up about this morning," Darcy said.

"Quinn." It wasn't a question.

He almost said something but didn't.

"I should have told you. I'm sorry."

He nodded.

"He wouldn't vote on your transfer until he's worked with you. I need to fill this position, and I want it to be you, but Quinn is the sergeant in the task force, and he has a veto."

"He's said no already?"

Darcy was surprised. Virago didn't answer right away.

"He's expressed his concerns about your past—"

"But I was cleared by IA," Darcy interrupted.

She raised her hand. "He hasn't voted. He just stated his apprehensions. I told him you were good police and..."

Darcy locked eyes with her. "And?"

"I shared your file from Seattle."

"Why?" He shifted his feet and realized his whole body was tense.

"Because you had a stellar career there and you have been in California less than a year. I wanted him to know you, to vote on who you really are, not the detective who got a cushy job because his brother-in-law is the Santa Clara sheriff."

"Ouch."

She tilted her head while keeping eye contact.

Darcy knew she was right. He scratched his left temple. "Does he know about my eye?"

"Lynch, everybody knows about your eye." After a minute she added, "It's taken me a while to get the unit going. I can't get anybody new from the PD until the six-month rotation is up, and that's why I only got Quinn part-time. This is the first opportunity I've had to have you two working together."

He turned but looked over his shoulder. "It's common courtesy. You should have given me a heads-up that Quinn was there."

"I was hoping to make it less awkward. I didn't tell him either if that's any consolation. But yes, I made the wrong call."

Darcy nodded and opened the door to leave.

"Detective, don't screw this up. I really want you on the team," Virago said.

CHAPTER 6

Darcy left Virago's office and met Sorensen at his desk. "Where's the coffee in this place?" he asked.

"I'll show you. Maybe I'll get lucky and find something other than green tea."

"No Red Bull?"

The SJPD was definitely changing Sorensen.

"Don't you read the news? The heir of Red Bull is a cop killer. He ran over and dragged an officer underneath his new Ferrari. No, man, I'm over Red Bulls." After a second he added, "Besides, they don't have crap here. Not even Dr Pepper."

The kitchen was barely big enough for a small fridge, a dishwasher that looked like a relic from the eighties, and a tile counter that had seen better days. The walls were gray, the same color as the hallway, and a couple of open shelves held random mugs and a few tea boxes.

"English Breakfast?" Darcy handed Sorensen a brown box.

"Same difference." Sorensen ignored it, opened the fridge, and inspected the leftovers.

Darcy suspected none of them were his. He put the tea back and filled his mug with black coffee. It was steaming. He smelled a hint of hazelnut.

"Flavored coffee? What kind of wimps work here?"

"No clue. You know me, I don't fraternize."

Sorensen walked out of the kitchen.

That was true. Darcy had had a hard time connecting with his partner. Sorensen seemed to go out of his way to not make new friends. Either you'd known him forever, like Virago, or you would never get to know him. Except Jon, whom Sorensen took under his wing, probably because he saw him as his own kid.

"Seriously, man, don't transfer."

Darcy started to wonder if his partner wasn't joking. In any case the choice was Quinn's. And as of now it didn't look good.

When they got back to the bullpen, Virago was waiting for them, leaning on one of the desks.

"Where's Quinn?"

"With Madison."

"No. I called the morgue, and he left a while back."

Sorensen shrugged.

"While we were at the scene, he mentioned something about waking up some informants," Darcy said.

"I've called him a few times, but he didn't answer." Virago dialed from the closest desk phone. "Sergeant, come to the station right away. We need to put together a plan." She hung up and shook her head. "Crap. I really wanted him here." Facing Darcy directly, she added, "As I mentioned, Quinn's been working at the Gang Suppression Unit for five years. His rotation is coming up. That's why he's only at CATCH half-time. Anyway, he's our gang expert, and I wanted him to give you guys a crash course."

"Commander, can we not say that word?" Sorensen asked.

"What word, Detective?"

35

"You know… *that* word."

Darcy looked from one to the other. He knew they were both pulling each other's legs, but he didn't know what about. So he watched, his mouth molding into a smile.

Virago planted both fists on her hips and opened her stance a little as she faced Sorensen.

He kept the stare. "No need to get defensive or nothing. It just sounds like one of those bad Hollywood movies… Just saying."

"I didn't come up with the name of the unit, the chief did," Virago said. "So you better embrace it and say it with pride. Or"—she paused for effect—"you can always transfer to robbery or traffic. I'm sure they'll be happy to have you."

Darcy ended their little game. "If you really think this is a gang case, why isn't GSU running it?"

"This is CATCH's first big case," she said with special emphasis on the name. "The chief gave it to us before we saw the tag. The murder occurred in San Jose, but the victim worked for the Santa Clara Crime Laboratory. He felt it was the perfect case to get the SJPD and the Sheriff working together." Virago locked eyes with every single one of them for a split second, then added, "It's high profile. I wouldn't be surprised if he's throwing us into the deep end, hoping we'll swim."

"Quinn's expertise will come in handy," Sorensen said. "If he ever shows up."

Virago checked the time. With a sigh, she pulled her cell and tapped the screen until the phone started ringing.

"Sergeant Walker, I need a favor."

CHAPTER 7

Oscar had no idea what time it was, but he was sure he'd walked for several hours before he found the dirt road. He'd followed it, and after a few more miles he saw a mailbox, but the road veered right, and there was no house in sight. The box was bursting with junk mail. He thumbed through it, growing increasingly desperate when he stopped and double-checked a blue envelope.

"Yes," he said out loud.

The Valpak was addressed to "our friends at," with the full postmark. Now he hoped there was an empty house somewhere along the road, and that it had a working phone.

He shoved the envelope in his pocket and followed the curving path, which finally led to an old summer home at the end of a small clearing. There were no cars parked in plain view and no garage. The house was dark, but he watched it for some time, afraid of approaching it in case it was inhabited.

The walls of the rambler were wood, dry and gray, and seemed ready to crumble with the slightest touch. The windows were dusty and a few had cracks. He ambled up to it and peeked inside. The dirt made it hard to see anything. He circled around, trying all the windows, but they were locked. When he came back to the front, he tried the door, with the same luck.

He wondered if there was an alarm but decided the house wasn't fancy enough to deserve one. He broke the opaque window just above the lock. His boots crunched the glass as he stepped inside. He was right: there was no keypad or any other indication that he needed to worry about the CHP showing up.

The main entrance led directly to the living room. There was a loveseat in front of an ancient TV, a pre-IKEA-era coffee table, and two large poufs that at one time had been blue but now were grayish. He saw a phone jack, but there was nothing plugged into it.

He followed a short hallway into the kitchen. A small nook to the left hosted a metallic picnic table and four folding chairs. An old beige phone hung on the wall by the pantry door. He crossed his fingers before he picked it up and almost cried when he heard the dial tone.

CHAPTER 8

While they waited for either Walker or Quinn to show up, Darcy and Sorensen started working the whiteboard. Darcy wrote down the case number, the date, and printed and pinned Carol's DMV head shot and a couple of crime scene photos he'd taken with his phone.

"Where's Jon?" Darcy asked, finally sitting in the guest chair.

"School. He graduates this summer."

"You think he'll stay?"

"At the PD? Who knows? He's a smart kid. He'll have his pick of offers." Sorensen's chest swelled.

Darcy scanned the board. It looked measly. No leads, no plan. He checked his watch. Almost seven hours since he got to the scene, and they had nothing except a possible connection to gangs. Why not investigate this as a homicide? He was sure there were nuances, but they were wasting valuable time waiting for some "expert" to get them up to speed. And if it was a gang case, why not let GSU take it?

He was about to say that when a man walked into the bullpen.

"Where can I find Commander Virago?"

His voice was deep, and he was tall and lean, like a basketball player. He wore the black PD uniform and pushed the top of his bulletproof vest down, as if it bothered him.

"Sergeant Walker," Virago said, exiting her office. "I'm glad you could help us out."

She looked like a little girl next to him when they shook hands.

"I shouldn't after how you treated me when I was your recruit." He laughed.

"And look at how fine a sergeant you've turned out."

Walker addressed the detectives.

"This woman was the hardest field training officer the department has ever had. Officers still talk about her."

Virago laughed and waved her hand.

"You were at the Sheriff's?" Darcy asked Walker.

"No. I was at the PD. A million years ago."

Virago ended the conversation by making the introductions.

Darcy was curious about what had made the commander transfer to the SO and then back to the PD, but he would have to ask her another time.

"Do you want a high-level view of all the gangs in the area, or are you interested in any one in particular?" Walker asked while he shook hands with the detectives.

"This is not just for educational purposes," she said. "We got the Carol Montes case."

"I've heard." After a second he added, "To be honest, it surprised me. No offense."

Virago shook her head. "None taken. I think we all were. But we'll have to worry about the politics another time. Tell these guys what you can about the Mexican gangs."

What would happen if Quinn showed up while Walker was giving them the rundown? Would he be pissed? Relieved? Darcy had never heard of a sergeant being MIA for hours, especially during an active investigation. He stopped thinking about him and watched as Walker jumped right in.

The sergeant planted his feet wide apart and squared his shoulders toward them but seemed relaxed, comfortable in his own skin. He adjusted his vest again and turned toward the board.

"You found this at the scene?" he asked, pointing at a photo of the "6" on the counter top by the grill.

"Next to the body," Sorensen said.

"The Diablos' signature. Made with blood?"

"It seems that way. Waiting for confirmation from the crime lab."

Walker nodded and then faced them. "Okay, here's the local Mexican street gangs crash course."

Darcy took the last sip of coffee and wished he'd refilled it before the lesson, even if it was flavored. Sorensen leaned back in his chair and put both feet on the desk. Virago rolled her eyes and went back to her office.

"Actually, let me back up a little," Walker said. "I'm not sure if you know, but GSU has been working with the DA's office and the crime lab to target street gangs in San Jose. GSU does the street work, Carol Montes processes the evidence, and when we have enough, we bring the case to Deputy District Attorney Matthews and his minions to prosecute. We've had incredible success. Quinn is part of our unit. You should get more details from him when you have a chance."

Sorensen looked at Darcy, his expression saying, *Good luck with that.*

Walker explained that gangs usually targeted rival gangsters or their own people for violating one of the many rules they lived by. When civilians got hit, it was almost always collateral damage. Gangs rarely went after law enforcement, because it was too risky. They knew every agency would go after them until they were all convicted or dead.

"What kind of rules are we talking about?" Darcy asked.

"Anything from not screwing another gangster's girl, to paying taxes to the prison bosses, to not ratting on a homie. The punishments for violations span from paying a fine to being beat up or even killed, depending on the offense. And let me tell you, these guys have no qualms killing people. It doesn't matter if they are from their own gang or a rival one. They just don't see the value of life the same way the rest of us do."

Darcy glanced over at Carol's crime scene photo on the board.

"There're two main Mexican gangs in San Jose. The Culebras, or Snakes, and the Diablos, or Devils." Walker scribbled the names at opposite sides of the whiteboard. "I'll go over the Snakes first quickly, since it seems that this may be a Diablos crime. But I think it would be good for you to have an overview of both."

"If this is going to take long, I'll need to take a leak," Sorensen said. He got up from his chair.

"I could use some coffee." Walker followed Darcy to the kitchen.

"Damn," Walker said after taking a sip. "If you want something drinkable, come down to our office on the second floor. We have Philz."

Darcy laughed. "That's high-end stuff. I'll take you up on it next time. This swill is disgusting," he said, but he refilled his mug.

When they got back, Walker continued. "The Snakes control a good part of East San Jose. They are a faction of the Mexican Kingsnakes, the prison gang run by Alejandro Jimeno, who goes by Bullet. At some point they got too lazy to use the full name and started going by the Snakes in the early 2000s."

42

Walker dug into his duffel bag and pulled a few files out. He leafed through one and selected two mug shots, which he pinned right below the gang name.

"Every prison gang has a street leader. The Snakes have Gustavo 'Chavo' Buenavente, twenty-nine. In the gang world everybody's known by their moniker."

Darcy stared at the photos. Chavo's neck was almost as thick as his face was wide. His head was shaven, and he had thick, black brows. A tattoo of a snake circled around his neck, the fangs shiny and menacing, the forked tongue almost licking his earlobe.

Walker tapped on the tat clearly visible on the profile shot. "Every member has one of these somewhere on their bodies." He paused and looked at his audience, then explained. "If a kid wants to join a gang, he'll get jumped in. It's an initiation where he is beaten by several members or required to commit a crime to prove his commitment to the gang. If he passes, he gets a fancy snake inked as a gift."

"Do they all look the same?" Sorensen asked.

Walker thought for a moment. "No. The designs and sizes vary, but they're all snakes." He turned to the board. "Chavo should have a rap sheet longer than the state of California."

"Should have?" Darcy asked.

Walker sighed. "His underage mischief soon escalated to armed robbery and aggravated assault. He served a four-year sentence in Pelican Bay Prison. He was tried and convicted as an adult before he turned seventeen, based on the heinousness of the assault. Since he got out, he's been a suspect in several assaults, rapes, and at least three murders, but we haven't been able to nail him on any yet." He scratched his chin, as if that helped him think. "We've been close on a few occasions, but each time the witnesses either recanted or disappeared."

"I thought you said your unit was very successful," Sorensen said.

Darcy cringed. This man couldn't help himself.

"We are, but we're not perfect. And this asshole has been really lucky. Or something." The sergeant pushed his vest down again. "Chavo is vicious. The word on the streets is that he's as good with knives as he is with guns."

"And leaves no evidence?" Darcy asked, a little surprised.

"We've brought him in for questioning several times, but as I said, we *know* some of the things he's done but don't have evidence good enough to nail him. And nobody's talking."

Walker went back to his file and picked a new photo. "The gang's signature is a snake wrapped around a knife. They tag it somewhere close to the victim. Or you can also see it spray-painted all over walls around their territory."

The new photo showed the body of a twentysomething kid on his back, his shirt red with blood. There was a crude drawing of a knife and what could be interpreted as a snake around it in black paint on the wall behind him.

Walker set the dry-erase marker down, and it rolled on Jon's desk. He picked it up before it reached the edge and put it back at the bottom of the whiteboard.

"What's their main business? Drugs?" Sorensen asked.

"The Snakes have ties with the Mexican cartels and own a big piece of the illegal drugs market. They do extortion too, but they're not very sophisticated, mostly targeting mom-and-pop stores for protection."

Walker dug out a different file from his bag. He walked to the empty side of the whiteboard and picked up a different marker. Before he started writing, he pinned a new photo under the Diablos name.

"This is Oscar 'Guero' Amaro."

CHAPTER 9

After Oscar washed himself up at the bathroom sink, he found a dresser in the bedroom and rummaged through it. He picked a black long-sleeve T-shirt and almost passed out from the pain while trying to put his injured arm into the sleeve. He discarded it and went to dig in the closet for something easier to put on. A plaid flannel shirt with snap buttons? Why not? He caught a glimpse of himself in the mirror and almost laughed.

"I never thought of myself as a lumberjack."

He grabbed his old bloody T-shirt, carried it to the living room, and laid down on the loveseat while he waited for his homie to show up. He dozed off. The sound of an approaching car jerked him awake. He went to the window and peeked out until he spotted the old Honda Civic he knew so well drive around the curve in the dirt road. He opened the door and used the frame for support while his compadre got out of the car.

"Holy shit! What the hell happened to you?" Pascual ran to help him.

Oscar took a couple of steps toward his homie, but before he reached him, everything went black.

An intense burning feeling in his shoulder woke Oscar up. He tried opening his eyes, but the sunlight coming through the window made him squint. He felt pressure where the burn was eating him alive and saw a rainbow of colors but was unsure if his eyes were open or closed. *Am I going crazy?* He swatted his right arm but didn't reach high enough to whack away the other man's hand.

"He's waking up. You have to hold him steady until I finish."

The voice sounded familiar, but he couldn't quite place the owner.

Two hands pushed his body against a flat surface. A musty smell made his nose twitch, until he sneezed.

Oscar wanted to cover his face from the light, but his arms wouldn't respond. He opened his left eye a sliver and saw the stained glass, bathing the small room in myriad colors. As he adjusted to the brightness, he opened the other eye and saw Pascual's face above him. Oscar kicked his legs, trying to sit up.

"Stop fighting, bro," Pascual said.

"Am I dead?"

"If you don't stop moving, you might be soon," the voice from before said.

Oscar scanned around him, trying to find the man who was speaking. The shadowy figure against the window came into focus. It was Father Gonzalez, his black sleeves pulled up to his elbows, his hands covered in blood.

"I'm in church?"

"The rectory."

The burning sensation started again when the priest dabbed something against his skin. Oscar grunted and tried pulling himself free but wasn't able to.

"Oscar, stop. I'm trying to stitch you up."

He finally got it. He stopped moving and went into a daze, sort of enjoying the pain, as if he deserved it.

About ten minutes later the priest made him sit up. His head spun, and he had to grab the mattress to steady himself. It was thin and firm, but he managed to squeeze it with his right hand hard enough to avoid falling back down.

Father Gonzalez started bandaging his shoulder. "I did the best I could, but you really need to go to a hospital."

"No can do. Gangsters don't see regular docs, unless they want to go to prison. Not a place I ever want to go back to. Besides, nobody stitches up people better than combat medics."

Father Gonzalez shook his head. "Being an army doctor on deployment overseas is one thing, being a surgeon in the rectory with a basic first-aid kit is completely different."

The father wiped the blood off his hands with an already-dirty towel. Oscar smiled, mostly to comfort him. He looked around the priest's personal quarters. He'd never been there before. He'd always imagined that it would be more spacious, filled with antiques and relics. Instead, there was a twin-size bed, where he was siting, a wooden chair without a cushion by an equally spartan desk, and a medieval print of Mary with baby Jesus on the wall.

"Hmm," Oscar said.

"What?" Pascual asked.

"I thought all priests had a cross in their rooms." Oscar looked up at the father, who was standing in front of him.

"It's behind you." Gonzalez smiled and looked over Oscar's head.

He started to turn, but his shoulder protested, and he decided that it wasn't important to see what it looked like.

"It was a through and through, right?" When the father nodded, Oscar went on. "You did a great job. See, not bleeding anymore." He pointed at the white bandages.

Gonzalez shook his head. He grabbed a large bottle of Tylenol and offered it to him.

"I don't have anything better for the pain."

"I think we both know I can get my hands on something stronger if I need to."

The priest looked down at his shoes and left the pills on the narrow desk. "You need to get some antibiotics. And I'm not joking about that."

Oscar nodded. He knew that much was true. Bullet wounds were notoriously dirty, and the hours he spent in the woods probably made things worse.

"You lost a lot of blood. You need to take it easy for a few days. If the bleeding starts again, you'll have to go to the hospital."

"Okay, doc."

Father Gonzalez checked his watch. "I'll be in confession for the rest of the morning. If you want to talk..."

"Another day."

He nodded. "You can stay here as long as you need to."

"*Gracias*, Father."

When the priest left, he pushed the bloody towels to the floor and asked, "What day of the week is it?"

"Tuesday."

Oscar was relieved that he'd only been out hours and not days.

"Everything's still in place with our plan?"

"All is set."

CHAPTER 10

Walker stared at the new photo and tapped it with his knuckle.

"The rumor is that Oscar Amaro is only half Hispanic. He goes by 'Guero' because he looks white. Nobody actually knows for sure if he's Mexican. He's the street boss of the Diablos, the main rival gang of the Snakes."

Guero did look white. Light skin complemented by green eyes. His hair was black and wavy, not quite long enough to reach his shoulders. Darcy had seen many Spaniards with that complexion during his year abroad in Spain. Guero could be Caucasian or mixed. It was impossible to tell just from looking at his picture.

"The Diablos are the street faction of the DDs, or Devil Disciples, the prison gang. Their reporting structure is very militaristic, and nobody who appreciates their life would dare question an order that comes from the boss: Big Chon. The Devils have been around the Bay Area for many generations."

"Why are there two Mexican prison gangs?" Darcy asked. "Why didn't they join to fight the others?" He felt stupid for asking the question.

"They come from different backgrounds. The DDs are American born. The Snakes were a bunch of first-generation immigrants who started settling on the DDs' territory. The Diablos went after them, claiming that the new guys were illiterate, stupid, and trash, and didn't want people to think they were the same. The Diablos assaulted and abused the new *vatos*, trying to push them out of the area. But the pressure didn't work, and the newbies started uniting in self-defense, ultimately forming the Mexican Kingsnakes. They've hated each other ever since."

Walker finished his coffee and waited for more questions. When none came, he continued. "Guero's an odd case. He's highly respected by his superiors and underlings because he makes them loads of money. On the surface he looks mostly legit, and he owns a couple of very successful strip clubs. We caught wind of gambling and prostitution in the back and some small-time racketeering."

Sorensen lowered his feet to the floor and got up to stretch his back. "I thought the Devils were in the drug business. I remember arresting a few for possession with intent to sell way back when."

"You're right. The Devils ruled the drug underworld in San Jose for decades, but when this guy became the leader a couple years ago"—he pointed to Guero's photo—"they seemed to let that business go. That's when the Snakes took over the connection with the cartels."

"Why would the Devils let the drug scene go to their rivals?" Darcy asked, and checked his mug. It was empty. "I worked vice back in Seattle for a few years, and I find it hard to believe that an entire organization gives up a very profitable enterprise just like that."

Walker nodded. "I think he's found a way to make more money with less risk. To be honest, this Guero guy is a genius."

Sorensen scoffed.

"I'm serious," Walker continued. "He started with one shady club down on Fourteenth Street and got two more in less than three years. I've heard he's bidding for a casino license, and he's not even thirty yet. We think they're using the businesses to launder money from other illegal activities. Something is earning the DDs a lot of dough, but we haven't figured out what that is yet. We don't have enough for a warrant, let alone to make a case stick."

Walker pulled Jon's chair out and sat on it, his back to the whiteboard.

"Something illegal that is giving them a lot of cash and it's not drugs?" Darcy said, baffled.

"Correct." Walker didn't seem defensive, just matter-of-fact.

"Okay, so maybe Guero is business savvy," Sorensen said. "But they haven't gone straight... Wasn't there a drive-by shooting last year that the Devils were wanted for?"

"Ah that." Walker fiddled with his file until he found what he wanted, then got up and pinned a crime scene photo of a run-down house with two bodies lying on the front porch.

"It was about a year or so ago, before you came to the Sheriff's," Sorensen told Darcy.

Walker strode around the desks and reached for the massive bucket of Red Vines. Before he took one, Sorensen said, "I wouldn't do that if I were you."

Walker smiled and took one.

"Quinn doesn't like to share."

Darcy had to make sure his mouth hadn't dropped open. Sorensen always went out of his way to piss others off, and now he was worried that Walker was taking candy from Quinn?

Walker chewed on the Vine and said, "I know. He has a tub down at GSU too." He took another one before he put the lid back on. "We all take from it, because he especially told us not to." He smiled and went on. "A couple assholes shot up the house, killing these junkies and injuring one more inside.

51

The Devils had been so quiet. We didn't believe the intel at first, but the tales didn't change. Everything pointed to them, but we had no evidence to bring anybody in. Eventually, the leads dried up, and we weren't able to make any arrests, so the case is still open."

Sorensen peered over his shoulder toward the entrance of the bullpen, then fetched a Red Vine too. "Natural selection at its best. The streets of San Jose are safer without these junkies roaming them."

"What was the motive? Why risk calling attention to themselves to kill a couple addicts?" Darcy asked.

"About a week before the drive-by, a girl from the Lonely Lady Club, the newest of Guero's enterprises, got raped and brutally beat up."

"The Snakes?" Darcy asked.

Walker nodded. "Eventually, the one survivor from the drive-by confessed to the rape and said the dead guys were also involved."

"Street justice." Sorensen twisted the Vine into a knot and put it in his mouth.

"Guero was sending a strong message that nobody fucks with him," Walker said.

CHAPTER 11

Sorensen felt his stomach rumble. Walker turned toward him, and he knew he'd heard it too.

"I'm hungry. I can't think anymore," Sorensen said.

He stood and grabbed his jacket.

Virago poked her head out of her office. "If you're done here, go check Carol's house. Find out why she was at Berto's when it was closed."

"After lunch you mean, right?" Sorensen said to the commander's back.

She turned and gave him that stare of hers that said, *Really?* He mumbled a curse, because he knew better than to open his mouth and should have kept his eyes on the exit route.

"Takeout. We can eat and drive," he said, heading to the door, followed by Lynch and Walker.

Sorensen pressed the elevator button, but nothing happened.

"Can you believe this shit? Still broken. I swear I'm about to file a formal complaint with the department. How long does it take to fix this crap?"

"At least we're going down," Lynch said.

"Yeah, but when we come back, we'll have to go up."

"It may be fixed by then."

"It won't. It always takes days. Right?" he asked Walker, who shrugged.

"I've never noticed. We all take the stairs," Walker said.

"Oh for God's sakes, you too?" He started going down. "Seriously, Lynch, stay at the SO."

He almost meant it.

When they reached the second floor, Walker said, "If you guys think of anything else, let me know. And if you need extra people on the ground, we can probably spare a few guys to help find out who did this to Carol. We all liked her."

"Thanks, man. We'll let you know," Sorensen said.

They both shook Walker's hand and headed to the garage.

Sorensen went directly to his car and beeped it open. He got in the Jeep and waited for Lynch to sit.

"I guess you're driving."

"Don't I always?"

He headed toward the Coleman Avenue In-N-Out Burger drive-through.

"And I guess we're getting burgers."

"Got a problem with that?"

He knew Lynch was playing. It was nice having him around. He had a naïveté about the California way of life that Sorensen liked.

After a few minutes they merged onto Highway 87 South and headed toward Almaden Valley, where Carol Montes lived. He savored the last bites of his Double-Double and crumbled the paper in a ball while he steered with one hand.

"This is why automatic cars rock." Sorensen pointed to the gearshift and eyed Lynch chewing on his Protein Style Burger. "What's bugging you?"

"What isn't?"

Yes, what isn't? Sorensen thought.

When they reached Santana Court, Lynch said, "Looks like a quiet neighborhood."

The street had only six lots on each side, and it ended in a wide cul-de-sac with a house with a four-car garage that seemed out of place compared to the other, more modest homes. Lynch checked his phone and pointed to a white two-story house to their right.

Sorensen pulled the Jeep into the driveway. They got out and he checked the garage. It was locked, so he peeked through the high window.

"It's empty."

"That makes sense. We found her car close to the scene."

Lynch walked to the front door and shook his head, indicating that it was also locked. He then disappeared to check the perimeter.

Sorensen took a few steps back. The front lawn was green and well trimmed. There was no fence. A long flowerbed framed the porch. Two wooden chairs with bright, colorful striped cushions faced the street. The curtains on the main window were drawn, as well as those on the second floor.

It didn't take long for his partner to reappear.

"Everything seems normal," Sorensen said, and rang the bell. After a few seconds he banged on the door.

"Anybody in there...? San Jose PD." Looking at Lynch, he said, "I still haven't gotten used to saying it. If I don't stop and think, I'll blurt out 'Santa Clara County Sheriff.'"

"Do you really regret the move?" Lynch asked as he picked the lock.

"No, I just complain because that's what I do. You know that."

Sorensen checked behind him. No neighbors nosing around.

The lock clicked and the door gave way. Lynch pushed it open.

Sorensen pulled his gun out of the holster and waited to enter until his partner had done the same.

"Are you playing hard to get with Virago, or have you decided not to come over?" he asked, clearing the hallway.

"It's not up to me." Lynch walked in behind him. "Clear," he said, going deeper into the house. "I don't think I made the best first impression with the gatekeeper."

Sorensen thought about their interactions at the crime scene earlier in the day.

"Yeah, it didn't go too well this morning."

"Thanks for making me feel better."

Lynch's voice sounded muffled, as if it were coming from far away.

Sorensen checked the fridge. A half-empty bag of broccoli, a few carrots, a half-dozen brown eggs, 2 percent milk, three leftover boxes from a Chinese place, and nail polish.

"What is it with women storing nail polish in the fridge?" He shook his head. He always found this in single women's fridges, and it never ceased to amaze him.

He moved back to the living room and started going through Carol's mail.

"I don't know," Lynch said.

"Uh?"

"The nail polish. I don't know. Saffron does the same thing."

"Virago wants you back," he said, returning to the previous conversation. Lynch didn't respond, so he continued. "At the very beginning I didn't respect you very much. You know, when you were milking the system just playing desk cop at the SO. But after you decided to get your hands dirty, you really pulled your weight."

Sorensen wasn't much for giving compliments, but even though he was a hard-ass to Lynch, he had to admit that the Seattle expat had earned his stripes.

"Hold on a second. Can you repeat that while I record it?" Lynch came back from the hallway, and shoved his phone in Sorensen's face.

Sorensen stopped riffling through the mail in the wicker basket and gave Lynch the bird. "I didn't say nothing," he said, and moved away from the letters.

He took in the entire room. It was clean and tidy. There wasn't an iota of dust on the bookshelf. There were no dirty dishes in the sink, no knickknack out of place, no sign of struggle. Either somebody came and wiped everything, or Carol Montes had OCD.

"Let's go upstairs," Lynch said.

Sorensen followed him into the master bedroom. Lynch looked into the walk-in closet.

"Carol didn't have a shoe fetish." Lynch pointed at the rack. "Look, only seven pairs, and two are sneakers."

"I never thought of her as fashion conscious," Sorensen said. "She seemed pretty conservative, almost as if she liked flying under the radar. I always assumed it was because she was shy."

He thought about the few times they'd met either at the lab or in court.

Her clothes were arranged by color. There was at least an inch between hangers. The floor-to-ceiling shelves on the right-hand side held neatly folded sweaters.

"I'm tempted to take a photo and send it to Saffron. She'd never believe that there are women who don't stuff their closets full of clothes."

Lynch shut the door.

"I got three girls at my house," Sorensen said. "Don't come crying to me."

He wasn't even sure why he'd said that. His wife and kids weren't that bad.

They walked into the last room. A small desk and chair stood by the window. A moody modern art painting took most of the opposite wall. The bookshelf was filled top to bottom with science books.

"Let's check the garage." Sorensen closed the desk drawer.

They went downstairs, then through the laundry room. Both washer and dryer were empty.

Lynch opened the door leading to the garage and, stepping inside, said, "Look at that."

"I thought Quinn said that Carol didn't have any firearms."

Sorensen reached the medium-size Lincoln Series Liberty gun safe, set below a set of shelves mounted on the wall.

"It's locked."

"Did you see any notes with passwords hidden anywhere? Maybe scribbled on a paper stuffed in the desk drawer or the nightstand," Lynch said.

"No. I'll check the kitchen."

Darcy headed out of the garage and rummaged through all the cabinets but didn't find any passwords.

"Let's get it over to Rachel," Lynch said when he came back.

"You want to take it to CSU without knowing what's inside? Use your magic tool kit, for God's sakes."

"Do you see a lock?" Lynch pointed at the set of numbers. "It's hard to pick a keypad."

"Is it bolted to the floor?"

Sorensen pushed the safe to see if it would move. It didn't.

"Leave it for CSU." Lynch headed back into the main room. "You knew Carol well?"

"No. Not like Rachel or Mauricio. I didn't work many gang cases at the Sheriff, and this is the first one since I transferred to SJPD. As that's all Carol did, there was no reason for us to interact much."

He watched Lynch make a last sweep around the living room. "There's not a single picture in this house."

His partner was right. There weren't any photos of Carol or of any other people.

Sorensen thought about his own home. Melissa had insisted on covering the walls with family photos showing the progression of time, starting with their wedding and moving through the kids growing up. Carol was single and didn't have kids, but... Not even a couple of photos of girlfriends at a happy hour or a weekend getaway pinned to the fridge?

When Lynch pulled out his phone to call CSU, Sorensen felt his own phone vibrate, then heard a ping coming from Lynch's phone too.

"That can't be good," he said, reaching for his device.

"It isn't," Lynch said, reading the text. "Let's go."

CHAPTER 12

Oscar woke up, and this time he had no trouble figuring out where he was: home. He'd slept deeply for a couple of hours and couldn't recall any dreams but did remember everything from the night before. He rubbed his eyes and then touched his shoulder. It hurt, but the bandages were still white. He sat and felt sore, his muscles protesting with each movement.

The leather of his favorite black sofa felt sticky against his sweaty legs. As the living room came into focus, he looked around and for the first time realized he'd never bothered to make his house a home.

The 65-inch TV mounted on the wall across from him was turned off, and his reflection stared at him, faint as if he were a ghost. He leaned back and put both feet on the solid wood coffee table. He was thirsty but didn't feel like walking the few feet that separated him from the fridge, which was on the other side of the kitchen island.

As if sensing he was awake, Pascual came into the room.

"I got you chow at El Grullense." The burritos made Pascual's hands look like a child's. "And antibiotics. Two pills every eight hours," he said, throwing the beige bottle on the cushion next to where Oscar was sitting.

Oscar felt nauseous. He rejected the food but took the pills.

"Get me some water."

His compadre filled a glass and handed it to him, then sat across from Oscar and started to peel the wrapper off one of the burritos. The smell of rice and carne asada made Oscar's stomach growl. Maybe he didn't feel so sick after all. He watched Pascual take a huge bite, filling his cheeks with beans.

"Okay, fine," he said as if he were being forced to eat at gunpoint.

"You don't have to chow, bro. More for me." Pascual winked.

Oscar leaned over to grab the burrito and the stitches pulled at his skin. He readjusted his posture and grabbed the burrito with his right hand instead, grateful that Pascual pretended he hadn't noticed. Oscar peeled off the aluminum foil from one end. The moment he took the first bite, his entire body felt warm. Everything was better.

"Best idea you've had all day," he said with a full mouth.

"I know. You should give me a raise."

"I might."

"Wanna talk about it?" Pascual asked, crumpling the silver wrapper into a ball and pointing at Oscar's shoulder.

He didn't know what to do. He kept very few things from Pascual... But this may have to be another one to add to that short list.

"But please leave out how you got that fancy shirt you were wearing," Pascual said, laughing. "Man, that was some ugly-ass shit."

Oscar had no idea what he was talking about, but before he could ask, two of his soldiers busted into the room. He only recognized Angel, the older of the two teenagers, and wondered if Pascual had made new rotations to the guards outside his house.

"Check the TV," Angel said.

"Why?" Pascual asked.

61

"My mom just called me. News about Jefe's case."

Angel reached for the remote, but Pascual snatched it before the kid could touch it. Oscar looked at Pascual and nodded for him to push the green button.

CHAPTER 13

Darcy turned on the police radio while Sorensen drove with the spinners on. The radio crackled, but nothing came through.

"I think it's broken," Sorensen said.

"You think?" Darcy sighed and checked his phone for updates, but the screen was blank.

"The Santa Clara Hall of Justice is only fifteen miles away. We'll be there in a sec." Sorensen stepped on the gas. "How are you getting along with your new boss?"

"Not really new anymore. You guys left three months ago," Darcy said.

Sorensen waved his hand. "You know what I mean."

Darcy looked out the window. Most cars let them go by because of the flashing red lights.

"Howard is definitely not Virago," he said.

Sorensen laughed. "That's the understatement of the century."

"I catch him watching me. It's creepy. I almost wonder if he has a thing for me."

Sorensen laughed and coughed at the same time and almost choked. "Stop saying this shit. You're killing me." He slapped the steering wheel. After a few seconds he said, "He's freaked out by you."

"Me?"

"Oh please. He's terrified that you'll tell your brother-in-law how incompetent the poor bastard is."

"That's ridiculous."

Sorensen glanced at him. Darcy returned the look but didn't hold it, afraid Sorensen would play a staring contest and crash the car into the median.

"I don't even like my brother-in-law that much." Darcy felt defensive as he spoke. "But even if I did, I wouldn't tell him anything. I just want Howard to leave me alone." He shook his head. "He meddles with every little detail of my investigations."

"Maybe you should say something to him."

"To Howard?"

Sorensen smirked while he merged into the Taylor Street exit without slowing down. The tires screeched as they took the turn.

"I meant the sheriff. Having a moron for a boss only makes your life harder. Trust me. I almost left the SO because of that once."

This was the first time Sorensen had mentioned anything like that.

"When was this?"

"Ages ago. Virago replaced the loser and I stayed."

Darcy was about to ask for him to elaborate when they arrived at the Hall of Justice. The entire block was surrounded by patrol cars from the SO and the SJPD. Darcy looked at his partner as the car slowed down.

"There's a whole lot of brass for a 207," Sorensen said, as if he were reading Darcy's mind.

"Yeah."

Several officers were crossing the street in front of them, probably to start the canvas.

"Did you get any details of who got kidnapped?" Darcy said.

Sorensen shook his head. "The courthouse is the SO jurisdiction. You should be telling me what's going on. Don't you get updates on your phone?"

"Haven't you heard? When Howard took over the acting captain position, he said he was going to establish a better communication process, sending information better targeted to the deputies via text messaging. His aim was to reduce civilian interceptions over the air."

Sorensen pulled the key out of the ignition but didn't say anything.

"You agree?" Darcy asked.

"To some degree I guess. Nowadays every idiot out there can monitor everything we're doing. That's not good either."

"I don't know." Darcy opened the car door but didn't step out. "Three months later we get less radio and no texting. So we get all these resources deployed for a possible kidnapping we know nothing about. I wish I came into the scene with more intel." As if on cue his phone rang. "It's the boss," he said, getting out of the car. "I'll meet you inside."

"And you complain... he's handing you the information personally." Sorensen winked as Darcy closed the door.

"I would rather get it any other way."

He swiped the green button on his phone as he sprinted toward the main entrance.

CHAPTER 14

"I'm almost there," Darcy told Howard.

"Hurry up. Everybody else is here."

The captain ended the call.

"Damn it." Darcy had too many questions.

He sped up the pace as he tapped the Call button. When it went to voice mail, he hung up.

Darcy reached the beige six-story building and went inside. The metal detector beeped as he walked through it, flashing his credentials. He hurried along the dull hallway to the elevator, swerving around people being escorted out.

The fourth floor looked busy, but there was a certain sense of controlled chaos. Per protocol, all civilians had been moved to jury rooms and were being interviewed or dismissed. Only law enforcement was allowed close to the scene.

About fifteen feet in front of him he saw two deputies nod and turn toward one of the courtrooms, leaving acting Captain Howard by himself. The man wore an ill-fitting steel-gray suit and the same scuffed burgundy shoes he always did. Darcy wondered if his boss was too oblivious to know that just wearing a suit didn't automatically make him look professional.

"Who got kidnapped, the governor?" Darcy asked as soon as he was within earshot.

"What? The governor got kidnapped too?" Howard's voice cracked at the end. He frowned as he rubbed his hands over his pant legs.

Jesus, Darcy thought. "No. It seems that all of the SO and the SJPD are here, so I'm assuming the 207 is about someone big," Darcy said, looking around.

"Ah, you're being funny." Venom spewed from Howard's mouth. "You think a material witness in a gang case doesn't deserve all hands on deck?"

Darcy wondered if the man was truly offended or just pissed because he'd fallen for the comment about the governor.

"I only got the 207 code and the location on the text," he said. "Can you fill me in on the details?"

Even if Sorensen was right that too many civilians could listen to the police on the scanner, going blind into a scene was not a better alternative. A flood of messages providing more information should have followed the first one. But Howard hadn't implemented that process yet, and Darcy wasn't holding his breath that he ever would.

"What took you so long to get here?"

"I was down with Sorensen at—"

"You were playing cops with that stupid CATCH unit? I'm putting you as lead on this case. This better become your priority. I expect hourly updates. The media's all over us. Your frigging brother-in-law, the Santa Clara county sheriff, is all over me, so now I'm all over you. This is yours, Lynch. You have to solve this mess yesterday."

"This is a kidnapping, right?"

Howard's urgency seemed misplaced. How could his acting captain justify making a kidnapping take precedence over the investigation of Carol's murder? Or was this the AC's pathetic way to reinstate "ownership" of his resource and make

67

sure that Virago knew Darcy still worked for him, not CATCH?

"What, this is not sexy enough for you?"

Howard's tone was as inappropriate as his implication.

Darcy made a ninety-degree turn and headed toward the crime scene tape. He wasn't going to get anything valuable from Howard anyway.

"Go solve this case," Howard said to his back. "And remember, hourly updates. Got it?"

Before he reached the cordoned-off area, Darcy heard Sorensen calling out for him. He waited, and they both walked to the deputy, who was guarding the bathroom door. His name tag said "Gimeno."

"The victim is Nhu Tran. She was testifying in a gang homicide, the Diego Ochoa case." Gimeno put his notebook back in his chest pocket and stroked his short beard.

Darcy had heard more about gangs in one day than he had since he'd moved to California.

"Tran came to the bathroom. There was a male deputy escorting her, so he didn't go in. He waited. When she didn't come out after fifteen minutes, he called for her. There was no response. Finally, he went in and only found two women, but both said Tran wasn't there when they went in."

"Any other witnesses?" Darcy asked.

"We're waiting on the footage from the cameras. Nothing else so far."

"Of course not," Sorensen said, and walked into the bathroom.

Before following him inside, Darcy addressed Gimeno. "I want to talk to the deputy who escorted Ms. Tran and the two women he found when he went in."

CHAPTER 15

The restroom was wide. The scrambled-egg color of the walls and the tiny tiles arranged in a checkered pattern on the floor made Darcy think of the generic government buildings of the seventies.

Sorensen was standing by one of the windows. The glass was protected by chicken wire.

"Nobody just goes *poof*," he said.

Darcy heard the metal judder.

"You were looking for me?" a young man dressed in the SO khakis asked. "I'm Deputy Lawrence."

"Come on in. We don't bite," Sorensen said.

Lawrence shook Darcy's hand but didn't walk all the way in to greet his partner. The deputy stood close to the door and crossed his arms behind him. The kid wasn't twenty-five yet, and it was obvious he was fresh out of the academy. Darcy watched him as he told them pretty much the same story they'd heard from Gimeno.

"You said there was a cleaning crew when you guys arrived?" Darcy asked.

"Yes, the sign was by the door. I told Ms. Tran that we had to go to another restroom, but she said she couldn't hold it.

Another lady sneaked in when we were talking, so I assumed it was okay." Sweat beaded his forehead and reappeared as soon as he wiped it off with his hand.

"Did you go in to check that it was safe?" Sorensen asked.

Lawrence didn't answer right away, but the perspiration was even more obvious as his face turned red.

"It's the courthouse. I... I got a text and didn't think about going in," he said.

"You didn't think?" Sorensen stared back at Lawrence, spittle building in the corners of his mouth. "Why do you think the SO is the laughingstock of all the other agencies? Because morons like you give the Sheriff the reputation it has."

"Sorensen," Darcy scolded.

Walking toward Lawrence, Sorensen went on. "Did you think keeping a witness safe—the main witness at a gang murder trial for God's sakes—was something you could do while texting your buddies?"

"Enough." Darcy took a step toward his partner.

Sorensen stopped walking and turned away. Then, as if he were talking to himself but wanted to make sure everybody heard him, he added, "She's probably dead by now because this asshole was too busy texting."

Lawrence's eyes opened wide with apprehension. "Do you think she's dead?"

"How do you think most witnesses in gang cases end up? WITSEC? No. They end up in a fucking ditch."

Lawrence looked like he was about to throw up.

Darcy placed himself between Lawrence and Sorensen. "What can you tell me about the case?" Darcy wanted to distract him. "Do you know if there were any hits put out on her life?"

70

"No. I don't know much. I was just replacing Kooch. He called in sick today, and they told me to come in. I was doing overtime. Today's not even my shift day."

"Stop the whining. No one cares," Sorensen said from the opposite wall. "Is there anything useful that you can tell us, or was your buddy sending you dirty pics of his girlfriend?"

"Uh? No. What?"

Lawrence was now drenched in sweat.

"Enough." Turning back toward the deputy, Darcy said, "Please focus. Was there anything at all that seemed out of place, that looked weird, even if you can't put your finger on why?"

Darcy moved, forcing Lawrence to rotate with him, so his back was to Sorensen. He needed the kid to concentrate, and his ex-partner wasn't helping.

"No, sir. I'm sorry."

Mauricio, the lab tech, walked into the bathroom with a tool bag that was half his size. "Good morning, gentlemen," he said, his intonation rising at the end of the sentence. "Kidnapping?"

"More like MIA," Sorensen said.

"Ah. I wonder why they called it a kidnapping then." He set his bag on the floor.

"Because the response is much better," Sorensen said. "Look at this zoo. Everybody and their mother are here." He puffed and concentrated on one of the sinks. "For a stupid MIA case."

"I thought you said she's probably dead." Lawrence grabbed a paper towel, which he used to wipe his hands.

Darcy looked at Sorensen. He needed to stop alienating Lawrence.

"What?" Sorensen mouthed to Darcy, shrugging his shoulders.

71

"I haven't seen a witness disappearance at the courthouse in a while." Mauricio dropped on all fours and grabbed something between two stalls. "Look what we have here, a button." He stood up and showed it around, as if showcasing a jewel resting on the palm of his hand.

"Could be nothing," Sorensen said, going back to the last window and checking the metal again.

"Such a ray of sunshine, Detective Sorensen." Mauricio placed the button in an evidence bag and sealed it. "Why are you here anyway? Don't you work for SJPD now?"

"I do. I was with this guy when the call came in," he said, pointing to Darcy with this thumb. "So I decided to come and supervise."

"Right." Mauricio winked at Darcy.

Sorensen stared out the window. "I don't think anybody saw anything from across the street. The chicken wire's too thick."

"Tell us about the case she was testifying in," Darcy said to Lawrence.

Before the deputy could respond, Sergeant Marra walked in. His smile widened as he crushed Darcy's bones with his handshake.

"What the hell are you doing here, buddy?" Sorensen asked him.

"I was supposed to testify after the missing witness. I was the sergeant at the scene of Ochoa's murder." When he met blank stares from Darcy and Sorensen, he explained. "Diego Ochoa was that dealer who got shot a couple years ago in the alley behind the Lonely Lady because he was supplying drugs to Jefe's pregnant lady."

"Jefe as in the ex–street boss of the Diablos?" Sorensen asked.

"The one and only."

Two crimes connected to the Diablos in the same day? Darcy looked at Sorensen. He didn't believe in coincidences.

Marra looked back at the door and shook his head. "I'm not all that surprised that Nhu Tran pulled a Houdini."

CHAPTER 16

O scar shifted on the sofa. Feeling his shoulder stiffen, he grabbed the bottle of Tylenol Pascual had taken from the priest and washed the tablets down with a mouthful of water.

Over the news anchor's voice, Angel said, "That ho disappearing will be good for Jefe, right?"

Nobody responded.

Pascual leaned on the counter, still holding the remote control. "Go sniff around. Be stealthy, copy?" he told the two soldiers, but addressed the mandate to Angel, the older one.

They left the room, closing the door behind them.

"It can get messy," Pascual said.

"A risk we had to take."

Oscar took another bite of his burrito, happy that the news had shifted his homie's attention away from the conversation they were having before. He was not ready to explain what happened to him the previous night.

Oscar finished his food and checked the time. "I got to go see Dominique."

Pascual turned but didn't block his way. "You think that's a good idea right now?" He looked down at Oscar's shoulder. "I can go."

"Nah. I need the fresh air. Besides"—Oscar pointed at the news—"I want you to make sure no shit goes south with Nhu."

He got off the sofa and went to the bedroom, heading directly to the closet. He slid the door open and kneeled in front of the gun safe. Oscar punched in the code and checked the contents: a 9 mm, a .40 caliber, three shotguns, and five revolvers. He decided to leave the firepower behind and reached for the bottom, where he had a hidden compartment. He opened it, pulled a few stacks of bills, and stuffed them in his gym bag.

"Two hundred G should do it," he said barely out loud.

He locked the safe and shut the closet door. Walking by the kitchen, he stopped to grab the bottle of pain meds on his way out the door.

"Boss, going...?" The soldier guarding the door took a step back when he looked up at Oscar.

Unintentionally, Oscar touched the surgical tape that covered his forehead and cheek wounds. He stuffed both hands in his hoodie pockets and went down the porch steps.

The teen said behind him, "Angel told me you put him on a big mission. Can you give me something big to do too? I'm ready."

Oscar stopped and turned around. "You Angel's little brother?" he asked, noticing the resemblance.

The kid nodded. "I go by Crow."

Oscar wasn't sure if he was pissed that Angel couldn't keep his mouth zipped or pleased that Crow was so eager to prove himself.

"Need a driver?" The kid asked, but almost immediately his shoulders shrunk and he looked away.

Oscar's banged-up face probably made Crow think that offering help was the right thing to do, but you never questioned the capabilities of the boss. He should teach him a lesson about respect. But there was something about the kid he liked. No reason to make him feel like shit for being human.

"You ain't old enough to drive, fool." Oscar headed back to the garage.

"Sixteen last month." The kid ran up to him. When he was by his side, he stood tall, as if that would make him look older, and shoved his driver's permit toward Oscar.

That made him laugh. "Nobody drives my Tesla. You should know that if you wanna be my number-one soldier." He punched Crow's shoulder and entered the garage.

The black-on-black Tesla Model S with the 22-inch wheels and tinted windows was parked next to his Ducati. The car woke up once he put his foot on the break, then he backed into the street. His shoulder protested with every turn of the wheel.

A few minutes later he cursed himself. He pulled over to the side of the road and stopped the car. It was more than likely that the police had already linked him to Berto's place. The Tesla and the strip clubs were the only things that were connected to his name.

"What's wrong with you?" he said to himself, and squeezed the leather steering wheel with his right hand.

He checked the dashboard clock. He didn't want to drive back. He was already late and it never went well when he made Dominique wait. He scrolled through his contacts until he found Crow.

"Boss, what you need?" the kid asked.

"Meet me at the corner of..." He checked the street sign ahead of him. "Alicia Street and Lagos. And bring your car."

"I... I don't have a car."

"Get someone else's." Oscar tapped the red cross on the screen, turned off the motor, and waited.

"Fuck me," he said when a bird pooped on the windshield.

He turned on the motor and the wipers, and drove a few feet forward, blocking part of a driveway, but safe from trees.

Crow arrived about ten minutes later in a beat-up rust-orange Datsun and pulled over next to the Model S.

"Is it hot?" Oscar asked.

"I didn't steal it. It's my cousin's."

Oscar looked at his perfect and beautiful car and then eyed Crow. Taking the Datsun's keys he said, "Watch my baby until I come back."

Crow extended his hand. "I can drive it home if you want."

"Trying this shit again? Didn't I just tell you no a minute ago?" Oscar laughed but didn't give him the keys. "You're not sitting in it. You're just watching it." Oscar got in the Honda and added, "If I see your ass print anywhere on it when I get back, I'll beat the shit out of you. Got it?"

Crow took a step back from the Tesla. Oscar smiled and drove off.

The Datsun smelled of cigarettes and marijuana. He admonished himself again for not making sure that everything was okay with the car. Was the registration current? Did the brake lights work? Was there a gun or dope hidden somewhere in it? He looked up at the sky and prayed the police wouldn't stop him. He may have been safer driving his own car.

"Rookie mistakes," Oscar said out loud.

He pushed the thoughts away and concentrated on getting to his destination without making any traffic violations. About twenty minutes later he reached Mountain View. He wasn't sure if it was the stink of the car or the pain from the bullet, but he felt woozy as the warehouse came into view.

Oscar parked a block away, put his hoodie on, and zipped it up to the neck. When he reached the door, he punched in the code and let himself in.

"You're late. You know I don't…" Dominique retreated a foot or two. "What happened to your face?"

"Nothing."

Dominique fidgeted. If Oscar hadn't known better, he would have thought the engineer was high on speed.

"You're late," he said again, and started pulling on his right eyebrow. He did that so often, Oscar was surprised he still had any hair left.

"You need to chill. Things happen. The world doesn't revolve around your schedule." Oscar walked up to Dominique, his body blocking the fluorescent light from the ceiling, throwing a shadow on the engineer's face.

"But you wanted to meet at noon. You said you would come at noon, and it's almost four. I thought you weren't coming. I thought maybe you got in trouble with the police. You could destroy my company."

"D, stop that shit already. We've gone over this a million times. We're doing a simple business transaction. I'm investing in your company and I'm using your product. There's nothing illegal about that."

"Do you have the 333 Exemption I told you to get?" When there was no response, Dominique went on. "If you don't get the Certificate of Waiver from the FAA, you can't operate drones commercially. I know you are not just flying them for fun in your backyard. So you're flying them illegally." The bravado in his voice waned as the words came out. "These drones are way too powerful to just fly for fun."

"You have nothing to worry about, okay?" Oscar looked around the vacant warehouse. "Come on, show me the new toys."

Dominique hesitated but finally went to the metal shelf by the back wall. He pulled out a box and set it on the floor as if it were an injured bird. He opened it, and Oscar saw that the drone's metal frame was matte, just as he'd requested.

Oscar opened his bag and pulled out the cash. "Two hundred K should carry you for a while."

He set the money on the shelf where the box had been.

"Oh no, no. Cash?" Dominique moved back, as if the money were a contagious virus.

"Come on, just take it."

Dominique crossed his arms, but his feet remained in place.

"D, really. Stop with this shit. Next time I'll pay you in Bitcoin, but for now just take this."

The engineer left the money where it was and headed toward his desk. He walked as if his limbs were too long for him and he had problems coordinating his arms and legs. Oscar followed him.

Dominique pulled out his chair and sat on it, bumping into the desk. The 27-inch monitors came to life. On the right side there was a black window filled with lines of code from top to bottom. On the left there was a 3-D view of a prototype Oscar hadn't seen before.

"What's that?" he asked.

"Nothing." Dominique fiddled with the keyboard until the design disappeared from the screen.

"Don't fuck with me. I asked you a question."

After a very long sigh the engineer tapped the keys and pulled up the image. The specifications of the drone looked very similar to what they were producing already, but there was a box underneath that was new. He didn't know what it was at first. Then he realized he was looking at their new prototype.

"I didn't want to show it to you until I had the proof of concept built. But this will be the future of surveillance. The three cameras capture the images from slightly different angles, making matching much more accurate. The video is streamed directly to the cloud, where the servers automatically process and analyze the images, sending the results back in milliseconds."

CHAPTER 17

The courthouse bathroom felt crowded. Darcy, Marra, and Sorensen were by the door. Mauricio was at the opposite side, inspecting the sink drain. Deputy Lawrence was leaning against the wall by the windows. But the witnesses Darcy had asked for were still not there. He checked his watch. It had been almost ten minutes already.

"Why aren't you surprised about Nhu's disappearance?" Darcy asked Sergeant Marra.

"Jefe doesn't want her to testify. She's the one who turned things against him in the original investigation."

"Why not kill her? Simpler, faster, cleaner," Sorensen said. "Okay, maybe not cleaner."

"Then everybody would be looking at him. This way the defense attorney can always claim that she got cold feet and split," Marra said.

Darcy addressed the deputy. "Lawrence, can you check why the witnesses are not here yet?"

The deputy used his radio to call out the status. The response came muffled. He leaned over the receiver. When the crackling stopped, his face was white. "Sir... apparently they left."

"What?" Darcy, Sorensen, and Marra said at unison.

"Get their home addresses right now," Darcy said.

Lawrence pushed the button to speak into the radio, and after a few interactions he said, "So... nobody knows who they are."

"Oh, for fuck's sakes. Can this get any worse?" Sorensen asked.

After Marra volunteered to get a few of his guys to find the witnesses, Darcy and Sorensen decided to go back to the station.

Quinn wasn't there, but Jon was. Darcy wondered if he might end up having to ask for Jon's help to find the witnesses if Marra didn't get lucky. Jon's uncanny way of uncovering connections that many investigators missed was one of the kid's biggest assets.

"Detective Lynch, good to see you. Are you working the Carol Montes case with us?" Jon asked, getting up from behind his desk and shaking Darcy's hand.

"It looks that way."

"Awesome. It'll be like old times." Jon shoved his hands deep into his pants pockets.

Darcy noticed that his hair was shorter, and his button-down shirt was tucked into his khakis. When Jon was at the SO as an unpaid intern, he wore Converse shoes, and his polo shirts were always loose over his belt.

"Are they treating you well here?" Darcy asked.

"Yes, it's great. And I'm getting paid," he said with a gleam in his eyes.

Darcy laughed. "As you should be. When are you graduating?"

"June. I'll switch to full-time then."

"You're going to stay?" He was only mildly surprised.

"Unless they kick me out... I love this job."

"You may have to get sworn in," Sorensen said.

"Like, go to the academy and carry a gun?" Suddenly Jon didn't look so excited.

"Yep."

Darcy grinned and mouthed "no" under his breath. Sorensen was concentrating on some document, so he didn't see him.

Jon looked from one to the other, shuffled his feet, and said, "I was able to find another homicide related to the gun that was used at the restaurant, matching the slug we found there."

"Another gang hit?" Sorensen stopped riffling through papers and looked up.

"That was the thought, but it was never solved. Six years ago Sergio Gonzalez was killed with the same gun. They never found the weapon, obviously."

"Another lowlife being taken out of his misery." Sorensen picked up the mug on his desk and smelled its contents as if he was afraid to find spoilt milk. "As far as I'm concerned, these gangsters are doing us a favor ridding the world of each other's scumbags."

Darcy and Jon looked at him.

"What?" Sorensen shrugged. "It's true, and you know it. So long as they only kill mobsters, the world's a better place." When he still got no visual or verbal agreement, he added, "You're just too PC to admit it." He leaned over the side of his desk and poured the cup of old tea into his garbage can.

"That's gross." Darcy laughed.

"He does it all the time," Jon said.

"And until they bring something decent to drink, I'll keep doing it."

Sorensen took a Red Vine from Quinn's desk. He started chewing, and as soon as he sat down the sergeant came into

83

the bullpen. "Oh shit." Sorensen stuffed the whole Vine in his mouth and chomped on it.

Darcy couldn't help but enjoy Sorensen's predicament. He'd never seen his partner sweat over doing something that would piss anyone off.

Quinn reached them, stared down at the tub of Red Vines, and asked, "Who the hell touched my stuff?" The top of the container was not fully closed.

Darcy looked at Sorensen, who stood and walked to the board, probably trying to swallow before getting caught. He exchanged a look with Jon and saw that they were both savoring the moment.

"You, kid, was it you? Buy your own damn candy for fuck's sakes." Quinn huffed and shoved the lid down so hard it bulged into the container.

Jon's faced turned red, but before he could defend himself, Sorensen asked, "Did you get anything from your CIs?"

"Not much, but the one thing that's consistent is that nobody's talking about what happened at Berto's."

Sorensen caught Quinn up with the ballistics match Jon found. "Some ganster killed Gonzalez, the gun went dormant for six years and resurfaced last night."

"I remember that case. Nothing to it. We never found the guy. He probably hid the gun with Grandma while he got snatched up for something else. Now he's out and using his toy again."

They fell silent for a few seconds. Darcy stared at the whiteboard, still mostly bare.

"Did any of your CIs talk about the disappearance of Nhu Tran?" Darcy asked. "The witness that went MIA from the courthouse."

"Not only the khakis lost the witness, but now you want the SJPD to solve the case for you too?" Quinn asked.

His condescending tone hit Darcy like a glass of cold water thrown in his face. He was used to some interdepartmental rivalries, but the sergeant's attitude was getting old. He wondered if Quinn was making a special effort to put the SO down because of Darcy's brother-in-law, or if it was something more personal.

He massaged his left temple and took a deep breath. They'd never met before today. Maybe their first impression hadn't been the best, but it didn't merit such debasing.

There were a lot of things he wanted to tell Quinn, but none of them would bring him any closer to what he needed.

After exhaling for a long time, Darcy continued. "Nhu Tran was the main witness against Jefe. Carol was going to testify in the same case against him. So I figured that at least this 'coincidence'"—Darcy drew air quotes—"merited some discussion."

"Whatever," Quinn said under his breath, but loud enough for everyone to hear it.

Darcy walked to the other side of Quinn's desk. "I figured that you, being the gang hotshot and all, would have put two and two together and asked questions about both cases. But instead you've been gone the whole day, and you brought back nothing." Darcy opened the tub of Red Vines, took a handful, and threw the lid on Quinn's desk. It bounced on the keyboard and hit Quinn in the chest.

He took a bite on a Vine and walked out of the office.

So much for keeping my thoughts to myself.

CHAPTER 18

Oscar was a lot more excited about the new prototype than Dominique, who seemed shy about it. The young man bounced in his chair, only stopping when Oscar took a step back.

"This is big shit, D. Why aren't you more psyched?"

Dominique turned to look up at him but didn't quite make eye contact. "It's not ready. You know I don't like to talk about things until they're ready."

The v.2 was progressing much faster than Oscar had expected. "I guess those guys you hired back home are working out."

"It would be better if they were here."

This was another of Dominique's complaints. He had wanted to hire engineers to work with him in the warehouse, but Oscar had enough worrying about D keeping his mouth shut. He didn't want anybody outside of his crew to know that they were involved in the drone business.

"I'm proud of you, D. This may be the commercially viable product you've wanted from the beginning."

Oscar patted Dominique on the shoulder. Even if he didn't have much use for the v.2s, he was proud of the geek.

After they carried the two boxes of the v.1 model to the car, Oscar left. His nose picked up a stale whiff of marijuana, and he stepped on the gas, missing his Tesla even more. He rolled the windows down and breathed in through his mouth.

He'd only bought the Model S after Dominique convinced him that it was an amazing car. He'd been skeptical, but when he took it for a test drive on the highway and experienced the variable ride height as the car sped up past 100 mph, lowering itself for better aerodynamics, he was sold.

He looked back in the rearview mirror, as if he could still see the warehouse, and thought about the progression he'd witnessed with the drones in just two years. He was pretty impressed with the fairly small start-up. Dominique was a genius. He smiled.

"Damn," he said aloud. Who would have thought he would ever be involved in technology? And it all happened because he and his homie got hungry way too late one summer night.

Oscar had gone to a barbeque at Pascual's aunt's. It had been a hot day, and everybody had gathered around the pool in the shady backyard. The two of them had chilled in lounge chairs, drinking beer after beer. Before they knew it, it was past midnight and everyone had already gone home.

"I'm hungry," Pascual said, heading toward the back door.

"Don't wake your aunt. Let's go to el Grullense."

"Downtown?" Pascual checked the time. "Is it even open?"

"It is." Oscar started walking to the car.

It took them twenty minutes to get there because Pascual stopped at all the yellow lights. When they finally parked on San Carlos Street, right around the corner from the outdoor ordering counter, they were both glad that they hadn't run into any DUI traffic stops.

The red and cinnamon color of the walls and the green roof looked different shades of gray under the night light.

The menu was brightly lit. There were seventeen specials and additional sides. Oscar had tried everything at one point or another and knew all of it was good. There were several people in line waiting to order, and a few others sitting at tables by the side of the building.

A twentysomething ordered and took a few steps to the side to wait for his food. Oscar looked at him. He was wearing flip-flops, khaki cargo shorts, and a red T-shirt with black trim that had something written on it he couldn't quite make out. He smirked. Only three types of people ate at Mexican joints that late at night: cops, drunks, and engineers.

A group of four guys started shouting out items from the list. The one right in front of Oscar nudged his buddy and pointed at the engineer. His white wifebeater was a size too small, stretching across his back. His biceps and shoulders were covered in tattoos.

"Hey, yo. 'Expendable'? What the fuck's that?" he asked.

One of his buddies chuckled, his rotund stomach wobbling as he laughed. Another one wiped his hands on his dirty jeans. Was he getting ready to fight? The fourth mate, the one with the greasy ponytail, just watched.

The engineer ignored the question but moved backward, increasing the distance between him and the group.

"I'm talking to you," Wifebeater said, breaking away from the group. When he reached the guy in the red T-shirt, he pushed him, making him stumble. "I'm going to show you, 'Expendable.'"

Oscar took a step forward, but Pascual grabbed his arm.

The thug lifted his fist, and Oscar saw a rather crude tattoo of Jesus before it came down to smash the engineer's face. The geek toppled onto the ground and tucked into a ball. Dirty Jeans cheered from the sideline, backed by the fat guy.

Oscar sized them up quickly. Wifebeater was the biggest. Dirty Jeans was tall and lean but had no muscle mass. The fat guy was too slow to be a real threat, and Ponytail didn't seem too eager to get involved.

Oscar broke from Pascual's grip and ignored him when he said, "Not your war, bro. Let it go."

Oscar grabbed Wifebeater in a blood choke, lifting him off the engineer. Before he'd managed to completely subdue him, he felt the first few punches on his ribs. He turned around, swinging the guy's body almost as if he were a heavy rag doll. Dirty Jeans moved out of the way before getting hit.

Pascual tackled the fat dude to the ground and pounded on his face until it was pulp. He only stopped when Ponytail jumped on him. Pascual slid away from the fatso and managed to get up, then started hitting Ponytail with rapid hooks to the torso.

Oscar slammed Wifebeater against the pavement, kicked him in the stomach, and turned to punch Dirty Jeans straight in the nose. His eyes closed, probably from the pain of the impact, and his nose bled like a fire hose. Even though they were at a disadvantage, it didn't take long for Oscar and Pascual to claim victory. The four men crawled away. Oscar ran toward Wifebeater and kicked him in the ass so hard the man fell on his face a few feet from their car.

"Your food's ready," the plump woman behind the counter told the engineer in a sheepish voice once the car had disappeared.

Oscar walked toward him and extended a hand to help him get up to his feet.

"Thank you."

"Don't mention it," Oscar said as Pascual reached them.

"Can I pay for your food?" the kid asked with a strong French accent.

Oscar waved his hand and walked to the order window.

"My name's Dominique Badeaux," he said, still standing where they'd left him.

Oscar didn't reply, wanting to order.

Dominique walked toward them, his long arms stiff, almost glued to his sides. "I really don't know how to thank you."

"It's cool, man. Don't sweat it," Oscar said after he ordered the Burrito Chilito.

Dominique didn't go away. He grabbed his food and waited until Oscar and Pascual picked a spot. He sat at the table next to them. Oscar could see the guy wanted to talk but probably didn't know what to say. He didn't feel like having a conversation with a stranger. He was beginning to be sorry he'd helped the guy. It was one thing to save him from getting the shit beat out of him, and another to become BFFs.

"What does the T-shirt mean?" Pascual asked.

Oscar would have kicked him under the table, but he settled for a dirty look. Pascual ignored him. The engineer pulled out the bottom of his red T-shirt, as if he needed to get a better view of the "Expendable" black letters.

"It's from *Star Trek*. The red uniforms are the only ones who get killed. So they are expendable." He smiled at them, as if what he'd just said made all the sense in the world.

Pascual and Oscar looked at each other and worked on finishing their food.

When they were almost done, Dominique said, "I've never been hit before. I just moved here five months ago." He touched his ribs and winced.

"France?" Pascual asked, not caring that Oscar had sent him signals to stop talking to the engineer.

"Yes. I came to work in Silicon Valley. I have a start-up."

"How original," Oscar muttered under his breath.

"What about?" Pascual asked, once again ignoring Oscar's burning stare.

CHAPTER 19

Oscar, Pascual, and Dominique ended up talking that night until dawn. A few days later Oscar made him a proposal. Dominique's prototypes were currently nothing more than a bunch of code in a computer, but the French expat needed money, and that was something Oscar had a lot of.

He told Dominique he wanted to invest, but only if he could get his hands on at least ten units as soon as they were ready to fly.

"What would you use them for?"

"You don't need to worry about that."

D clenched his jaw and locked eyes with the floor. "I moved here for two reasons." He started pulling on his eyebrow while still focused on the tip of his shoes. "It's a lot easier to get a tech start-up going in Silicon Valley than in Berlin or Stockholm, and none of the other cities in Europe are as technologically advanced. But the most important reason is my dream to create the ultimate surveillance drone and sell it to the US government."

Oscar waited, pretty sure of where Dominique was going.

"It's been hard for me to get seed investments, because I don't have a live prototype. Your money would help me a lot moving things forward, but I won't take it if you'll use my drones for anything illegal."

Oscar could have walked away at that point. If he were a good guy, he would have. But D's hopes and dreams were much lower in his priority list than his own goals.

"I'm not sure what I'll do with them. But you have my word I won't use the birds for anything that would hurt you or your company." When D finally looked up at him, Oscar added, "I genuinely want to invest because I see potential in this." He still got nothing from the engineer. "Look, dude, I'm a smart guy. This is a good play for me. I won't screw you."

After another long silence while he pulled a few more hairs off of his eyebrows, Dominique took the $250K from Oscar's extended hand, sealing the deal. The next day Dominique called his father in France to convert a section of his manufacturing plant into a drone-making factory. And that was that. Oscar had become an angel investor of Faucon, or "hawk" in French. He chuckled. He was an angel and a devil. You couldn't get any more schizo than that.

His first thought had been to use them to transport dope. Pascual thought it was too risky, because drones were all over the news. Oscar dismissed him, claiming that the watchdogs were far from figuring out how to regulate the civilian side of the industry. But as months passed, he came up with a different use for the birds.

He invested in a command center, hidden in plain sight at an office complex off of First Street and Trimble. Pascual found the two brightest and most technologically savvy soldiers and set them up in the bright and sunny space, full of cool gadgets, toys, the latest computers and monitors, and loads of sugary drinks and junk food.

A few months later, when the first alphas were ready, Dominique came to the command center for the launch. Before he even considered flying one of the birds, he insisted on giving a long explanation about why his drones were special.

"Not only have I been able to solve the short battery life without adding substantial weight to the UAVs." He stood in front of his audience. "And made them fortyfive percent more quiet. But my drones also use a technology based on how insects see—the compound eye—that allows them to actually 'see' where they are going. This is huge," he alleged, standing tall with his finger up in the air to command further attention. "The drones are able to react without a pilot's command to avoid collision should something unexpected come their way."

The four gangsters shared furtive glances as they listened to Dominique talk. It wasn't that they weren't impressed or interested. It was mostly that 90 percent of what the engineer was saying was going over their heads.

After the lecture, Dominique did the honors. They watched the drone take off on one of the monitors. The engineer entered a few commands. The drone changed direction, climbed to 400 feet, and then flew back to exactly the place it'd lifted off from.

Spider, the older of the two soldiers, got to try it next. The previous hours of instruction Dominique gave them came to fruition. In what felt like only minutes but was probably longer, the drone took off, flew around the neighborhood, and returned safely to the roof. They all cheered, and then Palo stood up.

He pulled his sleeves down, but they didn't quite reach his wrists. His pant legs were as ill-fitting, showcasing two inches of discolored socks. He looked around his audience, maybe waiting for permission. After he completed the mission as successfully as Spider, they celebrated the perfect launch of the Hawk v.1 project with too much alcohol.

"Have you decided what you're going to do with them?" Dominique asked with a slight slur.

"Nope," Oscar said.

Pascual looked away.

D raised his almost-empty glass. "Do something cool. This is only the beginning."

They toasted to that.

Before Dominique passed out, Spider drove him home. When he came back, Oscar told them what they were going to do with the drones. It would be something much more lucrative and less risky than running "packages."

CHAPTER 20

Darcy exited the SJPD building, threw the handful of Red Vines in the garbage, and walked the block up to the Sheriff's Office. When he entered the bullpen, a few people turned their heads to look at him. The open space, jam-packed with double desks facing each other, small monitors, old computers, and black desk phones, was brimming with activity.

Before he got to his desk, Acting Captain Howard waved him into his office. Darcy closed the door behind him and wished he'd gone straight home.

"Where have you been all day?"

Darcy exhaled through gritted teeth. He wasn't sure if he was more annoyed at his boss's question or the unspoken implication.

"I've been working the case with the task force."

"So what do you have? Where are we? I told you, *we* need to find this woman, not SJPD."

"Every law enforcement agency is working on these cases—"

"They're connected?" Howard interrupted him. "Why haven't you informed me? I told you I wanted hourly updates."

"We don't know yet. There's a strong possibility."

Howard's stern stare told him he was still waiting for answers.

"Don't be ridiculous, Howard. You can't seriously expect hourly updates."

Howard didn't blink. "But I am serious. I mean it. We solve this case, you understand me? *We* solve this case."

Darcy wanted to slam the door behind him but at the last moment thought better of it.

He reached his desk and turned his laptop on. It was dead. He cursed, plugged it in, and went to the kitchen to get something to eat. The fridge was empty and there was nothing edible in the vending machine. He made a new pot of coffee and waited for it to brew. When he got back with a full mug, the computer booted up, and he started working on the warrant for Nhu's phone dumps.

He stopped typing to take a sip of his coffee, then leaned back on the chair and rubbed his right eye. Once, after he'd been working on a case for almost forty-eight hours straight, he rubbed both eyes without even thinking. The pain he felt, when his glass eye chafed against the socket, was almost as bad as what he felt when he'd lost it. He'd never done it again.

Stepan Kozlov.

Every time he thought about his missing eye, he remembered Stepan Kozlov and the day he had killed Gigi and stabbed Darcy's eye. He felt a sting, almost as if the Russian arms smuggler was stabbing him again.

Saffron's warm voice pulled him out of the nightmare from across the bullpen.

"I knew you would be here. Are you okay?" she asked.

"Yes. Just starving," he said when he saw the two bags of Chinese takeout in her hands.

He met her halfway to the entrance, just then realizing that most of the people who had been there earlier were already gone.

"I love you, you know that?" He kissed her on the lips and wrapped his arms around her, cracking the green parka she wore way into the spring.

"And not just because I bring you food I hope." She winked.

He took the bags from her and placed the containers around his keyboard. Once they were both seated, he grabbed the box closest to him.

"You got honey walnut prawns? You really are the woman of my dreams." With a mouthful, he added, "You have no idea how hungry I am."

"I figured you wouldn't be going home for a while." She put a healthy portion of fried rice in her mouth. "I was following the news. They're not saying much about what happened at the courthouse, just that a material witness in a homicide case has gone missing."

"Yeah, it's been a strange day. One awful homicide, and now this MIA case." He looked at the board out of habit, hoping that there was nothing on it that would turn Saffron's stomach. It was blank, and for once he was glad about that.

"I heard about that case too. The food at Berto's was awesome," Saffron said.

"You too?" He pointed at her with the chopsticks.

"What?"

"How come neither you nor Sorensen have taken me there but you both love the place?"

"You haven't been here that long," she said, covering her mouth while she talked.

"Seven months is not that long? Really? That's your story?"

"Eat your food," she said, and made a zip-it gesture with her fingers.

He laughed. He liked being around her. She always lifted his mood, no matter what horrors the day brought.

"Anything I can do to help?" she asked.

"Keep feeding me."

"That's easy. No, seriously."

Darcy shared with her a lot more about his job than he had with any other girlfriend. He knew she understood his world, because she'd been a victim in one of his earlier cases.

"Tell me about this restaurant," he said.

She chewed while she thought. "It's been around forever. It's a dive." She pushed the rice closer to Darcy. "But the food is fresh and the place smells amazing. And for Mexican food, I think he cooks pretty healthy. I've never had better fajitas in my life."

"Sorensen raved about the burritos." He took the carton she'd offered. "Done?"

"All yours."

"Was it a neighborhood hangout?"

"No. People from all over the South Bay went there. Berto's was the only reason to venture into East San Jose." Saffron threw the chopsticks in the garbage and interlaced her fingers on her lap. "A few months ago I went with a few friends from work, and it was closed. We knocked because we could see light inside, but the door was locked and the blinds were drawn. Nobody came, so we left. We bitched the entire ride back to San Pedro Square." She smiled. "I checked online afterwards and found out it was closed on Mondays. I should have looked before we went." After a pause she added, "Do you think he'll reopen after the crime scene gets cleared?"

"Who knows? He was very distraught this morning." Darcy wiped his mouth with a paper napkin and left to throw the empty containers into the kitchen garbage.

"You have a long night?" Saffron asked when he came back.

"Probably."

99

"Do you want me to hang around or go by your place to walk Shelby?"

Darcy scratched his chin, feeling the five-o'clock shadow prickling his fingers. "Would you mind staying over tonight?"

She got up and kissed his cheek. "Not at all. I'll wait up for you."

He took her hand and held it for a few seconds. Their eyes met. He felt the warmth of her body close to his. "I'll walk you out."

"Really? I thought you liked to sit back and check my butt."

Darcy laughed. "Yes, I like doing that too."

At the elevator they kissed one more time and she took the stairs.

As he walked back to his desk, he heard his cell ring. He picked it up. It was Rachel.

"Detective, I tried reaching Sorensen, but he's not picking up. Anyway, I've been going through the evidence. We have several kitchen knives. It's a restaurant, so nothing unusual about that, but I found two interesting things. There was a six-inch hollow-edge chef's knife that had been wiped clean, though I found traces of blood—"

"But that's not large enough to be the murder weapon."

"Detective, you know that every time you interrupt me, you owe me a caramel macchiato, right?"

"True. I better shut up then."

"Smart man." Her voice was light, and he knew she was teasing. "As I was saying, the interesting thing was that *only* one knife was wiped clean. There were no prints, but we found traces of human blood where the blade meets the handle. We're processing it right now."

It was somewhat noteworthy, but only valuable if the blood was Carol's or someone's who didn't work there. He would have to wait for the results before he got too excited.

"We matched prints on the other knives. There were Berto's of course, and two people who were in the system for petty theft and possession from a while back." Darcy heard her leaf through some papers. "One is Carlos Nunez and the other Jimeno Olano. They both work at the restaurant."

"I'll follow up on them tomorrow," he said, and wished he was home already.

"We got another print," she added. "This one's of Oscar Amaro."

"The Diablos shot caller?"

"The street boss, yes. We found his prints on three knives and the spatula."

"But no blood on any of those knives?"

"Nope. There were traces of food. Fish, onions, peppers, mushrooms."

Darcy thought about the food they found by the body.

"He was cooking?" He stood and paced along his desk. "Is he friends with the owner?"

"I can't answer that from the evidence." Just as Darcy was about to hang up, Rachel added, "We have many more prints, so expect this to take a while."

"Understood."

"Oh, and Detective, we opened the gun safe from Carol's garage."

"Anything interesting?"

"Maybe. There was only one thing inside. A big file folder—one of those that look like accordions."

"I haven't seen one of those in ages."

"Me neither. Anyway, it was bursting at the seams, held together by a luggage band. I'll try to take a quick peek tomorrow, but I may have to punt the whole thing to a junior tech."

"Why don't you have someone drop it off here? I can take a look at it."

Rachel didn't say anything for a few seconds. "Shouldn't I send it to the PD?"

"Sure. I'm working with CATCH. We'll take a look."

"I appreciate it, Detective. Not only do I have all the evidence to process, but I have to retest everything Carol did for Jefe's case so I can testify on her behalf."

CHAPTER 21

Oscar couldn't believe that he had already been in business with Dominique for almost a year. He glanced over his shoulder to see the two new swanky drones he was about to add to his fleet of eight flying around Silicon Valley, scouting for houses to burglarize.

As he turned into Alicia Street, his heart skipped a beat when he didn't spot Crow. Oscar drove past the Model S and saw the kid sitting on the curb beside the car's trunk. Crow looked up, his fingers still tapping all over the phone's screen. Oscar left the keys in the ignition when he got out of the Datsun, then gave Crow fifty dollars for keeping his baby safe. He drove to the command center and parked inside the garage, where he could hide his car from satellites and patrolling police.

Pascual was already downstairs with the dolly to carry the new drones inside.

"How's the wound?"

Oscar moved his left arm and was sorry he had.

"It's fine."

He brushed past Pascual into the elevator and used his electronic fob to get up to their secure floor. When the doors opened, they took a right and headed down the hall. Oscar swiped the badge and walked into a room that looked more like a CIA surveillance center than a gangster's pet project.

"How's it going?" Oscar asked.

"Great, boss," Spider said, not lifting his eyes from the eight monitors. When Oscar got closer, he pointed at the top-right one. "We're about to go into that house."

Pascual checked his watch. "It's dinnertime. Are you nuts?"

"No. Been scouting the house for a couple weeks. The entire family just left on vacation. They had so many bags, I thought they were moving. A fucking limo picked them up."

"They'll have high-end security systems," Pascual said.

"Gato's crew will be in and out before the alarm reaches the dispatcher. We've been peeking into each window for a while. We know where everything is."

Oscar looked at Pascual, who shrugged, equal parts coy and impressed.

"We haven't failed yet, boss," Palo said.

And that was true. Since they started using the drones for burglaries, they hadn't been caught once.

Oscar looked around his command center, proud of what he'd built. He was even more pleased about what Dominique's toys were doing for him, his standing in the gang, and his ever-increasing wealth.

So far, being an angel had paid off.

He leaned over on the desk, to the left of his homeboys, and saw Pascual do the same on the right side. The action on the screen was about to begin.

"Game on," Spider said, adjusting his headphones. "Gato, you ready?"

Oscar tapped him on the shoulder. "Speakers, dude."

Spider unplugged the headset from the computer. "Can you hear me okay?" he asked.

"All good." Gato's voice came in as clear as if he were standing next to them.

"There's a spot half a block up, between a red and silver car. Park there."

The screen in front of Oscar showed the stream from the drone that was spying on the target house. To its right, a different drone had eyes on the black Escalade transporting Gato's crew. He'd learned long ago that when going to rich neighborhoods it paid to blend in. The car backed into the space, and after two quick adjustments they stopped and all four doors opened at the same time.

"The target's the brown house, second to last."

The thugs wore dark clothes and their heads were covered with hoods. Each carried a backpack.

Right before they reach the mark, Spider said, "Move to the back of the house, on the north side of the pool, by the bushes. There's a shack and a ladder leaning against it. The second-floor window right above the back door is open a crack."

"Got it." Gato shared the instructions with the crew, and in less than a minute the four teenagers were inside the house.

"The bedroom has jewelry on the dresser, but most of the expensive stuff is in the left drawer of that table thing with the mirror and all the makeup."

Oscar took a step back to take in the full operation. There were four drones focused on the mission. Three were flying around the house, following the burglars as they raided each floor. He marveled at Gato's crew, at how methodical their approach had gotten. Each targeted a room, took whatever they found of value that they could carry, and moved on to the next one. They never stumbled upon each other or repeated sections of the home.

Palo focused on the fourth drone, the one with a "satellite" view of five blocks, with the house in the epicenter. That one allowed them to watch for police cars and unwanted visitors.

When the first kid started climbing down the ladder into the backyard, Oscar checked his watch. By the time they made it back to the car, the whole operation had taken less than eight minutes.

"How long have you been watching that house?" Pascual asked.

"I dunno. We've been on this one awhile," Spider said as he typed a few instructions, and the drones flew away from the scene.

Oscar smiled. The scheme had started more like a game than anything else. He hadn't even been sure that it would work. The one thing he told his guys was that they could never hit the same neighborhood in the same quarter. This way the incidents would look random rather than alerting the police of a burglary ring. It had been Spider's idea to have a set of drones focused on the next target while the rest scouted new areas.

As the kids grew more comfortable with the operation, they started delivering much more than Oscar had ever expected. These teens had gone from drug runners to sophisticated criminals.

If Dominique ever found out what his babies were being used for, he would probably jump off the Golden Gate Bridge. There were some things that were best kept secret.

"Make it go higher." Oscar tapped at the monitor to his left.

Spider directed the drone to rise with a few commands. The view zoomed out and the area widened.

"Do you see that?" Oscar asked Pascual, pointing at a dark rectangle moving down the lower part of the image.

"Yeah... it's the police."

"Exactly. If we had enough of these things in the air, we would know where the blues are at all times."

"Whoa." Pascual's eyes were still glued to the moving car. "This is going to change our world. Nobody—and I mean nobody—can ever know what we are doing here," Oscar said, making sure each one of them understood that violating that trust would cost them their lives. The three gangsters nodded.

"It's only a matter of time before others catch up. But for the time being, let's milk it all the way."

Oscar handed each of them a thick envelope.

CHAPTER 22

After they stuffed the money in their pockets, they focused back on the screens. The patrol car was heading toward the house, but Gato's car was already several blocks away, driving in the opposite direction.

Every time Oscar was in the command center, he felt engulfed by the action going on so far away from him, but it felt close, palpable almost. As if he could change the world without leaving the comfort of his own chair.

From the corner of his eye he saw the time on one of the monitors. He had to go.

"I need your car."

"I'll drive you," Pascual said.

Oscar extended his hand with the palm facing upwards.

"You shouldn't be driving." When Oscar's expression told Pascual he was running out of patience, he handed him the keys. "When are you back? We need to do something with the package."

"You go there now." Oscar checked his watch and calculated how much time he would need. "I'll meet you there at midnight."

Pascual made a driving motion with his hands.

"Take Uber." Oscar knew his homie could get a ride from a slew of soldiers he trusted.

He drove to Meadowfair Park but avoided going through "the Hole" in East San Jose, an area that was mostly industrial during the day but was flooded with police cruisers at night. He thought about his Tesla. He would have to keep it hidden for a while. He knew the police were going through every inch at Berto's, and it was just a matter of time until they found evidence that he'd been there, and not as a patron. In fact, he was surprised they hadn't gone by the clubs yet, with all the blood he'd left behind at the crime scene.

He reached the park and took a spot under a tree on Barberry Lane. It was dark, and the car blended in with the ones already there. He looked over at the school. The gates were open. It was well lit, too much for his taste. The public restrooms to the side of the gates were also bright, but he knew they were locked to keep the bums from shooting up or sleeping inside.

Oscar stayed put until he saw the familiar white van pass and pull over a couple of yards in front of him. He got out of the car and walked on the grass, away from the street. There was no moon. A gray sheen covered the sky as far as he could see. It was uncommon for the South Bay to be overcast.

Halfway in, he stopped and waited. He could hear the man walking toward him. He was shorter than Oscar, heavier, but moved at a brisk pace.

When he felt his presence just a few feet away, Oscar turned around and said, "Thank you for meeting me."

Berto didn't say anything. He had his hands deep in his jacket pockets, the right one much bulkier than the left. That was when Oscar comprehended that Berto had totally misunderstood the reason for the meeting, and he started laughing. He howled for a good minute and his cheeks started hurting. He bent over, trying to regain some composure.

Wiping the tears off his eyes, he said, "No, old man, I didn't call you here to kill you."

Oscar saw the restaurant owner exhale, as if he'd been holding his breath since he left the car.

"I have to ask you, did you ever tell anyone I hang at your place on Mondays?"

Berto shook his head.

"Old man, you have to tell me if you did."

"Nobody knew. I never told anyone."

The clarity in his eyes and his sad expression told Oscar he was honest. "I need your help."

Berto looked slightly relieved, but his hands remained in his pockets.

"Okay, first of all, I didn't kill that woman, but I was there when she was murdered. We had to keep our meetings secret, and that's why I was using your place every week. Chavo and two of his homies came in and attacked us." He pointed at his own face but wasn't sure there was enough light for Berto to see how messed up it was. "They killed her. Berto, they killed her in front of me." His throat closed up as he said the words.

Berto looked down at the freshly cut grass. It was moist from the sprinklers.

"They shot me and tied me up. I couldn't help her. They made me watch while they..."

"You should have told me. I came into my restaurant and found her there." Berto choked up and hugged himself. "It was awful. I don't think I'll ever be able to go back there again."

"I know, I'm sorry. I couldn't warn you. Chavo dumped me in the Santa Cruz Mountains. I didn't make it back home until midday, and then it was already too late."

"Did you love her?" Berto asked.

The question surprised him. He'd never thought about it before. At that point he realized for the first time since he'd met Carol that he did.

"Yes. I did." Oscar felt an incredible void in his chest, the realization that he'd lost her forever.

"Berto, I'm going to take care of you. You know that. If you don't ever want to go back in there, I'll get you another spot. Anywhere you want."

Oscar grabbed Berto's shoulder and squeezed. The intensity he felt carried through his grip.

"When you're ready." Oscar released his hold. "But now I really need your help. The police are going to find out I was there. They're going to ask you questions."

"They already have."

Oscar took a step back. Of course they had. He should have realized that. Maybe it was too late.

"What did you tell them?"

"Nothing. Just what I saw when I went in."

Oscar stared down at him. He was much taller than Berto. The man looked up. His eyes were still sad but no longer scared.

"Did you say anything about me?"

"No. They asked me if I knew the woman. I said no." He shivered. "I didn't really look at her."

Oscar walked around in a circle, thinking. Maybe it wasn't too late. "I need your help," he told Berto again.

CHAPTER 23

Oscar got into the car and watched Berto walk to his, hunched over as if carrying an incredible weight on his shoulders. There was no way the old man would hold strong when drilled by the police. He needed to wrap things up and get the hell out of town.

One loose end was "the package," as Pascual had called her.

Nhu Tran had been an amazing dancer. She was petite, well endowed, and her almond eyes could hypnotize the most steadfast of men. But she had a weakness, and Oscar had capitalized on it. Her child had been born with severe retardation due to her cocaine addiction. She'd managed to get clean, but her tips from dancing were not enough to cover the kid's expenses.

Oscar offered her a deal. If she told the police that she'd seen someone who looked a lot like Jefe kill the drug dealer behind his club, he would get her the best care available for her son, give her a lot of money, and ensure that she would never have to testify.

After the police took her statement and he was confident that they weren't going to come back for additional corroboration, he gave her fifty G as a down payment and sent her to Florida, where her son could attend the Devereux Advanced Behavioral Health center in Viera.

He hadn't heard from her since, until she called him out of the blue a couple of weeks ago. The police found her and served her a subpoena to come and testify at Jefe's discovery. They told her they considered her a flight risk and that they would be escorting her back to California. She'd rang him the first chance she got.

Nhu was crying and accused him of lying to her. He tried calming her down. He offered her money. A lot of money. But she said it wasn't about that. She couldn't lie on the stand. Jefe would have her killed, or worse, hurt her kid.

"You don't have to worry about Jefe," he'd promised her. "Call me tomorrow. I'll have a plan."

Oscar hadn't had a lot of time to come up with something, but looking back, he was pleased it had worked. Nhu was at the safe house, waiting to be shipped somewhere in the country where she could be reunited with her son.

Los Diablos had been operating just fine without Jefe, and he had to make sure things stayed that way. If the only witness suddenly recanted, Jefe would probably be back on the streets looking to personally kill him, no matter what Big Chon had ordered.

Oscar touched his shoulder. It was sore but didn't hurt as much as before. He reflected back on the previous night. Chavo had known somehow he was there. Nobody knew that except Berto. Not even Pascual.

As he got closer to the safe house, he thought about how his world had taken a 180-degree turn in the last twenty-four hours. He needed to figure out what was going on. Since his return to San Jose twelve years earlier, he'd never been in a situation that he hadn't seen coming one way or another.

If he didn't know for sure that the Snakes hated the Diablos with passion, he may have contemplated the possibility that Jefe had reached out to Chavo to go after him. But

113

that was impossible. There was nothing that could make the two gangs work together.

He parked a block away from the safe house and walked in the shadows to the side door. A light appeared on the other side of the peephole. Then it disappeared. A second later the door opened.

Pascual said, "She's a mess."

CHAPTER 24

Wednesday

Darcy decided to start the day in peace by avoiding Howard and went straight to SJPD. It was barely seven thirty, so he'd expected the office to be empty but wasn't entirely surprised to find Jon.

"You're here early," Darcy said, taking Sorensen's chair.

"I'm here late." Jon massaged his neck.

"You've been here all night?"

"Well... I found something, and it was like one of those threads, you know? You see it sticking out, so you pull and pull on it until you realize the whole sweater has come undone."

"Okay..."

"Sorry, my grandma used to knit." Jon blushed.

Darcy savored his coffee while he waited for Jon to go on. He took another long sip and realized how little he was looking forward to a hazelnut refill.

"Anyway, you want to see?" Jon asked. His voice wasn't as high pitch as it normally was when he found something that could break a case.

Darcy rolled Sorensen's chair around the desks, and Jon pushed the edge of the monitor toward him. The screen was filled with open tabs, one on top of another. It was hard to see how many, but there were probably twenty or thirty.

"What are we looking at?"

Jon tabbed through a few windows. He settled on one, but before opening it, he turned and pointed at the board.

"I thought it would be a good idea to do some research on Jefe."

"You were working on my case?" Darcy was touched. He figured he'd be working on it alone.

"It never hurts to look into things." Jon smiled. "Carol was testifying on Jefe's case. If Quinn busts my balls, I'll say that at least it merited a quick pass to see if I found any less-than-obvious connections." Jon faced Darcy as he was taking another sip. "But next time, you have to bring me a coffee too."

"Deal." Darcy raised his paper cup and then pulled out his phone. "I'll text Sorensen to do a run before he comes to the office."

Jon smiled. "He won't do it."

"Never hurts to try," Darcy said, but knew the kid was right.

Jon pointed at the open file on his monitor. "I checked all of the cases against Jefe. Nothing out of the ordinary for a gangster. Robberies, drugs, assaults, etc. He was wanted for a previous attempted murder but was never charged. He's been in and out of prison most of his life. Jefe's gone up the ranks in the Diablos, mostly as muscle. There were several hits inside Folsom and Pelican Bay attributed to him, but the DOC and the DA don't usually prosecute, so he was never charged. But they earned him stripes with the Devil Disciples' bosses. It seems that every time he got out of prison, he'd been promoted. The last time he got out, about four years ago, he managed two regiments, one in East San Jose and a much smaller one in Fremont."

"East Bay... So the Devils are expanding."

"Looks that way. Quinn will know more. Anyway, he was doing pretty well until he got rolled up for killing Ochoa. He's been awaiting trial since then."

"You know why it's taking this long? I thought these guys pushed for speedy trials, hoping the DA doesn't find additional evidence to charge them with the gang enhancements."

"Maybe it's because this is his third strike." Jon clicked on a few files until he found one showing the gun used in the Ochoa shooting. "The gun was wiped clean. Everything except a partial of the right thumb here." He pointed to the top of the silver hammer.

"It's rare these days to find prints on guns," Darcy said.

"I know. And look at this picture." He tabbed through several more screens. "See this?" He pulled up a surveillance photo of Jefe from a few years back. Three other guys stood by him while he paid a street vendor for a taco.

Darcy noticed the hand holding the money. "He's left-handed."

"Exactly." Jon jumped out of his chair.

"He could be ambidextrous."

"Maybe."

"But why would he go into an alley to kill a low-level drug dealer holding two guns?" Darcy finished his coffee.

"Ochoa was not only half of Jefe's size but consumed more merchandize than he sold." Jon turned to face him.

"He wouldn't have put up much of a fight." Looking back at the gun photo with the print, Darcy added, "And the defense attorney didn't bring this up?"

"I've checked all the documents presented already and haven't seen any mention of it so far, but I bet he'll argue it in court." Shrugging, Jon added, "But I think everybody will think the same thing—that Jefe's ambidextrous."

"Was he?"

"Only about one percent of the population truly is. I haven't found a single shot in which he's using his right hand to do something you would normally do with your dominant one. I don't think he is."

CHAPTER 25

Sorensen walked into the station, waved hello to the clerk, and stepped into the elevator, happy that it was working again. Quinn was already inside. They nodded to each other, but neither said a word.

He hated working with new people. He should have thought about that before transferring to SJPD, but for him it had been about moving with Virago and staying away from that moron Howard. Though working with Quinn hadn't been that great either, and the sergeant wasn't making any efforts to win anybody over.

He thought about Lynch. It'd taken him a while to warm up to the Seattle expat, but now that his old partner and Quinn were not getting along, he was dreading the possibility of someone else joining them in the task force.

When the doors of the elevator opened, they both walked into the bullpen, still in silence.

"Jon found something interesting," Lynch said in lieu of a salutation.

"Really?" Quinn asked, the skepticism tangible in his tone.

Jon told them about Jefe being a lefty but leaving a right thumbprint on the hammer.

"There're a million reasons why his print could be there," Quinn said.

"And one could be that he was framed." Sorensen knew exactly what Lynch and Jon were thinking.

Quinn rolled his eyes.

"Think about it. It could be," Lynch said.

"There's no reason for it. Ochoa was supplying drugs to Jefe's pregnant girl. He had plenty of motive and opportunity. Besides, this case has already been thoroughly investigated." Quinn opened the drawer and rummaged through it, then slammed it, empty-handed. "Gangsters don't get 'framed.' A soldier may take the blame for something he didn't do, but you won't get someone at Jefe's level to do that."

Quinn must have felt they were all unconvinced, because he got up and marched to the kitchen. Halfway there he said, "Jefe killed the lowlife who supplied his baby's mamma. Gangsters kill for a lot less." He turned and looked straight at Lynch. "We did solid police work on this. We have evidence and a witness your guys lost. You're barking up the wrong fucking tree."

Sorensen scanned the board. After a few seconds he got up and tapped on Oscar's photo. Ignoring Quinn's comment, he said, "Is it possible that Guero framed him to go up the ladder?"

"I've told you already, that's not how gangs work," Quinn yelled from the kitchen. "If Guero wanted to take Jefe's spot, he would have killed him, not framed him. End of story. Move on."

Sorensen looked at Lynch and then at Jon, who was fidgety, as if he felt guilty for sparking the confrontation between the detectives. Sorensen patted his shoulder. At the Sheriff's, Jon had been the golden boy. Here, Quinn was not taking anything for granted.

"Why are you being so dense? I think it merits a second look. It's not a reflection on your work on the case," Sorensen said.

Quinn walked back into the bullpen and gave him the finger. "Screw you and whatever you're implying. My investigation was solid. The case is tight. I'm the sergeant of this task force, and I'm telling you to not waste any more time on this."

"Listen, asshole, I don't give a shit who you are." Sorensen turned from the whiteboard to face him. "If you don't want to follow leads, why don't you ask Virago to assign you somewhere else?"

"I'm working on it, but in the meanwhile I'm not having you fuck things up with a solid trial coming up. If you can't handle command, I'll be happy to sign your transfer to traffic enforcement." Quinn set his mug on the table and then squared his stance, facing them.

Sorensen almost laughed. He wanted to be mad, but Quinn's attitude was so childish it made him feel as if he were back in junior high. He brushed his blond curls away from his forehead and turned to the board, deciding to let it go.

But then, not totally surprising himself, he said, "You're a dick, and I don't give a shit if you think you're lead of the task force or a fucking beauty pageant. I worked homicide long enough to know that people kill for all kinds of reasons, gangsters or not. Jefe could have been framed, and we're going to look into that."

"Oh, I get it. You don't have enough work to do, is that it?" Quinn grabbed a stack of folders and dumped them on Sorensen's desk. "Here, why don't you take these?" When Sorensen didn't say anything, he added, "I worked Jefe's case. Carol worked that case. Matthews put together the prosecution. It's solid. I'm ordering you to stop meddling with a case that's about to go to trial." Quinn crossed his arms and stood tall. They were the same height.

Before Sorensen had a chance to respond, Quinn added, "You know what? You're off the case." He pointed at Lynch.

"Go help the deputy here with his missing person, and leave me alone."

Nobody said a word. Sorensen looked at Lynch, who was watching the exchange while rubbing his left temple. Jon made himself busy typing on his keyboard.

Quinn picked up his jacket and headed to the door without saying another word.

The three remained silent until the sergeant disappeared into the hallway outside of CATCH.

"What an asshole," Sorensen said.

"Captain Virago won't kick us out of the task force, right?" Jon asked.

"No way." Sorensen sat down.

"I'll call Rachel and ask her to look a bit deeper into this, since she's preparing to sub for Carol at the trial," Lynch said.

"Good idea." Sorensen was still fuming from the exchange with Quinn.

"I'll keep digging, see if I find anything else that seems weird," Jon offered.

"Sounds good." Addressing Lynch, Sorensen said, "Let's go and talk to Berto."

Lynch checked the time. "It's not even eight thirty yet. You think he'll be up?"

"With what he saw yesterday, I don't think he's sleeping much."

"True." Lynch chuckled as they walked out of the bullpen.

Sorensen pushed the elevator button.

"By the way, you got my text?" Lynch asked.

"No."

"You just ignored it."

"Yep."

"It would have been nice for you to bring coffee."

"I know." He punched the elevator button again.

"You're almost as much a dick as Quinn is." Darcy laughed. "You sure you don't want to take the stairs?"

"For the one day that the elevator is working? No, thank you."

He got in. Lynch left him behind and took the stairs.

When he reached the garage, Lynch was already heading for his car.

"Dude, I'm not going to a low-income neighborhood in a Shelby Cobra."

"We'll have to go in yours again." Lynch backtracked to the Jeep.

"At least I get to drive."

"What issues do you have with my driving?"

"You have to ask?"

Sorensen looked at Lynch for a second before he shut the door. He knew he couldn't rehash the time his partner almost got Jon killed without getting mad all over again. As he drove by the Cobra, the candy-apple-red paint glinted in the light.

"I haven't forgotten about what happened to Jon," Lynch said, also looking at his car.

Lynch knew better than to go on a hot pursuit of a car full of paramilitary goons fleeing from a bank. "I haven't either."

His voice was cold. He'd mostly forgiven Lynch, but he still couldn't talk about it.

"I never—" Lynch started.

"I know. You've apologized enough times already. All I care about is that it never happens again."

Sorensen pulled out of the parking lot.

"It won't." Lynch looked out the window.

123

"I've seen the bullet hole," Sorensen said. "It's a good reminder."

"That's why I left it there. Thirty-four bullet holes. Thirty-three got fixed."

They rode in silence for several miles. When they took the Curtner exit, Lynch asked if he needed directions.

"Nah. This is my city. I know every nook and cranny."

They fell silent again until the radio crackled.

"It's working again?" Lynch asked.

"On and off. Shut up so we can hear what's up."

"Report of 10-57 at George Washington Elementary School. The RP said he heard two shots but it could be more. No visual of the shooter," the dispatcher said in a steady voice.

"Shit," Lynch said.

"That's right around the corner." Sorensen stepped on the accelerator.

Lynch turned the spinners on as they drove through a red light. They took a left at the second stop sign and then turned the sirens off to approach in silence. Two blocks later, Sorensen stopped the car at the corner of Pulgas and Lenora.

They both bolted from the car and grabbed the vests from the trunk. As soon as they came around the brick wall, they could see the playground behind the chain-link fence. There were several dozen kids and a couple of teachers standing by the opposite wall. On the ground a little girl lay bleeding.

CHAPTER 26

Oscar woke up feeling restless. He'd tossed and turned all night, unable to find a comfortable position. He'd been thinking about Nhu. Pascual's comment about her being a mess had been the understatement of the year.

He went into the house and met her in the living room. She looked like she was using again. She was drenched in sweat, could not stop crying and yelling, and at one point she launched at Oscar and started hitting him. He grabbed her flailing arms and held her tight until she calmed down.

"I never thought you would have to come back to testify," he told her. "I was sure Jefe would plead guilty if they took out the third strike. And when he didn't, I was sure the police would never find you."

When she stopped crying and seemed to be listening, he let her arms go and continued. "When you called, I told you I would take care of things, and I have. You're here. Nobody knows where you are, and we'll get you out of the state and reunited with your son in a day or two."

She looked up at him. Her eyes were still wet, but the intensity of her stare told him she was sober.

"I need you to listen to me real carefully." He squeezed her hand.

She nodded.

"My guys are going to get you out of California, and you will never, ever have to come back, but I need you to sit tight, relax, and not be any trouble. Got it?"

"Yes," she whispered.

Oscar left shortly after that. He had other things to concentrate on that were a lot more important than babysitting a stripper.

The knock on the door brought him back to the bright morning and his aching shoulder. He massaged it and yelled, "What?"

Pascual walked into the bedroom.

"What's up?"

Pascual was wearing shiny sweats and a white ribbed wifebeater. He looked more like an Italian mafioso than a Mexican one. He was sweating, but it didn't look like sweat from a workout. It looked like nervous sweat, the kind you get when the police take you in for questioning and you have no idea which mess they got you in for.

Oscar pushed himself out of the bed. The light breeze from the window felt good against his naked body.

Pascual turned the TV on. "There was a shooting at the George Washington School."

"One of ours?"

If the Snakes were going after his guys, he would have to start a full-blown war with Chavo. He preferred to keep it simple, just between the two of them. But there was no way to know what that worm was up to.

"Don't have details. Maybe." Pascual turned to look at the news report. The live video was raggedy, coming from someone's phone rather than a professional news camera.

Oscar felt his jaw drop when he saw the gunman. "Is that Robbie?"

"*Pendejo*, it looks like him…" Pascual covered his mouth. "Damn."

CHAPTER 27

Darcy could see the blood on the ground but couldn't figure out where the kid was hit. The girl was lying on her back, facing away from him. Long black hair spread out on the ground. He kept walking by the concrete fence. Inch by inch the playground opened up to him, but still no sign of the shooter. Two teachers were by the school wall, almost kitty-corner from him, keeping the kids calm and glued in their spots. He took two more steps, but still no gunman.

Without looking back, Darcy snapped his fingers to get Sorensen's attention, then pointed straight ahead with his left hand and quickly looked over his shoulder, directing Sorensen to go around the building. Darcy kept moving forward. He heard more sirens in the distance and cursed. The situation could quickly turn into a bloodbath. He didn't have a lot of time.

Based on where the teachers were staring at, he knew the shooter had to be somewhere on the other side of the wall. When he reached the end of the solid fence, he peered deep inside the school yard and finally spotted him. He had to blink a few times to believe what he was seeing.

Darcy took a step back to take cover behind the wall and looked behind him. There were several people on the other side of the street. He motioned for a younger man with a scruffy beard, baggy jeans, and a backpack to come to him.

"You work at the school?" Darcy asked.

"Yes, teaching assistant," the man said, shy steps closing the distance between them.

"You know the kid?"

"Robbie. Robbie Vasquez."

"Do you know what started all this?"

"No. I was in the cafeteria when it happened."

Darcy checked his surroundings. "I want you to gather everybody on that side of the street. Do you understand me?" He pointed to where he and Sorensen had come from.

The teacher nodded and turned to guide them away from the school entrance. Darcy checked the street ahead of him. It was now empty, but several people in houses across from the school peeked out of their windows. He wished he could tell them that there was nothing to see, but of course there was. He even saw a few with phones, recording everything live and probably planning on selling it to the networks.

A few more patrol cars parked where the teacher was standing with the other bystanders. Lights flashed but no sirens. A couple of news vans also fought for space. Darcy was glad that the solid wall extended all through the east side of the playground, so they wouldn't be able to see anything until it was over.

Darcy continued onward until he left the safety of the brick for the cyclone fence. There was no longer anything protecting him from getting shot. He reached the entrance to the playground, never losing sight of the gun.

The kid couldn't be more than seven or eight years old. He was very skinny, with a worn-out green polo shirt and khaki pants. His hair was on the longer side, waving into his eyes.

"Robbie, my name is Darcy."

The gun he was holding moved from the teachers and kids by the wall over to him.

Darcy wasn't sure if the intensity in the kid's eyes was hatred or fear.

"Robbie, I need to ask you a favor. I'm going to walk over there and make sure this little girl's okay. Will you let me do that?"

After a very long second the boy nodded almost imperceptibly.

"Thank you. I really appreciate it."

Every step felt like a walk on the moon. The distance toward the bleeding girl closed so slowly he feared she might die before he could reach her. When he finally got there, and only losing eye contact with Robbie for a second, he looked over the fence and saw that Sorensen was already there, pointing his Glock at the eight-year-old kid. Behind him there were at least another eight to ten cops, but still no reporters. Patrol must be doing a good job keeping them behind the tape.

He kneeled down and checked the girl's vitals. She was still alive.

"Robbie, this girl is hurt." He watched the boy as he absorbed the words. "I need to get her to the hospital. Can I do that?"

"No." He straightened the arm that held the gun.

"I know you want her to be okay. You know her, right? What's her name?"

Robbie didn't say anything but pushed the gun toward Darcy as if that would help the bullets come out. He didn't shoot, but it was obvious he'd watched too many movies.

"I tell you what, let me get her to a hospital, and you and I can stay here as long as you want to."

"No. Don't touch her, or I'll shoot you too." Robbie cupped the Beretta with both hands.

The gun looked so big against his tiny body. Darcy was surprised he managed to keep holding it up for this long.

"I'm just going to take her to my partner over there, okay? Then you and I can talk about what's going on."

When Robbie didn't offer further resistance, he scooped the girl off the ground.

Facing the barrel of the gun, Darcy covered the girl with his hands as best he could and walked backward toward Sorensen. When he got to the gate, Sorensen took the girl. Darcy spotted Quinn a few feet behind his partner, pointing his weapon at Robbie.

Sorensen wished him luck as he walked back into the school yard. He passed the pool of blood and kept walking. The kid raised the gun as Darcy got closer, keeping a steady aim at his chest.

"Don't come any closer or I'll shoot you."

Darcy hadn't quite got to the point where he could tackle the kid yet. He stopped and kneeled down on one knee. He needed to be able to get to him if he had to in one quick move, but he also wanted to look at him at eye level.

"Robbie, I think the little girl's going to be okay, so you are not going to be in any trouble."

The kid didn't respond, but he was having a hard time keeping the gun upright. He rested his elbows against his body but still maintained the aim.

"Are you hungry? Thirsty?"

Robbie shook his head, the long black hair swaying as he moved.

"I want to hear what happened. Will you tell me?"

"Amelia's my sister. I hate her!" Robbie said, raising his elbows again.

"She's your sister? Man, why didn't you tell me that before? I have a sister. I hate her too," Darcy said.

Robbie looked confused. "You do?"

"Of course I do. Sisters suck. Mine is a pain in the butt. Always telling me what to do. Is Amelia older or younger?"

"She's younger. She doesn't leave me alone."

"Mine is older. Always bossing me around. Clean this, tidy up your room, eat your broccoli." Darcy shook his head.

Robbie started smiling. The gun was almost pointing down now.

"Do you have any other siblings?" Darcy asked.

"An older brother. He's badass."

"Oh yeah?"

"Yes, he's the youngest Diablo to get jumped in."

"How old is he?"

"Fourteen. They jumped him so hard, he came home black and blue. I want to be like him, but I'll make it when I'm twelve." Robbie moved the gun up when he realized it wasn't pointing at Darcy anymore. But that didn't last very long.

"I bet you won't have any problem beating your brother." Darcy watched as Robbie's hand swayed.

"You think?" Robbie's voice sounded genuinely pleased.

Once the gun pointed back to the ground, Darcy jumped and in less than a second had taken the firearm from Robbie and picked him up in the air.

"What are you doing? Let me go!" Robbie screamed in his ear, and kicked his feet against Darcy's shins.

Darcy held the kid's arms by the sides with a tight embrace and walked toward the gate. When he got there, he handed the gun to Quinn, who was running toward them. Robbie was screaming and kept kicking with his tiny feet. When they reached the first police car, Darcy secured the kid in the back and used a zip tie to cuff him, since there were no handcuffs small enough for an eight-year-old.

CHAPTER 28

Darcy closed the patrol car's door. Robbie was crying, and he didn't know how to console him. Sorensen came to meet him, his shirt and vest stained with Amelia's blood. He was wiping his hands, but the blood was resilient.

"Is she going to make it?" Darcy asked his partner.

"I don't know. She's hit pretty bad in the abdomen. She's only six years old."

"Good job out there." Quinn extended his hand.

Darcy shook it, feeling awkward.

"That's the grandma right there. The mom went with Amelia in the ambulance." Quinn pointed at a woman who was as wide as she was tall.

"Have you talked to her yet?" Darcy asked.

Quinn shook his head.

"Let's go." Darcy took the wipe Sorensen offered.

"I know her. Let me do it."

Quinn pushed his way through them, but for the first time he invited them to follow.

Darcy didn't complain, and Sorensen just shrugged. It was easier to have someone lead who already had rapport with the family.

"Señora Vasquez," Quinn said when they got within a few feet of her.

"Ay, Sergeant Quinn. Robbie's a good kid. I don't know what happened."

"Were the kids fighting?"

"Just the usual stuff. She follows him around, always wants to do what he does. He gets so irritated."

"The gun—where did he get it?"

"I don't know. We don't allow guns in the house."

Quinn stared down at her for a long while. "Señora Vasquez, let's cut the crap, yes? Every male in your family's a Diablo. Robbie just boasted about Julio being jumped in. This is very serious."

"No, no. You know how kids are, always making stuff up. He doesn't know nothing. Julio got into a fight at school and made up that story to impress his little brother. I swear."

Quinn's expression said it all. "Señora Vasquez, please don't insult me."

"Ay, no. I never want to do that." She wrung her hands and started crying. "It's true, Sergeant Quinn. My daughter has good kids. No gangs. I swear, no gangs."

"Where did Robbie get the gun?" Quinn pushed.

"I don't know. I don't know." She covered her face with both hands.

Darcy noticed how the wedding band cut into the fat of her finger. The only other jewelry was a small gold cross hanging from her neck.

"Señora Vasquez, I need you to find out how Robbie got the gun. Okay?"

She nodded and started wailing.

Quinn turned and walked away from her. Addressing the two detectives, he said, "Her husband's doing life in Pelican Bay. Robbie's father got killed by his own people because he wanted to get out of the life, and the eldest grandson, Julio..."

Well, you heard—he's in now too." He shook his head. "She's good people. She's been working at the market for longer than I can remember. But the daughter... We thought she'd gone legit when she got a job at a dentist office."

"That sounds legit enough," Sorensen said.

"Yeah, until we realized she was stealing identities."

"What?"

"Exactly. It took the ID theft guys a while to solve the case. Marianna was feeding the customers' personal info to her boyfriend, who was selling it out."

"Gangs into identity theft. Seems more sophisticated than what I would have expected," Darcy said.

"Easy crime to commit, and it pays well. Depending on how much information they have, they can sell it from ten to fifty dollars a pop. That's what most of the 'legit' women do. They have clean records, they get admin jobs and help their men out with this little side business."

Darcy held up the gun inside an evidence bag. "Given the family history, Robbie could have found the gun at home."

Quinn looked across the street at a small one-story house with fading tan paint as if he could see inside it.

"I don't know, there're a few parolees living here. They're not the smartest, but they've been around the system enough to know better than to have guns on the premises when we can search without a warrant or advance notice."

Darcy turned to look at Robbie inside the police car. "He got it from somewhere."

CHAPTER 29

Oscar got dressed. He was mildly curious about the school shooting, but not enough to risk going there in person. The Diablo community was tight, and the Vasquez family had a long history in the gang. But if the little brother was stupid enough to play with guns, that was someone else's problem. Not his beef, especially not now.

Pascual came back into the house. "Everything's ready."

"Grab some clothes." He held the empty duffel bag in his hand.

His shoulder was still hurting and his face throbbed. He opened the Tylenol bottle and chewed on four tablets. He needed his head clear so he could set up his next steps.

"What do you want to bring?"

"A couple days' worth of clothes. Just enough until things cool down."

He thought about where he should go. He'd invested in a couple of properties around the South Bay and used them as storage or hideouts when his soldiers needed time off from law enforcement.

"I think we should go to the one at Almaden. Is it empty?" Oscar asked.

Pascual was deep inside Oscar's closet. He brought out a few T-shirts and polos, two pairs of jeans, some socks and underwear and stuffed it all in the bag. "No, we moved Nhu there this morning. We need another day or two to set everything up for her."

Oscar looked at him. He'd expected the package would've been taken care of already.

"Don't give me shit. You want her out of the state? I'm gonna do that, but it's got to be done right."

"A'right." Pascual was a good planner, always covered all the angles, so he let it go. "Where the hell are we going, then?"

Pascual grinned. "You'll see." He looked smug.

Oscar shook his head, smiling. Pascual had never let him down. He massaged his shoulder and felt the soreness subside a little.

"You want anything from the safe?" Pascual asked, staring into the closet.

"No," Oscar said, already walking out of the bedroom.

They got into the beat-up car Pascual had borrowed and headed up the street.

"You need to get your girl a new ride. This's a piece of shit." Oscar looked around the vehicle.

"As soon as you give me a raise, boss."

"You get raises all the time."

Pascual laughed. When he merged into the highway, he stole a look and then broke the silence. "I know it's your business and all, but you're gonna need help to take care of whatever happened."

"And what do you think happened?" Oscar didn't feel like having this conversation but knew he couldn't put it off forever.

"I think the Snakes jumped you. And I think we need to teach those motherfuckers some respect."

Oscar didn't say anything.

"And—"

"And what?"

"We could get twenty guys right now to beat the shit out of those worms."

Oscar thought about it. Yeah, they could get in a couple of cars and spray some houses, sure. But he didn't care about the Snakes. He only cared about three *putos*.

"Do you know who did it?" Pascual asked.

"It was Chavo and a homie of his with a scar on his face. And someone else I don't know."

"That's Joker, like in Batman, because of the scar."

"It doesn't even look like the Joker scar," Oscar said.

"Don't look at me, bro. I didn't come up with the name."

"Fair enough." Oscar laughed. "It's a stupid-ass name."

"I know where he hangs." Pascual kept his eyes on the road and added, "We can get him right now."

Oscar looked out the window. The mountains were starting to get brown already.

"Come on, man, let's do it."

"You know where he's at?"

"That shithead's a dope fiend. I know where he hangs." Pascual checked the clock on the dashboard. "I'm sure he's still passed out. It's not even eleven yet."

Oscar watched the cars on the road. It looked like every other morning, and yet everything was different. He only hesitated about getting Pascual's help because what Chavo did was personal, not business. He rotated his shoulder, feeling the bone grinding inside the socket. The logistics would be easier with Pascual. He didn't want to admit it, but he could use his help.

"Let's do it."

CHAPTER 30

Darcy was about to tell Quinn that he wanted to go into the Vasquezs' house when the sergeant got a call and turned away to answer it. A few seconds into the conversation, Quinn started yelling, then kicked the ground, spraying gravel all the way to the opposite sidewalk. Darcy watched his face turn red as he spat insults into the handset. He then hung up and walked to his car, still cursing.

"What's going on?" Sorensen yelled after him.

"Nothing."

Quinn slammed the car door so hard, his Mustang rocked. He sped away, screeching tires like a teenager racing on a Sunday night.

"If he keeps this up, he's going to have a heart attack," Darcy said to Sorensen.

"Better angry than depressed."

Darcy thought about this. "You mean—?"

"Off the record I heard a rumor he had to take some time off a few years back."

It wasn't uncommon for cops to fight depression, but it was extremely rare for them to take time off. He wondered how Sorensen found out but didn't ask.

"What do you think that was about?" Darcy made a phone gesture to indicate he was referring to the call, not the depression.

"No idea. If it's case related, we'll find out soon enough."

Maybe, Darcy thought. He turned to the Vasquezs' house. "Let's have some unis take a look inside."

Sorensen addressed the closest guys. "We're okay to enter and search. Take a thorough look at the place, but don't damage anything. I want the full report in my inbox by end of day."

They nodded, and Sorensen motioned for Darcy to follow him back to the car.

"I need to book Robbie." Darcy stood by the patrol car that still held the kid.

"Have Lowe do it. He has experience at juvenile hall. We need to get the gun to the crime lab. Maybe we'll get lucky and find out who had it before Robbie."

About twenty minutes later Sorensen dropped Darcy off at the lab.

"I'll dig into the Vasquezs' family while you talk to Rachel," Sorensen said.

Darcy went up to the second floor, and Mary greeted him with her dazzling smile, behind the tall reception desk.

"Handsome, when are you going to take me out on a date?" she asked.

"As soon as you're single," he teased back.

"Deal." She buzzed open the door to the lab. "Rachel's at the very back as usual."

"How did you know I wanted to see her?"

"Baby, I know everything."

She blew him a kiss, and he bowed before going inside.

The white walls and the chemical smells reminded him of his lab in Seattle, making him a little homesick. Except for those two things, the labs weren't alike at all. This one had longer and narrower hallways that spread around like a maze and was about double the size.

Mauricio came out of an office, staring at a piece of paper. Darcy spun around him to avoid a collision.

"Hey, man," Darcy said.

"Sorry. I was checking some evidence from Berto's place. There's something that doesn't add up."

"What do you mean? The last thing we need is issues with what little evidence we do have." Darcy rubbed his left temple.

Mauricio turned to look back at the office he'd just left. Heaps of bags covered the workspace. "Little evidence?" He put both hand on his hips.

"Evidence leading us somewhere."

"I'm working as fast as I can." His voice sounded drained. Then he waved his hand. "No reason to get your panties in a bunch yet. Let me look more into this before I raise any official flags."

"But what doesn't add up?" Darcy insisted.

"I'm not sure yet. I need time, okay?"

Darcy nodded. "Anything else you can share?"

"The smears on the floor, broken table, and chair—oh, and the booth—were definitely human blood but too contaminated to get anything more specific. We brought the booth in. I hope we'll have some testable specimens after we break it into pieces."

"Okay. Call me the second you find something."

"As always," Mauricio said, leaving him with hope, against his better judgment.

Darcy continued to the end of the hallway to give Rachel the gun Robbie used to try to kill his six-year-old sister.

CHAPTER 31

Sorensen arrived at the SJPD bullpen in a daze. He'd never pointed a gun at a child before. He thought about his kids. They were a pain in the ass, but he still saw them as innocent. A kid able to fire a real gun and then threaten others had lost all of his innocence in a second.

He reached his desk and let out a very long sigh. After that he felt empty, but this time it had nothing to do with hunger.

"Detective Sorensen?" said someone at the door.

"Who's asking?"

"I have some evidence for CATCH."

Sorensen recognized the man as one of the junior techs from the crime lab. He moved his keyboard off to the side to make space for the box. "What is it?"

"I don't know. Rachel said it's related to Carol's case."

His voice lowered when he said her name. Sorensen didn't know if it was intended to show respect, or sadness, for the loss.

"You knew her well?" Sorensen asked.

"I worked with her on several cases when I first joined. But I got assigned to Boyd down at the garage, so I didn't get lucky enough to learn more from her."

"None of us did, son." Sorensen stood to open the box.

The technician nodded in agreement and turn to leave. "Detective…" he said from the door.

"Yeah?"

"She was a great woman and an awesome scientist. Please do right by her and find out who killed her."

"I'm trying," Sorensen said.

He wanted to. He wanted to avenge Carol as much as everyone but also knew that many crimes went unsolved. He never made promises he couldn't keep.

After the young man left, Sorensen cut the tape of the box with a pair of scissors and opened the cardboard flaps. On top of the accordion file was a note from Rachel.

What we found inside Carol's gun safe. Lynch said CATCH could take a look. We're maxed out at the lab. Thanks. R.

He set the note on top of the keyboard and pulled the dossier out of the box, realizing that it was heavier than it looked. He removed the thick elastic band that held it together and took a quick peek, but instead of going through it, he went to get a drink first.

When he came back, he was surprised to find Quinn in the bullpen, and even more so to see him pawing through the file on his desk.

"What are you doing?"

"I saw the note from Rachel. I was going through the evidence."

"*I'm* going through the evidence," Sorensen said.

"You weren't here. This is time critical. Besides, what asshole leaves important evidence unwatched while he goes to take a leak?" Quinn didn't move.

"This is a secure area and I went to get a drink." Sorensen raised the steaming mug of swamp juice.

When he reached the desk, he stepped right next to Quinn, so close that their elbows were touching. He felt weird doing that, but this was his territory, and nobody was going to infringe on it.

"Creep," Quinn said under his breath, moving away.

"Asshole," Sorensen replied loud enough for his sergeant to hear it.

Quinn reached his desk and took a Red Vine. Pointing to the accordion with it, he asked, "What's in there?"

"I don't know yet. I just got it."

CHAPTER 32

Pascual took the next exit and headed toward the hills, taking the roundabout way to Milpitas. They passed the Jungle, and Oscar looked at it as they drove by. It was mostly hidden by trees. Hundreds of homeless had taken over this section of the city and set up their tents. It was a huge community. It was also the most disgusting place in all of San Jose.

"I heard the other day that the city's going to clean it up," Oscar said.

"The Jungle?" Pascual asked.

"Yeah."

"It won't last. Those homeless will come right back." Pascual glanced over to where the trees hid the tents.

"I lived there for a few weeks," Oscar said, still looking out the window.

"You shitting me?"

"When I came back from Detroit, I was homeless for a while. Someone told me about this place, so I went to check it out."

"Why didn't you stay with Jefe?"

"His dad was in prison, and his mom had a new boyfriend, who didn't want another mouth to feed." Oscar pulled his wavy hair away from his face, but it didn't stay put for long.

"Anyway, it doesn't matter. I got out of there fast. That place was brutal." He sighed.

"I never knew much about it," Pascual said.

"There was a sign written on a chipboard door, tied to a tree by barbwire, that said, 'Come in and you will die.'" He shook his head, trying to forget. "And that's how it felt when you were there—like you were dead. Most people were high or in withdrawal. The crazies would twitch and talk to themselves or scratch their own skins so hard they would bleed. One day I saw this guy smashing his head against a tree over and over, yelling something only he understood."

Pascual took a last look at the Jungle as they finally passed it. "Can't believe that, bro. You in the Jungle. Crazy."

"Don't go telling people about that, a'right? Nobody knows that shit. I don't even know why I told you."

"On my mom's grave." Pascual crossed his heart. "You and Jefe were close growing up?"

"Like brothers. Then I went to Detroit."

"That was when your grandparents died?"

"What's all this questioning shit? You writing my biography or something?" Oscar knew most of his regiment knew bits and pieces of his past, but no one knew the whole story, and he wanted to keep it that way.

"You and all these secrets..." Pascual said. "Fueling the Guero myth."

Oscar laughed. "And what myth's that?"

"We're here," Pascual said instead of answering.

"This one?" Oscar pointed to his right at a one-story house with graffiti for a paint job.

"No. Man, why would I park outside the house of the guy we're about to whack? What kind of amateur do you think I am?"

Oscar laughed, an honest laugh that came from the gut, which made his shoulder hurt.

Pascual leaned over Oscar and removed the sideboard of the passenger door to grab a gun.

Before he could stick it inside his pants, Oscar said, "That's a nice piece. Where did you get it?"

He took it and turned the Nano around in his hand. It felt solid, but the Berettas always did. It was a little too small for his hand, but he liked it.

"One of the young ones got it in a burglary a couple weeks ago. I thought it was perfect for hiding inside my girl's car," Pascual said, putting back the side panel.

Oscar pulled the magazine out. It was full. "You have another piece for me?"

"You said to not carry anything on the way to the hiding place, so no."

"And that's why you have the Nano?" Oscar punched Pascual on the shoulder, hard enough to sting. "I got a knife in the bag."

Oscar fished out the switchblade with the mother-of-pearl handle. He looked at it, twirled it in his hand. He opened it, closed it, and slipped it into the pocket of his baggy jeans. It was the perfect weapon for the job he was about to do.

CHAPTER 33

Darcy reached the end of the hallway and looked into Rachel's empty office through the glass wall. He was about to turn around to look for her in the kitchen when he spotted her. She was hunched over, peering into a microscope, at the opposite end of the room, almost hidden by the piles of evidence. Her back was to the door, and all he could see was her short, permed silver hair.

He stepped inside without knocking. Even though he couldn't see the earbuds from where he was, he knew she was listening to classical music and wouldn't hear him anyway.

"Rachel," he said, walking toward her. "Hey, Rachel," he repeated.

When she still didn't answer, he placed a hand on her shoulder, making her jump off the chair.

"Detective Lynch, haven't I asked you a million times not to do that?" she asked, still holding the lapels of her lab coat against her chest, as if that would protect her from harm.

"I always call your name, but you never hear me. You have the music playing a bit loud if I may say so," he teased, pointing to the buds dangling from her coat pocket. He could hear Carmina Burana playing from where he was standing.

She fetched her phone and paused the music, then rolled the earphones into a bundle and set them on the desk.

Darcy offered the gun. "From the school. I was hoping you could process this ASAP."

She stared up at him, then did a 180-degree sweep, assessing the evidence she was in the middle of processing.

"It's just the gun, DNA, and prints. Prints first and the casing. We don't have the bullet yet, so ballistics can wait."

She pursed her lips but finally extended her hand, palm up. "I would appreciate one of those caramel macchiatos just about now."

"On my way." He turned toward the door. "Chocolate-chip cookie to go with that?"

"Sounds like you really want this processed." She winked. "I'll be in Room B. I don't want the cases getting mixed up."

"I'll meet you there in five."

"If you can get me the bullet soon, I'll process that too," she said before he left.

Darcy gave her a thumbs-up from the other side of the glass and headed out of the lab. When he reached the reception area, he said to Mary, "Coffee run. Want anything?"

"I thought you would never ask." She smiled and handed him a small pink Post-it with a very long order and hearts over each i.

Less than fifteen minutes later Darcy was back with a tray and a few pastries. He handed Mary the double ristretto venti nonfat decaf mocha with whipped cream. The smile on the receptionist's face was worth the looks from the patrons behind him in the Starbucks line. Then he gave Mauricio his soy latte and a slice of banana bread and finally headed over to Room B. He sat Rachel's machiatto and two cookies on her desk and settled down to enjoy his venti Americano.

Rachel closed her eyes for a second as she savored the drink, then turned around in her chair and grabbed a white card with a gray print. She raised it facing Darcy.

"This makes me really sad," she said. "A tiny fingerprint like this lifted from a gun."

"I know," Darcy said.

"Is little Amelia going to make it?"

"Still in surgery." Sorensen was good at keeping him updated.

"I found an adult print. Running it right now." Rachel glanced over at the database scanning through existing prints. "I wonder what the DA's going to do. Sending an eight-year-old to juvie just sounds preposterous."

"And yet he had a gun and knew how to use it and almost killed his six-year-old sister and could have killed a few other kids," Darcy said, but had mixed feelings.

Her eyes settled on the lid of her coffee. "Just horrible." Looking back at him, she added, "I found several good prints on the gun. I'm running the best three right now."

"Anything on the casing?" Darcy asked.

"No. And the bullet hasn't arrived yet."

Darcy checked his cell. "On its way from the hospital right now."

The distinct ping of the database finding a print match called their attention to the monitor. Darcy got out of his chair and walked closer. He had the same booking photo pinned on the whiteboard of the SJPD bullpen.

CHAPTER 34

Oscar looked up and down the block. There was nobody in sight. Three vehicles were parked in the street, and only one, an old light-blue van with a banged-up bumper, was pulled into a driveway. The yards had long ago dried out in the California sun. Most houses were boarded up or looked like they were about to crumble to the ground should a light gusty wind blow the wrong way. If Oscar didn't know any better, he would wonder if anybody actually lived there. But yes, it was inhabited. The neighborhood had been taken over by squatters toward the end of the last bust and never quite recovered.

"Joker crashes in the second house from the end. The one with the snake painted on the boarded window." Pascual walked fast, holding his pants up with his left hand.

Oscar did a 360 near the car. It was hard to see if anybody was peeking into the street, since there were no window curtains to move, and the few that had glass reflected the street back at him.

Pascual stopped half a block up and said, "Today?" He rushed up the street and snuck through a hole in the chain-link fence. "Let's go through the side," he said, climbing on a mountain of dirt and garbage next to the large south-facing window.

"Are we gonna fight a bunch of worms?" Oscar asked.

"Nah. Maybe a few tweakers. Most of the Snakes who used to live here got pinched or killed. The few that still have it together moved back to the East Side. Nobody wants to live in fucking Milpitas, fool." Pascual wiggled the board until it came loose enough for the two of them to slide through. "Game time."

The smell of dirty socks and chemicals hit Oscar like a punch in the face. He never understood how people could do meth when it stunk like that. He breathed through his mouth and blinked a few times until his eyes adjusted to the darkness. There was an old stereo in the opposite corner. The tape deck was open, probably broken. The brown sofa was stained, and yellow foam spilled from the seams. Someone was sleeping on it, curled up like a fetus. It was hard to see if it was a man or a woman. Pascual pushed the bony shoulder. When the person moaned but didn't wake up, he moved on, giving Oscar a shrug.

There were several dirty magazines and dozens of empty discount beer bottles and cans spread over the coffee table and the floor. Two burnt glass pipes rested against a crusty pizza box. They left the living room and treaded down the hallway, decorated with colorful graffiti. The first door was open. Oscar looked inside and found Joker passed out on a mattress on the floor. A woman was sleeping next to him. They were both naked.

Pascual tapped Oscar. He motioned down the hallway with his hand. Oscar nodded and waited for his lieutenant to clear the house. He leaned on the doorway and watched Joker sleep.

"There's another loser at the end, but he'll be no trouble," Pascual said when he got back.

Oscar walked into the room and kicked the mattress. Joker moaned. He struck it again, this time so hard the man's scrawny body bounced up. Pascual closed the door behind him. Joker woke up and turned his face, the scar redder than Oscar remembered. It looked like an earthworm.

"What the…?" he said, and then crawled over the woman, who was still passed out. He pushed his back against the opposite wall, as if he could make himself go through it if he tried hard enough.

Oscar pulled out his knife. The blade made a daunting click when the switchblade opened.

"Oh no, man. No, no," Joker said.

"Yo. Wake up, bitch." Pascual shook the *chola* awake with his foot.

When she did, she also receded to the wall, but her half-mast eyes were foggy, and she had a hard time keeping them open. The queen-size mattress was too wide for Oscar to grab Joker. Instead of climbing on the unsteady surface, he grabbed the pad and pulled it with all his strength, then threw it to his left. His shoulder pain flared up, and for a second he thought he was going to pass out.

Joker and the girl fell backwards on the floor. Oscar closed in on him, while Pascual blocked the exit route.

"You're going to die today," Oscar told Joker.

"No, man, no. Please. Let's work something out. What you want? Dope? I have about a G in different flavors."

Oscar kept his expression blank.

"You want her? The bitch's yours. Take her. Do whatever—"

She trembled, as if surprised that Joker would sell her out.

"You're a sick fuck." Oscar's voice was hoarse. He moved the tip of the knife to Joker's throat.

Pascual grabbed the woman's skinny neck, holding her in place.

"Where's Chavo at?"

When the response didn't come, Oscar punched him with all his strength in the sternum. A red fist-mark surfaced on Joker's white chest.

"Don't know, man," Joker sobbed when he got his voice back.

"You're not getting the point, shit stick." Pascual pointed the Nano at Joker's head.

"I'm gonna kill you unless you tell me where Chavo's at." Oscar dug the tip of the knife into the side of the junkie's trachea.

The woman was having a hard time staying awake. Pascual shook her a few times. She sobered up for a second, eyes wide with fear, but then fell back into a drugged-up stupor.

"I can't. I don't know where he lives. He moves around all the time. He's paranoid that way."

Pascual moved closer, still holding the girl up. He pressed the barrel of the Nano against Joker's cheek.

"Don't kill me. I don't know where he is. I swear," he begged while trying to decide if he needed to keep an eye on Oscar or Pascual, but unable to do both. "I'll tell you where Toro is. He knows, man. I'm sure he knows. He's a lot closer to Chavo than I am. He's the fool you want. Not me."

Oscar turned the knife clockwise, the blade digging into Joker's skin a little deeper.

"Toro's at his old man's house, down in East San Jose."

Pascual pushed the barrel harder into Joker's cheek. It was obvious he needed further inspiration.

"Okay, man, okay. His house is the one with the big garage. He fixes old cars there."

"I need the address." Oscar broke the skin and watched a drop of blood slide down the dirty neck.

"Stop, stop. I... I think it's by Springbrook and Murillo."

Oscar looked at Pascual and nodded. Then the soldier slapped the girl awake.

"Bitch, this is what happens to the fools who disrespect a Diablo."

Oscar took a step back and added, "You tell Chavo I'm coming for him."

Pascual released her. She stumbled and hit her head against the wall but kept her eyes on her boyfriend.

Oscar thrust the knife into Joker's gut so deep he felt the warm blood bathe his fist. Joker bent over, his eyes white, surprised. Oscar pressed the man's chest against the wall while he shoved the knife inside the abdomen over and over again. He only stopped after he'd lost count of how many times he'd stabbed him.

With his bloody fingers he wrote a "6" on the wall.

CHAPTER 35

Darcy pulled out his phone and, still looking at the photo on the screen, called Sorensen.

"We got a match on the print from the gun at the school shooting," Darcy said.

"Let me guess... Some low-level gangster."

"Not quite."

"Oh?"

"Oscar 'Guero' Amaro." Darcy watched Rachel log the information in the case file.

"I'll start drafting the warrant for his arrest." Sorensen paused, then added, "On your way back?"

"Yes. I'll be there in ten."

Before leaving the lab, Darcy stopped by Mauricio's office. There was something nagging him. He knocked on the door, and the tech waved him in.

"Have you run any other prints from Berto's yet?"

"I've been focusing on the other evidence. It's a restaurant, so there'll be millions of prints leading nowhere. Why?"

Mauricio's voice had a trace of defensiveness that was unusual for him.

"I'm interested in any prints from Oscar Amaro besides the ones Rachel found in the cooking utensils."

"Okay, but... there'll be dozens from thugs. It seems that they liked the food at Berto's as much as the rest of us." Mauricio placed one hand on his hip while he pushed his dark-rimmed glasses up his nose with the other.

"I thought it wasn't a particularly big gang hangout."

"Just a popular place."

Why would Carol go to a restaurant frequented by the same people she spent her life putting away?

"Did you know Carol well?"

Mauricio sat back on his stool, grabbed the coffee Darcy had brought him earlier, and took a sip. It was empty, and he threw it in the garbage. "She kept to herself. But she was a real pro, one of the best lab techs I've ever known. In fact, she taught me most of what I know about DNA."

He was lost in thought for a few moments, then went to close the door. "You know, things have been very strained here with the budget cuts. We used to only focus on our expertise—Carol did DNA, Rachel did prints, I handled all of the obscure substances. Anyway, since we had to tighten our belt, Lou shifted the approach. Now we're assigned specific cases, and we process all of the evidence from that case, no matter what types they are. Because of this, we talk to each other a lot less. And since she wasn't a social butterfly, we didn't have a lot of interactions. But she was Lou's prodigy. Have you talked to him?"

"Virago has. Do you know when he's due back from Burundi?"

He checked the wall calendar pinned over his computer monitor. "Not for another two weeks, but with Carol's murder... I'm sure he's trying to get back."

Darcy saw the set of knives neatly stacked side by side on the large metal table. "Do you have any idea why she would be at Berto's?"

"Besides the food?" Mauricio asked, not even joking.

"Yes, besides the food."

"No idea. And the place was closed on Mondays..."

"I know. Even weirder." Darcy brushed his hair back and realized he needed a haircut.

He was frustrated. So little made sense in this case.

"Maybe a special event. Berto had them sometimes."

"But we haven't found any other bodies, and no witnesses are coming forward."

"That doesn't mean there weren't any." Mauricio shrugged. "No idea, man." He turned to get back to work. "I'll let you know when I get something."

Darcy got the hint, but before leaving he asked, "Anything from the blood on the booth?"

"It was wiped clean pretty well, but they weren't thorough enough. There was a pool of something that looks like blood in the crease, where the back and the seat meet."

"I thought you were going to ping me when you processed the booth."

"It's processing. I was going to call you if I got a DNA match." Mauricio turned to look at Darcy. He looked more worn out than pissed.

"I'm sorry. I know. You always do. I'm going to the SJPD. Oscar Amaro's prints are all over the gun in the school shooting. We're going to try to pick him up."

"Loads of gang cases these days."

"No kidding."

"Do you think it's all related?" Mauricio asked.

"Too close for comfort, but we have nothing solid yet."

Once on the street, Darcy decided to stop by the SO to see if he'd received a hard copy of Nhu's phone records, since there was nothing in his email inbox. He was annoyed that it was taking the phone company this long to comply.

The bullpen felt strange. There were other detectives there, but everybody was minding their own business. He felt disconnected from them and was looking forward to going back to the CATCH office.

He fired up his laptop and sent a follow-up email asking for the records again. He tapped his fingers on the desk and then started another warrant—this one for Guero's phone records. He reread it, fixed a typo, and emailed it to Judge Ewan.

Darcy waited a few seconds, hoping that at least one of the documents would have a light-speed turnaround, but none did. A minute later he closed the lid and put the laptop in his bag.

CHAPTER 36

Oscar washed the blood off his hands in the bathroom sink and watched the water turn from darker red to pale pink to clear. On their way out of the tweaker house, they made a quick sweep to make sure that none of the residents had woken up.

When Oscar walked outside, the sun made him squint. Pascual dragged the woman out of the house. Oscar noticed that she'd put on her sweater inside out, and her dirty jeans looked so big he thought she might have taken Joker's by mistake. Pascual shoved her into the backseat and when he turned said, "Your shirt, bro."

Oscar looked down. There was a large crimson stain across his abs. He took it off, rolled it into a ball, and threw it into a plastic bag he found in the trunk. Once they were all inside the car, he couldn't help but look at Joker's girl. Her teeth were brown and she smelled like rotting flesh and vomit. Oscar rolled down the window.

As they drove out of the run-down neighborhood, Oscar stared into the passenger mirror and said, "You better take the side streets again."

Oscar looked down at his chest. The seven .223 rounds he had tattooed underneath his right pectoral were covered by the wifebeater. One per kill. He needed a new one for Joker. But he would wait until he got Chavo and his compadre and get the three inked at the same time.

They drove a few miles to a gas station that had bathrooms outside the main premises. They parked as close to the door as they could, and Pascual checked to see if it was locked. It wasn't, and the three of them got in.

Oscar spun the woman by her arm until she was facing him. He grabbed her chin and watched her struggle with the mixed emotions fighting in her burnt-out brain. "Remember what I said. Tell Chavo I'm coming for him."

She nodded. The car ride had woken her up. She was sweating. Oscar let go of her face and wiped his hand on his pants. She pulled up the sleeves of her sweatshirt. Her skinny arms were covered in goose bumps even though it was muggy and felt like eighty degrees inside the bathroom.

"Can you give me something?" she pleaded. "You know, to help me remember..."

Oscar looked down at her, then nodded at Pascual and left the bathroom.

A few seconds later Pascual met him by the car. "You never know when you gonna need smack."

"It'll be a shitty day when you get caught with that crap on you."

Pascual drove to the pump, but before he got out of the car said, "Not after Prop 47, bro. Personal use of drugs is just a misdemeanor. And I'm not on parole or probation. It's all good." When Oscar didn't say anything, he added, "I only carry for things like this. It's like the gun in the car. Happy to have it when needed."

He had a point, so Oscar let it go. Pascual stepped out and unscrewed the gas cap.

"We need gas?" Oscar asked.

"This is America. We always need gas."

CHAPTER 37

Darcy took the stairs down to the street and felt his phone vibrate. The email with the phone records had finally arrived. He considered going to CATCH and dealing with it there, but he didn't want to get distracted, so he retraced his steps and went back to his own bullpen.

The file wasn't that long. Nhu had probably changed numbers when she left the Bay Area. After a quick check, he was disappointed that nothing stood out. But he printed the few pages that had potential for a closer look.

A new email popped up, the warrant for Guero's phones. He was more excited about that. He attached it to the form he'd already created for the phone company and followed up with a call to make sure they took a lot less time with this request than they had with Nhu's.

Darcy checked the map and pinpointed several cell towers close to the strip clubs Guero owned, as well as Berto's place, around the time of Carol's murder. Then he called Jon.

"Can you get me whatever phone records we have for the Ochoa murder, the one at the back alley of Guero's club?"

"You know who won't be happy..."

"Be discreet. I don't want you to get in trouble with Quinn on my account." Darcy paused. He knew he was asking for a lot.

"Are you looking for anything specific?" Jon asked.

"I'm interested in the phones that pinged the cell towers at the time of the murder."

"I doubt that would be on the file. I think we can find Guero's and Jefe's records, since they were suspects pretty early on, but I doubt they'll have many more."

Darcy didn't respond. Jon was probably right.

"I can do a new search, but you won't be able to use it in court."

"I can worry about that later. I care more about finding if there's anything that leads me somewhere."

"Understood," Jon said.

Then Darcy added, "Can you add in your search any records for the towers around the other two clubs?"

"Will do," Jon said.

He was hoping to identify as many of Guero's numbers as possible. If one pinged a tower close to Berto's, he would be able to connect him to Carol's murder. This gave him an idea, and he decided to prepare another warrant for the towers around the school where Robbie shot Amelia.

Knowing that the information would take time to arrive, he shut down his laptop and left for the PD. On the way there his phone rang. The caller ID said "Santa Clara Sheriff." He was sure his brother-in-law was calling to check on the case, just like Howard. He wanted to ignore the call but decided that alienating the acting captain was enough of a career-limiting move.

"Damon, what can I do for you?"

"Two things, Lynch."

Darcy cringed. His brother-in-law always called him Lynch, even in social settings. He wasn't sure if it was because of deference to their working relationship, or because he wanted to maintain a certain distance between them. He waited to hear what he had to say.

"I wanted to check on the case and confirm that you'll be coming to the concert."

"Yes, Saffron and I will be there." He paused, trying to decide how to diplomatically tell his boss he had nothing, when another call popped up. It was Mauricio. "Listen, I'm getting a call from the lab. Let me catch you up later, okay?" And he switched callers before waiting for a response.

"I got a hit on the DNA from Berto's booth," Mauricio shrieked on the phone.

Darcy was just stepping inside the CATCH office and saw Sorensen and Jon focused on a monitor. There was no sign of Quinn. He put the phone on speaker and planted both hands on the desk across from his partner. Jon and Sorensen looked up, listening.

"The blood, it's from the same guy as your school shooting gun print: Oscar Amaro."

Darcy felt his neurons firing. This placed him at the scene, and not just as a patron. He started pacing, noticing that he did that a lot more at the PD because he felt weird sitting in Sorensen's guest chair.

"Carol must have fought him," Sorensen said.

"And after he's hurt, he sits in a booth?" Darcy asked. It didn't make sense. "Have you been able to test any of the blood that was wiped out from the floor?" he asked into the phone.

"No. It was too damaged by the bleach. Besides what we just got from the booth, the only blood that was testable was Carol's, on the other side of the counter." When no one said anything, he added, "I'll call you if I get more," and hung up.

"Should we go public?" Darcy asked.

Sorensen looked over his shoulder toward Virago's office. "Yo, boss," he yelled.

Darcy saw Virago look up from her computer monitor. Her expression almost made him laugh.

"Excuse me? Are you hanging out with lowlives so much that you've lost your manners?" She remained at her desk.

Sorensen walked to her door but didn't go inside. Darcy wasn't sure if it was so they could hear the conversation or if he was afraid Virago would throw something at him for being rude.

"We found Oscar Amaro's blood at Berto's. Thinking about leaking it to the news, see what shakes."

She took her glasses off and massaged the bridge of her nose. "It may spook him."

Sorensen turned toward the others. "We have no idea where he is."

"I wasn't able to find a current address," Jon said.

"Quinn had eyes on the strip clubs for a day now, and Guero hasn't shown his pretty face," Sorensen said.

"Quinn got surveillance on him?" Darcy was surprised that this was the first time he'd heard of it.

"Not officially. He has a couple CIs checking things for him," Sorensen said, waving his hand. "Captain—I mean, Commander." He bowed his head toward her. "If we waste too much time chasing dead ends, we may need a provisional arrest warrant to go fetch him in Mexico. And we all know those are not easy to get."

"Lynch, do you think you can spin this with that media connection of yours?" Virago asked.

Darcy looked over at the board, disheartened with how little they had even after two days of investigation. "Maybe someone will talk. Apparently Berto has a lot of pissed-off customers because they can't have the best burritos, or fajitas, or whatever in the state of California anymore."

"The world. The best burritos in the world," Sorensen said.

"Okay. Your call." She put her glasses back on.

Sorensen went to the kitchen and came back with a cup of green tea. Instead of drinking it, he stole a Red Vine from Quinn's desk.

As if on cue the sergeant came into the office, and Darcy saw Sorensen steal a glance at the box of Red Vines, probably to double-check that the lid was properly closed.

"Any luck?" Darcy asked.

"No. Nobody's talking, even after I threatened jail time for parole violations."

Darcy checked his phone, mostly out of habit, hoping to have something new from Rachel, but there was nothing.

Sorensen updated Quinn with what they were planning.

"Should we say Guero's a person of interest or...?" Jon asked.

"Do it already," Virago's voice came loud and clear from her office.

"Damn, I didn't know she could hear us from all the way there," Sorensen said.

"I can hear everything," Virago responded.

Darcy smiled. He'd missed working with them. Just as he grabbed the desk phone to call Janet Hagen, his contact at Channel 6 News, he got a call from Howard on his cell. He tapped the Ignore button and waited until Hagen answered the phone.

167

CHAPTER 38

Oscar walked around Pascual, stretching his legs. He inhaled deeply and then coughed, expelling the gas that had filled his lungs. As they refueled, he realized he felt a sense of peace for having killed Joker. He had planned on avenging Carol's murder, and he was well on his way. Even if the bitch in the bathroom didn't have direct access to Chavo, news in the gang community traveled fast.

The worm should have killed him and left Carol alone. But instead he started a personal war, and Oscar was going to make him pay.

He watched the pump's numbers rolling, until his eyes settled to the screen on top of the pump with news about basketball. Sports led to weather. Maybe rain tomorrow? That would be good. California was always in a continuous drought. The weather was interrupted with breaking news. Oscar was sure it would be something about the school shooting, but what he saw froze his blood, and he was unable to move. Then he lifted his hood and drew on the strings.

His mug shot filled the entire screen, and the newscaster explained that he was wanted in connection to the homicide of the Santa Clara County Crime Laboratory technician Carol Montes. Pascual didn't finish refueling. They both leaped into the car and sped away.

About a mile or two from the gas station, Pascual suggested stealing a car, in case someone had spotted him and called the police.

"We can't risk driving a hot car." He shook his head.

"You're right, bro."

Pascual drove straight to the house he'd rented in Fremont for Oscar to lay low. The rambler was about sixty years old, well kept, and had a solid six-foot wooden fence hiding the enclosed property. Pascual pulled into the driveway and got out to open the garage door, then drove the car inside and closed it. The energy-efficient bulbs took a while to become bright enough, so for a few seconds they sat in darkness. Neither had said a word the entire drive.

"I got this on Airbnb," Pascual said. "Well, a Dr. Whitmann did." He smiled for the first time since the news. "Those damn drones have boosted the home invasions and the identity theft business to the next level."

Pascual was right.

They walked into the living room. It was bright and spacious but not fancy.

Pascual set the duffel bag on the sofa. "The fridge's stuffed too. Want a beer?"

"I'm good."

Pascual took one and sat to Oscar's right. Out of habit they both propped their feet up on the ottoman, and Oscar noted that their boots were caked with the filth from the tweaker house.

"You know I'll follow you to the grave," his lieutenant said.

Oscar massaged his shoulder but stopped when he realized that he was calling attention to it. He knew his man was dying to know what was going on. In a way he wanted to tell him everything, but he couldn't bring himself to.

"I have to know if you killed that woman." Pascual wiped the sweat off the beer bottle.

"I didn't," Oscar said after a long moment.

"It looks bad, though. She gets killed at Berto's, you're shot the same night. And now the police want you for it."

"I was there." Oscar brushed his hair away from his face. "Chavo was there."

"You were..." Pascual stopped talking. "Wait, you were there with Chavo? What the fuck, man?"

"No. I was there with Carol."

Pascual spilled his beer. Oscar wanted to laugh but didn't have it in him.

CHAPTER 39

Darcy watched the news Jon was streaming on his computer and hoped they'd done the right thing.

"This will make him nervous, and hopefully he'll start making mistakes." Sorensen rolled his chair away from Jon's.

"Quinn, where do we get this guy?" Virago asked.

"He hasn't set foot in his clubs, and nobody has seen him in any of his known locations."

She raised her eyebrows. "I didn't ask where he wasn't. I asked you how we find him."

Darcy saw Quinn's jaw clench.

"Guero has been out of the state only once. He was sent back east to a distant aunt when his grandparents died. He fled Detroit and returned to San Jose when he was sixteen. I doubt he left behind any friends. My bet's on Mexico."

"He'll need money," Sorensen said.

"He has plenty stashed away." Quinn circled around the group toward his desk.

"I want you guys to hit the pavement. He's got to be nervous. He's bound to screw up somewhere, and I want you guys ready when he does."

Virago's voice was grave. Her words were more a plea than an order.

Quinn grabbed his jacket from the back of his chair and headed out without another word.

"What an asshole." Sorensen looked at Virago while he said it loud enough for Quinn to hear it.

The sergeant flipped him off and without turning said, "You slow me down."

Virago shook her head, telling Sorensen to let it go.

Darcy was surprised that a sergeant would get to act like such a child without any admonishment. But Virago looked frustrated, and it wasn't Darcy's place to say anything.

Jon went to the printer and offered them a stack of papers. "I'm sure he won't be there, but this is all I could find on Oscar's strip clubs and his other assets. He has one house in his grandmother's name, who's deceased. And he has a car to his name, a Tesla Model S."

"A Tesla?" The more Darcy learned about this guy, the more Guero surprised him.

Jon nodded, "Twenty-two-inch wheels, black on black."

"That's not a cheap car," Sorensen said. "Business must be good."

"He seems like a smart guy. He's taking business classes at San Jose State University." Jon leafed through the papers until he found the class registration form and lifted it for them to see it.

"A smart gangster. We're fucked finding this guy."

"He's getting As too."

"For God's sakes, stop already," Sorensen said.

"Girlfriend, wife?" Darcy asked.

"Not that I could find. And he doesn't use social media." Jon slouched against the chair.

"Of course not. He couldn't make it easy for us." Sorensen headed for the door. "And I thought gangstas like bragging."

"He's different." Darcy met up with Sorensen.

Jon leaned over his keyboard, already typing. "I'll keep digging."

Sorensen pulled out of the parking lot. "You know, we never followed up with Berto after that initial interview. Unless you have some other brilliant idea, I think we should have another chat with him."

Darcy didn't, so they headed out to Berto's place. When they arrived at his house, nobody answered the door. Darcy circled the perimeter, but the backyard was empty. When he met Sorensen back at the front porch, the detective was on the phone.

"I'm calling his cell."

After the beep, Sorensen left a voice mail.

"What does a restaurant owner do when he can't be at his restaurant?"

"How the hell should I know? Play golf? Get a happy ending at a shady massage parlor?" Sorensen went back to his car and turned on the engine even before Darcy got in.

Darcy called Jon. "Have they released Berto's crime scene yet?"

"Yes, this morning."

"He's back at the restaurant."

Sorensen put the car in gear and raced out of the street.

"The commander wants to talk to you. Hold on," Jon said.

Darcy exchanged a look with Sorensen and waited for Virago to get on the phone.

"The guardian ad litem just showed up. I want you to interview Robbie."

"He got a court-appointed advocate?"

"You're surprised? Only his grandma stood by him at the school. I don't think anybody but the guardian gives a crap about this kid."

Darcy thought about Robbie crying in the backseat of the patrol car. He was just a boy. "How's Amelia doing?"

"She got out of surgery a little bit ago. It looks like she'll make it."

Darcy exhaled for a long time. "Okay, I'll do it."

He hung up.

Sorensen drove back to the station but complained the whole way there.

"You know, Quinn may have a point. I'm getting tired of chauffeuring you around. Maybe we should take separate cars from now on."

Sorensen stopped by the main entrance of the SJPD.

"You're not staying?" Darcy asked before getting out.

"I'll go talk to Berto."

"Okay."

Darcy valued Sorensen's perspective from the other side of the mirror and wished he would stay, but it was obvious his partner had made up his mind, so he didn't push it.

CHAPTER 40

On the way down to the basement, Howard called him again. Darcy ignored it. A minute later the phone vibrated with a voice mail. He knew it would be a nasty one.

If a conversation with his captain would generate something valuable, Darcy would be more willing to have it. But the fact was that all the AC did was patronize him without offering viable alternatives. It didn't motivate Darcy to waste any time with his superior. At some point he would have to talk to him, but that time wasn't now.

He stopped by the recording chamber and watched for a while. The interview room was painted an indistinct blue, or maybe it was gray. Robbie and his county-appointed guardian were sitting next to each other on the far end of the metal desk. The boy had wet streaks running down his cheeks. There was an empty Pop-Tart wrapper on the table and a small carton of grape juice with a tiny straw sticking out from the hole. Robbie had chewed on it.

The officer manning the door opened it, and the lawyer stood to greet him.

"Alvaro Cañas, guardian ad litem."

He extended his hand. It was small but strong and rough, as if he'd been a carpenter or a construction worker in a previous life.

"Darcy Lynch. Santa Clara Sheriff's Office."

He sat on the opposite side of the table, facing them.

"Sheriff?" Cañas asked.

"Joint task force." Darcy addressed the lawyer. "I understand no family members are here with him."

"That's correct. The state will be proceeding forward with foster care, as I'm sure you won't be pressing charges."

An optimist, Darcy thought, and looked at Robbie. The kid was hunched over, concentrating on the food wrapper. A large tear fell on the table and splashed on the metal surface.

"Robbie, how're you doing?" Darcy hunched over the table to get closer to the boy without towering over him. "Do you want anything more to eat or drink?"

The kid mumbled something unintelligible and shook his head.

"I have good news. It looks like Amelia's going to be okay."

"Really?" Robbie's face lit up as he looked up.

Darcy nodded. "I think she would really like to see you when she wakes up. Would you like to see her too?"

"Yes. I'm really sorry. I didn't mean to hurt her." He started crying again. "The man said it was a toy."

"What man?" Darcy asked.

"The man who gave me the gun. I was in the school yard, fighting with Amelia because she wouldn't leave me alone. A car stopped by the fence and a man called me over."

"Did you know him?"

"No."

"Did he know your name?"

"Yes."

"Have you seen him around the neighborhood before?"

"No. But he told me he hangs with Julio."

176

"Your brother?" When Robbie nodded, Darcy went on. "So he stopped by the fence and then what happened?"

"He called me over. Told me Julio was his homeboy, but that he heard I was tougher than my bro, that he knew I would be someone in Los Diablos."

His eyes lit up when he talked about the prospect of being in the gang.

Darcy's heart sank as he thought about the many kids who didn't know any other life, and becoming a gang member was their highest aspiration.

"And then what happened?"

"He told me if I started putting in work, I could get jumped at thirteen or even sooner. That's like earlier than anybody I know."

Darcy realized Robbie didn't quite understand he was talking to the police or get the implications of what he was saying. Even though this kid had almost killed another human being, he was still eight years old.

"What did he want you to do?"

"He showed me the gun. He said that I could start repping by waving it around and scaring my teachers."

Darcy looked at Cañas.

"Repping means 'representing' the gang. This is often done early on as a way to show your commitment," Cañas explained.

"So you took the gun," Darcy said, encouraging Robbie to go on.

"I didn't at first. But he told me it was a toy. All I had to do was pretend it was real and show how dangerous I was so everybody would respect me."

Darcy was surprised by the guardian's blank stare. He didn't know if it was because the lawyer wasn't disturbed by anything he heard anymore or if he had a great poker face.

Robbie sat on his hands. "Before I took it, I asked if I had to pay for it. He laughed and said no, that he wanted to give it to me as a present because he knew I would be a kick-ass Diablo, that I would be a super-*soldado*."

Darcy felt a burning rage build in his gut. Whoever did this had set the kid up to hurt himself or others at the school on purpose. "Then what happened?"

"He gave me the gun and left."

"Do you remember the car?"

"It was white, old. Four doors."

"Did you happen to see the plates?"

"They were blue with the yellow letters—you know, like the real old ones—and had a Mystery Spot yellow sticker on the bumper."

Darcy wrote the information in his notepad. "The man who gave you the gun, what can you tell me about him?"

"I don't know."

"What was he wearing?"

"A baseball cap."

"Any logos?"

Robbie shook his head.

"Do you remember the color of his eyes?"

"Brown?"

Robbie looked at Cañas, hoping for confirmation. The lawyer nodded for encouragement.

"Did he have any tattoos on his face?"

"No. One on his neck, but I couldn't see what it was."

"He was wearing a jacket?"

"A hoodie."

"Was he white or Hispanic?" Guero looked white, so Darcy had to ask.

"He was Mexican. I don't talk to gringos." Robbie immediately blushed when he looked at Darcy.

Darcy smiled to let him know he wasn't offended. "Do you know Guero?"

"Everybody knows Guero," he said, as if the gangster was some kind of celebrity.

"He looks white..."

"But he's not."

"And you're sure it wasn't Guero who gave you the gun?"

"It wasn't. I know Guero—I told you. I don't know the guy who gave me the gun, but he said he was my brother's homeboy."

Darcy let it go. "Did you see any other tattoos?"

Robbie looked down at the table. He reached out for the Pop-Tart wrapper, but before touching it he retreated and sat on his hands again.

"Robbie, anything you can remember can help us find this man."

The kid looked up at Cañas and started crying. Darcy waited for a few moments.

"He had a snake inked on his left hand," he whispered, so low Darcy wasn't sure he'd heard him right.

"A snake?"

Robbie shifted in his seat.

"Are you sure it was a snake?"

Robbie looked defeated and concentrated back on the table.

"Robbie, this is very important."

"He said he was Julio's homie. It can't be a snake, it can't be. I know that, but that's what I saw," Robbie yelled.

The gravity of what he'd just said was probably sinking into his little eight-year-old brain. He then crossed his skinny arms on the table and plunged his head on them, sobbing so hard his entire body shook.

"You think this man may have been from the Snakes and not from Los Diablos?" Darcy asked.

"He said he was Julio's friend. He said it was a toy. It was supposed to be a toy. Then I shot it and it wasn't. I even dropped it, but when I saw Amelia was hurt, I had to pick it up and defend myself." Robbie's words came through muffled.

Cañas leaned over and put an arm around him. That was the first sign of warmth the guardian demonstrated since he got there.

CHAPTER 41

Sorensen found Berto in his restaurant behind the counter, on his knees, scrubbing Carol's leftover blood from the floor. His wife and kids were spread out, washing, sweeping, and polishing. The city's crime-scene cleaners only covered public areas, so Berto was stuck doing it himself, unless he wanted to pony up the money for the bill.

"Detective Sorensen with San Jose PD. We talked yesterday." He stood on the other side of the counter.

Berto's complicated hairdo had come undone, and a long lock of brittle hair hung loose, exposing his balding head. He removed his heavy rubber gloves and wiped his sweaty hands on the apron. "I remember. What can I do for you?"

"Is there a place we can talk?" Sorensen looked over at Berto's family, who had stopped working and were staring at them.

The man nodded and headed toward the back door. Once outside, Berto leaned against the restaurant wall, and Sorensen blocked the way out of the alley. Not because he thought the man would run, but because he hoped the mental suggestion of being trapped would make Berto more cooperative.

"I have to tell you, I'm a bit confused about what happened here."

Berto rubbed the back of his neck but said nothing.

"There's no sign of forced entry. I know you have an alibi, but come on, your family? Of course they would lie for you."

"Wait, what?" Berto looked up at him. "You think I did this?" His right eye started twitching. He blinked until it stopped.

"You have a better explanation?"

"I... I had a break-in a couple weeks ago. I didn't realize that the spare keys were taken. I thought my wife had them, you know?"

"You had a break-in?" Sorensen made his voice match the disbelief he felt.

"Yes, several weeks ago."

"I haven't seen any reports."

"I didn't call the police. They didn't take anything. Well, I mean, besides the keys and a few dollars from the tip jar."

Sorensen arched his eyebrows as high as they would go. He was enjoying this exchange because it'd been a while since he'd met such a bad liar.

"Let me get this straight. Somebody breaks into your restaurant, steals your spare keys and a couple Washingtons, and you don't call it in, because... And not only that, but you didn't even discover that your keys were missing for days, or change the locks once you did. And you didn't think it was important to tell the police about any of this, considering what happened here two nights ago."

Berto scrutinized his fingernails.

"They left a snake," Berto murmured.

"I'm sorry?" Sorensen leaned closer.

"They tagged a snake on the wall."

"When they broke in? Show me."

"I washed it off."

"Of course you did." Sorensen paced back and forth, shaking his head.

Berto took a step to the left, putting some distance between them. A slight breeze must have made him realize that his hair had come undone, because he rushed to comb the long strands into place. None stayed put.

Sorensen stopped walking after invading Berto's personal space. "This is what I'm thinking: you're a terrible liar, so you're either covering for someone, probably your buddy Oscar Amaro, or"—he tapped his shield and raised his voice to make sure Berto got the point—"you're trying to get away with the brutal murder of one of our own."

The man covered his face with one hand while he pasted his hair back into place with the other.

CHAPTER 42

Darcy wasn't able to get anything else out of Robbie. The boy wouldn't stop crying, and at one point it looked like he was going to choke on his own phlegm. He told Cañas that he would come back in a few hours, and the guardian promised to stick around. Darcy took them to the station's kids' room, even though it was only for victims, because he didn't have the heart to leave them in the sterile interview room. He made sure there was an officer guarding the door.

He then walked upstairs to Virago's office, picking Jon up along the way.

"Robbie originally thought he was getting a toy gun from a Diablo," Darcy said, closing the door behind them.

"Originally?" she asked.

Darcy went through the interview but paused right before the punch line.

"And?" Virago pushed.

"Robbie said the guy who gave him the gun had a snake tattoo on his hand."

"A snake?" Virago leaned in and placed her elbows on either side of the keyboard.

"But a Diablo wouldn't have a snake..." Jon looked confused.

"Exactly. Right on the web of the hand." Darcy pointed at the same spot Robbie had shown him earlier.

"The gun had Guero's prints all over it, though," Virago said.

"Anybody else's?" Jon asked.

"Besides the kid's, no."

"Do you believe him?" She played with her mug but didn't drink from it.

"He's eight years old. He's capable of lying, but I think he's too distraught to conjure a story like this."

Virago's eyes got lost somewhere on the opposite wall. Darcy figured she was assessing her own kids' ability to lie.

"Is it possible he could be making it up?"

"Maybe. But he got really upset when he realized that the guy who gave him the 'toy' wasn't a 'friendly.'"

Virago lifted an eyebrow. "Look at you, mastering the lingo," she said, only one side of her mouth raised, as it always was when she mocked people.

"Wait until I awe you with the handshakes. Then you'll be really impressed." Darcy mimicked something but soon stopped, as he was sure it looked as pathetic as he felt doing it.

Jon and Virago laughed. Then Virago picked up the phone and punched a number.

"Quinn, you're on speaker. Lynch and Jon are with me."

"What's up?"

Virago shared the updates on Robbie's interview.

"Do you think it could have been a Snake posing as a Diablo?"

"I've never heard of such a thing," Quinn said. "Gangs boast about their hits. They would never give the credit to a rival mafia. That's how they earn respect and the soldiers move up the ranks."

Virago looked at Darcy.

185

He shrugged, letting it go, but his gut told him the kid wasn't lying.

"I can check on the description of the car. Maybe we'll get lucky," Jon said.

"Do that." Virago looked down at the phone. "Quinn, check if your contacts have heard anything about this."

"I'll bring a couple fools in. The station seems to help with memory recollection."

"Very well. Oh, and look for the brother, Julio. I want us to have a chat with him." She ended the call and focused on him. "Lynch, where are we with Nhu's kidnapping?"

"Nowhere."

She didn't smile anymore.

"I got nothing, Commander."

"You better get on it." She rested her elbows on her desk, pushing the keyboard forward. "Let Sorensen and Quinn pursue the leads on Carol for a while. If you don't get something on the witness case, Howard's going to start banging on my door, and you know how much I hate that."

She turned to the monitor. The conversation was over.

"I think you can take Sorensen's desk," Jon offered after closing Virago's door.

Darcy wanted to avoid having to deal with Howard, but since his computer was at the SO, he had no choice but to go back.

The short walk to the Sheriff's cleared his head. Virago was right: he needed to focus on Nhu's kidnapping. When he entered the bullpen, he was happy to see that the AC wasn't there, and only a few desks were occupied. He logged into his laptop, and while it booted, he skimmed through the printouts of the phone records he'd requested.

A new email popped up. It was nothing related to the case. A departmental change or some crap like that. But he realized he had another unread email. Jon had sent him the records of all the numbers that had pinged the towers close to Berto's place around the time of Carol's murder.

He called the intern. "I just got the records. Thank you."

"It's a lot of numbers…"

"Can you run some query magic for me?"

"I thought you would never ask."

Darcy smiled. The kid was awesome. "Is there a way to figure out if some numbers show up at specific locations at the same time?" Darcy asked.

"You mean the same numbers in different locations?"

"Yes. Sort of." Darcy thought about it. He knew what he wanted but wasn't sure he knew how to ask for it. "What I would like to see is if we can find people who were together at different locations."

"I think I can come up with an algorithim to figure out if there are numbers that show up at the same places around the same times."

"What if I only have the locations?"

Jon hummed for a second or two. "I can do that, but it'll take longer."

"ASAP is good. I have a few numbers, but I'm more interested in the ones I don't have yet. I'll email you whatever I have and the warrants as soon as I get them so you're covered."

He hoped the intern would be able to surprise him, as he often did.

CHAPTER 43

Oscar wasn't surprised at Pascual's reaction. He knew his homie was trying to figure out all the possible permutations of why he'd been at Berto's with Carol. And knew that not one of them would come close to the truth.

Pascual wiped the spilt beer off the ottoman with his pant leg and took a fresh sip while he eyed Oscar.

"You planning on swallowing this time?" Oscar asked.

"That depends, bro. You gonna tell me what this is all about?"

Oscar watched him. "Let's go get this *puto.*" He got up from the sofa. "No confessions today. We got work to do."

Pascual cursed, but Oscar wasn't sure if it was disappointment because he wasn't confiding in him or unfulfilled curiosity.

"Where do you want to go? The blues are looking for you."

Oscar thought about his picture on the news. And as he did, he thought about Dominique. He pulled his burner and punched his number.

"You're wanted by the police."

He was surprised the engineer had answered the call. His voice sounded steadier than Oscar would have expected.

"A misunderstanding."

Silence.

"I want the prototype," Oscar said.

More silence.

Oscar heard Dominique pacing and knew he would also be pulling at his eyebrow. At this rate, the twentysomething MIT graduate would soon have no hair left.

"I'm not asking. I need you to use that fancy 3-D printer you got with all the money I gave you and get me five v.2s."

"The software is not ready."

"Don't make me remind you who owns your company."

"You just did. You always remind me, as if I didn't already know. And doing that doesn't make the code any more ready."

"I don't care that it's in alpha state. It'll be like a test run."

"It has a lot of bugs. It won't be ready to enter alpha until the beginning of next month."

"Does it fly?"

"Of course. The base flying code is the same as the v.1. The flight features are flawless."

"Exactly. This will just be like an early test of the facial-recognition function. I promise we'll log all the bugs we find."

"It's too early." Dominique's voice started high pitch but broke before he finished.

"I'll come by and pick up five..." Oscar looked at his watch, as if that would tell him the information he needed. "By 10 a.m. tomorrow."

"That's impossible," Dominique shouted, but the back-and-forth pacing was causing him to be out of breath.

"Okay, fine. I will come by eleven and pick up three. You can give me the other two by the weekend."

Oscar hung up. He knew Dominique was freaking out, and he didn't want to hear it.

"What was that about?" Pascual asked him.

"I don't know about you, but I doubt Chavo's gonna be home waiting for us after Joker's *puta* spreads the word that I'm coming for him."

"He's shitting his pants hiding somewhere." Pascual shook his head. "I never got why you told her. Made our lives more difficult."

"Wasn't fucking thinking, broski," Oscar said, too pissed with himself to come up with an excuse.

"No shit," Pascual said, and raised his bottle.

"So, I think it's time we use technology to help."

Oscar went to get his own beer.

CHAPTER 44

Darcy knew Jon needed time to figure out the cell tower information he wanted. So he decided to check the notes from the conversation they'd had with Mike Walker to see if anything stood out now that he had more context.

Gangs were all about respect, within and outside of the clan, Walker told him. The wrong look or a simple insult from a rival could cause a bloodbath. Trying to get out of the life, as they called it, or ratting to the police would be an automatic death sentence. All the orders came from high-ranking members in prison and were delivered via kites, which were messages that got passed along by the inmates and eventually made it to the outside world via a visitor. The gangs only existed to make money for the parent faction in prison. In a way it all looked like a big pyramid scheme.

Nothing jumped at him. Darcy moved on to Nhu's file. There wasn't much in it, and he still hadn't got any information from Lawrence on the witnesses. He called him.

"When are you bringing the two women you found in the restroom?"

"I... We haven't been able to locate them yet."

"Do you have IDs?" Darcy got being a rookie, but he didn't have much patience for laziness.

"We..."

"Yes or no. It's a simple question." He started to sound like Sorensen.

"No."

"Have you watched the courthouse footage?" Darcy subdued a long sigh from becoming audible. "Send it to me now." He slammed the phone down.

Howard walked into the bullpen. His brown shirt looked slept in, but it was more likely that he hadn't bothered to iron it.

"I don't have anything yet."

"Why not, damn it? Where have you been all day?" He stood by Darcy's desk, staring down at him.

"Working the case."

"Which case? Not this one. If you'd been working this case, you would have something by now. Aren't you the Sheriff's rock star?" When Darcy didn't respond, he continued. "Get me something today. Remember what I told you: we solve this case, not that stupid-ass task force. Got it?"

"Loud and clear."

He wondered if his boss felt the need to repeat himself because he was so often ignored.

Howard walked to his office. Darcy was relived when he heard the door close. The AC was known to bark commands from his desk, and he wasn't in the mood to hear them.

Focusing back on the file, he printed a few photos of the courthouse bathroom and the hallway where Nhu was last seen. He also pinned her DMV photo. To its right, he drew squares and put a question mark inside each. Below, he wrote "witness," just to make an extra point that he didn't have any information on them, because they'd been released before anybody got their names. The last thing he put up was Jefe's mug shot.

Short of an hour later, the courthouse thumb drive arrived. Apparently, it was too large for email. He wasn't surprised that Lawrence didn't deliver it personally. He sifted through the folder and decided to start watching the footage from the hallway first. As the file loaded, he glanced at the statements they'd collected. Out of the twenty-some witnesses they'd interviewed, nobody had seen anything, except for the cleaning service cart and the yellow post stating that the bathroom was closed to the public. There had been dozens of people walking those hallways, and not one remembered seeing Nhu Tran.

The video showed her walking with Deputy Lawrence. They stopped by the bathroom; he pointed at the sign. They chatted for a few seconds. A woman walked up to them, paused when she saw the "Closed for Cleaning" message, but went in anyway. Nhu said something to the deputy and then followed her into the bathroom. After a couple of minutes the first woman left. One more arrived, paused, then continued walking. Lawrence was on his phone the whole time, not even looking up when people approached his location.

A portly woman with bleached blond hair ran to the door, almost ran over the sign, and disappeared inside the bathroom. There was no activity for the next couple of minutes. The cleaning lady came out, pushing the cart, and disappeared down the hall. A short while after that Lawrence went in.

Darcy watched the video again. He paused when the cleaning lady was leaving the bathroom. There was something odd. Something didn't add up. He rewound it. The door of the bathroom opened. The cleaning cart emerged and turned left on the hallway, disappearing from view.

"That's it," Darcy said out loud, and slapped the desk.

A couple of heads turned, but he didn't care.

He rewound the video and paused it just as the cart started disappearing from the frame. He captured a screen shot of the image filling the monitor. The sign announcing that the bathroom was closed stood by the door. The cleaning lady had forgotten to pick it up. He printed the photo and also tagged it up on the whiteboard.

He rewound the video to see the cleaning lady arrive and was not surprised when there was no clear shot of her face. She came in, set the sign by the door, and went inside. There was nothing more to it until she left, leaving the sign behind.

Darcy called Mauricio. The CSI told him that he was maxed out helping Rachel with Berto's place, and the case had been reassigned to Carlos Vega. Before Darcy could get any intel on the new guy, Mauricio ended the call.

Darcy rang Vega, and after a quick introduction he asked, "Any updates on Nhu Tran's case?"

"Is that even a real case?" Vega asked.

This told him everything he needed to know about the lab tech. "Why would you say that?" he asked, more disappointed than miffed.

"There's no sign of foul play. My take's that she didn't want to testify and split."

"She was in protective custody."

"Yeah, but one of my buddies was part of the crew that picked her up. She didn't want to come back to California, much less testify."

"Did he say anything else?" Darcy wondered if that had been the same guy who let the two witnesses go home without getting IDs.

"Not really. That was about it."

"Give me his contact info."

Vega provided the digits and said, "He's in Mexico now, on vacation."

Darcy cursed under his breath.

"Seriously, I bet you she split," Vega insisted.

"I'm glad you've solved the case for me. Now can you send me the scene photos and any evidence results you have so far?"

"No reason to get snappy. I was just offering my opinion."

"When your opinion counts as evidence, I'll be happy to hear it. Until then, shut up and do your job."

Darcy slammed the desk phone down. He should have waited until he got the email with the findings, but he was too frustrated to stay on the line. A few minutes later his in-box pinged, and he was happy to see that Vega had followed through. He opened the attachments, but there was nothing of value in them.

He called Marra. "Sergeant, Lynch here."

"What can I do for you?"

"Nhu's disappearance at the courthouse... Are your guys trying to find the witnesses who were inside the bathroom?"

"Don't get me started. I chewed everybody's ass at the courthouse, and they weren't even my guys. Seriously, what kind of shop is Howard running at the Sheriff's?"

Darcy smiled at Marra's rant. He felt the same way.

Marra's tone eased off. "Based on the videos, we've identified one as a court reporter and the other as a member of the jury pool. I thought your people would have told you this already."

"Nobody tells me anything around here."

"So, when are you coming over to the dark side?" Marra asked.

Darcy was surprised that he knew about the possible transfer.

"I don't know if that'll ever happen... Quinn has to vote."

"You're screwed, bro."

"That good, uh?"

"Yeah. Anyway, you want me to bring the witnesses in?"

"Have you talked to them?"

"We did, but they had nothing. I'll send you the reports."

"What about the cleaning lady? Has she been identified yet?"

"There were four on the roster for that shift. As luck would have it, we've located three, and one is missing."

"Are you serious? And nobody told me this?" Darcy was pissed.

"We reported this to Howard. He said he wanted updates to go directly to him. I expected he was flowing the info downstream."

"He hasn't." And for the first time Darcy was sorry he'd been ignoring Howard's calls. Though the ass hadn't left him any voice mails either. What a dick.

"Okay, let me have my lead officer call you and get you up to speed. You'll get whatever we get directly from him moving forward. In any case, the missing cleaning lady is Samantha Lee. Nobody has seen her since she punched in Tuesday morning. Her house is pristine, and we have a unit waiting there in case she shows up."

"Have we got a warrant for her bank records?"

"There's a thing called probable cause... She could be taking a vacation right now for all we know."

Marra was right, but they both knew there was more to it.

"Better go beg one of your buddy justices for a warrant if you're really itching for it," the sergeant said. "As Howard keeps reminding everyone, this is a Sheriff's case, though for some reason he doesn't mind when we find out leads."

"And I appreciate it," Darcy said.

"I know, buddy."

Marra hung up.

CHAPTER 45

Sorensen guided Berto into one of the interview rooms and closed the door. He looked around to see who was still in the office and spotted one of the junior detectives.

"Do you mind watching my guy in Room One for a couple minutes? Got to talk to the boss."

"Sure."

The detective walked inside and sat across from Berto but didn't say a word.

Sorensen headed for Virago's office. She looked up at him as soon as she saw him walk into CATCH.

"I brought Berto in."

Her right eyebrow rose while she waited for him to continue.

He gave her a quick rundown of their conversation at the restaurant. "I don't think he did it, but he's obviously lying about something, and now he's clammed up."

"A little scare tactic may work," she agreed. "Have you asked Quinn what he thinks?"

"Haven't seen him around." He wanted to say more but waited to see if Virago opened the door. When she didn't, he proceeded. "I don't know what the guy's up to, but he's MIA more than he's not and has come up with nothing. So far, useless."

"Give him time. I think he's a lone wolf, but I've heard great things about him. Maybe he'll surprise you."

He wasn't convinced but decided to let it go.

"Anything else?"

Sorensen shook his head and opened the door but then turned and said, "I think he wants to join us."

"Who?"

He wondered if he wanted to go there.

"I think Lynch wants to join SJPD."

"Has he said anything?"

Her voice gave no hint of what she thought about it.

"Not with so many words. No."

She pursed her lips and stared back at him. He felt as if she was gauging him. "Do you want him to?"

He looked away toward the empty bullpen, then combed his curls back. "He's practically working with us now."

"That's not what I asked."

"I like him better than Quinn."

"That's also not what I asked." She leaned back into her chair, the right side of her mouth turned up into that smirk of hers.

"Fine. Yes. I think he's a good cop. He works well with Jon too."

And before she could push for more details, he walked out to put the fear of God into Berto.

199

CHAPTER 46

Darcy watched the courthouse videos a few more times. He could clearly see the cleaning cart, but there wasn't a single shot of the woman's face or anything else that might prove his theory. She wasn't wearing protective gloves, and he was sure he would find Nhu's prints all over the handlebar, but that would take time.

The question was whether she ran of her own volition, or if someone had arranged it to make sure she wasn't available to testify. Could Nhu have orchestrated the theatrics with the cleaning lady by herself? Did she pay her, or were they friends?

Or could Jefe be connected enough with the outside world to have set this up? After talking to Walker, he knew it was highly probable. But if so, why not just kill her? That would have been a lot easier. He made a note to check on Jefe's prison visitors. If not Jefe, who else would want her to disappear before she could testify in the preliminary hearing?

Darcy checked the time. It was almost 8 p.m.

He called Jon. "Any updates on the phone records?"

"I'm running into some discrepancies with my queries. Trying to figure out what's going on. I won't leave until I have the info for you."

"We can pick this up tomorrow. The data's not going anywhere, and I'm not doing anything more tonight."

"Are you sure? I don't mind."

"I think two all-nighters in a row are a bit much. Go home. And thanks for doing this for me."

"You're welcome." After a pause Jon added, "It reminds me of when we all worked together. When are you going to join us?"

Darcy doubted he ever would. "We'll see."

They hung up. Darcy looked around the bullpen. There were still a few people scattered around, but he decided to give it a fresh start in the morning. He would focus his energy on finding Samantha Lee and figuring out her connection to Nhu. Lee would lead him to his missing witness, he was sure of that.

As he got ready to leave, he thought about Robbie. The guardian had called him to let him know that they'd moved the boy to juvie. Darcy had been disappointed because he wanted to talk to him one more time, but the day had gotten away from him. Another thing to tackle tomorrow.

The snake... He remembered Robbie's comment about the snake tattoo on the guy's hand.

Darcy decided to stay for a few more minutes. He grabbed the mouse and logged into the tattoo database. For decades law enforcement had photographed all the tattoos of the criminals they arrested. The database was now national and extensive.

He selected only one parameter to see what he got. Better start wide and narrow it down from there. He wrote "snake" on the search bar. A couple of seconds later 534,887 results popped up. Too broad. He selected the option for "gang." 107,365. That was better, but still. He played around with different settings, narrowing the geographical area, the time frame, and the location of the tattoo on the body. Fifteen snake tattoos on or close to the web of the left hand and for known gang members in California from 1980 to the present. He sent the images to his phone and decided to call it a night.

On his way home he texted Saffron to check if she was already there. Shortly after, his phone pinged, and he smiled. But it wasn't Saffron. It was his sister, asking why he was ignoring calls from the Santa Clara Sheriff. He almost typed "Because I can" but decided against it and didn't reply.

She pinged him again. "If you keep ignoring us, I'm going to make you pay for dinner on Friday."

He laughed. He would make sure to call her in the morning. His to-do list for tomorrow was growing by the minute.

When he opened his front door, he knew Saffron was home. A whiff of hot air almost made him feel short of breath.

"Woman, what is this, a sauna?" he asked, placing the keys and his gun on the kitchen counter.

Shelby barked and greeted him with a wagging tail. He scratched her behind the ears until Saffron came. She didn't say anything, but her smile lit up her face, fine wrinkles framed her eyes, and her soft, dark hair bounced past her shoulders. She offered him a generous glass of wine, but before he took it she placed it next to the Glock and embraced him. She felt warm, inviting. He kissed her neck and felt her goose bumps form against his lips. She wiggled in his arms, his touch tickling her.

Saffron ran her fingers through his hair, and he felt the entire weight of the day melt away.

"I love you," he said to her.

"I know," she said back, her smile wider still.

He picked her up and, still kissing, sat her on the counter only a few inches from the wine. She locked eyes with him and bit her lip. He wondered if she had any idea how sexy she was when she did that. Saffron started unbuttoning his shirt. He played with her hair.

When the shirt fell on the floor, she traced his torso with her fingers. His blood pressure rose, and he pushed himself against her, then pulled her top over her head. She was wearing a thin black camisole.

"That's still too much clothing," he whispered.

She giggled. The phone rang. He ignored it.

"You should check it," she said.

"No."

"Your captain always gets mad when you ignore her calls."

"She's the commander now, but she's not my boss, and Howard's a douche. I never answer his calls," he said between kisses.

"It may be someone else."

Her voice lacked conviction. He was nibbling on her shoulder.

The phone stopped ringing but started again immediately.

"You really need to check it." She exhaled, tilting her head back, exposing her long neck even more.

He put both hands on the small of her back and pulled her closer to him. After kissing him, she leaned on the counter and wrapped her legs around his body. She was barefoot. He wanted her. He leaned over, pressing his body against hers, feeling her warm skin against his.

The phone rang again. Three times back-to-back was never good.

She grabbed it and handed it to him. "You need to."

"I know." He checked the number. "Shit," he said, and tapped the green button to answer.

CHAPTER 47

Oscar knew that he should be hiding rather than driving the streets of East San Jose. Of course he could've had Pascual put together a team of soldiers to go look for Chavo. But he didn't trust that a spark wouldn't ignite and blow the whole thing up before he was able to get there and take care of the worm himself. Chavo killing Carol was personal. He needed to end Chavo's life himself.

So there he was, in the passenger seat of a rusty burgundy Honda Civic his second-in-command had borrowed from a homeboy, hoping to encourage Toro to tell them where Chavo was hiding.

"You know the city has cameras everywhere, right?" Pascual reminded him for the nth time.

Oscar ignored him but pulled his cap down lower over his head. "I got to do this, Pascual. I just gotta."

The night was clear and crisp, full of stars. Not the best night to kill somebody.

Pascual took a right as they crossed the light. "It's a couple blocks up."

Oscar drew out two ski masks from his pocket. He handed one to his buddy, and after taking off his cap, he slid the other on, adjusting the holes over his eyes. Then he reached behind him and grabbed the MP5.

"You too." Oscar pointed at the wool mask on Pascual's lap.

Pascual obliged. "When we turn left, the house's the third on your side. Let's hope Joker's not a liar and Toro spends a lot of time in his garage." He slowed down, as if he needed the extra time to go over the plan, even though they'd rehashed it ad nauseum. "If he's not there..." he said as the car decelerated.

"We'll have to come back."

Oscar watched the block. There was no one in sight up or down the street, but he could see light coming from Toro's open garage. He hoped the snake was working on a beat-up car. It would suck to destroy a beauty.

Pascual stopped the car, and Oscar got out. As the Honda rolled away, he watched until he saw the tip of the MP5 appear out of the passenger window. Oscar ducked between a fence and the side bushes and headed for the south side of Toro's house. He had reached the back porch when he heard the first spray of bullets.

CHAPTER 48

By the time Darcy made it to the Santa Clara County Jail, the place was already packed with personnel from the Sheriff's Office and the Department of Corrections, including Acting Captain Howard. As soon as he saw Darcy, he walked over to him, index finger extended, as if he needed to call extra attention to himself.

"What happened?" Darcy asked, trying to divert the accusation he was sure was coming.

"Someone offed Jefe."

"I got that from the phone call," Darcy said. "Any other details?"

Howard looked behind him and waved over a corrections officer. A man who resembled the Hulk, except for the skin color, met up with them.

"Details," Howard said to the CO.

Darcy introduced himself, sure that Howard wasn't going to do it. Connor shook his hand and directed him toward the crime scene. They passed the security doors that led from the jail to the tunnel that connected the building to the courthouse. As soon as the doors opened, Darcy saw a couple of techs already collecting evidence.

"After the whole thing with the missing witness yesterday, Jefe's pretrial motions were put on hold. Today, late in the afternoon, he was called in to the courthouse for a meeting with the judge. The defense attorney had to leave for something but asked us to wait, because he wasn't going to be long."

Howard caught up to them. Darcy wished he'd stayed behind.

"Before the lawyer came back, the judge was pulled into something else too but also told us to wait. This is why it got so late. Finally, they all came back and talked for a while in the judge's chambers When they were done, they told us we could bring Jefe back to jail."

Darcy made a mental note to talk to the DDA to learn more about that meeting. "What happened then?"

"Kim, the deputy who was escorting Jefe, had a call that there was another inmate who also needed transport. Nene, a low-level gangster from the Diablos. The system didn't raise any flags, so we decided to take them together. We do this all the time." Connor scratched his chin, as if that helped him collect his thoughts. "Anyway, Kim and Bocco, the deputy who was assigned to Nene, met at the courthouse side and headed together into the tunnel. About a third of the way in, Nene starts convulsing. Bocco kneels down to help the dude, but the second he gets close, Nene pushes him to the floor and sneaks past him, then reaches Jefe and stabs him with a shank."

"How the hell did he get a shank into the courthouse?" Howard asked.

"We don't know yet, sir. We're looking into it."

"Then what? Because there's a whole lot of blood here," Darcy said, a foot away from where the assault had occurred.

"Nene continues stabbing Jefe. Bocco got back on his feet as Kim pulled his service weapon and starts yelling at Nene to stop."

"He didn't try to separate them?" Howard asked.

207

"Bocco reached them and tried to restrain Nene. In the process he got stabbed in the forearm and the gut." As he said this, Connor looked down at the AC, then clenched his jaw, probably to prevent himself from saying more.

"Is he going to be okay?" Darcy asked.

"In surgery now. This is why we don't interfere. We instruct to stop, and if they don't, we halt the threat with whatever means necessary," Connor explained.

"Did Kim shoot?" Darcy asked. The amount of blood on the floor could belong to three people.

"He did. And managed to stop the threat, sir."

So now Bocco was in surgery, and Jefe and Nene were dead. Another open-and-shut inmate casualty case.

"Can I speak to Kim?" Darcy looked up the long hallway. It had been a ballsy move for Nene to hit Jefe here.

"He's at the jail side," Connor said. "Are you ready to go back?"

"Yes."

As they walked to the jail, Darcy wondered what the meeting with the judge had been about. With the case in shambles, was the DDA pushing for a longer continuance, or was there something else they needed to consider?

There were only a handful of people who would have known that Jefe was being transported back so late in the day. It didn't look like a crime of opportunity. If it was planned, the list of suspects should be fairly easy to narrow down.

CHAPTER 49

Thursday

Sorensen had interviewed Berto until almost 2 a.m. Less than six hours later he was sitting at his kitchen table, feeling worn-out and ancient. He was surprised—disappointed, really—that he hadn't been able to break the old man. Even the junior detective had tried, playing a rather underwhelming version of bad cop with no results. They got nothing more than "Somebody broke into the restaurant and took the frigging extra keys."

Whatever.

"Babe, more tea?" Melissa's voice brought him back to the present. "You look like you could use some caffeine..."

Sorensen pushed the mug over to her, and she refilled it with steaming water.

"Rough night? I didn't hear you come in," she said, sitting across from him.

"Just disappointing. I have this guy who's lying, and I can't figure out why."

Her blue eyes were soft, sweet, her hair up in a loose bun. She extended her hand toward him, and he met her halfway. Her skin was soft. He thought about how much he loved her. She was his rock.

"You'll figure it out. You always do." She got up, gave him a bear hug, and kissed his cheek. He held on to her arms until her second kiss told him he needed to let go. "Kids, it's time to go to school," she yelled, walking out of the kitchen.

Sorensen decided to not drink the second cup of tea and dumped it in the sink. He took his Glock and badge and yelled, "I'm off. Be good today, okay, kids?"

"Yes, Dad," their voices came from different parts of the house.

That always made him smile.

As soon as he turned the engine on, a familiar ping told him he was low on gas. He would stop on the way to the station.

Halfway there, Virago called him. "Do you know what happened at the jail last night?"

"Nope." He rubbed his face while he waited for the light to turn green. He'd forgotten to shave. *Oh well.*

Virago updated him.

"Holy shit. We haven't had a homicide at the jail in a long time," Sorensen said when she was done.

"I know."

"Lynch on it?"

"Yes." A long pause followed. "You're gonna help?"

"Haven't been asked."

"I'm asking you now."

Her voice didn't show it, but they both liked pulling each other's legs.

"Isn't it the Sheriff's jurisdiction?"

"I'm going to claim it under CATCH in connection to Carol's murder."

"Your replacement okay with that?"

"Who gives a shit?" she said. "Talk with Lynch. I want you both in my office ASAP."

"Quinn?" Sorensen merged onto Highway 85. Traffic was stop-and-go. He thought about using the spinners but instead kept inching away.

"He's already here," she said.

Sorensen turned his lights and sirens on.

CHAPTER 50

Darcy was pleasantly surprised when Virago told him last night that she was going to get Jefe's murder investigation under the task force. The less he had to deal with his current boss, the better. He wasn't sure if Howard was incompetent or thought his micromanaging style would turn his acting gig into a real position. But Howard wasn't helping the investigation, so not having to report to him on this case made Darcy feel better.

When he reached Virago's office, Quinn and Sorensen were already there. Her face was tense, making her ponytail look tighter than usual.

"It looks like I missed something," Darcy said.

Quinn looked down at the floor.

Sorensen shook his head. "We didn't get the case."

"Jefe's case?" Darcy asked. "Why? Who took it?"

Had Howard fought to keep it from the task force?

"I called the PD chief to make our pitch, and he didn't even let me finish. He told me to stop all avenues of investigation and hand over whatever we already had directly to him."

Silence.

"Maybe your bro wanted it?" Sorensen looked at Darcy.

He laughed. "I don't think your chief has ever cared about what the sheriff wants."

Sorensen smirked.

After reflecting on the news, Darcy added, "It makes no sense."

Quinn was noticeably quiet.

"I'm sure the SO will close the case under the DOC advisement, since the perpetrator and the victim are both dead. Why do they care if we investigate?" Sorensen asked.

"They're not closing the case. But I was told very clearly that we're not to roceed." Virago made eye contact with each of them. "We follow orders, so I want no rogue crap, okay?" After everybody had acquiesced one way or another, she went on. "I want everybody's focus on Carol. We still don't have the killer, and Lou's going to chew our asses if he gets home and we have nothing."

"Is he on his way back from Burundi?" Sorensen asked.

"He's trying."

Darcy thought about the courthouse disappearance. "We all think Carol, Nhu, and now Jefe's cases are related, right?"

Virago looked at him. *Tread carefully*, her eyes said.

Sorensen shifted his weight from one foot to the other. "All I'm saying is that it's going to be rather difficult to investigate without any crossover."

"Try." She took her glasses off and massaged the bridge of her nose. "Try really hard, Detective." After a pause, she added, "We're done here."

Darcy shook his head and walked out first.

"Trying to piss off the boss?" Sorensen whispered.

That hadn't been his intention. "I thought it was a valid point." Looking at Quinn, he asked, "It doesn't bother you?"

The sergeant had yet to say a word, and Darcy didn't think it was because he gave a crap about pissing off Virago.

"Nope," Quinn said once he realized the question was addressed to him. When he reached his desk, he opened the drawer and took an extra magazine. "Commander, I'm off to do some investigating."

"Where?" Sorensen asked.

"None of your damn business."

Quinn took a Red Vine and chewed it on his way out.

"He's the worst partner I've ever had," Sorensen told Darcy. "And I thought I reached bottom with you."

"That should teach you." Darcy sat on the guest chair. "I hate to say this, but I smell some fish."

"Quinn's escapades?" Sorensen asked.

Darcy fought a smile. They were a lot more on the same page than he'd realized.

"Yes."

"Me too." Sorensen looked toward the door. "I say we follow him."

CHAPTER 51

Sorensen led the way down to the parking lot. A few steps from his car, he stopped, realizing that there was no way they could follow Quinn. Lynch was walking close and almost bumped into him.

"Watch where you're going, man," Sorensen said, sounding more aggravated than he felt.

"Sorry. Was reading an email from Jon. What's up?"

Sorensen stood between their two vehicles, looking from one to the other. "I think we have to call Uber." One hand pointed at his Jeep and the other at the flamboyant Cobra. "I've taken him in my car before, and everybody knows yours."

Lynch stood there. "You have a point."

Sorensen looked at him. "I always have a point." He did a 180. "While you come up with a brilliant plan, let me go back upstairs. I want to grab the file they found in Carol's gun safe."

"I almost forgot all about it. Anything interesting so far?" Lynch asked.

"I haven't had time to look. Quinn seemed awfully absorbed in it, though."

Lynch gave him a quizzical look. "I don't know, man. I had it on my desk and left for a second, and when I got back he had his paws all over it." Before he disappeared through the door, he added, "Let me get it, and we can take a look over breakfast."

"I guess we're not going fishing," Lynch said.

"Should have come up with that plan sooner. He's long gone by now."

Sorensen panted as he walked up the stairs. He hadn't really planned on following Quinn, but there was something odd about the dude. Always MIA and bringing no leads. If he had such a good reputation, as Virago claimed, either the SJPD had a very low bar, or Quinn had some magic in the past that he wasn't able to live up to now. Regardless, something did smell bad.

Once he reached his desk, he opened the bottom drawer, and his heart bolted when he found it empty. Then he remembered he'd left the file in Virago's office for safekeeping, since he'd lost the key to his cabinet long ago.

He tapped on her doorframe and walked in without waiting to be invited.

"What?" she asked.

"The big file I left in your office..."

"That accordion thing? Carol's, right?"

"Yep. I'm going to check it out. Where is it?"

"Quinn took it."

Sorensen's blood froze. Virago looked at him.

"I left a note saying it was mine. Why did you give it to him?" His voice was strained, and he didn't even try to mask his exasperation.

"He said he knew Carol more than anybody else in the team and may be able to connect some dots better than you guys."

"What the fuck?"

Sorensen didn't know what else to say.

"It makes sense," she said.

"That folder was mine. I was going to look through it. It may be the only real lead we have."

"It's not like I threw it in the garbage. Call Quinn and tell him you want it after he's done with it."

"After?" Sorensen pushed.

"Yes, Detective. After."

He stormed out of the office. Not only was the asshole not sharing anything he might be learning from his escapades, but now he was stealing possible leads from them.

He walked down the stairs, pissed that they hadn't followed the douche.

CHAPTER 52

Darcy was on the phone with Jon when Sorensen came back to the garage. He was empty-handed, which probably explained the disgust splashed on his face. Instead of asking, he put the phone on speaker.

"I reviewed and cross-referenced all of Guero's phone records going back a few years. Nothing there, except the absence of anything interesting," Jon said. "There's not much in terms of calls or texts. I'm sure he's doing the heavy lifting of his communications with burner phones we haven't identified yet."

"Who's he called?" Darcy asked.

"Pizza, several calls to his clubs, and a couple to the movie theater down at Oakridge Mall. Things like that."

"Incoming calls?" Sorensen asked.

"A few from the club. There were a couple from a number I traced to a Ramiro Rato. He was a bartender at the Lonely Lady Club until just about after Ochoa got murdered."

Darcy's interest was piqued. "Recent calls?"

"No. From around the time he was still working there."

"Calls from other employees?" Sorensen asked.

"Whatever came from the club's landlines."

Darcy looked at Sorensen, then spoke into the phone. "Send us Rato's address. It's worth a chat."

"I would have rather gone fishing," Sorensen said.

"You were going fishing?" Jon asked.

"Long story, kid. Anything else?" Sorensen beeped his car open.

"I'm still working on the data..."

Darcy knew what Jon was referring to.

"But I was thinking that if I get all the cell activity surrounding Guero's clubs and homes, I have a higher chance to find other numbers he might be using."

Sorensen's stare was as cold as ice.

"Good idea. You're being careful, right?" Darcy maintained eye contact.

"Working from home. All good."

"Thanks, buddy. Work fast."

Darcy hung up.

"You better not be getting the kid in trouble," Sorensen said.

"I just have him checking some numbers. Nothing we'll use in court."

Sorensen scoffed. "No shit." He motioned for Darcy to get into the Jeep. "Let's go talk to the bartender."

About fifteen minutes later they pulled into the lot of a ten-story building. The place looked nicer on the outside than it did on the inside.

"I used to come to domestic disturbances in this building way too often when I was on patrol," Sorensen said. "This place's pretty mixed, which is interesting. You'll see when you walk through the hallways. You go from curry to fajitas to kimchi all within a few feet."

The elevator doors opened, and the first whiff of food hit Darcy like a punch in the face, even after Sorensen's warning.

They turned the first corner and saw Apartment 705. He was glad the trek to their destination was short.

After three heavy knocks, each subsequently louder, an unshaven, dirty-haired, and topless Ramiro Rato opened the door. The smell of stale beer emanating from his body was worse than the mixture of ethnic foods from the hallway. Darcy allowed his nose to adjust to the smell and widened his eyes to get used to the dim light inside the apartment.

"Can we come in?" Sorensen asked when Rato didn't say anything.

He stepped to the side, and the two detectives walked in. The living room was stuffy, as if Rato hadn't opened a window in weeks. A few plates with dried-out food and several empty beer cans spread out over the coffee table and parts of the floor. Darcy wondered when the first cockroach would make an appearance.

Rato sat on a La-Z-Boy chair that was covered with mail coupons and dirty magazines. A fire engine speeding by on the street almost muffled the crackling noise of the papers being crushed under his weight.

"Feel free to take a seat." He pointed to the sofa across from him.

Old, crusty noodles stained one side of the cushion, while a tubby cat occupied the other, sleeping curled in a ball. Neither detective took him up on his offer.

Darcy noticed that the only tattoo on the man's upper body was an American flag behind an eagle and an anchor. The letters "USN" were inked on the top of a band that circled the three items. "You served in the navy?"

"Ages ago."

Darcy took in the sordid place and felt sad. "You used to work for Guero."

"Yep."

"But you don't have any gang tats?" Darcy asked.

"I only worked for the guy. He hired me as a bartender. I was a damn good one too. He promised me a spot at the casino once he got it going."

"Why did you quit?"

"Who says I did?"

"Why did you get fired, then?" Sorensen leaned against the wall.

"Who says I did?"

"Oh for God's sakes, cut the crap. We don't have time for this shit," Sorensen said. "You worked at the Lonely Lady for over two years, then suddenly a couple weeks after the murder behind the club, you no longer work there. What happened?"

Rato leaned over and grabbed the closest can. He shook it to see if there was anything inside and took a sip. Placing it back on the coffee table, he said, "Nhu was my girlfriend. A couple weeks after the murder, she disappeared. *Puff.* No note, no text, no call. Just gone."

Darcy waited for him to continue, but Rato looked lost in thought. "And?" he finally asked.

"She left the cat behind," he said, staring at the orange mat of fur.

Darcy thought about Lola, the fish he had inherited pretty much the same way from an ex-girlfriend.

"And?" Darcy pressed.

"And what?"

Sorensen puffed.

"Come on, tell us what happened." Darcy knew this guy was going to make them work for the information.

Rato scratched his armpit. After a very long sigh, he began, "She tells the police she saw the killer, and then she disappears. I thought she was dead."

"Why would you think that?"

Rato looked at Darcy for a long time. It wasn't a defiant look. It was more one of disbelief.

"You know who Guero is, right?" When Darcy nodded, he said, "I thought he'd killed her too and got rid of her body."

"You think Guero killed the drug dealer?" Darcy wanted to look at Sorensen but kept his eyes on Rato. His facial expressions weren't telling much, but he didn't want to miss any, just in case.

"I don't know, man. Ochoa was dealing behind the Lonely Lady. It was Guero's club, and the police arrested him." He shifted in his chair, crunching the papers underneath. "A few days later, Nhu goes to the police and tells them she saw Jefe do it. So they let Guero go, arrest Jefe, and then Nhu disappears. And from what I hear, that was the beginning of Guero's real stardom in the Diablos. Can you read between the lines?"

"Why did you get fired?" Sorensen asked.

"I looked for Nhu and I started asking too many questions. Guero finally told me to mind my own business or else."

"Or else what?"

"I'm sure you can fill in the blanks, Detective." He looked up at Sorensen.

Darcy noticed that Rato was having a hard time focusing, as if he was myopic and couldn't quite see that far.

"I don't think Nhu saw anything. I doubt she was even there," Rato said.

"The police report said she went there to score."

"There's no way." Rato shook his head. "She'd been clean for almost three years before the murder."

"Maybe she relapsed? It happens all the time," Sorensen said.

Darcy cringed. His ex-partner really needed a sensitivity course.

"What part of 'she was my girlfriend' didn't you get?" His voice was bitter but had an undertone of defeat.

"Don't be naïve. You know junkies fall off the wagon all the time."

Rato turned his arm and exposed a line of old track marks. "Yes, I know. I left the life ten years ago. I was Nhu's sponsor. She didn't relapse. Not then, anyway. I don't know what happened after she left."

"You are sure Guero killed Ochoa?" Darcy asked.

Rato shrugged. "Everybody knew that Ochoa was supplying Jefe's girl. Guero was his second-in-command... I always found it interesting that they arrested Guero first. Then Nhu comes forward, and suddenly Jefe takes the hit and my boss goes free."

Darcy and Sorensen had talked about the same thing. Even Quinn had admitted that the whole thing smelled at the time, but they had the print evidence against Jefe and the eye witness, so the prosecutor went ahead with the case.

"Guero is right-handed, right?" Darcy asked.

"I think so," Rato said.

He thought about the print Carol found on the gun that killed Ochoa. Jefe's right index finger, even though he was a lefty.

"Nhu never confided in you at the time?" Darcy asked.

Rato shook his head.

"But you tried talking to her?" Sorensen pushed his bulk off the wall and looked down at Rato.

The ex-bartender belched, grabbed the can he'd just drank from, and crushed it. "I never had the chance. One day she was here, the next she was gone. When I started looking for her, Guero gave me a few warnings. The last one put me in the hospital for three days. I quit after that."

"If her testimony cleared Guero, why would he care that you look for her?" Sorensen asked.

"Now that I know she was alive all this time, I think he just wanted her far away from here so she wouldn't change her story. Detectives, I'm telling you, she didn't see anything. I think Guero paid her to say that she did. It's the only explanation of why she came forward, why she disappeared, and why Guero wanted me to stop looking for her."

The silence went on for a while, feeling heavy in the dark living room.

"Did you talk to Nhu when she came back to testify?" Darcy asked.

"I didn't even know she was in town until I saw the news."

Rato rubbed his eyes, but Darcy thought it was more from being tired than sad.

CHAPTER 53

Darcy thought about Rato and the desperation he must have felt when his girlfriend vanished. And now she'd disappeared again. Sorensen seemed to be lost in his own thoughts too, so they drove out of the garage in silence.

Rato had mentioned that Nhu had a kid with developmental problems. He decided to check it out when they got back to the office. Maybe there was a way to track her via his special care. He made another mental note to follow up on the two witnesses Marra found for him and check on the BOLO of Samantha Lee. She was the best lead to finding Nhu Tran. And finding Nhu may be the key to figuring out who really killed Ochoa and why a suspicious print was found on the smoking gun.

"You don't think that investigating Nhu's case is a waste of time, right?" Darcy asked.

"The investigation takes us where it takes us." Sorensen flipped on the blinker.

"But we're supposed to focus on Carol." Darcy hadn't been paying attention to where they were going and suddenly realized that they weren't heading to the office.

"I'm not going to turn a blind eye if we get anything on Nhu or Jefe. Are you?" Sorensen asked.

"Don't I always?" Darcy pointed at his glass eye and grinned.

Sorensen laughed. "That was almost funny."

Darcy believed that Jefe, Nhu, and Carol were related, and not just because the three of them had been involved in Ochoa's case way back when.

Sorensen pulled into the parking lot of the 4th Street Bowl.

"I guess we're having brunch?" Darcy found amusing how his partner was so driven by food.

Sorensen didn't bother to answer the rhetorical question and opened the door, making the cowbell clank. The diner was long and narrow and mostly full, but the bowling lanes at the back were empty.

"Detectives, good to see you."

George left his post by the grill and came to greet them. His apron was dirty and his hands greasy. He wiped them in a small towel that hung from his waist.

The owner was not quite fifty yet, but the lines in his face made him look much older. His hair was black and shiny, the bangs coming down to midforehead, while the sides were longer, covering his ears.

"How are things, my man?" Sorensen said as he reached the last booth and sat facing the entrance.

Darcy sat across from him, bothered again that he was always the one with his back to the door.

"All good. Business is good, kids are good. No complaints."

George's eyes closed, creating two thin lines as he smiled. "The usual?" he asked when Sorensen pushed the menu away.

"Yes."

"Me too," Darcy added.

George set two large glasses of ice water on the table. As soon as he walked away, Darcy pushed the thick folded napkins, plates, and silverware out of the way and pulled out a pen from his jacket pocket.

"I can't even have breakfast in peace?" Sorensen crossed his arms over his ample torso.

Darcy ignored him and drew a line across the top of the paper place mat. Then he started adding the events in sequence.

"Ochoa gets killed in the alley. Tran comes forward. Then Carol matches the print on the gun to Jefe. Quinn doesn't really buy the whole story, but the DDA thinks the evidence is compelling enough and proceeds with the indictment."

George came with breakfast but didn't interrupt them. Sorensen stuffed two strips of bacon in his mouth. Darcy sipped his coffee while he waited for his partner to acknowledge they were on the same page.

"Yeah, I'm with you. What do you want, step-by-step acknowledgement? Jeez."

"So my question is, if it was your case, would you have stopped investigating?"

Sorensen grabbed another strip of bacon but stopped before putting it in his mouth. "No."

"Me neither. And Quinn doesn't strike me as the type who would have either."

"But he did," Sorensen said.

"Why did he stop?" Darcy asked.

Sorensen motioned George to get him more water. "You know how it goes. The DDA had the case, you have twenty open on your desk, you pick the next one."

Darcy placed the pen on the table and looked up.

"He has a great reputation in SJPD. The Gang Suppression Unit has something like a ninety-five-percent conviction rate," Sorensen said, probably aware of where Darcy was going.

"But if the cases are like this one—a bit too perfect—that percentage rate may be due to something different than good police work."

Darcy felt uncomfortable uttering the words out loud.

Sorensen munched in silence. Darcy felt the knot in his stomach grow tighter. He never liked suspecting a fellow detective, but…

After both eggs and the country potatoes were gone, Sorensen said, "It's one thing to think it's fishy that every time he goes out to 'talk to his CIs' he comes back with nothing, but another to think he's cooking cases."

Darcy nodded. "I know."

"Maybe he has a little something on the side—you know, like a beat wife." Sorensen chuckled. Before Darcy could complain, Sorensen added, "I know. There's no way that man has a woman in his life, unless it's a pro."

Darcy thought about it. It could be an explanation for his absenteeism but not for his success rate in the gang unit.

"I'm not serious, man. It was a joke."

"Maybe we need to have Jon check out some case trends." Darcy looked down at the place mat, considering what he wanted to write next.

"If Quinn finds out we're checking on his cases, he's never going to approve your transfer into the SJPD. This is a lot bigger than taking his Red Vines."

Darcy laughed, remembering the tub's lid bouncing off Quinn's desk and hitting him on the torso. "I think that sealed the deal. I'll never recover from that." He started drawing again. "We have Jefe arrested for killing Ochoa, and we have Tran as a witness and the print on the gun sealing his fate." He encased the three names inside a circle. "We also have Guero as a suspect for Ochoa and for killing Carol, with his blood at the scene." He drew an arrow from the gangster's name to the dealer and to Carol.

Sorensen watched as Darcy thought out loud. At the very opposite side of the place mat Darcy wrote "Quinn" and saw his partner's eyes widen. Darcy studied the names and thought about the connections between them. On one side they had crooks, on the other Carol working hard trying to put them away. And Quinn? There was no evidence that he was nothing but one of the good guys too. And yet... He thought about Carol's accordion file.

"When is Quinn going to bring back Carol's folder?"

"No idea. But his voice mail is about to explode with my messages."

Darcy pulled his cell and called Virago. "Commander, we need Carol's folder—"

"Before you go on, I already heard it all from Sorensen, and I don't want to hear it from you too. Quinn has it, and he's going to be following a lead in Seattle."

"He's what?"

He would have put the phone on speaker if they weren't in a restaurant. He wrote on the place mat, "Quinn going to Seattle," and spun it around. Sorensen almost jumped out of his seat, his cheeks flushed red.

"Why aren't you sending me? That's my former beat. I have contacts—"

"I expect you to be a team player and facilitate his investigation there," Virago interrupted him.

Darcy was speechless.

"Are you sending him because I'm not in your team?" he asked after a few seconds of awkward silence.

"You're part of CATCH, that's why I'm asking you to grease the way for Quinn in the Emerald City."

Sorensen pulled out his own phone. "Text from Jon," he mouthed, then after he read it he pushed it across the table so Darcy could see it.

"'Drive-by shooting last night in East San Jose,'" Darcy read, then addressed Virago: "Fine. He can call me if he wants anything."

He tapped the red button, ending the call.

"The address is within the Snakes' territory," Sorensen said.

"Let's go."

Darcy left two twenty-dollar bills and they headed out the door.

CHAPTER 54

Oscar woke up feeling stiff and cursed for having fallen asleep on the sofa. He got up and meandered through his temporary house until he found the bathroom. The light was bright, and he squinted until his eyes adjusted. He stared at his reflection for a long time. His skin and features were Caucasian, even his eyes were green. He had no traces of Hispanic ancestry.

When he was little, his grandmother called him the White Devil because he was rowdy and white. It had nothing to do with the gang. The nickname stuck through the years, but he stopped using it when she died and he was sent to Detroit. When he came back, he changed his moniker to Guero. Nana would have hated it if she thought her nickname had been an omen for who he would become.

He took his shirt off and checked his wound. It was healing. Pain spread through his back when he lifted his arm. He ignored it. The scabs on his facial lacerations were getting smaller, and the bruises looked more magenta than blue. Leaning over the sink, Oscar stared into his own eyes. They were bloodshot. He rubbed them. They felt sandy, so he stopped.

He took a short shower and changed into black jeans. As he put on the wifebeater, he saw a streak of pink. The wound

231

had started bleeding. He pulled off the shirt and was about to dab the blood when Pascual came in.

"There's coffee and muffins in the kitch— " He rushed to help Oscar. "Shit, it's bleeding."

"You think?" Oscar said, more as a joke than to be an ass.

Pascual pulled out a handful of cotton balls and pressed them against the wound until it stopped bleeding. "You want to wrap it up?" He threw the soaked mess into the trash.

"No. I'll just put on gauze and a Band-Aid."

"I'll do it." When Pascual was done, he backed off so Oscar could finish dressing. "The priest might be right..."

"Not much I can do about it. Unless you know a doc who makes house calls, you're the best I've got."

"You're screwed then, man." Pascual laughed.

Oscar grabbed another wifebeater. "Help me with this shit."

His compadre pulled it down. "You never told me the story about the tat," he said, pointing down to Oscar's ribs with his index.

"Yeah, I have. They're all 187s."

"I know that. I mean the red one."

Oscar looked down at the ink on his skin, even though he knew exactly what Pascual was referring to.

"That's blood." He tapped on the last bullet.

"I got that."

Oscar grabbed his belt. As he slid it inside the loops of his jeans, he said, "I got that bullet tattooed deep red when I killed my father. It didn't seem right to have it gray, like the others. I never want to forget who I got that one for."

When he turned to Pascual, Oscar almost laughed. "You seen a ghost or something? Close that stupid mouth."

"I thought your old man died of a heart attack."

"Not Nano, you moron. Nano took care of me. I'm talking about my biological father."

"I never knew he wasn't your real dad." Pascual sat on the edge of the bed. "Why did you kill your father?"

The only person Oscar had ever confided this story to was Serena. And she took it to the grave when she died in the car accident. He wasn't worried about sharing it with Pascual. He felt cautious only because it had been his secret. It was something he kept deep inside with all the resentment and hatred you can have for the person who made you.

"Come on, dog, you know all my dirt," Pascual said.

Oscar left the bedroom. When he entered the kitchen, he poured two generous cups of coffee and waited for Pascual to show up. He slid one mug over the counter and grabbed the other one. If he told him why he killed his dad, he would have to tell him everything else. After he took a sip of the black steaming liquid, he decided it wasn't the time for stories.

"I need breakfast," he said instead of "Once upon a time..."

"I got breakfast." Pascual opened the box of Safeway muffins.

"That's not breakfast. I'm going out. Wanna come?"

"Bro, don't be an ass."

Pascual placed himself between Oscar and the door.

"Do you see this thing?" He pointed at his stubble. It pricked his hand, and he knew it still only looked like a long five-o'clock shadow. "Nobody will recognize me."

"You wanna get caught?" Pascual challenged him.

Oscar stopped and turned to face his compadre. He knew he was being stupid but couldn't stay put. Thinking about his father had made the urgency to kill Chavo even greater. Once that was done, he would get the hell out of San Jose. But none of that could ever happen while hiding in an Airbnb eating Safeway muffins.

"Let me get you something from the Black Bear Diner," Pascual said.

"If you get me the volcano with extra bacon, I'll stay in the car."

Oscar put on his jacket.

CHAPTER 55

Sorensen's rant about Quinn stealing Carol's folder and being sent to Seattle was getting on Darcy's nerves. He was pissed too—hell, he had a lot more reason to feel chafed than Sorensen—but Virago had made her decision, and even though he didn't agree, it was what it was.

Darcy wanted to concentrate on the drive-by. He was intrigued by the new crime. As soon as Sorensen pulled over behind a line of patrol vehicles, Darcy jumped out of the car. He ducked under the tape after logging in and searched for the sergeant in charge. When he saw Marra, he felt relieved.

"What the hell are you two doing here?" the sergeant asked, coming over to meet them.

"I have no clue," Sorensen said, catching up.

The sergeant looked at Darcy. His question wasn't rhetorical.

"Is the victim a Snake?" Darcy asked.

"You could say that." Marra laughed.

Darcy cursed himself. "You know what I mean."

Marra punched his shoulder and motioned for them to follow him. "The shooting happened almost twelve hours ago." He stopped by the bloodstain on the floor inside the garage. "It looks like Mike 'Toro' Guzman was hit with two different firearms." He pointed to the blood spatter and then moved his finger toward the wall. "The drive-by's aim was low. I think they were going for the legs."

Darcy checked the inside wall. "The hits are concentrated on the south side." There were at least ten or twelve holes about three feet high that stopped abruptly in the middle of the wall. He pointed to the other side of the garage. "Was there a car here?"

"You'll cry when you hear this. The shithead was working on a gorgeous 1979 blue Camaro that ended up like your Cobra after the commandos shot it up."

Marra walked to the empty space in the garage.

"Sad," Darcy said.

"We've found no casings but recovered a few 9 mm from the wall," Marra continued. "The body had a through and through to the head that hit the ground right here." He pointed at a spot covered in blood. "And guess what? It was at close range, like an inch or two of close range."

"They came inside to finish the job?" Sorensen asked.

"Madison would have to confirm, but that's what it looks like."

Marra looked around the empty space as if he was searching for something else he wanted to show them.

Darcy knelt next to the blood. He could clearly make out the hole in the cement. CSI had already removed the bullet. He got up and checked the damage to the wall. The spray had made a pretty steady horizontal line.

"And this Toro guy was a known gang member?" Darcy asked.

"Yes. From the Snakes," Marra said.

"Any leads?" Sorensen checked the classic car calendar with the naked ladies sprawled over the hoods pinned up on the wall. There was nothing written on it.

"We have no witnesses. Apparently everybody in this neighborhood had vision and hearing problems, because to not hear this shooting, you must have been legally deaf."

"They weren't out of town? That's what I get when I canvas," Sorensen spewed, full of sarcasm.

Marra nodded and went on. "There's one camera on this street, a couple houses up, but the owner had it for show. We'll have to round up the usual suspects to see what shakes."

"Do you know of any hits put on the victim? Any history on him?" Darcy asked.

Marra squared his stance to face both detectives. "Don't know if he was a guest on any blacklists yet, but he was a dipshit. He's been in the can a couple of times for burglary, possession, and assault. He was on parole and was peeing clean."

"I'm sure it's pee from his girl's kid," Sorensen said.

"Aren't they all?" Focusing back on Darcy, he asked, "Why the interest?"

"The kid at the school shooting yesterday," Sorensen jumped in. "He told Lynch that the guy who gave him the gun had a snake tattooed on his hand."

"No shit," Marra said, surprised. "This guy didn't have any ink on his hands."

Darcy nodded, not that he was expecting it either. But he was wondering how two rival gangs ended up so intertwined in totally different crimes. Guero's blood was at Berto's. A gun with his prints was used in a school shooting, but apparently it was supplied by a Snake, and now there was a drive-by followed by a close-range execution. It didn't look like an open gang war yet, but there was more to it than random murders.

"Thanks, Sergeant," Darcy said, then addressed Sorensen, "We need to talk to Robbie," he said, itching to leave the crime scene and head to juvie.

CHAPTER 56

Once inside the car, Darcy called Cañas to make sure Robbie would be available when they got to juvie.

"I'm not available until tomorrow afternoon," the guardian said.

"You're kidding, right?" Darcy looked out the window.

"I'm sorry, but I have other cases. I can't just drop everything and be at your beck and call. If you remember, we were at the station the whole day yesterday waiting for you to come back."

"You understand that this is a homicide investigation?" Darcy asked.

"Did Amelia die?"

Darcy exhaled and stopped rubbing his temple. He avoided looking at Sorensen, because his partner hadn't bought the Snake angle yet. "No. She's okay. This is in connection to Carol Montes's death."

Sorensen kept his eyes on the road.

There was silence on the other end. Finally, Cañas asked, "Is this confirmed?"

"You know we can't say, but we're investigating both as possibly being connected."

Sorensen took a left onto Guadalupe Parkway. Darcy hoped the trip hadn't been in vain.

After another long moment, the guardian relinquished.

"Very well. I'll be there in thirty minutes."

Sorensen parked.

"We should go to the courthouse and get a soda," he said. "There's nothing to do here until he gets on-site."

Darcy wasn't thirsty. He just wanted to talk to Robbie for a couple of minutes.

"Let's go in. Maybe Cañas will be early."

"And maybe he'll be late."

Darcy ignored him and headed for the large glass door. They signed in at the front desk, gave Robbie's full name, and walked to the assigned interview room.

"Why are you so sure the kid's not making it up?" Sorensen asked while they waited.

Darcy thought about it. His gut feelings were normally nothing more than experience telling him to look into something more carefully. Sometimes he could figure out what, sometimes he couldn't. This time his feelings were strong, but he had nothing more than that.

Before he could reply, his phone rang. It was Mauricio.

"Tell me you caught a break," Darcy said, and hit the speaker button.

"I don't know if it's that good," the CSU tech said, "but at least it's interesting."

"I'm with Sorensen. Go on."

"The gun used in the school shooting—remember that I processed it superfast because you wanted to get the prints?"

"Yes."

Darcy paced and waited.

"Well, I went back to do a more thorough job and found a tiny bit of glue on the trigger."

"What do you mean, glue?" Sorensen asked.

239

"It was a very small amount, as if it got caught while pulling the trigger."

The two detectives exchanged looks. Darcy was disappointed when Sorensen's expression didn't match his hope.

"Can you get anything else out of it?" Darcy asked.

"The composition is the same as Super Glue. There're millions of tubes of that stuff being sold."

Sorensen flopped in a chair. "Was the gun damaged?"

"No. I checked several times and even asked Rachel to do a pass just in case."

"Was there any DNA on the glue?" Darcy knew the adhesive had nothing to do with a broken gun.

"Processing right now. I'll let you know."

Mauricio hung up.

Darcy was trying to curb his excitement, but if there was usable DNA...

"He used the glue to cover his fingerprints," he said.

"Not unheard of."

Sorensen sounded bored.

"Why aren't you even amused by this?" Darcy pulled out a chair but then decided to keep walking along the wall.

"I think you're chasing a wild goose. What can I say?"

"We've seen weirder things. I know Quinn said there's never rival gang collaborations, but there's something here. I expected you would want to turn over every rock."

"I'm here, aren't I?" Sorensen pushed his curls away and met Darcy's eyes. But he looked annoyed and that didn't make Darcy feel any better.

When Cañas finally came, Darcy saw the kid's face turn somber when Robbie realized it was them, and not his family, waiting for him. Cañas explained that the detectives had a few more questions and that he needed to be completely honest with his answers. Robbie nodded and shoved both tiny fists inside his sweatshirt.

"How are you holding up?" Darcy asked.

He would have preferred to sit by Robbie, but Cañas had already taken the spot, so he sat across from the boy. Sorensen gave them space and stood by the door, picking on a hangnail.

"When can I go home?" Robbie asked.

"I don't know. But your sister's doing really well. She'll come and visit you very soon."

The kid nodded but kept staring down at the desk.

"Robbie, I need your help again. Do you think you're up for it?" Darcy asked.

The boy's nod was almost imperceptible.

"Great, thank you. I'm going to show you some tattoos. Would you tell me if you recognize any of them?"

Robbie shrugged. He looked as if he was about to cry.

Darcy pulled his phone and tapped until he got to the photos he'd taken from the database. He showed the first one to Robbie, who shook his head. Darcy swiped the screen of the phone, each time getting a negative response. He was growing hopeless, even though he had a few more photos to get through.

"I..." Robbie said when Darcy got to the one before last, the one with the bluish prison color.

"What?" Darcy asked, and felt Sorensen move closer to them.

"It was that one." Robbie inched his way toward Cañas, as if looking for protection, or maybe simply warmth.

"Where do you recognize this tattoo from?" Darcy asked.

"The gun. The *puto* who gave me the gun had that tattoo on his hand," Robbie yelled.

"Are you sure?" Darcy asked.

"Yes," he screamed, and shoved his face into Cañas's chest, smearing large tears all over his sports coat.

CHAPTER 57

Oscar stayed in the car as promised while Pascual got the food. He racked his brain trying to figure out where Chavo could be. Toro hadn't been any help, and he was running out of ideas.

He thought about the previous night. How Toro's muscles felt fighting against Oscar's weight when he pushed his knee on the worm's chest. He pressed harder on the sternum as he waited for Toro to give up Chavo's location. When he didn't, Oscar placed the barrel of his gun against the man's forehead and offered him one last chance.

"I got no idea how we're gonna eat all this shit in the car," Pascual said, opening the back door and placing the bags of food in the seat.

"Let's go to D's. We can share it with him."

Pascual got in and held on to the steering wheel.

"After having your mug shot plastered all over the news," he said, "Dominique's probably more freaked out than ever about doing business with you."

"Bro, he doesn't have a choice. Let's go there and play nice. I need those drones."

Pascual didn't start the car.

"I wasn't debatin'."

"What makes you think he hasn't called the cops?"

"Don't be an idiot. He has at least as much to lose as we do. He's been providing drones used in burglaries all over the Bay Area, he's been associating with known gang members, and his entire business is funded with gang money."

"Well, when you put it that way..." Pascual smirked as he started the car.

Oscar enjoyed the drive in silence and the smell of freshly made pancakes, eggs, and cinnamon rolls. When they reached the warehouse, he punched in the code and they walked in.

Dominique sat in front of the two large monitors on his desk. The engineer had on huge headphones and was absent-mindedly pulling on his left eyebrow as he stared into the screen. He jumped when he finally saw them.

"If you don't want surprises, you should listen to music over regular speakers." Oscar pointed to the Beats.

Dominique took them off and stood. "They're not ready yet. I told you."

Oscar ignored him and kept walking. He was several inches taller and about double in body mass, so by the time he reached him, the engineer had stumbled backward into his chair and was looking up like a scared puppy. He knew that intimidating the geek wasn't the most efficient way to go. But now he didn't have the luxury of time, and he believed he'd explained his needs sufficiently clearly already.

"Really, they're not ready. They'll break," Dominique said.

Oscar looked over his shoulder at the large metal desk on the north end of the wall, where the 3-D printers were humming. "They'll break how?"

"The facial recognition has bugs."

"What kind of bugs?"

"All kinds of bugs. I haven't been able to write all the test suites yet. I've only run unit tests," Dominique said with more vigor in his voice than Oscar had ever heard before.

Oscar weighed the pros and cons. He didn't have anything else. He would rather have a fleet of faulty drones out there looking for Chavo than nothing at all. What was the worst thing that could happen?

"We'll be your beta testers."

Dominique pulled on his brow. Oscar knew all he had to do was wait until the silence became uncomfortable. When it did, the engineer exhaled audibly and tapped on the keyboard a few times until he found the window he needed.

Oscar drummed his fingers on the desk while he watched Dominique enter commands on a terminal window. Even though he had no idea what he was doing, Oscar was fascinated by the magic created by entering a bunch of gibberish into a machine. If he survived this and didn't end up in prison, he would spend some time with the engineer and maybe even learn to code.

After a few minutes Dominique stopped typing and said, "I need a picture of the person you want to find."

Oscar searched on his phone for what he wanted: a few recent photos of Chavo Buenavente, care of social media. It never ceased to amaze him how stupid most gangsters were. Their desire for notoriety superseded everything else.

"Send them to me," Dominique said.

Oscar picked the best face shots of Chavo and was careful to exclude any photos that displayed firearms, which were many. The engineer opened each on his computer. The face of the man who'd killed the most important woman in his life stared back at him.

In most of the pictures, Chavo's eyes looked like thin slits. If his other features weren't so clearly Hispanic, he would have pegged him for Asian. The snake circling his neck was only partially visible.

"Why do you want to find him?" he asked as he tapped on the keyboard.

Oscar almost told him that he wanted to kill him but didn't. Dominique would probably freak out and sabotage the drones somehow.

"His mother died and he needs to know so he can go to the funeral."

Dominique nodded. Then a few seconds later, as if he had to process the information, he added, "You can't call him?"

"No. He's hiding from the police. But his mother was a good person, and he needs to show his respect, even if he's a criminal."

"That makes sense," he said, almost to himself.

Dominique pressed Enter and stretched his arms over his head, watching as the code executed on the screen. Oscar and Pascual watched too, though they had no idea what was happening.

"The update has been uploaded. You need to tell me the area we should send the drones to. But as I said, I can't guarantee that we'll find him. There are bugs."

"How large can the grid be?" Oscar asked.

"They still have to recharge, like the v.1s., so I wouldn't have them fly too far, or they won't make it back. I managed to limit the increase in power consumption by only ten percent, but that's one of the things I want to spend more time improving."

They decided on a grid starting over East San Jose. If that didn't bear any results, they would reconsider opening that up by adding more charging stations. But that would take a day or two.

"What do my guys need to do?" Oscar thought about his command center, where his crew monitored the home break-ins.

"Let them fly, and wait and see," Dominique said.

CHAPTER 58

Darcy thanked Cañas and told Robbie that he would bring his sister for a visit as soon as she was out of the hospital. He couldn't shove them out of the room fast enough. Sorensen must have noticed, because instead of following them out, he closed the door and faced him.

"You look like the ugly girl who just got asked to the prom by the quarterback. What the hell's going on?"

"This tattoo." Darcy shoved the phone displaying the photo toward Sorensen. "It belongs to Chavo Buenavente."

He didn't remember the last time he'd felt this good about finding a possible lead.

Sorensen tilted his head.

Darcy went on. "I was right. It didn't make any sense that Guero would give a loaded gun to one of his own to shoot up a school while his prints were still on it. Chavo's connected to this somehow. Why did he have a gun with Guero's prints, and why did he give it to the kid?"

"He could have found it."

Darcy took a step back, trying to assess whether his partner was kidding.

"Just saying. Guero could have ditched it, and Chavo could have found it. It happens."

"Oh yeah. That's totally consistent with the fact that Guero is the closest to a genius we've seen in a criminal." He stuffed the phone in his pocket. "Besides, what are the chances of that?"

"Low."

Darcy gave him the look and kept it until Sorensen fessed up. "Okay, nil."

"Exactly."

"It happens in the movies all the time, though." Sorensen shrugged, but by now Darcy knew he wasn't serious.

"At least let's pick Chavo up in connection to the school shooting," Darcy said.

"If we find him."

"Jesus, can you be any more pessimistic?"

"Just my realistic self."

Sorensen led the way out of juvie. Before reaching the gates, he lifted his index and disappeared into a hallway. When he came back, he was holding two cans of a power drink Darcy didn't recognize.

"These are my new faves," he said, showcasing the black-and-green can.

Sorensen got into the Jeep and his stomach rumbled. Darcy couldn't help but laugh.

"Why is it that every time I work with you I starve to death?"

Sorensen turned on the engine and soon took a right on Taylor Street.

"What are you talking about? We eat all the time," Darcy said. "I put on weight when we work together."

"You must have a really slow metabolism."

Sorensen took Coleman Street and then pulled into the In-N-Out drive-through.

"We just had brunch."

Sorensen waved his hand. "You don't have to get anything." Then he spilled out his order into the speaker box.

Darcy pulled out his phone and called JC, his contact at the parole board. They'd met a few months prior on a case, and since then Darcy had relied on her when he needed intel on possible suspects who'd been inside. He told her about the meeting with Robbie and the ID of Chavo's tattoo.

"That's huge. Let me pull it up." Darcy heard her typing on the keyboard. "Yes, I recognized this. Apparently he tattooed that ugly thing himself one of the times he was inside." She laughed.

"I bet he's soon going to regret it."

"He's been out for a while. Unfortunately, he finished his parole last year, so we have no current intel on him." Her voice had no traces of the amusement from before.

"Shit."

Sorensen paid the drive-up cashier and inched his way to the pickup window.

JC continued. "Chavo's a person of interest in multiple crimes, but nothing tangible and definitely not enough probable cause for a manhunt."

"Send me his known addresses and whatever you've got on known affiliates."

"Will do."

Darcy hung up and realized Sorensen hadn't ordered anything for him.

"That was rude. Not even a Coke?"

"Just looking out for your girlie figure." Sorensen opened a packet of ketchup and dug a french fry in it. His phone rang. "Can you take that?" He had one hand on the steering wheel and the other was slick with grease.

"Hello, Rachel, I'm with Sorensen in the car. He's driving." He put the phone on speaker.

"That's never stopped him before," she joked.

"Let me rephrase: he's eating, drinking, and driving."

"Ah." She laughed. "I found something. I want to talk to both of you, but I would rather do it in person."

"We'll be there in five," Sorensen mumbled with his mouth full.

CHAPTER 59

Rachel instructed Sorensen to close the door behind him. Darcy was surprised that she'd directed them to Lou's office, as if her lab wasn't discreet enough. She looked even smaller when she sat behind the desk, even more so because Lou was gigantic in comparison and had set up his office to suit his large frame.

The blinds were drawn, but some light seeped through. She waited until they were both seated.

"Rachel, I've known you for a long time, and you've never taken me to the principal's office. You're freaking me out," Sorensen said.

She looked sullen. "What I'm going to share needs to remain in this room until I know more."

Darcy nodded, letting her know he understood, and saw Sorensen do the same.

"As you know, I had to retest all of the evidence in Jefe's case because I was going to testify for Carol." She folded her arms on top of Lou's desk. "I got some results earlier today. At first I pushed them aside, since we won't be going to trial now that he's dead. But then I decided to take a quick peek, since I already had them."

"Right." Sorensen had a trace of impatience in his voice.

"I'd been especially careful with the gun, as you asked me to be," she said to Darcy. "Yes, there was the partial print of Jefe's right index finger on the trigger guard. We all knew that. What was interesting was that I found absolutely nothing else. The gun was wiped clean. There was no DNA, no other prints, not even smudges."

"And?" Sorensen asked.

She paused, as if she was trying to figure out what to say next. "In my experience, when people clean guns they are particularly careful to wipe where the fingers normally go. It is extremely rare to find prints on a clean weapon nowadays."

Darcy knew that he would annoy Sorensen if he looked at him, so he refrained, but he was feeling more and more hopeful with the latest developments.

"Are you drawing any conclusions?" he asked.

She sighed for a long time. "I don't know yet. But I find this very peculiar." She paused. "To be honest, it feels like a plant to me."

"Carol's?" Sorensen asked.

"I hope to God no," she responded.

"Rachel." Darcy didn't want to make her fears more real, but he had to share what Jon had discovered. "Jefe was a lefty."

She leaned back in Lou's leather chair and played with the gold stub in her ear.

"Anybody who knew Jefe would know that," Darcy said. "It's unlikely that a Diablo planted the print, assuming he knew how."

"Have you found any evidence connecting Carol to Jefe's case in any way that is not purely professional?" she asked.

"No. But we haven't had a reason to look either. I guess that's all changed now," Sorensen said.

They promised Rachel that they would keep the information under wraps until she could look more into Carol's work. In the meanwhile, they would dig quietly on their side.

When they reached the CATCH bullpen, Sorensen closed the door and gave Jon the rundown of what they just heard from Rachel. She'd been okay with them bringing Jon up to speed, as they all trusted him and needed his unique skills.

"Am I looking for anything specific?" Jon asked.

"Poke around with an open mind. Do the usual—Carol's bank records, emails, etc.—but then see if you can come up with something brilliant. You know, your typical outside-of-the-box thinking." Sorensen patted Jon on the shoulder. "And remember, not even Quinn hears about this."

Jon paused and looked from one detective to the other. "You don't really think...?"

"We don't know, kid. We just don't know," Sorensen said.

CHAPTER 60

Darcy checked his phone and was pissed when he didn't see the additional cell tower records in his inbox. What was taking the carriers so long? He decided to leave Sorensen and Jon at the SJPD and drive to the parole office to have another quick chat with JC.

The five-story building was gray and dirty, as if large strings of snot had slithered down and had never been wiped off. He wrote down his name and badge number on the sign-in sheet and went through the metal detectors.

The elevator was full and he considered waiting for the next one but jumped in and regretted it as soon as the doors closed. The man standing next to him smeared sweat against his coat jacket. He cursed for not taking the stairs, but six floors was a bit too much, especially when he wasn't showing off for Sorensen.

When the doors opened on the top floor, he walked directly to JC's cube.

"What's going on? You never come in person."

She had a bone-crushing handshake. Her auburn hair was long and shiny, reminding him of Saffron's. She had a healthy tan and warm, vibrant eyes.

Darcy lifted a few files from the chair, stockpiled them on top of another foot of papers on her desk, and sat. "Gustavo Buenavente."

"Chavo. Yes."

"Tell me more about him."

"He's a lifer." She talked and typed at the same time.

"I thought he was out of prison?"

Darcy felt as if he'd had a bucket of ice water thrown over his head. Could he have it wrong and Chavo was inside?

"No." She shook her head and smiled, as if Darcy had said something cute. "What I mean is that the only life he knows is with the gang. He comes from generations of Snakes. He only adheres to the brotherhood's code. He doesn't give a crap about society's morals."

"Give me specifics."

"He's gone up the ranks fast because he's hit, dismembered, or killed anybody he's been ordered to, or anyone who's gotten in his way."

"And he's not inside?"

If Chavo was this dangerous, why weren't they going after him with everything they had?

"He's careful. Or lucky. Or both."

There were very few criminals who were lucky.

"What's Chavo after?"

"Respect, power, money, women. The same as everybody else."

Darcy smiled. "Damn, I wish I'd come to you earlier. I didn't know you knew so much about gangs."

"I try to go deep on my guys. You end up learning all kinds of crap." She pointed at her files, her own version of *Encyclopedia Britannica*.

"If he's not on parole anymore, do you have any tabs on him?"

"Unfortunately, no." She pulled her hair and twisted it into a bun, then held it in place with a number two pencil. "I've been thinking about this tattoo you told me about. You okay if we call Walker, the Gang Suppression Unit sergeant? He's the best we've had in years."

Darcy nodded. "I just met him. I'm glad he's that good. We need all the help we can get."

She dialed from her desk phone. "Hey, Walker, your buddy Chavo, what's he been up to?"

"That shit stick?" His voice was deep and clear, displaying the same air of authority Darcy saw when they met at CATCH.

"The one and only." JC laughed.

"He's been MIA for a couple days. Haven't heard why, though."

"Do you have any intel about Chavo hanging around in schools?" Darcy asked.

"Perv stuff?"

"More like the shooting at the George Washington School."

"You're shitting me." There was a pause, as if Walker was thinking. "No known history of that. He's more your regular mobster, but with an extra mean streak, and does the hits himself to maintain his rep of total freak."

"You think he's capable of instigating a school shooting?" Darcy asked.

"I thought you guys got a Diablo kid for it," Walker said.

"We do." Darcy thought about how much he wanted to share. "The boy identified a snake tattoo on the guy who gave him the gun. We matched the ink to the one on Chavo's hand."

Nobody spoke for a long minute.

"That's definitely enough to bring him in," Walker said.

Darcy straightened his back. That was exactly what he was hoping to hear. "How fast can you make that happen?"

"If I knew where he was, you could be face-to-face with him in minutes. But..."

"We should double-check his known locations. Maybe he was just sleeping off a high," JC said.

"Nah, we've been checking regularly. I'll rile up the guys and put together an arrest warrant. He's very dangerous, so it's better if the MERGE unit serves it."

"SWAT? Really?" Darcy asked.

"No doubt."

"How long will that take?"

"Don't worry. When we find him, we'll be ready."

CHAPTER 61

Sorensen sensed someone brush by his desk so close he felt the wake left by the body moving away. He looked up. It was one of the younger detectives. One he hadn't exchanged more than a word or two with since he'd started at SJPD. He was still staring at the man's back when Quinn appeared behind him.

"Nice of you to show up."

Quinn ignored him, took a Red Vine, and sat on his desk. Sorensen watched him chomp on one end and wondered if the sergeant would be able to tell that he'd licked at least half of them before he put them back.

"I thought you would be on your way to Seattle by now."

"Waiting on the paperwork," Quinn answered.

"You go off on your own an awful lot. You must be getting good leads."

Jon got up. Sorensen felt bad for making the intern feel uncomfortable but wanted to shake Quinn up a little.

"It's time you shared with the rest of us."

"Why don't you do your own intel instead of sitting your fat ass on that chair all day long?" Quinn tapped on his laptop.

"Go fuck yourself."

Sorensen stood and went to Virago's office. Her door was closed, but Sorensen barged in without knocking. She was on the phone, and her look told him he wasn't welcome, but he didn't leave. He'd followed her to SJPD and this place was shit, so she owed him something.

He sat and waited. She was doing most of the listening. Finally, she said, "Got it" and hung up. She pushed her glasses on top of her head and rubbed her eyes, smearing mascara all over them. "That was the chief."

Sorensen nodded. He knew more was coming without having to probe.

"He wanted to know where we were with Carol."

"We have Guero. We just need to find him," he said.

"And what are you doing about that?"

"All we can. But the more important question is, what's Quinn doing?"

She put her glasses back on. They didn't quite hide the blotches.

"He's off all the time and hasn't brought back anything in four days." Without saying more, he looked behind him to make sure the sergeant wasn't listening. "Commander, he's hiding something. Either he's hiding leads or covering some shit he doesn't want us to find." He paused. "Either way he adds no value, and now you're sending him to Seattle. To do what? You should get him off the case."

She looked out into the bullpen. "I have an idea." She got up and yelled for Quinn to join them.

When he reached her office, he walked in and leaned on the doorframe.

"Close the door."

It wasn't an invitation.

He did but didn't sit.

"I want you both to get me some solid leads on Carol." When they both started complaining, she raised her hand.

259

They stopped. "This is an order. Get out of my office and bring me a break in the case by end of day."

She focused on her monitor, and Sorensen got up, knowing they'd been dismissed.

"Crying to Mommy," Quinn said after closing the door. "What a pussy."

Sorensen turned and, putting his whole weight behind it, threw a hook that landed square on Quinn's right cheek, sending him backward. Quinn lost his step and fell on a desk. The monitor tumbled on the keyboard, and the chair rolled a few feet away. Quinn steadied himself, but before he could launch at Sorensen, Virago came out of her office.

"Enough!" she yelled.

Sorensen grabbed his jacket and headed to the elevator. "I'm driving."

"The hell you are," Quinn said behind him.

"There's no discussion."

"I'm the sergeant."

Quinn punched the elevator button three times.

"I came to SJPD with all my years. I have seniority."

Sorensen pushed through the opening doors, as if getting in the elevator first would automatically grant him his wish.

CHAPTER 62

Darcy left the parole office and called DDA Matthews. His secretary told him he was in court, so he decided to drive to Chavo's girlfriend's last known address. If he was hiding anywhere, it was probably somewhere where he could get booty.

The San Andreas apartment complex looked like any other low-income housing. The four-story buildings with small windows and tinier balconies flanked Jefferson Park. To the left-hand side there was a playground and benches spread along a dirt path that was shaded by trees. He noticed a group of teens gathered around a worn-out picnic table. They looked his way when they heard the Cobra approach. He cursed for not getting an undercover car before venturing out into gang territory.

He parked and approached the group. They all wore the same oversized hoodies and sagging black pants. One of the kids threw something on the ground and stomped on it. Another handed something off to the only girl. Someone said something Darcy couldn't quite make out, and three teens walked away from him. Three others stayed. He found that curious and wondered if they would sprint in opposite directions when he got closer.

But they didn't. The two males looked up at him, defiant with their dark eyes. The girl looked down at the ground.

Maybe she was shy, or maybe she was high and was trying to hide it.

"Hey, guys, how you doing today? Can I talk to you for a second?"

He felt stupid the moment he asked, but Walker had told him that when talking to gangsters, it was better to keep it respectful but casual, especially if he was trying to relate to the younger ones.

The older boy, who looked barely seventeen, chewed on the string of his hoodie and lifted his chin up at him. "What up?"

"Nice ink. You design that yourself?" Darcy pointed to an interesting emblem on the guy's forearm. He figured it was less contentious to focus on that than on the tail of the snake that peeked out of the collar of his hoodie.

"You here for tat referrals?" He laughed.

The others joined in, but the giggles sounded flat.

"What does it mean?" Darcy felt out of place dressed in his light-gray suit and driving his red-candy-apple Cobra.

He was considering leaving when the kid crossed his arms and squared his body toward him. If he left now, he would be seen as weak and would never be able to command respect from the Snakes. So he evened out his weight on both feet, making himself an inch taller even though he towered over them by almost a foot. He pushed his jacket back and rested his palm on the butt of his gun. It was a subtle move, but they all noticed it.

The air changed. He felt them stiffen. He watched their hands and forced his to stay in place instead of loosening the safety. He needed to figure out how to de-escalate the tension before he ended up as another gang statistic.

Emblem leaned back on the picnic table, the strain lifting a smidge. "I just got it for my girl."

The female shifted away from him, and Darcy understood Emblem wasn't referring to her.

"You guys heard about the school shooting?" Darcy made eye contact with each of them except the girl, who wouldn't look up.

Nobody said anything.

"A six-year-old girl almost died."

"Some *joto* hit her. Got nothing to do with us."

"I know. We got him already."

The tension was still palpable but felt less dire.

"Why you bothering us about that shit?"

The other guy grunted and nodded in support. The girl was so quiet, Darcy wondered if she would only talk if they gave her permission.

He pulled a printout of Chavo's hand tattoo and passed it around. "Do you recognize this?"

The two guys shook their heads. The girl looked at the photo, then at the guys for guidance.

"Never seen that before," Emblem guy said.

"Yeah, never," said the other.

The girl shook her head, her long ponytail swaying from side to side.

"Really? Because it belongs to Chavo Buenavente. I hear he's the shot caller around here."

"Well, I ain't fuckin' lying." Emblem puffed out his chest.

"I just thought you'd recognize the ink."

"What you want with him?" the other kid asked.

Emblem gave him a look. The teen zipped his hoodie all the way up and sat on the table next to the girl.

"I think he has information that can help us nail the *joto* who hurt the little girl."

Emblem smiled when Darcy used the derogatory term to refer to the Diablos. That had been another suggestion from Walker.

"The kid's in jail. Heard it on the news," Emblem said.

"Wait, aren't you the guy who went into the school?" the kid sitting asked.

For the first time the girl looked up at Darcy. She also recognized him.

Damn news and everybody's phone cameras.

"Yeah. I thought I seen you somewhere. You're like a fucking celebrity or som'thing." Emblem pushed himself off the table, as if he needed to get a closer look at his face.

Darcy shifted his weight from one foot to the other. Was this good?

"Not cool enough for an autograph, though," Emblem said.

Darcy laughed. The three kids laughed too, and this time it was genuine.

"Come on, guys, throw me a bone here," Darcy said.

"What you want with Chavo?" Emblem asked.

"Seriously, what I said. I think he can help us put a Diablo away."

"He won't talk to you." Emblem's body stiffened again. Darcy wondered if he'd telegraphed something, but he hadn't moved. "Snakes don't talk to police. Got nothing for you."

He crossed his arms, and Darcy saw the word "snake" tattooed across his knuckles. One letter on each finger except the index, which held a scrunched "KE."

"Maybe I can ask him myself."

"Chavo's not here, and he won't tell you shit." Emblem pulled his pants up from the belt, not quite covering his red boxers. "Are we free to leave?"

Darcy nodded. As they started walking away, he stepped in front of the girl. "Can you stay for a minute?"

She looked past him to the leader.

"She can't. We gotta go," Emblem said, and took a few steps toward Darcy.

"I was asking her."

Darcy didn't move.

"You talked to her already." Emblem took off his hat. "SFE" in black block lettering was spread across his forehead.

Snakes for Ever? Darcy wondered. *Really?*

Emblem wiped the sweat and put the hat back on, pulling the visor all the way down to his eyebrows.

"I saw the hand-to-hand when I came over. It looked like dope. This is gang territory, and I have enough to search her. So you either leave and let me talk to her alone, or I'm going to frisk her. And you know that'll give me enough to book her."

The girl looked up to the kid and shoved both hands into her denim cut-offs. The white pockets stuck out of the frilled jeans.

He waited. Emblem nodded at the girl and started walking to catch up with the other kid. They didn't leave the park but stopped right before the road.

Darcy looked at the girl. He didn't know what to say and wished for the first time since meeting Quinn that he was there with him.

She sat down where she was before. He took a place at the other end of the table and rested his elbows on his knees. They were both staring out into the park, in the opposite direction of where the two boys were. He knew that wasn't the smartest thing to do, but he thought that standing in front of her would only make her more defensive. He glanced over at her and almost laughed when he realized that she probably felt as uncomfortable as he was.

"Is he your boyfriend?" He already knew the answer from watching her body language.

265

She smiled and shook her head, but her cheeks flushed.

"Oh, I see. You're someone else's girl, but you like this guy."

"Noooo," she said, her body swinging from side to side, but now her cheeks were bright red.

"Oh come on, you can tell me. I won't say anything."

She continued to shake her body but finally said, "Okay, maybe a little."

"Is he into you too?"

She covered her face with both hands. "I don't know." Her words were muffled.

"He's very protective of you. I think he likes you back." Darcy looked over his shoulder. Emblem guy met his eyes from a distance. "What's your name?"

"Lila."

"Like the flower?"

She nodded and pulled the sleeve of her hoodie to display the purple lilac tattooed on it.

"That's very pretty. When did you get it done?"

"When I turned fifteen. Three months ago."

He nodded and looked out into the park again. "Lila, I know Chavo hangs around here."

She lifted her knees and wrapped her arms around them, curling up into a ball.

"You have siblings?"

She nodded.

"Older or younger?"

She took a long time to respond but finally said, "An older sister and two younger brothers."

"The girl who got hit at the school was six. How would you feel if it'd been one of your brothers?"

Her body started rocking.

"Please help me find Chavo."

Lila started turning her head.

"Don't look at them. This is between us," he said before she could communicate distress back to the boys. "I know you don't want me to search you, because you know I'll find dope."

"If you put your hand—"

"I can have a female officer here in less than five minutes," he said, and then added, "I don't have anything against you. I have no interest in arresting you either. But right now I need to find this guy, and I know you can help me, so I'll use whatever I can to get the information I need. Even if that means taking you to jail."

She looked to her right, to a set of buildings. Darcy knew she was looking at Chavo's girlfriend's apartment.

"Please," he said.

"He's down with my cousin," she said, and hid her face in her hands.

"He's there now?"

The girl shook her head. "I haven't seen him for a few days."

"Is that normal? Does he live with her?"

"No. He has his own place over by Monterey Highway."

Darcy recognized the street from the list of known addresses JC had provided him. It looked like he wasn't getting anything he didn't already know.

"When is he going to visit your cousin again?"

"Never. My cousin kicked him out because she found him sexting some ho from Oakland."

"Ouch."

"Yeah, she beat him good." Lila laughed. "I don't think he'll come back anytime soon."

"Do you know where else he might be kicking it?" Darcy ran his fingers through his short hair and waited. "Come on, Lila, help me out here a little more and I'll go. I promise."

"Okay, fine, but you can't tell nobody I told you." Her eyes met his for the first time. Her pupils were dilated, but the anxiety in them didn't escape him.

Darcy nodded.

"Say it. You have to say the words." She kept looking at him.

"I promise I won't tell anybody I heard this from you."

"The last time Chavo came to see my cousin—you know, the day she caught him sexting." She stopped until Darcy urged her to go on. "He bought my cousin's car. He gave her eight hundred dollars."

"What car did your cousin have?"

"A really old Corolla. Brownish with a gray front fender," she said.

CHAPTER 63

After leaving the warehouse, Oscar and Pascual argued about what to do next. Pascual finally conceded, and they headed to the command center to watch the drones work. In a way, that was probably the safest place they could be, and his lieutenant knew it.

Dominique had sent the v.2s flying from the warehouse and piloted them until Oscar had enough time to brief Spider and Palo and they could take over.

The two soldiers ran to the door when they arrived, eager to see the new toys. The excitement in the boys' faces quickly faded when Oscar told them about the new mission.

"If we're not using them for the rich houses... what we looking for?" Spider asked.

"Something else," Oscar said.

Both kids stared at the screen, which was split in two. The left side showed a satellite view of the streets the drone was flying over in East San Jose. The right displayed a rapid sequence of facial images.

"What exactly?" Spider asked, staring at the faces.

"None of your biz, fool." Oscar noticed that Pascual's voice lacked the intensity he normally used when putting one of the guys in his place.

Spider wasn't quiet for long. "But how can we do the job if we don't know what we're doing?"

"Hey, *puto*, you're gonna have no job if you keep asking questions. Understood?" Pascual said.

Spider shrugged and looked at Palo, who shrugged back.

After a short while the soldiers got immersed in a burglary and forgot all about the new drones. Oscar had kept an eye on the v.2s, but the faces on the monitor had started to blur in front of him. One after another popped up on the screen, looking very much like something coming from a spy movie. Several parameters were listed on the screen—the distance between the eyes, size of the ears, even the ethnic bone structure.

The data was compared to what the system had already calculated for Chavo and computed the likeness of the found faces. So far the closest they got was a 42.75 percent match. Not enough to go on a chase. And a simple eye inspection showed that the match wasn't Chavo. Oscar was getting discouraged.

The more he thought about this whole thing, the more he realized it didn't make any sense. What was he thinking? The chances of one of the two drones and Chavo being at the same location at the same time were minute. He needed the whole fleet hunting him down.

He called Dominique. "What do I need to do to get my ten v.1s upgraded to v.2?"

There was no answer.

"D, I'm running out of patience."

"The v.2s have three cameras instead of one, they fly more steadily, there's less vibration, and therefore they can scan faces much more reliably. That's why I tweaked the hardware for the v.2s. The cameras are better too."

"But you could push the software upgrades to the v.1s," Oscar said, now looking at the ten monitors showing the drones' home invasion targets.

"Technically that would be possible, but you probably won't get good results."

Oscar thought about the word "probably."

"Are you saying that they can work, but not as well, or that they won't work at all?"

He was much more interested in finding Chavo than making money with the robberies, but if there was no point, he would rather leave the drones working and shower Dominique with the earnings to get more v.2s faster.

"I also improved the streaming performance. The v.1s won't be able to transmit the images to be processed as fast. They won't work as well. Far from it."

Dominique sounded defeated. Oscar thought about it for a while. He could give it a try. If it was futile, he would only lose a day or two of profits.

"I want you to push the software. Now."

"Okay," Dominique said almost inaudibly. "You have to land the drones. Then it'll take about thirty minutes or so."

Oscar thanked him, but Dominique had already hung up. Pascual called Gato to tell him the crew had the rest of the day off.

"You should throw them a bone. They were counting on today's cash," Pascual told Oscar after hanging up.

"Sure," Oscar said, not really paying attention.

Palo and Spider landed the drones. Oscar and Pascual stared at the black monitors for what seemed like days, while the two kids played Ping-Pong.

Exactly a half an hour later, there were a few flickers, and the screens came back to life. Soon after the drones took

271

off, the monitors started displaying new faces, with vertical and horizontal dimensions. There was something new too. Chavo's photo was tucked in the bottom-right corner. Oscar cursed. The one thing he hadn't counted on was that Dominique could have done an update to the user interface. He was upset for not thinking of that.

He'd wanted to keep the identity of his search target secret until he was able to get him. It never occurred to him that Dominique might add a way to do a quick visual check as a feature enhancement. He made a mental note to tell the geek to run any updates to the UI by him before pushing anything live moving forward.

Too late now. Oscar's crew knew who the drones were after.

"I know that guy." Spider stared at the monitor, as if mesmerized by the image. "He's a dumb-ass worm."

"We all know him," Pascual said.

"No, I mean in person. He used to go to my dad's store. He was always short of dough and never paid my dad back."

"Where's your dad's store?"

"By Jefferson Park."

"Send the v.2s there now," Oscar said.

Spider entered a few commands. One drone continued on a straight path, and the other veered to the right and began a steep climb to avoid a building.

Maybe the UI update had been a blessing after all, Oscar thought as he watched the drones fly to their new destination.

CHAPTER 64

Sorensen drove to East San Jose, following Quinn's direction. He wasn't sure where the sergeant was taking him, but since Virago had forced them to go together, he'd decided to shut up and see what precious intel Quinn was hiding from the rest of them. Not that he expected him to share anything of value.

Eventually, Quinn pointed to the curb for Sorensen to park and got out of the car. "I got to take this," he said, answering his cell.

Sorensen locked the car and walked behind the sergeant. Not too close to make him uncomfortable, but enough to try to catch some of the conversation. But before he could make any sense of it, Quinn saw him and hung up.

"What the hell? Spying on me?"

"What are we doing here?" Sorensen looked up the street. There was an old man walking away about a block up.

Quinn shook his head. "This is main Diablos territory. I have a couple CIs we can rough up. If anybody knows anything, it would be them."

"Why didn't you come here earlier if that's the case?"

"Who says I didn't? They were too high to be coherent."

Quinn opened a chain-link fence, and a silver pitbull came running toward them, barking. He extended his hand, palm

273

facing down. The dog stopped close enough to smell him, then sat and panted until Quinn scratched him behind the ears.

"Droopy, you in?" he yelled toward the back of the house.

Sorensen wondered if the dog would sniff him too or eat his entire hand for dessert. He decided to not find out. The dog turned and ran behind the house. Quinn followed, and so did he.

A guy who didn't quite look twenty was idling inside an inflatable pool. The water too shallow to cover his scrawny body, his arms and legs hung outside the pink-and-yellow plastic sides. He was squinting in the sunlight.

"What up, Sergeant Quinn?" He shaded his face with a wet hand.

"The hit at Berto's."

"Terrible thing. From what I hear, they did a number on her."

His voice was singsongy, and Sorensen had to fight back the urge to kick the plastic pool.

"What else have you heard?" Sorensen asked.

"Who's this fool, bro?" Droopy asked Quinn.

Sorensen looked over his shoulder at the dog sitting under a tree, in the shade. He crossed his arms instead of using them to pull the pimp out of the pool by one leg and beat the shit out of him.

"What's the word on the street?" Quinn asked again.

When Droopy didn't speak, Quinn pushed. "I'm talking to you, you're talking to me. I asked you a question."

"Fine, bro. No need to get all mad and shit. Diablos didn't do it. We staying the hell out of this mess."

"You're not taking responsibility for this one even though your boss Guero was all over the crime scene?" Sorensen asked.

"Your dude here's misguided. I've already told you," Droopy said, addressing Quinn. "All of us ate at Berto's. Hell, all of San Jose ate there. You don't want the Diablos for this."

Sorensen wasn't that surprised that the gang was refusing to take responsibility for the hit, even though it would have given them a lot of street cred. But then again, Droopy could be lying or not know anything at all.

After a few more useless interactions, they went back to the car. Sorensen had a slew of questions of his own.

"How much do you trust this guy?" he asked.

"Not at all," Quinn said.

"Then why the fuck come all the way here?"

Sorensen put the car in gear but didn't move. He was too tempted to push Quinn out once they started rolling.

"You wanted to meet one of my CIs, so we came."

"A CI you don't trust. Whoa, dude, I wonder what crap you're pulling to have the case close rate you have, because obviously it's not good police work that got you those numbers."

The force of Quinn's fist pushed his head a half foot in the opposite direction. His cheek burnt first, then started hurting, so much he felt his eyes water. Sorensen was glad the car window was open, or he would have smashed the glass with his thick skull.

CHAPTER 65

Darcy left Lila at the bench and walked toward his car. Emblem guy was leaning against the Cobra, his foot propped right above the wheel. He stared up at Darcy as he got closer. It was intriguing to see the teen daring him, trying to piss him off by disrespecting his car, and how unsuccessful he was being. After Ethan Mitchell's commandos put thirty-four bullets in it and almost killed Jon, the Cobra had become a reminder of what was really important in life. He loved his car, but not enough to fight over it.

When he reached the Cobra, he opened the door and placed a hand on the back of the seat, but before he got in he said, "You may want to move before I pull out."

Emblem guy pushed himself off the car and spat a few inches from his sneaker. Darcy placed the other hand on the dashboard and slid into the seat. When the key turned in the ignition, the car roared to life, and he drove off.

Before he turned right at the end of the block, he saw that Lila had joined the two boys and they were all staring at him. Darcy signaled and left the park.

A few blocks later he stopped at a red light and suddenly realized that he'd been holding his breath. After he exhaled for a long time, he pulled his phone out to check the information he had about Chavo's known associates. He wanted to have a chat with Lila's cousin.

Darcy entered the address of the dentist office where Consuelo Martinez worked and followed the directions. It was only a few miles away.

The strip mall hosted a cluster of small businesses. There was a phone shop, a massage parlor, a mom-and-pop grocery store, and at the very end the dentist office he was looking for. Darcy parked kitty-corner from it, under a tree. The lot was filled with old cars and pickup trucks in various stages of decay. A few kids ran on the sidewalk, playing tag.

Darcy waited until they had gone by and entered the establishment. The chimes were loud and all the patrons looked up at him. There was a woman sitting next to a teenager texting faster than anything Darcy had ever seen before, and an older gentleman with a farmer's hat on, flipping through an old magazine.

"Can I help you?" asked the receptionist from behind a wooden-laminated counter.

He immediately recognized her as Chavo's latest girlfriend from the DMV photos JC had printed for him.

"Miss Martinez." He flashed his badge as he introduced himself. "Is there somewhere we can talk?"

She sighed and looked over her shoulder. It was obvious she'd been through this before. "Dora, I'm taking my fifteen. Can you cover the reception?"

The woman nodded, and Consuelo motioned for Darcy to follow her outside. She went around the corner of the building and stopped only when she was in the shade.

"What is it now?" she asked. She sounded bored rather than frustrated or defiant.

"I understand that you are Chavo's girlfriend."

"No. I broke up with the two-time *cabrón* a few days ago."

"Is that when you sold him your car?"

She seemed surprised that he knew about that. He didn't press, giving her time. After a long moment she nodded. Darcy figured she was trying to assess how little she could get away with giving him.

"Was there a particular reason why he wanted to buy your car?"

"How should I know?"

"Why did you sell it to him? Weren't you broken up already?"

"I needed the money."

"Is there anything special about your car?"

"Besides it being a piece of shit? No. I don't think so."

"Did you date for a long time?"

"On and off for five years. I hate the man, but he comes back and sweet-talks me back into it."

She removed the purse from her shoulder. Long bright-pink nails pulled on the zipper. She dug out a pack of gum and offered it to Darcy. He shook his head, and she unwrapped two pieces and put them in her mouth.

"Consuelo, I'm going to be honest with you. Chavo is wanted in connection to the school shooting."

"No way. A Diablo kid did that. Everybody knows it." She popped the gum as she shook her head. The smell of strawberry reached his nose.

"We have pretty strong evidence connecting him to the crime. I really need to talk to him. Maybe that will clear him."

She laughed, and it wasn't a nice laugh. "You think I'm dumb or som'thing? I've heard this bull from cops before. 'Oh, I just want to clear his name.' Right."

This was going in the wrong direction. Darcy needed a new approach.

"I changed my mind. Can I have some gum?"

She rolled her eyes, as if he'd asked her for money or her child. She dug inside her purse and pulled out the pack. Darcy took a piece.

"Do you really hate Chavo, or is he your man?"

Consuelo looked down. Darcy could see her jaw crunching on the gum.

"I fucking hate his guts."

"Then help me."

"I'm no snitch. You know how it goes."

"Nobody needs to know. I just want to find him. A little girl got seriously injured. She could have died, and I know for a fact that it was Chavo who gave the gun to the shooter."

She shook her head. "That's not possible. I'm telling you. No way." She popped her gum twice.

Darcy detected less conviction in her voice.

"Has he ever hit you?"

She didn't reply.

"You know he can be mean, even vicious."

She played with the large hoop in her ear, still not looking at him.

"Tell me what happened when you sold him the car."

She spat out her gum. It landed an inch from the gutter.

"He asked for it. He said he wanted to fly under the radar for a while. He took my phone too, gave me another fifty bucks for me to get a new one."

"The same day?"

"No. He got my phone on Monday morning. If I had known what the ass was doing with his, I wouldn't have sold it to him."

Monday. Maybe that was why Chavo's phone didn't ping anywhere around Berto's at the time of the murder. Darcy wanted to kiss this woman. What if he'd gone to the restaurant with Consuelo's phone instead of his?

CHAPTER 66

Sorensen was glad when Quinn went straight home after their CI interview. He didn't feel like being around him for a second longer than he had to. When he arrived at CATCH, Jon ran him through what he'd found so far. Sorensen leaned in his chair and blew out air through gritted teeth. Neither spoke for a while.

Finally Sorensen dialed Lynch's number. "You need to come to the station."

"I was on my way to talk to DDA Matthews."

Sorensen rolled his eyes. "Why?"

"Long story. Also, can you put a BOLO on a car? I'll text you the info."

"What am I, your frigging secretary?" He scanned the desk for his energy drink, but it was long gone. A lukewarm Dr Pepper from earlier stood by his keyboard. "Okay, text it to me, but postpone Matthews. You need to come here now. It's related to our little research project."

"Oh?"

"'Oh' is right. Better be here in five." Sorensen hung up.

A few seconds later he received the information from Lynch and started working on the BOLO. It seemed that they both had news to share. He looked over to Jon. The poor intern looked green. Not much better than how he felt.

Jon left the bullpen and came back with a small bag of chips. "This was the last one." He opened it and placed it between them.

"I swear there are days I really miss the Sheriff's Office." Sorensen thought about the well-stocked vending machines with junk food and power drinks. "Screw this. Let's order food." Sorensen dialed from his desk phone.

About twenty minutes later Lynch showed up carrying three bags from Minato's.

"I didn't know you were moonlighting." Sorensen offered him a five-dollar bill.

"Keep the tip. When I saw the delivery guy downstairs, I knew it was yours." Lynch pushed the keyboard out of the way with one of the bags. "Do I actually want to know what you guys found?"

Sorensen shook his head as he dug into the shrimp tempura.

Jon shaved the splinters off the chopsticks and took one container with chicken Teriyaki.

"It's bad," Sorensen said with a full mouth.

Lynch sat on the guest chair. "By the way, did you get my BOLO out?"

"Yes, but you won't care after you hear what we're about to tell you."

Lynch started massaging his left temple. Sorensen wondered if he knew he always did that when he was worried or stressed. He would have to invite him to the upcoming Annual PAAF Poker Tournament.

After he took the last sip of his drink, Sorensen said, "We found some interesting stuff that may lead to loads of damage control."

"Are we talking really dirty?" Lynch's voice lowered to an almost-inaudible level.

Sorensen pointed at Jon with an open hand, inviting him to share what he already knew.

"I've been checking all of Carol's cases, going back to when she started at the county's crime lab fifteen years ago."

Sorensen leaned on his chair and derived some guilty pleasure watching Lynch's expressions change as Jon delivered the news.

"I only focused on the cases that were related to gangs. There were thousands. I noticed a strange trend." Jon looked up. He had Lynch's attention. "She worked all kinds of gang cases—the Hispanics, the Asians, even a few linked to organized crime, and a couple here and there with the Italian and Indian Mafias. I didn't even know there were Indian gangs."

Sorensen saw Jon blush, as if he felt he was expected to know everything. It was endearing to work with someone so smart and yet so humble.

"Anyway, out of all of the cases she worked on up to about two years ago, the conviction rate was high, almost ninety-five percent. Pretty much the same across all types of gangs. After that, the conviction rate for the Diablos gang cases dropped by thirty percent, most of the cases getting dismissals or acquittals. And these are only the cases the DA decided to move forward with."

Nobody spoke. They both stared at Lynch, who stood and started pacing.

"Have you checked other factors?"

"Yes, I cross-referenced with judges and accounted for different prosecutors and investigating officers, but none of those factors seemed to have any statistical significance. I also cross-checked with other lab techs, but the sample size was too small, since Carol pretty much worked all of the gang cases."

"Damn." Lynch paced by Jon's desk.

"That's exactly what I said." Sorensen reached for the beef chosenyaki.

"And you're sure you've only seen this change in the cases related to Los Diablos?"

Jon nodded. "The other cases, especially the Snakes, have actually increased by fifteen percent, though I haven't looked into possible causes yet."

Sorensen brushed the blond curls from his forehead. "I told you you would want to postpone meeting with the DDA."

"I've reviewed the numbers like twenty times." Jon fidgeted in his chair and clicked the mouse as he looked from the monitor to the detectives.

Sorensen stared at Lynch until his partner stopped wandering.

"Jon, you always do great work, but we need to be a hundred fifty percent sure before we go anywhere with this."

"A hundred fifty percent? Really?" Sorensen mocked.

"What?" Lynch looked confused.

"That's a stupid expression. A hundred percent does just fine."

"What are you guys talking so hush-hush about?" Virago said, walking into the bullpen.

The silence stretched for a bit too long, and Sorensen knew the time to tell Virago a lie had passed. Before he said anything, he double-checked that there was no one in the bullpen.

"Carol may have been compromising cases," he finally said.

Virago stopped cleaning her glasses with the tip of her blouse and put them back on. She looked at Sorensen, then at Jon, and finally at Lynch. Addressing the intern, she said, "Tell me everything."

Jon ran through the same information for the third time. Then Lynch told her about Jefe's print on the gun that killed the drug dealer. And Sorensen finished by adding what Rachel thought about that print—"Just a bit too clean to be real."

When they were done, she said, "This stays here until we have ironclad evidence that it is true. And then you share that with nobody until we figure out what to do."

They nodded, but no one said a word.

The elephant in the room was suffocating Sorensen. "What about Quinn?"

Virago set her black eyes on him, and he felt as if she could see right through him.

"This cannot be a one-person show," he added.

"Did you do the same calculation for the arrests?" the commander asked Jon, who looked small, as if he was trying to avoid being part of the conversation.

"Just preliminary work."

"And?" she asked.

"No findings yet."

"Nothing?" She walked to Sorensen's side so she could look at Jon directly.

"Nothing yet. I will have a full report before I leave for the day."

"Whatever you find, not a word to anybody but us, understood?"

"Yes, ma'am," Jon responded.

"Not a word about what?" Quinn asked, his rubber soles silent on the linoleum floor.

Sorensen cursed himself for assuming that the sergeant had called it a day.

CHAPTER 67

The lie Virago came up with was inconsequential, and Darcy could tell that Quinn didn't buy it, but the sergeant didn't push. An uncomfortable air surrounded them for a few seconds, until Quinn broke it.

"Commander, can we talk for a sec?" Quinn looked past them toward her office.

She nodded, and they both left. He closed the door.

Darcy felt Sorensen's eyes on him and looked up.

"What do you think that's about?" Sorensen asked.

"No clue."

"Damn, I was going to dig into the sergeant's old cases, but with him here..." Sorensen leaned back on his chair and interlaced his fingers behind his head.

Darcy filed yet another warrant—this one for Consuelo's phone—and emailed it to the judge on call. He didn't expect to get a reply until the next day but asked Jon to start looking into that number too when he had a chance to go back to triangulating phones with locations.

He was about to leave when he got a call from a number he didn't recognize.

"Sergeant Harjo, Reno County Sheriff's. You have a BOLO out on a Samantha Lee?"

"You found her?"

Darcy got up from the chair. He'd almost forgotten all about Nhu Tran.

"We caught her doing 65 in a 45 mph. She's in custody. We found a bag full of clothes and twenty thousand dollars in her trunk she wouldn't explain."

"How fast can you get her to Santa Clara?"

"We can send a car over tomorrow. Want us to ask some questions before we do?"

Darcy thought about it. Jefe was dead, and Nhu would not be testifying, even if they found her. There was no reason to press things tonight.

"That's okay. We can take over tomorrow when your guy gets here." Then he remembered the button Mauricio had found in the court restroom and searched for the photo in his computer. "Sergeant, can I ask you to take a look at her clothes and see if you find a missing button? I'll send you the evidence photo from the scene."

"You got it. I'll share the transport details tomorrow morning."

After they hung up, Darcy said, "I knew it," and shared the conversation with Sorensen and Jon. He was happy that his gut had been right.

"It's a bummer that Jefe's dead, though," Sorensen said. "Actually, not that he's dead—he was a scumbag—but that this was all for nothing."

"It's not for nothing. Lee was paid to aid a witness escape. I'm going to get her charged, and the DA better get a conviction."

Sorensen shrugged. Darcy wasn't sure if it was because he didn't care or because he didn't think the DA would push too hard either. Before he could ask, the commander stormed out of her office, followed by Quinn. Her jaw was clenched, matching her fists. Without a word she'd captured their full attention.

"DDA Matthews has been shot," she said.

Quinn grabbed his jacket. He looked almost as distressed as he had when Darcy met him at Carol's crime scene.

"Is he okay?"

"Alive—for now."

"Suspects?" Sorensen asked.

"None yet. He was eating at that Pho place on First, by the courthouse. He was gunned down leaving the restaurant."

"Witnesses?"

"Let's go. I don't have details." She was already by the door.

Darcy wondered if they would all jump in the same car, but when he saw Virago heading to hers and Sorensen and Quinn walking in the opposite direction, he went for his own car. Jon got in with Sorensen. It didn't surprise him. He doubted the intern would ever feel comfortable riding with him again, even though Darcy had learned his lesson.

First Street was cordoned off north- and southbound about a block off the restaurant. The light rail had also been stopped, and law enforcement were the only people within the perimeter.

Sergeant Marra met them by the fire truck.

"Commander." He crossed his arms and faced Virago, his feet apart, centering his weight. "He's in very critical condition. He was shot several times."

"They took him to RMC, right?" Virago asked.

"Yes. Left a few minutes ago."

"Any other victims?" Quinn looked up and down the sidewalk.

"No. The restaurant gets a lot of traffic for lunch, but it's fairly quiet at dinner. The owner was in the back. He didn't see anything."

"You believe him?" Darcy asked.

"They're pro-blue in this place. If he'd seen anything, he would tell us," Marra said.

CSU was already setting yellow numbered cones next to the evidence they found. There was a large pool of blood on the walkway, with some splatter across the wall. One of the storefront windows was shattered.

"This was a drive-by," Darcy said.

"Sherlock, sometimes your powers of deduction amaze me," Sorensen said.

Marra chuckled, and Virago walked toward the restaurant.

The fire truck left, leaving a large void behind.

A tall officer with black hair and darker skin came over to join their huddle.

"We have several security cameras nearby. We'll have the footage at the station in an hour," he reported to Marra, and left.

"You taking this case too?" Marra asked Sorensen.

"Sometimes I feel like I'm the only damn detective in the entire SJPD," Sorensen said loud enough for Quinn to hear it.

But the sergeant didn't take the bait.

"You have this guy." Marra pointed at Darcy with his thumb.

Darcy didn't feel like hearing Sorensen's snarky reply, so he left them behind and went to check the area where Matthews had been gunned down. The blood was dark and thick, and there was a lot of it. The DDA had bled for some time before the paramedics arrived.

Darcy walked up the street instead of going into the restaurant. *First Carol*, he thought. *Now DDA Matthews.*

CHAPTER 68

Friday

Sorensen shifted in the seat at the passenger lounge of the San Jose airport and wondered why they had to make the chairs so frigging small. He looked around as he sucked on the straw sticking out of his extra large Dr Pepper plastic cup. He was glad Quinn hadn't arrived yet. Or maybe the douche was waiting at a different gate just to avoid him. That suited him fine. He didn't really want to see the sergeant.

He thought about last night and how pissed he'd been at Virago. She'd waited until the wee hours, after all his energy had been spent at DDA Matthews's crime scene, to tell him that he needed to rush home to get a change of clothes, because he was going to chaperone Quinn up in Seattle.

"He's been going through that folder you guys found in Carol's gun safe—" she had said.

"You mean the folder I was going to look into?" Sorensen had reminded her.

She ignored him and went on. "He found some information that merits a personal visit."

"So why do I need to go?"

She raised her black eyes to meet his. Nothing more needed to be said, and yet he really wanted her to say it, to say something about Quinn. About his suspicions that there was something odd with the sergeant's behavior, and maybe by association the questions around Carol also extended to Quinn. And that was why Quinn couldn't go by himself, because Virago couldn't trust that he would go there to unearth Carol's discrepancies instead of hiding his own.

But all she said was, "Don't you want to investigate what's in the folder? Well, this is your chance. You can't have it both ways."

She got in her car, leaving him behind trying to concoct a brilliant comeback that never came.

So here he was, at dawn sitting in a crowded gate, waiting to board a nonstop flight to Seattle to dig into Carol's past.

Virago had assured him that Quinn understood that he would be bringing Sorensen up to speed. And since the sergeant wasn't there and they weren't sitting together on the flight, he expected the ride into the city to be fairly interesting.

CHAPTER 69

Darcy kissed Saffron, petted Shelby, and left for the office. The roads were already crowded, even though it wasn't 8 a.m. yet.

They'd been at the scene past midnight and then watched every tape until four. The videos clearly showed Matthews exiting the restaurant, a Honda coming around the corner drive by him, the DDA falling to the ground, and the car speeding away.

The plates soon identified a maroon Civic that had been reported stolen that afternoon. A couple of uniforms found the car a few miles away from the crime scene. They had towed it to the police garage, but nobody expected to find any prints.

Darcy's phone rang. He looked for his earbuds but couldn't find them, so he put it on speaker.

"Are you heading to CATCH?" Virago asked without any preamble.

"I am."

"I need to talk to you. Come by my office as soon as you get in."

"Want to give me the CliffsNotes?"

"I'd rather wait."

This didn't sound like her.

He checked the clock on the dashboard. "I'll be there in ten."

Darcy wondered what was so important that Virago wouldn't give him any highlights over the phone. It had to be related to his transfer to CATCH. He didn't make it. That was why she wanted to see him. Otherwise, she would be telling him the good news over the phone. Well, it wasn't as if it came as a shock.

He suppressed his disappointment and sped up to the office. When he got to the SJPD, he went straight upstairs. Remembering the flavored tainted water they tried to pass off for coffee, he regretted not having stopped at Starbucks for a decent cup.

Jon was already working, but neither Sorensen nor Quinn were there yet. Darcy wasn't that surprised considering how late they'd worked the previous night. After greeting the intern, he went to Virago's office.

"Close the door," she said.

He did and took the chair opposite to her.

"I sent Sorensen up to Seattle with Quinn."

"What? Why?"

Darcy felt as if he'd been punched in the gut. Quinn maybe, but sending Sorensen instead of him?

"I talked to Howard. He wouldn't have it, no matter how I presented the option to send you there."

"I could have talked to my brother-in-law."

"Out of anyone I know, I thought you were the most adamant about not using cronyism to get what you wanted," she said. "I may have assumed wrong."

That was a low blow. She knew he abhorred being connected to his brother-in-law in any way. He stood, ready to leave.

"I don't like leveraging him, but this is ridiculous. You know I have a much better chance of getting things done there, and much quicker, than both of them together."

"Given the option, I made the call and sent Sorensen."

"Fine."

"I expect you to grease their way."

"Sure." He opened the door and without turning said, "Anything else?"

"No."

He walked out. Originally, he'd wanted to update her on his conversation with Consuelo, but he was pissed and didn't feel like talking to Virago anymore. If it led anywhere, he would share it then.

CHAPTER 70

Now that Darcy knew that neither Sorensen nor Quinn would be in the office, he decided to squat there and work with Jon. He set his bag on the guest chair, sat in Sorensen's spot, but didn't connect his laptop to the monitor.

"Did you find anything?" he asked Jon while his computer booted.

"Nothing I would call 'conclusive.'" Jon sighed.

"Do you think we may have all this about Carol wrong?"

Jon didn't say anything for a few seconds. "There's definitely a shift in cases from about two years ago." Jon tapped the keyboard to get to the window he wanted. "The Diablos' arrest rate has a downward trend, similar to the one we saw for the convictions." Jon blinked a few times. "But there are many possible explanations for this."

"Guero taking over and going semi-legit probably made the biggest impact," Darcy said.

Jon nodded. "They only had a couple dozen drug-related arrests in the last two years, and they were all for possession, and then nothing after Prop 47." After a second Jon added, "I found something else, but I'm not sure it's related at all."

"What?"

"Shortly after Guero took over the Diablos, the home invasion reports skyrocketed all over the Bay Area."

Darcy had heard that burglaries were yet another enterprise gangs engaged in, but "skyrocket"? The Bay Area was a large region. Were the Diablos expanding their criminal activities into new territories?

"Hey, guys, can you come over?" Virago yelled from her office.

When they got there, she pointed to the phone, indicating that she was on a call.

"Lieutenant Kobe, from the Santa Cruz County Sheriff," she told them. Then, addressing the phone, she said, "I have Detective Lynch and Jon Evans with me. Please share with them what you just told me."

"We got a call about a break-in in at a house in the mountains a couple days ago. It's not a well-traveled area, and the owners only go there sporadically, so we don't really know when the incident occurred. The curious thing was that they only took a change of clothes and left the used ones behind."

Darcy looked at Virago.

She mouthed, "Just wait."

He continued listening.

"The clothes were bloody. Too bloody to be from a scratch. We also found a cell. The phone was dead, so we put it in a Faraday bag. Anyway, long story short, we sent the clothes to the lab, and we have a guy who's pretty tech savvy, so we got the phone running. The blood on the clothes was a match to Oscar Amaro. I believe you're after him in connection to the Montes murder."

He waited for a response. Virago told him to go on.

"The cell only had a few incoming and outgoing calls. I just emailed you those numbers."

Virago leaned back and took the page from the printer. She handed it over to Lynch, and Jon scooted his chair closer to see the list too. There were four numbers. One looked familiar. Darcy had seen it somewhere and pointed it out to Jon. The intern nodded, indicating that he knew it too.

"Lieutenant, this is really helpful. Can you send us the evidence, both the clothes and the phone?" Virago asked.

"Will do." Before he hung up, he said, "I hope you catch the guy who did this to Montes. We didn't work with your lab too much, but when something like this happens, it's an attack on all of us."

"We're doing our best," Virago said.

She ended the call.

"We know Oscar got shot at Berto's, but why the hell does he go from the restaurant after killing Carol to breaking into a small house in the woods thirty miles away to get a change of clothes, then leave behind a burner?" Virago asked while she massaged the bridge of her nose.

They left her office, and Darcy checked his notes to see if his memory was right. He had too many numbers in too many places, but then he spotted it.

"Holy shit," Darcy said, and showed Jon his notebook with the match.

CHAPTER 71

Pascual busted into Oscar's room.

"Guero, they found him. They found Chavo."

"No way," Oscar said, more alert than he'd felt in ages.

"Yes, one of the drones. It spotted him by Eastridge Mall."

"Still eyes on him?"

"Yeah. The frigging drone stays with the target once spotted. That Dominique dude's a genius."

Oscar smiled. He threw on some clothes and headed for the car. "Let's go."

His homie had already understood the futility of his complaints, so he didn't even try telling him to stay.

Pascual drove fast, but not crazy enough to get pulled over.

"We need updates," Oscar said, and called the command center.

"We just lost him, boss. He went into the mall," Spider said when he picked up.

"Send all the drones there to monitor each exit." He felt his shoulder as he made a fist with his empty hand.

"On it."

"Call me back when you spot him again."

He hung up.

Pascual decelerated. "It'll be risky for you to go into the mall. Maybe we can send some soldiers."

Oscar thought about it. If Chavo spotted them, it may spook him for good.

"You and me, bro. And the birds."

Oscar wondered what the *joto* could be doing at the mall. What store would he go to? If he could figure that out, maybe he could find him without hassle. He tapped on his phone and browsed. The shopping center was your typical American mall—same stores, same food court, same kids' area. Nothing out of the ordinary.

"What the hell's he doing at the fucking mall?" Oscar asked, giving up on his search.

"Tattoo shop?"

"Seriously? No reputable gangster gets inked at the mall."

Pascual laughed. "We're talking about a *gusano*."

"Good point."

"Because I doubt he's at Kay Jewelers, or whatever that place is," Pascual said.

"He has a bitch?"

"He don't buy jewelry, fool." Pascual laughed.

"Tru dat." Oscar leaned into the seat and felt the gun press against his lower back. "I want this *puto*, man. We have to get him."

The phone rang.

"Got him?" Oscar asked, and felt his body stiffen.

"No, but all the drones are in position."

"Okay."

Oscar would have to wait until Chavo was done with his business at the mall. He needed him alive, because he was going to make the last hours of his life hell on earth.

CHAPTER 72

Sorensen turned his phone on as soon as the wheels of the 737 touched ground. The first message that popped up was from Virago.

Lou got a ticket out of Burundi but won't get here for another two days. The connections are horrible.

Almost immediately another one appeared.

Seattle needs to wrap up before Lou gets here. Play nice with Quinn.

"Yes, boss," Sorensen said under his breath. "If it only were that easy."

He shoved the phone in his jacket pocket and unbuckled his seat belt as the plane pulled up to the gate. He wanted to be one of the first ones out. Virago wasn't the only one who wanted them back to San Jose ASAP.

Quinn disembarked a minute later. He was rubbing his neck, as if he'd fallen asleep in the wrong position. They headed over to the rental car booths, and the sergeant argued like the little bitch he was about who would drive.

"This is my trip. I'm driving. Period," Quinn shouted, pounding the counter.

Several employees had come out of the back office to see what the ruckus was about.

"I can add both of you to the policy," the shrimpy man in the green polo shirt offered.

"Don't waste your time. He's not driving," Quinn said.

"Oh for God's sakes. You're such an asshole."

Sorensen turned and wished he was back in California. He cursed Virago, then forced himself to let it go. Every minute they spent there was a minute longer he had to be with Quinn.

Neither buckled up when they got into the black Buick Verano. They drove in silence, until the skyline of the Emerald City came into view.

"That's pretty nice. I've never been here before," Sorensen said.

Quinn responded with a grunt, and Sorensen didn't care.

"Are you going to catch me up with why we're here, or do I have to read your mind?"

The sergeant glanced out his side window. Sorensen wondered how he would feel if he were in Quinn's shoes. He would be annoyed that the commander had sent someone along. If he had something to hide, he would have spent the whole plane ride thinking of ways to get rid of the guy or do what he needed to do without showing his hand. Neither was going to be easy for Quinn.

"The file from Carol's gun safe," Sorensen said, and bit his tongue before another admonition for stealing his evidence escaped his lips.

"I knew her."

"So?"

Quinn looked at him as if Sorensen was daring him. "Because I have history with her, I can see things where others wouldn't make connections."

Maybe. Or maybe he wanted to make sure there was nothing there he needed to cover his ass about.

"How well did you know her?"

"I've worked with her for many years."

"What did you find in the file? Why are we here?"

Sorensen was growing impatient. Ten minutes into the drive, and he still knew nothing.

Quinn's hands tightened around the steering wheel. "Carol never talked about her family or much about her past before she joined the crime lab. I always figured it hadn't been a great childhood, so I never pressed. One day we had just won this big case—three Snakes went to prison for killing two people and a baby and injuring two others when they shot them up in a drive-by. Anyway, a few of us went out to celebrate after the verdict, and Carol drank a bit too much. After everybody left, she started crying. Between sobs she told me that she had a baby once, but it died. After she blurted that out, her demeanor completely changed. She stopped crying, pulled away, as if surprised by what she'd said, and left the bar."

Quinn's words surprised Sorensen. He'd gone from completely reserved to sharing something very intimate. Maybe he was human after all. He decided to keep his comments to himself and let Quinn continue.

The sergeant took his eyes off the road for a few seconds to look at him. Then went on.

"A few days later I asked her if she wanted to talk about it. She froze, as if she didn't remember she'd told me, then faked a laugh and said she'd made it all up. I knew she was lying, and it was so completely out of character that I had to look into it. There was no record of a birth or death ever connected to Carol Montes."

CHAPTER 73

Darcy waited until Jon checked his data. He had the same match for the number they found in the burner at the cabin.

"Commander, you need to see this."

Darcy wasn't sure if he was excited or depressed.

"What?"

Virago's pace out of her office was slow. She looked tired, more stressed than usual.

"We are certain that this phone belongs to Guero, right?" Darcy asked.

She looked at him as if he were asking if it was possible that the moon landing was a hoax. "You just heard Kobe. The clothes they found at the scene are soaked in Guero's blood, the owner of the house does not recognize the phone, and Guero's prints are all over it. That's pretty 'certain' to me."

Darcy handed her the email printout with the numbers Kobe sent them and pointed at the third one, which he'd highlighted in neon green, then went to the whiteboard and tapped on the photo of the burner found in Carol's purse at Berto's.

"No," she said.

"There are incoming and outgoing calls from this burner"—he tapped on the photo—"to that burner." He pointed at the paper in Virago's hand. "The only number on Carol's phone is that one."

Virago sat down in Sorensen's chair. She pulled the rubber band out of her hair and redid her ponytail. She missed a strand that brushed against her shoulder.

"Carol and Guero were communicating via burner cells...?" She looked up at them as if hoping for a different explanation.

"We need to change how we're looking at this whole case. If Carol was working with the Diablos in any way, it doesn't make sense that they killed her—" Darcy said.

"Or it makes perfect sense that they did if she decided to not help them anymore," Virago countered. "That may explain why it was so visceral and why it felt personal."

"This could explain the drop in the Diablos convictions too," Jon said.

"Jesus. I can't believe this," Virago said. "Jon, start looking into her bank records and all of her email, both work and personal. I want you to go over everything—and I mean everything—and flag the smallest thing that looks remotely suspicious."

"You got it."

"I'm heading back to the SO. I can stop by the lab and talk to Rachel," Darcy offered.

Virago didn't respond for a long second.

"Okay, see what she can dig up about Carol. She's definitely not the person we all thought she was."

Darcy closed his laptop and slid it into his bag.

"I'll tell Sorensen," she said before he left. "Same rules—still not a word on this to anyone else."

"Understood."

Jon nodded.

Darcy did too and said, "Better make sure to give Sorensen a heads-up to keep his expressions to himself before you tell him, or Quinn will know something's up."

Virago smiled. "Good point."

Darcy's walk to the crime lab felt longer than normal. The more they found out about Carol, the darker she seemed. And nobody had a clue. He shook his head and mentally braced himself, preparing for the conversation he was about to have with the lead CSI.

He found Rachel in the kitchen. She poured two mugs full of coffee when she saw him come in.

Darcy took a sip. It tasted burnt. He swallowed and said, "Lou's office?"

Her eyebrows raised, but then she nodded and led him to it.

It felt darker than the previous time they'd been there. After a long sigh she settled in, and he told her about the phone numbers and watched her process the information.

Rachel shook her head slowly. "It just goes to show you, you never know people."

"That's a happy thought."

"Not feeling very upbeat right now."

He was taken aback. They'd worked a lot together and dealt with many awful cases, but he'd never seen her so down before.

"I'm sorry. I just can't believe Carol was working with the Diablos."

"Maybe there's an explanation."

"Sure. One that involves her being as much of a criminal as the people we bust our asses to put away."

Darcy knew Rachel was right, there could be other explanations, but it was hard to imagine one where Carol was innocent.

"Detective Lynch, when this comes out we're going to have defense attorneys question every single case she's ever worked on—maybe even every case this lab has ever done. It's going to be a nightmare that is going to cost millions of dollars and potentially lead to many criminals being let back onto the streets. This is so very bad."

Darcy stood. "Let's keep this under wraps until we've confirmed the evidence. No need to rush into anything."

Rachel looked up at him, not appearing very convinced.

CHAPTER 74

Pascual parked by one of the main mall entrances. Close enough to spot people going in and out, but far enough to avoid the cameras. Oscar knew that after his face had been plastered all over the news, every law enforcement agency would be looking for him, and that included the rent-a-cops at the shopping center.

"What now?" Pascual asked.

"We wait."

Pascual turned the ignition off and reclined the seat a few inches.

Oscar checked the rearview mirror. A woman with three kids in tow passed by.

"We need to find Chavo," he said.

"You really think this crazy shit with the birds is gonna work?"

Oscar shrugged. "I got nothing better."

"You're risking your life to get this worm. I get respect, but why not send the army? Why do this yourself? Why not wait until things cool down?"

Oscar had thought about all those questions too. "I got to do this now."

"You keep saying that." Pascual wasn't looking at him. "And risk getting arrested, or even killed?"

"If I get arrested, you'll do it for me."

He was only half joking.

Pascual scoffed. "You wrong, bro. If you get pinched, I'm starting a legit life with my girl somewhere with snow."

Oscar laughed. "Shut the hell up. You're allergic to the cold."

"Not the point."

Oscar turned the radio on, but nothing came out of the speakers.

"Only for show. Nice hiding place for the baby."

"Is there one now?"

Pascual nodded. "The Nano I brought for Joker."

Oscar felt his own Beretta rub against his back. "We have two, then."

"Three. There's one in the trunk."

They fell silent again. Oscar watched more people go about their business, their lives so normal, his so different.

Pascual scratched his arm, revealing a partial "VI."

"That was your first, right?" Oscar asked.

The soldier pulled up his sleeve all the way. "Yep." The ink covered his entire bicep. "I got it the day I got jumped in."

Oscar relaxed against the seat. "The toughest motherfucker you were. Not sure what happened to you after that."

Pascual laughed. "Still am," he said, and jabbed Oscar in the abs. "You lucky I don't go for that injured shoulder."

"You know better, *puto*." Oscar raised his fist in warning.

They both laughed like they used to do when they were teens.

CHAPTER 75

When Quinn told him that he wanted to go to the hotel before getting into the whole story of why they were in Seattle, Sorensen thought it was just another stalling tactic. But as soon as they checked in, the sergeant asked him to follow him to his room. Once there he opened his bag on the bed, which only contained Carol's accordion folder.

Setting out several piles of paper neatly bound together by clips and rubber bands, he said, "I looked at birth records for a long time, and nothing ever popped. So I thought that maybe what she'd meant was that she had an abortion."

Sorensen raised his eyebrows. "Did she?"

"There were no records of that either, but that is always harder to find. However, when I started digging into her papers"—he pointed at the bed—"there was something that caught my attention. She'd always told me that both of her parents were dead, and we had no kin to notify."

Sorensen was starting to get impatient. Who cared?

"Nothing in the folder was organized. It just seemed like a bunch of junk collected over the years for one reason or another. I started going through everything and soon figured out that it all started with this." He picked the first pile from the left. Quinn handed him the bundle.

An obituary was on top. There was a head shot of a man in his fifties.

Sorensen scanned the article and said, "'Samuel Lopez died of lung cancer. He was an icon to the Bothell community. His widow and daughter survived him.' Okay, so what?"

"The obituary came inside a letter. A letter from Carol's mom, attaching the article and asking her to come home for the funeral."

"Maybe she died after."

"I found her. Carol's mother answered my call."

Sorensen raised the papers in his hand. "You cannot possibly be telling me that we came all the way here to deliver the bad news to the mother in person?"

Quinn seemed taken aback. He looked down at the bed full of bundles and said, "You're a moron. Of course not. What I'm trying to tell you is that this clipping started Carol in a quest. Everything in this folder is about finding a missing person. Her child."

"I don't mean to be insensitive or anything, but you said the kid died or never existed. And why does any of this have anything to do with her murder?"

"That's what we're going to find out."

Sorensen threw the wad of papers on the bed. "We flew all the way here for this bullshit? How on earth did you get approval from Virago for this?"

Quinn headed to the door. "I never wanted you here. So you either follow me to go talk to the mom, or you can start early at the hotel bar. I don't give a shit either way."

Sorensen followed the sergeant. He didn't have a choice.

The ride to Bothell was long and boring. They couldn't even agree on a radio station, so they drove in silence most of the way. When they finally got there, Sorensen felt as if he'd been cooped up in a cage for hours.

The three-story house had a somber feel to it. Sorensen wondered if it was the chocolate paint or the stained glass that was part of the door. The front yard was almost nonexistent.

Quinn rang the bell. An elderly woman opened the door. There was an air of sophistication Sorensen wasn't expecting for some reason. Carol was always understated. This woman had a presence. He wondered if Quinn had it all wrong and they weren't related at all.

"Mrs. Lopez, Detectives Quinn and Sorensen," Quinn said, and took her hand.

After she shook it, she took a step to the side and said, "Please come in. I prepared some tea."

She directed them through a short landing into a spacious living room. The kitchen was to the right, partially visible behind an open door. The furniture was dark and the curtains looked heavy. Sorensen felt as if he'd stepped into a haunted house. It was eerie, almost as if it had been frozen in time.

Mrs. Lopez offered them a seat on the wide burgundy sofa and chose the matching chair for herself. She served the tea and offered the first cup to the sergeant.

Quinn exchanged a few sentences with the woman, and it was obvious that they already had some rapport. He soon got to the point.

"When we talked on the phone, you told me that your daughter, Carol, was sent to boarding school for the last two years of high school."

"Correct." Her eyes were at half-mast.

"What happened when she graduated?"

"She went off to college in Florida."

"I noticed that Carol had a different last name. Did you remarry?" Sorensen asked.

Mrs. Lopez shook her head. "Shortly after she enrolled, she started to become more distant. The calls came less frequently. The holiday visits soon stopped too. There was al-

311

ways a paper or a special project she needed to stay back for." She held the teacup with both hands.

"Mrs. Lopez..." Quinn urged.

She met his eyes. "Eventually she even stopped answering when we called."

"Did she say why?"

"I knew why. A mother always knows why. When she was fifteen she got pregnant."

Quinn looked at Sorensen. He didn't return the stare. He wasn't ready to give the sergeant any credit yet.

"She said that losing her baby was really hard for her and that she needed time to find herself. She wanted to be left alone until she could make peace with that."

"Is that when she decided to change her name?" Sorensen asked.

"I think so." When she refilled the cups with tea, her hand was trembling. "We had no contact for years. Then we moved to Bothell so I could take care of my sister when she got cancer. Soon after she passed, Samuel also died. I sent Carol a letter asking her to come to her father's funeral."

Quinn looked at Sorensen again. He kept his eyes on Mrs. Lopez.

"Did she come?" Quinn asked.

She nodded. "That's when I told her the truth."

CHAPTER 76

Sargent Harjo called while Darcy was walking from the crime lab to the SO. A truck drove by, and he pressed the phone against his ear.

The Reno sergeant told him that they had a forest fire they believed to be arson and they couldn't spare any personnel to transport Samantha Lee back to California. He also told him that they went through her bags and indeed found a button missing from one of her blouses. It looked like the one in the photo Darcy had sent him, but of course the lab would have to validate it once they had the item.

Darcy almost skipped a step. He knew it wasn't as important anymore, but it felt good that at least the Nhu case was wrapping up nicely. He told Harjo that he would arrange for a transport and would get back to him as soon as everything was ready.

He wasn't in a rush to get Lee back, but he still wanted to pursue it. Darcy left a message for AC Howard and hoped that getting his voice mail meant he wasn't in the office.

The bullpen was only half-full, and he grinned when he saw that Howard was gone. He checked the BOLO he had out on Consuelo's car, but there were no sightings of the old Toyota Corolla. He logged into his email and opened the one with the phone records he'd shared with Jon. There was something there—he could feel it. The intern hadn't had time to

313

fine-tune the queries, so he decided to spend a few minutes looking at the information he had. He knew Chavo's girl-friend's number, and he had the locations and the date and time of what he wanted.

He opened a spreadsheet and dumped all the records from the towers around Berto's at the time of Carol's murder. On another tab he pasted the numbers that hit the towers next to the school just a few minutes before the shooting. There were hundreds of rows.

He hit Command-F and entered Chavo's phone number. He got no hits on any of the lists. He then entered Consuelo's number and got a match on the first and second lists. The timeline made sense. Chavo had changed phones on Monday, sometime before Carol's murder.

He switched gears and entered Guero's number. There was the hit he expected on the list from Berto. That just cor-roborated the blood evidence they had at the restaurant.

When he keyed in Carol's burner, the only result that matched came from Berto's the night of her murder. Which he already knew, since they found the phone in her purse at the scene. He skimmed the other numbers on the spread-sheet, but nothing jumped out.

Darcy leaned back in his chair and stretched his arms over his head. He just got corroboration of what he already knew. There was nothing groundbreaking about this. He needed more.

"Hey, Jon," he said as soon as the intern picked up. "I know you're working on your massive query, but if I give you a spreadsheet with a couple tabs, can you do some quick magic to find out if we get a hit on multiple numbers and locations?"

"Sure, I can try. Send it over."

Darcy did and waited. He tapped his fingers on the desk. He tabbed through different screens on his computer. He wrote some notes on the whiteboard, but mainly he felt restless and couldn't concentrate. There had to be something in those phone numbers.

He wondered how long it would take Jon to run the searches. He should have asked him. Did he have time to follow a lead, or should he just wait by the phone? Could he even get coffee? Darcy shook his head. He was being stupid.

He went to the kitchen and poured himself a cup of coffee. He was glad it didn't smell like hazelnut. It just smelled like black coffee.

As he walked back, the phone rang. It was Jon.

"I just sent you something super-preliminary."

"I'm opening it right now."

"I'll continue to work on the other data. It's more comprehensive."

"Thanks, Jon."

They hung up, and Darcy dug into the email. There was a number he didn't recognize that showed up on the first two lists at the time of the incidents.

CHAPTER 77

"We got a match! The drone found Chavo again."

Spider's voice was so loud, Oscar had to pull the phone a few inches from his ear.

"Which exit?"

Pascual turned the engine on, checked the rearview mirror, and pulled out of the parking spot.

Spider made humming noises. Oscar squeezed the cell and bit his tongue.

"I'm... not sure. North?"

"Is that a fucking question? Give me the street the door faces," Oscar said.

Pascual stopped moving and waited for directions.

"Delaney. He's getting into a car."

"Shit, that's the opposite side. Go, go," he told Pascual.

The car sped toward the outside road. It was longer, but there were fewer stop signs and less people crossing.

"What car?"

"Blue Honda. Four-door. The drone lost him."

"What do you mean 'lost him'?"

"It's because it only does faces. Once Chavo went inside the car, it just went on to fly around again."

"Can you make it follow the car?"

"What? No. I have no idea."

"Call Dominique and ask him right now. But tell me, what's the last thing you saw the car do?"

"Turned right on Delaney."

Oscar hung up.

"He should be coming this way," Pascual said.

Oscar hoped Chavo hadn't passed them already.

"Get on Delaney here," he said, and pointed at the stoplight.

They both scanned the road. It was busy, but no blue Hondas.

"There, there." Pascual pointed out the window to his left.

Oscar saw the car. There were two shit sticks sitting in front, but neither looked like Chavo. Then he saw somebody in the backseat but couldn't quite make out the face behind the tinted window.

"Get closer."

The light turned green, and the car in front of them went straight. Pascual merged right into the wide avenue. Oscar watched the traffic, hoping the Honda would pass them quickly and they could get a good look at the third rider.

It took almost a whole block, but finally they were side by side. Oscar looked. The man in the backseat had his head turned the other way. He tried to see if he could spot the snake tattoo on the neck, but the hoodie was zipped all the way up.

"Look this way, *joto*, look this way," he said through gritted teeth.

The phone rang, startling him. "What?"

"Dominique says the drones are not programmed to track objects."

Oscar hung up.

"Make them pull over," Oscar said.

"You think I'm a cop or something?" Pascual asked.

"Get on their left. I'll make them."

Pascual slowed down, moved behind the Honda, and switched lanes one more time. Then he sped up to get side by side with the blue car. Oscar pulled his Beretta and pointed it out the window as soon as they were aligned with the driver. He still couldn't make out if the punk was Chavo.

The driver jumped in his seat when he saw the gun. Oscar waved it toward the curb. The three men in the car stared back at him. The one he wanted pulled the hood over his hat.

"Let me see your face, fool," Oscar yelled out the window, keeping the aim of his gun on his target.

"What for?" The driver leaned toward his window, daring him to fire.

"I want to make sure I kill the right guy," he said.

"You're not killing shit, bro. Otherwise, you'd shot us already."

The man on the back took the hood off, but his baseball cap still hid half his face.

Pascual extended his arm, his hand holding the Nano, also pointed at the driver's head. The Honda slowed down and finally pulled over. Pascual stopped right next to them, generating honks and screeching tires from the cars behind them. Oscar pointed his gun at the guy in the backseat.

"Hands up, all of you. No reaching for nothing, or I'll shoot you dead."

The driver put both hands on the window frame. The passenger rested his on the dashboard and the guy sitting on the backseat lifted them to his head, pushing the baseball cap further down.

"Chavo, be a man and show your fucking face," Oscar yelled at him.

The two *cholos* in the front looked at each other, then turned to the backseat. Then the three of them busted out laughing.

CHAPTER 78

Sorensen realized that he was hanging on every word coming from Mrs. Lopez's mouth. She spoke softly, as if she was embarrassed by what she was sharing.

"Samuel made me promise that I would never tell Carol, but I couldn't keep it from her anymore. When she came to the funeral, I told her that her baby never died."

Sorensen looked at Quinn, but he didn't look back. His jaw was clenched.

Mrs. Lopez was wringing her hands. She stopped to wipe a tear.

"There was this boy at school. He was a junior. She had a crush on him. I always thought it had been him. Carol never told us who the actual father was. Not then, anyway. Samuel was so angry when he found out she was pregnant. When she finished the school year, right before she started to show, we sent her away to live with my sister in Bothell until the baby was born. She was furious." Mrs. Lopez took a sip of her tea and savored it. "My sister was the midwife, and Samuel went to take the baby. He made me stay home. He didn't want me to get attached to the baby and pressure him to keep it. Samuel gave it to Father Mateo. He made my sister swear she would tell Carol that her baby died."

"What happened next?" Sorensen said.

He was glad Carol's father was dead. He would have had a hard time not punching the son of a bitch for what he made his own daughter go through. Losing a baby was one of the most horrible things that could happen to someone. Finding out a lifetime later that the baby was alive was almost unthinkable.

"Father Mateo found a good home."

"Where? With whom?" Quinn asked.

She shook her head so slowly it took a second for Sorensen to notice it.

"I don't know. Samuel said it was better that way. Carol never knew her father was there until I told her after the funeral."

"What happened when Carol found out her baby didn't die?" Quinn said.

She should be ashamed, Sorensen thought, not feeling remotely sad for her.

"Her face got so white, as if she'd seen a ghost. I didn't know what to do. She asked me to tell her everything."

"Which was what?"

"I didn't know more. As I said, Samuel kept me in the dark. He was afraid I would tell Carol."

"What did she do then?"

"She said she wanted to talk to the priest, but Father Mateo passed several years before Samuel." She finished her tea.

Sorensen leaned against the chair, though what he wanted to do was yell at the woman for being a coward and allowing her husband to take the easy way out.

Mrs. Lopez went on. "She was so angry. There was this look in her eye. I've never seen her like that before."

"You think?" Sorensen put as much sarcasm in his tone as he could.

Mrs. Lopez got up and went to the kitchen counter to grab a box of Kleenex. As she walked back, she dabbed her eyes, leaving her makeup untouched. "She packed her things. But before she got in her car, she told me..."

"She told you what?" Quinn said.

He was pacing by the wall like a panther ready to pounce.

"She told me who the father was. I didn't want to believe her. I thought she was lying to hurt me."

"Who was it?"

Sorensen feared the worst. If it hadn't been a kid from her school, could it have been incest, and that was why Samuel had been so insistent on getting rid of the baby?

"Don't tell me she was raped by her own father?" Quinn spat, thinking the same thing.

"Oh God, no. Of course not. But she was raped. By Larry Simmons, Samuel's business partner."

CHAPTER 79

Oscar cursed the entire drive to the command center. When they got there, he barged in. The door slammed against the wall, and the knob left a dent in the white plaster. The door closed with a thud and bounced opened again. Pascual walked in. Spider and Palo stood up from behind the desk, while Oscar spewed insults at no one in particular.

"Get that asshole on the phone. What kind of shit software does he think he's running?"

Nobody moved. He looked around and wondered why they were frozen.

"Why are you doing nothing? I told you to call Dominique," he yelled.

Pascual reached the desk and grabbed the burner they used at the command center but didn't dial. "He told you the software wasn't ready."

"Not ready? Not working at all. That's a huge difference."

"What happened?" Spider asked.

"That wasn't Chavo. That's what happened." Squaring himself with Pascual, Oscar added, "Give me the fucking phone."

Pascual handed him the device. "Let's get something to eat," he told the homies, and headed for the door, followed by the two kids.

Oscar sat on one of the chairs and stared at the monitors, trying to calm himself down before making the call. Faces flashed several times per second. He wondered how futile this operation was. He needed to go back to basics and deploy his crew on the ground. Pascual had been right all along. That was the only way to find Chavo. But what if people started asking questions or got trigger-happy and offed him before he could get his hands on him?

Oscar took a few long breaths. He needed to get a real answer on what the odds of successfully finding Chavo with the current software really were. He'd been driving this entire operation assuming it would all work out just because he wanted it to. There were flaws in his plan, and it was time for him to deal with them.

He dialed and listened to the tone while more faces popped up on the monitors. When Dominique finally picked up, they talked for a while, and Oscar managed to keep his frustration under wraps.

An hour later his three homeboys came back. Palo had a large spot on his T-shirt.

"Food too gross to keep in your mouth?" Oscar asked.

"Salsa. Too much of it." He dabbed the spot, but it was already dry. "What do you want us to do, boss?"

"Dominique says that it's normal to get some false positives. We can't rely just on the similarity percentage from the drone captures. You'll have to visually compare them to the target. He also reminded me again that the code is buggy, and it won't work as well as it will when we go live."

"He has a point," Pascual said.

"I know, bro. Still. He's going to have the whole team working on improving the software, but it can take days."

He moved to the couch and waited until Pascual joined him. Spider and Palo got back to work.

"I want to have some of the guys on the streets looking for Chavo too. Only guys you completely trust. Nobody outside of them can know, and no one touches a hair of Chavo. He's mine."

"I got a few we can rely on."

"Do it now. As soon as this is over, I'm going dark for a while."

Pascual started saying something but then stopped. Oscar knew what it was and didn't want to hear it, but Pascual ended up saying it anyway.

"You know we can take care of this for you, right?"

"I got to kill that worm myself."

CHAPTER 80

Darcy entered the number he'd just found into ViCAP. Not expecting much, he got up and went to the kitchen to get a fresh cup of coffee. He cursed when he found the pot empty. He made a new one and waited for it to brew.

He paced along the kitchen wall, realizing that he didn't feel comfortable in his own bullpen either. A lot of it had to do with Howard. He despised working for someone he didn't respect. At the same time he knew his chances at the SJPD were pretty much nil.

When he got back to his desk, he was surprised to see that ViCAP had a match to the number. It was connected to a homicide in Milpitas. That seemed a bit far to have a direct connection, but he decided to call the detective on the case.

After he introduced himself, he got to the point.

"I understand you're investigating the murder of Gilbert 'Joker' Diaz."

"I am."

Detective Gayler's voice was raspy, as if she had a cold.

"Can you share any details?"

"The crime occurred at a tweaker house, frequented by lowlifes wanting to score, get high, or crash if they'd been kicked out of wherever they normally stay." She paused. Darcy figured she was trying to decide how much to share.

"Joker was a known Snake. We found a rival tagging at the scene."

"Diablos?" Darcy asked.

"Yes. A '6' painted on the wall with Joker's blood."

"Classy."

"Typical."

Darcy thought about the "6" at Berto's place.

"Any leads?"

"Besides the entire Diablos crew?"

He knew the question was rhetorical, so he waited for her to proceed.

"We haven't seen a Diablos hit in a while. This is surprising. I hope it's not the beginning of a war."

"You've been working gangs for a while?"

"Homicide. Twelve years. I've seen my share." For the first time in the conversation, her voice sounded more proud than tired. "We're too small here to have our own gang unit, so we all pitch in."

"Can I come see you? I would like to get your take on a case I'm working on. I think it may tie into yours."

"Meet me at the Grind Coffee House. I need more caffeine."

Darcy checked the traffic while walking to his car. It was rush hour, and it would take him at least half an hour to get there.

When he pulled into the parking lot, Gayler was already waiting for him. She looked like a Valkyrie straight out of Wagner's *Ring*. She was nursing an iced drink with one hand and leafed through a notebook with the other. Her blond stringy hair was held in place by aviator glasses pushed up on her head. She must have recognized him too, because she stood the moment he stepped out of his car.

"Fancy," she said, looking past him at the Cobra. "What happened to it?"

He followed her gaze. She was referring to the bullet hole in the hood of the car.

"Professional hazard."

"I'm surprised they let you drive your own car at the SO."

"I've never asked. I just do it."

She laughed. "That should teach you."

He smiled and went inside to get her a refill and order something for himself. When he joined her back outside, the sun heated the pavement, but the table was in the shade, and a nice breeze lowered the temperature by several degrees.

"How did you hear about my case?" she asked after she took a long sip of her new iced latte.

"I was checking out a phone number. It belonged to your victim."

"And your case is?"

"Carol Montes. Ring a bell?"

"Crap, the lab tech. Yes. Worked with her on several cases. She was rock solid." She drank again. "Why do you think our cases are connected?"

"Long shot really. I was doing a cell tower check. Your vic was around my scene at the time of the murder."

"That's a long shot."

Darcy looked at his car. The sun reflected on it and made him squint. He drank half of his black coffee in silence. He wanted to run his theory by her. He could use another perspective.

"Hear me all the way out on this, okay?" he asked.

She nodded but then said, "For that I'm going to need a muffin. The blueberry ones are delicious."

Darcy left and got two, just in case. She peeled the wrapper, broke the top off, and took a healthy bite off the bottom half.

"I'm learning as fast as I can about street gangs in the Bay Area," he said.

She raised an eyebrow instead of asking with her mouth full.

"I'm a transplant from Seattle."

She nodded.

"We get to Carol's crime scene and find evidence that Oscar 'Guero' Amaro has been there, and not as a customer."

"It makes sense that he would be after her, given Carol's track record with gangs."

"Maybe. But the Diablos have been laying low for a while, so why the sudden hit?" Before she answered, he proceeded. "You heard about the school shooting?"

"Yes." She pointed at the second muffin. "You're going to eat that?"

"No, go ahead."

"I'm training for the Regionals." When Darcy didn't respond she added, "The CrossFit Games. Made the Open, now off to the Regionals. It's huge. I'm training three to five hours a day—that's why I'm hungry all the time."

Darcy didn't know anything about CrossFit, so he went on.

"The gun used at the school had Oscar's prints all over it."

"A bit weird that he didn't wipe them off before handing it to a kid to shoot up a school," she conceded.

"And Robbie, the shooter, identified Chavo Buenavente as the man who gave him the gun."

She put the piece of muffin on its way to her mouth back on the napkin. "That's triple confirmed?"

"He identified the tattoo Chavo has on his hand."

329

She crossed her arms and stared at him. "That's far from triple confirmed. You know how many people get the same artwork?"

"Not this one. Chavo tattooed it himself. I doubt there are any others like it." He looked at her to ensure she didn't think he was being condescending. "I got more. His phone pinged a cell tower in the vicinity of the school just before the shooting. And another one around the time of Carol's murder." He let that sink in, then added, "And so did your vic's number, on both locations at the same times."

"Are you thinking...?" she asked.

He nodded.

CHAPTER 81

The trip from Mrs. Lopez's home in Bothell to St. Peter Parish in Capitol Hill, a quaint neighborhood in Seattle, didn't take them as long. Sorensen was surprised that Seattle was so hilly. It was something everybody knew about San Francisco, but Seattle?

The landscape didn't keep him distracted enough. He had a million thoughts bouncing in his head. Quinn probably did too, because neither said a word until they parked.

"No wonder Carol changed her name." Sorensen felt heavy in his seat.

Quinn nodded and turned the ignition off. "I cannot even imagine how she must have felt. She gets raped by her father's partner, her parents tell her the baby's dead, and to top it all off, decades later she finds out he or she is still around. Whoa."

"Horrible," Sorensen said.

The first time Melissa got pregnant, she had a miscarriage. He'd never been so grief-stricken in his life. He couldn't even imagine what Carol must have felt.

"When we're done here, I want to go back to the hotel. Some of the papers Carol saved are starting to make more sense," Quinn said, and got out of the car.

"What I don't really get"—Sorensen pushed his thoughts aside and walked toward the main entrance of the church—

"is why you think this is all connected to Carol's murder." He didn't look at him, but he could feel Quinn's eyes burning a hole in the back of his head.

"Why are you so sure it isn't?" Quinn asked, brushing past him and grabbing the handle. He pulled the door open, but not far enough for either of them to go through.

"I'm serious. I don't really know why we're here. We should be back home, looking for Guero."

"You can go anytime."

Quinn walked inside, still giving him no answers. Sorensen shook his head and followed him. The church smelled of old wood and wax from the candles. There was a short hallway with checkered dark-gray and beige tiles flanked by a few rows of pews. In the center there were three marble steps that led to the altar, which stood tall in the middle.

The place was cool but not humid. Sorensen wasn't sure why he'd expected it to be. There were a few people scattered about, praying.

Quinn was a few feet in front of him already, walking fast, as if he knew where he was going. Before he got to the altar, a priest appeared from the right. The sergeant switched direction and met him right below a stained-glass window with an image of the Virgin Mary.

"We're looking for Father Robert."

"You have found him. How can I be of service?" he asked, and nodded as a salutation when Sorensen joined them.

They both showed their badges. Quinn made the introductions and then said, "Father, our understanding is that you took over the flock when Father Mateo retired."

"Unfortunately, it was when Father Mateo passed. It was very sudden, a stroke."

Quinn shook his head, probably in disappointment.

Sorensen asked, "Do you know if the father was in the habit of kidnapping babies from teenage girls and telling them their babies died after birth, or is that something that he only did once in a while?"

Father Robert took a step back and covered his mouth with an open hand. The look on Quinn's face reminded him of how Darcy normally reacted when he went straight to the point.

He didn't care.

"I beg your pardon?"

Father Robert lowered himself into the end of the pew.

"You heard me. About three decades ago Carol Lopez gave birth to a perfectly healthy baby. A few hours later Father Mateo and her aunt, who happened to be the midwife, told her the baby had died."

"Oh no," the priest said.

"Not only that, but Mr. Lopez had arranged for Father Mateo to drop the baby off with someone. We want to know who that someone was."

Sorensen took a step forward, invading the father's personal space, but he didn't seem fazed by it.

"I do not know of any such thing. But I still have a box with Father Mateo's things. He had no family, and I haven't had the heart to get rid of it."

"Please show us," Quinn said.

Father Robert led them to an office and went directly to a file cabinet. He opened the bottom drawer. It was empty, except for a cardboard box. It was about the size of a shoe box, but square. He picked it up and handed it to Quinn.

The sergeant opened the lid. It was full of papers.

"Can we take this?" he said.

"Of course. You don't need to bring it back."

333

Sorensen almost smiled. "Is there anything you can tell us? Anything you may have heard?" he asked, his tone softer.

"I... I was asked once by one of my parishioners to help them place a baby somewhere."

Quinn set the box on the desk. Sorensen crossed his arms.

"It was shortly after I started. They didn't ask me straight out. There was a lot of reading between the lines. I never complied of course and was never asked again—by anybody. I guess maybe they had made arrangements with Father Mateo, and when he died they came to me, expecting the same thing. I never made the connection until just now."

"How long ago was this?" Quinn asked.

"It was only a week or two after I started about seven years ago. The parishioners never came back."

CHAPTER 82

It'd taken Pascual about three hours to make sure he had the right people on the ground looking for Chavo. Oscar had been adamant that nobody should know why. All they had to do was find the worm, report his location, and not lose him until Oscar could get there. He wasn't naïve enough to think the plan would work flawlessly, but he didn't have many options.

He watched the monitors. The incessant stream of faces popping up on the screens every few seconds made him dizzy. He wasn't expecting miracles anymore, but it was better than staring at a blank wall and chewing his fingernails off.

"How are you getting reports from the field?" he asked Pascual.

"Matón is gonna call me every hour."

Increasing the frequency was pointless. Especially because what he really wanted was the unexpected call telling him that they'd found the worm.

"You trust that they can follow him without being spotted?"

Pascual looked at him. His face said it all.

Oscar almost laughed, even though it wasn't funny. He decided to not think about it anymore. There was no point. He couldn't be out there looking for Chavo himself, and even if he could, he was only one guy and didn't have any superpowers. Deploying the crew was the right move.

He watched the drones work. After an hour he realized he was getting a headache. He stretched his back and rotated his shoulders, loosening them up. The left one was still sore, so he stopped.

Oscar rubbed his eyes and focused back on the monitors. One caught his attention. The drone roaming Jefferson Park was flying higher up than the others. After a closer look, he realized it was climbing.

"Why is it going up? Wouldn't it be harder to see faces the higher the altitude?" he asked no one in particular.

"I think so," Palo responded.

The altimeter indicated that the drone had passed 250 feet and kept climbing. The frequency with which the faces flickered up on the screen slowed, and finally the last one picked up by the drone disappeared. The machine kept climbing, but now it began to spin on its own axis. The buildings captured by the cameras looked blurry on the screen.

"What the hell's happening?" Oscar yelled.

"I don't know. We've never seen this before," Spider said.

"Make it stop."

Oscar launched from the chair and grabbed the sides of the table. He felt his knuckles go numb.

The drone spun faster and faster, climbing with each turn. Oscar thought it would stall and crash, but it kept rising.

"Do something!" Pascual shouted.

"I don't know what to do," Spider yelled back, pawing the keyboard but not pressing on any particular key.

Then suddenly the monitor went black. The faint buzzing of hardware fans was the only noise in the room.

CHAPTER 83

The road from Saratoga to the Mountain Winery was twisty and shaded by tall trees. Darcy realized that he'd been thinking about his conversation with Gayler the entire drive. It was too much of a coincidence that Chavo and Joker pinged the same towers at the time of Carol's murder *and* the shooting at the school if they weren't there and together. He shook his head. He needed to keep digging. He had to know what Chavo, Joker, and the rival gang boss, Guero, were doing at Berto's and what any of that had to do with Carol, and even Robbie.

Saffron's hand was resting on his knee. He reached for it and squeezed. "I'm sorry."

"It's okay. You always get this way when we're meeting your sister and her husband." She turned her hand around and interlaced her fingers with his.

She was right, even though this time his brother-in-law hadn't entered his mind for even a second.

Instead of going into the case, he said, "He's too political for me. I always feel like he has an agenda he's trying to push. Even when it's just dinner."

They reached the top of the hill, and Darcy pulled all the way up to a teen directing the traffic. His hair was sandy blond, and his face was covered with red pimples.

"You have VIP parking. Take any spot along this side." He motioned to his left. "Enjoy the show."

"VIP parking?" Saffron asked. "Nice."

"Being associated with the sheriff comes with perks."

He parked close to the exit. They grabbed their coats and started walking uphill to the Chateau Deck Restaurant, holding hands.

"What do you think his agenda will be today?" she asked.

She was trying to engage him, but he was preoccupied. The case didn't make any sense, and he couldn't stop thinking about it.

"Honestly? He's left me a few voice mails saying that he wanted to talk to me." Darcy brushed his short hair with his free hand. "These last few days have been rough for the Sheriff's Office. First we lose a material witness, then a detainee ends up killing a pretty big prisoner and puts one of our deputies in the hospital in critical condition. I'm surprised he still wanted to do this concert tonight. Hell, I'm surprised he hasn't resigned."

"Maybe he wants to run some ideas by you. Get your opinion about how things can be improved."

His chest filled up with warmth. Saffron always looked on the bright side of things, thought the best of every situation. Not naïve, just an optimist.

"I think he's going to fire me."

She stopped walking. She looked worried, and he realized he shouldn't have said it, even though he thought it was true.

"Are you serious?"

Her eyes were greener than usual. The sun shined in her hair, and at that moment all he wanted was to be on a white sandy beach, where they could wear bathing suits all day long.

He leaned and kissed her, then put his arm around her shoulder and started walking again.

"I think he needs to make some changes, and I've always been seen as the guy who got in because of my blood connections. I'm an easy target."

"That doesn't make any sense. You've solved plenty of cases. He needs to get to the root of the problem, not can someone just to make a statement. Though firing Howard would be a good start." Her voice rose a few decibels, her tone indignant.

She made him smile. He loved this woman.

"I don't think he'll fire me in the middle of the concert, so let's enjoy the show," he said, seeing that his sister and brother-in-law were already sitting at a table.

Kate stood, hugged him, and kissed his cheek. Damon shook his hand. Saffron hugged both and sat next to Darcy. Their hosts had been considerate enough to leave the seats facing the Valley for them. The view was breathtaking, and he let out a long sigh as he took in the moment.

He noticed that Damon had already ordered wine for the table. He felt rebellious enough to order something else, like a beer, but then decided to stop being a brat.

"Very nice seeing you guys again," Kate said. "I hope you'll be able to come to the fund-raiser next month."

"Absolutely. We wouldn't miss it for anything," Saffron said for the both of them.

"Fantastic."

Darcy could see Damon was already bored with the small talk. He wondered if he would call him away from the table and bitch about his recent failures, or if he would do it in front of everybody. Neither would surprise him.

They ordered the meal, made more small talk about recent trips and inconsequential gossip, but the scolding never came. Darcy felt somewhat weird about that, and in a way wished Damon had brought it up over dessert so he could stop thinking about it.

When the bill came, Damon made a big deal about taking care of it but seemed disappointed when Darcy didn't fight him on it.

The entire hour and half the dinner lasted, Darcy wondered for the nth time how his sister had ended up with a guy like Damon. But then again they were one of the power couples of the South Bay, and that seemed to be very important to her.

On the way to the VIP booth, Saffron wrapped her arm around his waist, and he pulled her close to him.

"Breathe," she said. "Now with the music, there'll be no more conversation."

"I hope you're right, or I'll have to make up some murder somewhere I must go solve," he joked.

She got on her toes and kissed his cheek. "Maybe they really wanted to spend time with us."

He didn't respond but kissed her back.

The VIP area was near the stage. It was covered, and the seats were padded. There was room for about thirty people, but they were the only ones there. In the back a narrow nook to the side hosted a large platter with melon slices, pineapple chunks, and three different types of berries. Next to it there was a large cheese platter with dry fruit and crackers. At the other end of the table was the wine.

"The choices are Cabernet, Pinot, or Shiraz." Darcy knew he didn't have to bother with the whites.

"You know what I like," she responded, still holding his hand.

He poured two generous glasses of Shiraz and led the way to the seats. The concert was starting.

"Lynch, care to join me for a cigar?" Damon asked.

"Here it comes." He kissed Saffron before he stood up.

"Keep your cool, okay?"

"Bring your glass," Damon said.

They walked in silence until they reached the restaurant they'd just had dinner at. The place was deserted. It was breezy, and cooler than it had been just half an hour earlier. The sun had set, and dusk made the city below look enchanted. He wished he were there with Saffron, not the Santa Clara sheriff.

"You're not getting along with Howard," Damon said.

Darcy laughed. "You're direct. I give you that."

The sheriff waited.

"Not sure what you want me to say."

The feeling of being tested, or measured, came back. Darcy felt on edge, unsure of what quiz he needed to pass this time.

"I think he's a moron, but he was the next one up, and I had to give him the chance to fuck up," Damon said.

Darcy almost choked on his wine. "He's succeeding at that."

The sheriff kept staring out into the valley, as if looking at Darcy would make his confession more personal than he felt comfortable with.

There was nothing Darcy could add, so he sipped his wine and waited.

"The press is crushing us."

"It's been a complicated case," Darcy said.

"Are you anywhere close to figuring out what's going on?"

"You sound like Howard," he joked.

Damon laughed. It was one of the few genuine laughs Darcy had ever heard coming from his brother-in-law.

"I have a few theories. I think this case is not the straight gang case SJPD wants to make it."

The theory that he so easily shared with Detective Gayler wasn't something he was prepared to talk about with his brother-in-law.

"Say more."

Instead Darcy asked, "What happened to Jefe's case? I would have figured if anybody was going to take it from the task force it would be you."

Damon took out two cigars from his coat pocket and offered one to Darcy. He declined. The sheriff lit up and puffed a few times, closing one eye as the smoke danced around his face.

"Jefe was getting out of the life. There were only four people who knew."

"You are kidding."

"Nope."

"Virago didn't know?" Darcy asked, the pieces now making more sense.

"She didn't. It was huge. It involved everybody from Guero and his homies to Big Chon. Jefe was going to take down the entire Diablos organization. Imagine, millions of dollars in various criminal activities, spanning from burglaries to drugs, human trafficking, identity theft, and of course assault and murder."

Darcy took a sip from his wine. The dark liquid warmed his mouth. "Why didn't you tell me about this before?"

"Maybe if you ever answered your phone I would have."

"Touché," Darcy said, and raised his glass to his brother-in-law.

"That's not why I wanted to talk to you, though."

Here it comes. Darcy braced himself.

"I heard you're still on the short list for the CATCH transfer."

"I think your intel may be outdated."

"Not getting along with Quinn?"

Darcy smiled. Maybe his brother-in-law was more perceptive than he gave him credit for.

"Is that something you want to do, work at CATCH?" Damon asked, then added, "Because I see a future for you at the SO."

Darcy turned to look at him. He must have heard wrong. Before he could ask him to repeat it, both their phones beeped.

"Never good," Damon said, pulling out his cell.

"I know."

The sheriff got up to answer the call. Darcy tapped his own and saw one of the worst texts he'd ever received.

CHAPTER 84

Quinn drove the short distance from the church back to the hotel while he admonished Sorensen about his inquiry tactics with Father Robert. Sorensen tuned him out. What else was new?

They left the car with the valet and went to Quinn's room to go through the contents of Father Mateo's box. When the sergeant lifted the top, they both dug in. Quinn grunted like a caveman protesting when someone tried to steal the meat roasting in the fire.

Quinn pulled out a sheaf of loose papers, while something shiny caught Sorensen's eye. It was a chain with a pendant.

"You're Catholic, right?"

He shoved the saint into Quinn's face.

The sergeant inspected it for a long while. "I think it's Saint Maria, the saint of forgiveness."

"How appropriate."

Sorensen thought about all the babies the priest had given away.

After that they worked in silence, leafing through the contents. Quinn was making piles of papers, very similar to the ones he already had from Carol's folder. Sorensen was more focused on the trinkets that were in the box. Besides the saint, there were a few porcelain figurines, a cross, and a couple of coins with engravings he didn't recognize. At the bottom of the box he found a notebook. It was leather bound and stained with age and use.

"I think I just found Father Mateo's little black book," he said after browsing through several pages.

"What do you mean?" Quinn set the papers he was examining on the table.

"It doesn't say much, but..." Sorensen leaned over and pointed to the first page. Mateo hadn't drawn a table, but the entries clearly fell in a pattern. "The first column looks like last names, the second is *B* or *G*. I think we can guess what that stands for. The third is another last name, and the last is a date. It doesn't take a rocket scientist to figure this out."

They all followed the same arrangement. The first entry was over forty years ago. The last was just weeks before Father Mateo died.

Quinn took the book and examined it for a while, but he soon started flipping through the pages, first rather fast, then slower as he got closer to what he was looking for. He stopped on a page and traced each entry with his finger.

"Check this out," he said, keeping his index on the line he wanted the detective to see.

"Lopez. B. Flores. 10/31/1987," Sorensen read out loud. "I guess we need to find this Flores family."

"Damn the guy for not writing any addresses." Quinn scratched his beard.

"That would have been too easy."

CHAPTER 85

There wasn't a lot of information in the text, so Darcy called Virago.

"Air3 just went down?"

"Crashed. Over by Jefferson Park."

Her voice was terse, and he could hear background noise. She was on the move.

"Shot down?" Darcy asked.

"We don't know yet. Meet me there."

She hung up.

A few seconds later he got her text with the exact address.

Damon was already on the way to the VIP area and still on the phone. Darcy followed him, told Saffron he had to go, and made sure Kate would give her a ride home. He would have liked to sync with Damon but decided not to wait.

The ride down the hill at high speed was more perilous than Darcy would have wanted, but he had quite a bit of ground to cover. Once he reached Highway 85, he turned the spinners on and stepped on the accelerator. The drive seemed to take forever, but when he started running into other patrols heading in the same direction, he knew he was close.

He parked outside of the perimeter tape, behind a few other cars. Virago had already signed in but was out of sight. He went inside and headed toward a small cluster of people.

He was too far to see anything more than a pile of metal, a ton of officers running around, and the Hazmat SJFD unit at the ready. He could smell the Jet A fuel from where he stood.

He reached the group.

"How are the guys?" he asked Lieutenant Ramirez, a stocky man with a bushy handlebar mustache and piercing black eyes.

"They made it. Moro broke his shoulder, and Findley probably a leg and a foot. They are heading to the hospital, but it doesn't look more serious than that." He stroked his whiskers and looked over his shoulder at the helicopter wreck.

Virago came to meet them with Jon in tow. Darcy was surprised to see the intern, as he never came to the scenes, but then remembered that the commander always gave him a ride home when he worked late.

"Fine pilots they are to bring the bird down with only a couple broken bones," Virago said.

"Do we know the cause yet?" Darcy asked.

"The FAA will do a full investigation, but what we know so far is that they were heading toward Almaden and Duane, responding to a silent alarm at one of the businesses, when something hit them."

"They were shot at?" Darcy took a step toward Ramirez.

"No, something literally hit them, but it wasn't another aircraft or a bird."

Before anybody could ask more questions, an officer came running toward them. When she was within earshot, she said, "Lieutenant, I found this in the debris." She was holding an evidence bag with both hands, not quite waving it.

She was tiny, even shorter than Virago, her blond hair tied in a tight bun, and her face showed a mixture of eagerness and diligence. Her badge number was one of the highest numbers Darcy had seen. She was fresh out of the academy, probably still riding with a field training officer.

Ramirez took the bag and inspected it. "What am I looking at, Schulman?" he asked her.

"I think it's part of a drone." She pointed to something at the end of a rod. Her cheeks were red with excitement.

Darcy stared at the matte black arm that got wider and ended in a rubbery white mitten. A knob protruded from it. Another piece had broken off. It looked like it could have been a small propeller.

Virago looked at Jon. "What do you think?"

"It looks like one. What altitude was the helicopter flying?"

"About five hundred feet," Ramirez said.

"That's a hundred feet outside of the legal limit set by the FAA for drones," Jon said.

"Any more pieces that can be identified?" Ramirez asked Schulman.

"Not yet, sir, but CSU is working on it."

"Who told you this might be a drone?"

She blushed and, forcing herself to look up at the lieutenant, said, "I thought it might be. I'm taking a night class to learn how to fly drones, and I recognized the structure."

Ramirez set his black eyes on her. For the first time since they'd shown up, he smiled, and he patted her shoulder.

"Well done. Make sure CSU concentrates on getting the pieces together so we can identify where it came from. I want you to help. Your FTO is Costa, right?"

She nodded.

"Tell him I said so if he gives you any crap about it."

"Thank you, sir." She nodded at the group and headed back to the helicopter.

When she was a few feet away, she turned and looked at Jon. Darcy saw him smile and then hide his chin in his chest.

"If there's anything we can do to help, let us know," Virago told Ramirez.

"Will do."

"These drones are going to change a lot of things in the world, both for better and for worse," she said.

CHAPTER 86

Saturday

Quinn had insisted on meeting in the lobby at the crack of dawn, so Sorensen made sure he had at least thirty minutes to enjoy the buffet. He hated having to rush through breakfast, and he figured Quinn wouldn't have any. The waitress approached him with a jar full of freshly squeezed orange juice. He nodded and she refilled his glass.

Sorensen thought about Father Mateo's little black book. It became a whirlwind of a night after they'd identified Carol's entry.

Quinn reached for his own pile of papers and unclipped one of the bundles, placing each piece one by one on the bed.

"Carol hired a PI shortly after she came to her dad's funeral," the sergeant said, *offering the evidence to Sorensen.*

Sorensen examined the receipts.

"I don't think he found much, and if he did, he didn't give her a hard copy of his report."

"Dead end?"

Quinn picked up his cell and dialed the number on one of the invoices. An automatic voice told him that the number was no longer in service.

"It looks that way."

Sorensen called Lynch to get someone from the Seattle PD to help them with an address search, but he didn't pick up, so he left a message.

"Now what?" he asked.

Quinn shook his head and pretty much kicked him out of the room. Which was fine with him, because he was tired.

The hostess led a businessman to the table next to Sorensen's, bringing him up to the present. He took a healthy gulp of his OJ and wondered about Father Mateo. He'd been giving babies away for over thirty years. That was insane.

He was still thinking about the entries in the book when Quinn showed up. To his surprise, he sat down and waved the waitress to come by.

"Black coffee," he said when she was still a few feet away. "I can't believe the priest kept notes."

Sorensen chewed on a large bite of hash brown potatoes and said, "It makes sense, if he was a decent human being. That may have been his way to keep tabs on the kids."

"Or his way to keep his accounting straight."

"Indeed."

Sorensen didn't feel very generous toward the father either.

"I managed to find a few Flores families last night." Quinn pushed a sheet of paper with twenty addresses handwritten on it.

"You want to canvas all of them?" Sorensen asked a bit too loud, getting looks from the tables around them.

"You got a better idea?"

"I got a much more pressing investigation going on back home. That's what I got." Sorensen moved the chair back but didn't stand.

"Again with that shit? Go home. I can't deal with your whining anymore."

351

Quinn looked down at Sorensen's plate and got up. Before he left, he gulped the steaming coffee down as if it were cold.

Sorensen hoped it burned his trachea all the way down. He tossed the napkin on the table and with a long sigh followed the sergeant out of the hotel. They only had one car after all.

They walked to the valet, and Quinn gave the ticket to a teenager who should be in school rather than parking cars. They both waited in silence.

Quinn's phone rang. He pulled it out of his pocket and, after checking the caller ID, answered and walked away. Sorensen watched as his sergeant marched faster and faster up and down the driveway. He also raised his tone, but the words came out between gritted teeth, so it was impossible for Sorensen to make out what he was getting so upset about.

The rental arrived and the valet gave him the keys, distracting him for a second. Sorensen tipped him but didn't get in, still trying to pick up something from the call.

Finally Quinn hung up and stomped to the car. "Give me the keys."

Sorensen handed them to him and walked around to the passenger side.

"You got your wish. I'm going back to San Jose."

"What? Why?"

"You can find your own way home."

Quinn stepped on the gas and left Sorensen behind. After a few seconds he realized he still had his mouth open. He pulled his own phone and called Virago.

"Commander, what the hell?"

"Are you on your way to the airport?"

"No. Quinn took off without me."

She didn't respond for a few seconds.

"Quinn said you guys had a possible lead."

"I don't know if I would call it that, but we've uncovered a part of Carol I don't think anybody knew."

"So did Jon," she said.

"Does it have anything to do with Quinn?"

There was more silence. Sorensen knew she was weighing his years of loyalty versus what she should be sharing with a detective about their task force sergeant. While he waited for her to make up her mind, he went back into the hotel and sat on a leather lounge chair.

"Jon started looking into Carol's personal stuff. He found a rather rudimentary secret folder, where she had stashed a bunch of emails with Quinn."

"I knew it! I had the feeling from the beginning that he was dirty."

She let him gloat for a few seconds, and that was when he knew he was wrong.

"Are you done, Detective?"

"Yes. But you have to admit—"

"I thought you said you were done." She waited. When nothing more came from him, she went on. "The emails were of a more personal nature."

This took Sorensen aback.

"What?"

"Carol and Quinn had been seeing each other for over four years."

"So they were having a relationship on top of Quinn helping her cover up the Diablos cases? Whoa, I didn't see that coming."

"There's no indication of him jeopardizing cases."

"You pulled him off the investigation because he was seeing Carol? Isn't that a little extreme?"

"I suspended him because he should have never been lead in Carol's murder without disclosing that he was having a personal relationship with her. Especially after we found out that she was most likely compromising Diablos cases and getting them dismissed."

"Did he know that?"

"He says he didn't, but what kind of a detective is he if he's working with her day and night on the same cases and didn't know she was tampering with the evidence?"

"Ouch."

Sorensen got her point, but he knew humans tended to ignore things they didn't want to see.

"So, Detective, is it worth for you to follow the lead you guys have, or should you come back home?"

Sorensen thought about it.

"I'll catch the last flight in. I think it's worth a day."

CHAPTER 87

Oscar got out of bed, realizing that he was getting used to the new place. He put on a clean T-shirt and noticed that his wound still bothered him. He made a fist and felt a dull sting shoot through his shoulder to his spine. It was less pain than yesterday. Things were moving in the right direction, at least with that.

He thought about the drone. It never came back to life. He wasn't sure if the camera had broken, the drone crashed, or it just stopped transmitting. He'd called Dominique to ask him, but the engineer only said, "I told you there were bugs. You shouldn't have taken it before it was ready."

Funny for him to say that. He'd been ignoring Dominique's warnings, because when you were desperate, you took anything that might help, even substandard products.

Pascual burst into the room without knocking. "Did you hear about the chopper?"

Oscar shook his head.

"I think that's good news. It's a ghetto bird." Pascual grabbed the remote control and turned the TV on.

"A police helicopter?"

Oscar's interest was piqued.

"Yes."

"My fifteen minutes of fame are finally over."

355

"You still have to hide. Just because the reporters have something else to focus on, don't mean the blues have stopped looking for you."

Oscar nodded. "Have you heard from the guys on the ground?"

"Nothing yet. They're all looking."

"They need to look harder."

"Bro, ten G is a great incentive. They're looking as hard as they can. Trust me."

Oscar stroked his new beard. "I may leave this look. What do you think?"

"Just don't let it get long. It's gross."

Oscar laughed. "Let's go to the command center. I want to see how things are progressing."

When they got there, Spider was still sleeping on the couch, but Palo was hard at work, staring at all the monitors.

"Anything going on?" Oscar asked when they walked in.

"Same old. Two drones have come down for juice." He pointed to the screens with "Charging" plastered in the center. "But otherwise nothing new."

"The drone from yesterday come back to life yet?" Oscar asked, though the black monitor implied that it hadn't.

Spider woke up and stretched with a loud grunt.

"Bro, Guero asked you a question." Pascual hit Palo on the chest with a pen.

"Sorry. No. Still dark." Palo pointed at number twelve, which reflected his own image.

During yesterday's call with Dominique, Oscar had told him that he wanted five more drones with v.2 ready by the morning. He considered calling him but knew there was no point pestering Dominique for them yet.

He strolled to the sofa by the wall and flopped down on it, wondering what else he could do to find Chavo.

CHAPTER 88

Darcy called Virago to get updates on the Air3, but she had nothing new. He asked her if he should go to CATCH but was relieved when she said no, because he'd already made other plans.

He'd been pleased when Gayler told him she didn't mind meeting him on a Saturday. But when she got to the Southern Kitchen, in Los Gatos, it took her five minutes of complaining about the traffic before she calmed down enough to enjoy her first cup of coffee.

"How did you score this table?" she asked, looking around.

They were tucked away in a corner, away from everyone else.

"I'm a regular," Darcy said. "They treat me well here, and I told them we needed to work."

She nodded. "I've wanted to check this place for ages, but the line is always too long. With three kids, you don't get the luxury to drive for half an hour and then wait another to eat."

"I can imagine."

"News on the chopper?" she asked.

Darcy gave her the highlights about the crash and the latest on the pilots' recovery status, then added, "Still investigating the cause, but it looks like a drone may have crashed into it."

"Damn," she said. "Terminator. I'm telling you, the end of civilization is just around the corner." She shook her head, her wispy blond hair moving from side to side. "This is why I still have a flip phone."

"You do not," Darcy said.

"Oh, I do."

She pulled the device from her pocket. It was scratched almost beyond recognition.

"You know, the Computer History Museum in Mountain View would probably give you big bucks for it. That thing's a relic." He laughed.

"Were you saying something? I wasn't listening."

"I bet the battery lasts about five minutes."

She waved him off and put the phone away, her big smile showcasing a line of crooked teeth.

"Okay, enough already. Let's get to work," she said.

"I got some more interesting data from cell tower dumps."

He pulled out his laptop and entered his password. Jon had sent him an updated report.

She pushed the lid until it closed. "There's not enough space for food and that thing. Please put it away and talk like a normal human being while we eat."

Darcy chuckled. She could be Sorensen's sister. He stuffed the laptop in his bag. Instead he took a pen. Pushing the coffee cup to the side of the paper place mat, he started drawing.

"See, isn't that better?" she asked, obviously pleased with his new approach.

He drew a box and labeled it "Berto's," then drew another one, a bit larger, and called it "George Washington School." Next to each he drew a triangle with lines fanning out at the top.

"These are cell towers," he explained.

359

Gayler rolled her eyes but smirked. "I get that."

The food came, and the waitress took away the condiments tray so both plates could fit without covering Darcy's work in progress. He wrote down Chavo's and Joker's names under each box.

"Nothing new there," she said.

"So impatient. It's coming."

He wrote "Guero" under the Berto's box. Gayler nibbled on a piece of sourdough toast slathered with butter and strawberry jam.

"There're probably about a hundred throw-down phones pinging this tower around the time of Carol's murder." Darcy tapped on the square.

"It's not uncommon for gangsters to have several phones," Gayler said.

Darcy nodded. "I found another number that hits these two towers." He wrote down the new name. "Mike Guzman, a.k.a. Toro, was also here at the same time Joker and Chavo were."

He was pissed because he should have run the vic's number through ViCAP the moment he left the drive-by crime scene. But instead he hadn't connected Toro's number to Berto's and the school until he got the report from Jon.

"Who's that punk?" Gayler asked.

"Did you hear about the drive-by shooting the other day in East San Jose?"

"No shit." She lifted her mug toward the waitress, who came to refill both cups.

Darcy told Gayler about the spray of bullets at the garage and the hole in the floor right underneath Toro's head.

"The street cams didn't have anything, and no witnesses have come forward. So all we have are the shell casings and the odd MO," he told her.

"Drive-bys are a standard thing with gangs," she said. "Sounds like payback."

"But for what? The Snakes haven't killed any Diablos, so what are the Diablos retaliating about? And doesn't it strike you as odd that the drive-by finished with an execution?"

She shrugged. "It's probably not the first time."

"Maybe," he said, "but what if all this is about something else altogether?" He put the pen down and blew the steam off of his coffee before taking a large sip.

She leaned in her seat, wiped her mouth, and folded the napkin on her plate. Darcy realized it was empty, while his food remained untouched.

"You can have mine if you want."

"My tummy's happy." She readjusted her glasses over her head, catching a few strands of hair that had become loose.

Darcy stared at Detective Gayler over the coffee mugs, plates, and eggs Benedict. Her eyes were light blue and shined with the expectation that he would share something juicy that would be worth her time. He really hoped so, even though all he had were theories.

Darcy chewed on the tip of the pen and organized his thoughts, but before he had a chance to lay out his idea, the waitress came by.

"I'm sorry, Detective Lynch, but we have a long line..." The middle-age woman pointed behind her.

"We were just leaving. Thank you for letting us stay this long."

He placed a fifty on the table and followed Gayler out the door.

CHAPTER 89

When Darcy and Gayler got to the Purple Onion Café down the street, the host led them to a table outside by the back wall, and they both ordered more coffee. Darcy unfolded the place mat he'd been drawing on and straightened it out on the table.

"Chavo, Joker, and Toro go to Berto's on a night the restaurant is closed. Carol Montes is there visiting Guero."

He looked up and saw Gayler's eyes open wide. She grabbed her mug and brought it to her lips but didn't drink. If he told her the truth, he would be violating a direct order from Virago. Could he trust a detective he didn't know at all? He went with his gut.

"This is off the record and can never leave this table."

She sipped her coffee, then did it again. He could tell she was weighing how much she wanted to get involved in something she didn't know anything about and that could potentially crap all over her.

"This better be good."

"I think it'll solve your case," he said.

"Well, then, how come you didn't say that earlier?" she joked.

Even though Darcy believed it would, he knew she was making light of it because she also knew there was some-

362

thing much deeper, and darker, that would change their relationship forever.

For better or for worse.

"We have suspicions that Carol was sabotaging Diablos cases to get them dismissed."

"Holy fuck," Gayler said loud enough to get a dirty look from a dad sitting two tables over. "Sorry," she mouthed to him.

Darcy waited, letting everything sink in.

"You know this how?"

"Long story. I can fill you in one day, but for now just trust me."

She took a minute to process the information and all that it implied.

"That might explain why she was at Berto's with Guero, but what the hell were the other three doing there?"

"Bear with me."

She moved her chair to the left to avoid the sun that was hitting her eyes straight on. "Go on."

"What if the three musketeers go to Berto's to kill Guero, but when they get there and see Carol, decide to kill her instead and frame the Diablo?" he asked.

Her eyes widened. Her reaction was more one of curiosity than incredulity. Exactly what he was hoping for.

But then she said, "That's not gang MO. At all."

"Didn't I say 'bear with me'?"

"Okay, I'll shut up." She made a zip-it motion, leaned back, and crossed her arms.

"If you think about it, it makes sense. Chavo has a reputation for being rather crazy, so for him to go after Guero is not that outlandish. He has tabs on him somehow and takes two homies to make sure he can off him without problems. When he gets there, his wheels start turning. Why not get rid of the criminalist who's been giving his gang grief for a long time and make Guero's life miserable in the meanwhile?"

Gayler was still listening but didn't look that convinced.

"How else would Guero's own gun end up in the hands of Chavo?" Darcy continued.

"If what the kid says is true," she challenged. "And I can think of a dozen ways."

"Fine. What if Chavo takes Guero's gun and, to further play with him, gives it to a Diablos kid to cause mayhem? He knew we would tie the gun back to Guero."

"Hmm."

"This also may explain why Guero's clothes and burner showed up at a cabin in the Santa Cruz Mountains. Why would he go there on his own?" Darcy finished his coffee. His stomach churned, and he wished he'd eaten something earlier. "Let's say for argument's sake that what I've proposed so far is true. Guero's actions do follow gang MO. He goes after the men who framed him for a murder he didn't commit. He finds Joker, kills him, and then offs Toro."

While he talked, Gayler pulled something out of her messenger bag. It was her case file on Joker. She flipped through a few pages and then handed it to him so he could peruse the photos as she walked him through the scene.

"There's a whole lot of rage in those stab wounds," she conceded. "It'll be forever before we get any evidence processed, though. You know how things go when the victim is a tweaker."

"Any leads?"

"No. We got an anonymous call from a woman saying that someone had killed Joker at the Sevilla Road tweaker house. She hung up before the dispatcher could get more information."

Darcy thought about the 911 call.

"Was that before or after you found the body?"

"That's how we found the body. We wouldn't have gone into that dump otherwise."

"You think she might have done it?" he asked.

"Anything's possible, but I've listened to the tape a bunch of times, and it doesn't strike me as a confession. I think she witnessed something but was too high to know whether it was real but still had a sliver of humanity left to report it."

Darcy perused the file. "You think Guero could have done it?" He pulled the photo of the dirty wall with the maroon "6."

"A Diablo did it, that's for sure," she said.

"Guero has no homicide convictions. But he was originally arrested for offing Diego Ochoa, the drug dealer behind his club."

"Didn't they get Jefe for it?" she asked.

"Doesn't mean he did it."

Her eyebrows disappeared underneath her thin bangs. Gayler was tough, but he enjoyed the challenge.

"I think you'll find what I have to say about Toro interesting," Darcy said.

CHAPTER 90

There was something nagging Oscar, but he couldn't quite put his finger on it. He massaged his shoulder and rotated it, forcing his range of motion.

Everyone in the command center was staring at the faces on the monitors as if they were in a trance. There was nothing for them to do, just wait for a drone to find Chavo. Number twelve was still black. Oscar checked his watch and wondered if he should go over to Dominique's and pressure him to give him the drones already. But he knew it wouldn't make a difference. You couldn't have nine women make a baby in one month, as the engineer liked to remind him. He felt antsy and hated not having anything to do but wait.

Pascual broke the silence. "I still can't believe the home invasions work so well."

There was more frustration than admiration in his voice. Oscar knew it was because he was using the drones for the nonlucrative purpose of finding Chavo. He decided to ignore the resentment and take the compliment.

"It's such a no-brainer. We can monitor the household patterns without being seen and get the hell out before the police are even close."

"It's making us rich." Pascual made a dollar sign with his index finger.

Oscar looked over at the dead monitor. "Spider, you need to bring that drone up."

The homeboy looked up at him. His eyes were opened so wide the irises looked tiny.

"Boss, I don't know how. I've tried everything."

"Have you traced the bird?" As the last words came out, his throat closed shut. "Pascual, where did that police helicopter crash at?"

"Jefferson Park I think? I wasn't paying too much attention. I was just happy we'll have one less..." His smile quickly faded, as if he realized the same thing Guero was thinking.

Oscar pulled out his phone and checked the news about the crash.

"It was Jefferson Park, but it looks like it happened on the north side, by Mola Street."

"The drone went crazy," Pascual said. "It could have veered off course and gone up that way."

Spider was looking at them as if watching a tennis match.

"Puto, stop staring and pull up the last images we got on twelve," Oscar told Spider.

"It doesn't record."

"What do you mean, 'it doesn't record'?"

"We asked Dominique one day. He told us that he had disabled that feature so the police couldn't get any evidence of past crimes if any of the drones got caught."

"He wouldn't store the images in the drones, you idiot," Oscar said.

"No, in the cloud," Spider said. "The police could get to it with a warrant."

Oscar cursed and punched the desk. The keyboard jumped and a half-empty cup of coffee tipped over, its contents spilling on the surface and dripping onto the floor. Spider grabbed a stack of napkins he still had from breakfast and wiped up the mess.

"I thought Dominique didn't know what we were using the drones for," Pascual said, pacing back and forth.

"He doesn't know we're doing home invasions. But he probably thinks we're flying the drones commercially without the FAA exception, which is illegal," Spider said.

Oscar eyed Spider, impressed, but focused back on the subject.

"Are they identifiable?"

He got blank stares.

"Can the drones be traced back to Dominique?"

The three men shrugged. Oscar pulled his phone out, but before he could dial, Pascual snatched it.

"What the f— ?" Oscar said.

"Think, man. Do you want a drone traced to Dominique and an incoming call from your number?"

He waited until the question sank in.

"You're right," Oscar said.

He pulled out the burner they used in the command center and punched in the number. The phone rang and went to voice mail. Oscar didn't leave a message.

"We need to go there," he said.

"No way in hell. We're not going there."

Oscar was already halfway to the door. He heard Pascual curse and run after him.

Pascual drove like an eighty-year-old myopic woman. Oscar had to bite his tongue to avoid yelling at him to go faster. As they got closer to the industrial park, several police cars flew by at high speed. No lights or sirens.

Pascual looked at Oscar and pulled down his baseball cap. "Doesn't look good."

His second-in-command was right. It was stupid being there, but they had no choice but to get to the engineer. Saving Dominique was the most important thing, even if they had to leave the inventory behind.

Pascual turned left, slowed down, and, after two more streets, turned right, going the roundabout way. The industrial park spread over several lots. The next turn would be telling, as they would be entering Dominique's street, even though the warehouse was six blocks away. Before he made the final turn, he stopped the car.

"Go on," Oscar said.

"If we see cops, we turn left on the next street and get the hell out," Pascual said.

Oscar knew he would want to get a lot closer but didn't say it.

Pascual inched forward, and Oscar held his breath. As soon as the car turned, they saw a mass of police cars from different jurisdictions. No sirens, but red, blue, and white lights flashed from several yards away.

The car decelerated, and as it started to veer left, Oscar put a hand on Pascual's forearm.

"Man, we need to know for sure. Get a little closer."

"That's suicide. What's wrong with you?"

"We need to know. If they got him, if they're really there for him... we need to know for sure."

CHAPTER 91

Darcy didn't have all the *i*'s dotted and the *t*'s crossed in his theory, but he was convinced he was onto something. So he plowed through.

"What interests me about Toro's drive-by is the different shootings."

"Not uncommon with multiple perps," she said.

"Out of the twelve bullets shot at or below three feet from the ground, three hit the target in the legs. The thirteenth shot was a close-range through and through fired by a different gun."

Gayler's phone rang. She looked at it and answered. "I can't now." She checked her watch as she listened. "I'll be late. Start the barbeque without me."

Darcy heard a female voice on the other end but couldn't quite make out what she was saying.

"I know. I'm sorry. This is important. I'll be there as soon as I can. I love you." She ended the call. "Sorry. My partner gets antsy when we have people coming over."

"We can do this some other time," Darcy said, but didn't mean it.

"No. Go on."

He nodded. "Maybe Guero wanted to make sure he was dead—that's why he went in to finish the job."

"But if they wanted to kill him, why aim at the legs first?"

"Exactly. So maybe whoever killed Toro wanted to immobilize him first."

"But why?" she asked.

"Nobody has seen Chavo for a few days. Since Guero hasn't bothered hiding the other bodies, I doubt he's gotten to Chavo yet. And maybe he didn't kill Toro right away because he was trying to get the boss's location from him."

"More coffee please," she said to a waitress passing by.

She grabbed the file that lay between them and took a few minutes to search through it. Darcy wished she would talk out loud as she read, but she didn't.

Finally, she handed it to him. "Check this section," she said, pointing to the middle of the page. It was the transcript of the 911 call she'd referred to earlier.

"'Tell everybody I'm coming for him,'" he read out loud.

"I had no context for this before. It made no sense, but most of this call made no sense," she said.

He read a few lines before and after that statement, but there was no reference to who was coming after who.

"Did she witness Joker being killed?" Darcy asked. He set the file back down.

"She didn't quite say that. She said Joker was dead at the tweaker house. We don't have an ID on her. A dead end for now."

He mulled the information. "What if this warning came from Guero and he wanted to make sure Chavo got it?"

"That's what I'm thinking, but why would he do that?" Gayler swirled her coffee with a spoon, even though she hadn't put in any sugar or milk. "Any intel on Guero's location?"

"Also MIA. All of SJPD is looking for him. They still think he's good for Carol."

She looked at him sideways. "They haven't bought your theory?"

She didn't pull any punches. He liked her.

"Haven't shared it." He didn't want to get into the internal politics of CATCH and the added difficulty of trying to sell his theories when Quinn and Sorensen were off-site. "Anyway, we need to find Chavo."

"Wouldn't it be easier to align with the PD and find Guero?"

"Maybe. But nobody has a single lead on him, but I have a BOLO on Chavo's car." Almost to himself Darcy said, "I wish Howard had authorized the use of StingRay."

"That's pretty rad tracking technology. The Santa Clara Sheriff is one of the few organizations that have it."

"I know," Darcy said, pissed that the one time he needed it he couldn't use it.

He grabbed his phone and dialed. "JC, any luck locating Chavo?" He locked eyes with Gayler as he spoke. The phone was on speaker.

"Been keeping an eye out on the BOLO you put out. We had a couple spottings that turned out to be nothing."

The parole officer didn't seem bothered that he was calling her on a weekend.

"Traffic cam?"

"One. A patrol followed up but wasn't able to find him."

Darcy rubbed his temple. He couldn't believe they hadn't informed him of this.

"The other one was a uni, who pulled up behind a car that matched the description, but when he validated the plates it wasn't a match."

"Did he make the stop?"

"No. He was called to a domestic disturbance."

Darcy shook his head while he looked at Gayler. "What were the locations of the visuals?"

"The first one was around Eastridge Mall, the other on Santiago Avenue, by Welch Park."

"Keep me posted even if they don't pan out, okay?"

He tapped on the Maps app and searched for the mall. When he found it, he looked for the park and then pushed the phone over to Gayler.

"He's around here somewhere."

"But JC said the second sighting wasn't Chavo."

"Or he changed the plates."

He knew he was stretching everything to fit his theory, and that wasn't good. But he wanted to pursue it until it completely fell apart. He didn't have anything better, so why not?

"I'll see if I get Consuelo's phone pinging any towers around this area. It's a good place to start."

On the way out of the Purple Onion, Gayler said, "You know, it wouldn't be a bad thing if Guero gets rid of Chavo."

Darcy stopped walking.

When Gayler realized he'd stayed behind, she looked back. "Don't tell me you're one of those holier-than-thou dudes."

Darcy laughed. What were the chances that out of the entire law enforcement community in the Bay Area, he ended up working with Sorensen's twin?

CHAPTER 92

Oscar convinced Pascual to get a couple of blocks closer to the police perimeter. They craned their necks to see if they could confirm that the commotion was coming from Dominique's warehouse, as if there were any doubt.

"Man..." Pascual said.

"I know. Let's roll."

Pascual turned left and headed out of the industrial park as fast as he could without raising suspicion from the upcoming patrols.

Oscar checked the rearview mirror all the way to the highway. When they finally jumped back on Highway 237, he exhaled and said, "We need to find Chavo."

Pascual slammed the brakes, and the car skidded to the median.

"What the hell's wrong with you? No, we're not finding Chavo. Who gives a shit? You need to get the hell out. They got Dominique, and after he sings, they'll put you away forever. You are a two striker, and they'll get you with the gang enhancement too."

Oscar looked out the window. Cars passed by. A few honked because they weren't clear of the solid line.

"This is not your beef. I can handle it."

"This has nothing to do with that, asshole," Pascual said, shifting the car into gear and merging back into traffic.

"Let's go back to the command center," Oscar said.

"Sure. Whatever."

Pascual sounded defeated.

Oscar thought about his lieutenant. His second-in-command had been with him through the good and the bad for over a decade. But this was turning much uglier than he'd expected.

"Pull over. I'm going to drive you home."

"Fuck you." Pascual accelerated. "After all these years you don't get to throw me out." He looked at Oscar for much longer than was safe while at the wheel.

"Okay, but pay attention to the road. I don't want to die here."

Oscar laughed, but Pascual didn't join him.

They drove in silence the rest of the way. When they reached the underground parking at the command center, Pascual's phone rang. Instead of walking up with Oscar, he stayed behind to take the call.

Oscar reached the fourth floor but waited in the hallway. Just when he was about to give up, the elevator pinged and the doors slid open. Pascual was wrapping up.

"What was that about?"

His homie walked up to him, leaned against the wall, and planted both hands on his knees, then took a deep breath and squared himself to face him.

"You look like you're about to throw up." Oscar put a hand on Pascual's shoulder.

"I just don't know how to say this."

Oscar grinded his teeth. He wasn't up for another lecture on why he should leave town or why he was being stupid.

"That was Big Chon."

Oscar felt as if his best friend had punched him in the gut. Since Jefe had gone inside, Big Chon had always communicated with him directly. This was not good.

"You know what he said." Pascual looked away.

"Why don't you tell me?"

Pascual shook his head. "He said we have a business to run."

"And we'll get to it in a minute. Just a day or two more."

Oscar didn't quite plead, but he wanted his lieutenant to be on his side.

"You don't have that time. Big Chon wants the drones back in business now."

"They're my drones. Nobody tells me what to do with them."

Oscar started to walk away.

"You've lost your head, bro. You've lost your head for some *puta* you were screwing."

Before Pascual could react, Oscar turned and punched him as if he were a boxing dummy. Pascual's head slammed against the wall with a dull thud and his nose started bleeding, but he didn't hit him back. Oscar continued with hooks to the torso and within short breaths said, "Don't you ever call her that again."

Pascual managed to push him away and wiped the blood off his face with his sleeve. He left a red smear on his cheek. Oscar expected his homie to launch at him, but he didn't. Pascual combed his short hair back and walked to the elevator.

For a second Oscar thought his best friend shook his head, but he couldn't be sure.

CHAPTER 93

Gayler left to go to her barbeque but made Darcy promise that if things got interesting he would save her from an endless afternoon of boring conversations with her mundane neighbors. He agreed to keep her on speed dial and decided to go to the SO to check on the cell tower activity.

The bullpen was empty. Howard's door was closed and the lights turned off. Darcy thought about the short conversation he had with his brother-in-law. Where was he going with that? In a way he was happy they were interrupted. Whatever Damon had in mind, Darcy didn't need any more cronyism. But, he guessed, it was better than being admonished or fired.

He stared at the whiteboard. It was a mixture of Nhu's disappearance, Carol's murder, and miscellaneous information about the Diablos and the Snakes. He sighed for what felt like a full minute. The information felt more like disjointed clues leading nowhere than actual evidence.

His cell rang. It was Virago.

"We just arrested someone in connection to the chopper going down. I would like you to interview him."

Darcy looked at his screen full of phone records that needed to be parsed. "Why me?"

"You're the only one available. You want to be part of CATCH, then act like it." When there was no response, she added, "You were there with me, Moro and Findley could have been killed. Just see what he says. If it drags or he invokes, you can move on."

He closed the lid of his laptop and stuffed it in his bag. "I'm walking over right now."

"Meet Marra in the interview rooms. He's bringing in the suspect as we speak."

He walked the short distance to the SJPD and let himself into the basement. There was nobody there, so he went up the stairs to the third floor. He figured Marra would bring the suspect to Homicide, which had the best setup for interviews.

"And we meet again," the sergeant said when Darcy approached him. "You here to do the honors?" he asked, pointing at the suspect inside Room 2.

Darcy nodded. The young man was probably taller than he looked. He was thin, his skin too pasty for a California resident. He was hunched over, his eyes half-closed, focused on his interlaced fingers, which were resting on top of the metal table.

"What happened to his eyebrow?" Darcy asked, noticing that the left one was missing.

"We found him that way." Marra smirked.

"What do you have so far?" Darcy asked while eyeing the suspect.

"The drone that crashed into Air3 was traced back to this guy's warehouse. You should see the place. It's like a set from a sci-fi movie."

"Start-up?"

"Looks that way. But weird enough, it looked like a one-man show, though the place was gigantic." Marra pulled out his phone. "Check out the pics. I only took a few, but it gives you an idea."

The warehouse was about five thousand square feet and of new construction. The walls were concrete, as was the floor, and there was no color and no natural light coming in. It was mostly empty, except for a computer, a large desk that seemed thwarted by the size of the two monitors, and a wall covered from floor to ceiling with shelving. The drones were neatly stacked on each shelf and equally spaced from each other.

"What is this?" Darcy pointed at a white spot in the last photo. It was too pixelated for him to make out what it was.

"A mattress on the floor. It looks like the dude lived there too."

Darcy handed the phone back to Marra and looked at the suspect. Living and working by himself in a huge warehouse. And now his drone had taken down the Air3. What a way to end a promising career.

"Where's Officer Schulman?"

"Back at the scene," Marra said.

Darcy nodded and called Jon. "Are you busy?"

"No," he said after a bit too long. "What can I help with? I was just going for a run."

"We have someone in custody for the Air3 crash. Can you head out to his warehouse and check the place out?" As if he needed extra incentive, he added, "Officer Schulman's there already."

Darcy told himself he was sending the intern over because he knew the two of them could get him more information in an hour than the rest of the team put together, and not because he was trying to be a matchmaker.

"You want me to work with her?"

Jon's voice increased in pitch as he finished the question. It almost made Darcy laugh out loud.

"Is that a problem?"

The moment Darcy asked, he felt like Sorensen and wished he could take it back.

"No. I mean. I just thought you wanted me to continue looking into Carol's data."

"That can wait. I'm going to interview the suspect, so I need intel ASAP."

When the conversation was over, Marra handed Darcy a few printouts. "Here's the prelim information we have on this guy. The scumbag is a Dominique Badeaux. He hasn't said much, but I think he speaks enough English."

"Good. Waiting for a French interpreter on a Saturday would take forever."

Darcy went to the kitchen while he leafed through Badeaux's paperwork. He filled a small plastic glass with tap water and walked back.

"Will you be watching?" he asked Marra.

"Dying to see what you can do."

Darcy placed the water glass in front of Dominique. There was nothing else on the table. He introduced himself, but the young man didn't say a word.

He wished he'd grabbed a cup of coffee for himself. At least that would give him something to do while he watched Mr. Badeaux's reactions.

"One of your drones crashed into a San Jose Police helicopter."

The young man looked up for the first time. His expression was a mixture of fear and incredulity.

"I can't even begin to tell you how bad that is for you."

Dominique searched for any remaining hairs on his eyebrow. When he realized there were none left, he switched to the right one.

"It looks like you have no permits for flying drones. Which means you were operating them illegally. You'll be facing both civil and criminal charges. And you are not a US citizen, but we'll make sure you spend a long time in prison and pay millions in restitution. Then we'll kick you out of the country and you'll be banned from ever coming back."

Dominique mumbled something. He had a strong accent that made him even harder to understand.

"Didn't catch that," Darcy said.

"It wasn't me."

"We traced the drone to your stash. You founded Faucon. The drone was yours. This is pretty much a closed case."

Darcy was much bigger than the suspect. He knew the geek was intimidated enough, so instead of leaning on the table, he relaxed against the chair and crossed his arms.

"They're my drones. But I wasn't the one operating them. I have an investor, who took them from me before they were ready. I warned him. I told him they had bugs, but he wouldn't listen. He took them. He stole them. It's his fault."

"Tell me who this person is," Darcy said, and really wished he'd brought coffee with him.

CHAPTER 94

Oscar waited on the other side of the command center's door for a few minutes, sure that Pascual would come back. He walked to the elevator, wanting to be there when the doors opened, unsure whether he would hit or hug his compadre when they did. The elevator hummed, and he smiled to himself. He knew Pascual wouldn't abandon him, even if he'd pushed him to do so. But the elevator came and went, passing by his floor without opening.

He scratched his chin. His beard was itchy and he didn't like it. When he finally opened the door to the command center, he found Spider and Palo playing a first-person shooter game on the monitor that had gone unused for a couple of days.

"This is how you spend your time when I'm not watching you?" he yelled.

"With the new gig, there's nothing for us to do," Spider said, and shut down the console.

"Pack up. We're moving," Oscar said.

The two kids froze.

"Come on, we don't have time."

He walked around to figure out what he needed to take and what could be left behind. He knew Dominique would tell the police who and where they were, so they didn't have to worry about wiping off prints or DNA.

Oscar watched as Spider started turning off and disconnecting the monitors.

"If the drones don't record, how would we know if one finds Chavo while we have everything disconnected?" he asked.

Spider stopped, with a cord in his hand. While he thought about it, he started coiling it up. "I think it would follow him until he gets into a building or a car. Like what happened the other time, when the guy we thought was him went to the mall and then later to the car."

Oscar thought about how close he'd been to killing the wrong guy.

"So the moment he takes shelter, we'll lose him." When no one answered, he said to Palo, "Help me take all the stuff to the cars."

Down in the parking lot, he realized he would have to use his car to transport some of the equipment. Palo and Spider commuted together, and their little beat-up Hyundai wouldn't hold twelve monitors and three passengers. Taking his own car would be too risky, but he didn't have time to get a soldier to bring a van.

Once they'd brought all the equipment down and loaded Spider's car, Oscar walked around the garage. He could steal something and probably make it to the safe house before it was reported. Then he could hide it in the Airbnb's garage until he could get someone to ditch it somewhere.

There were only two cars parked on their floor. He chose the Jeep over the Acura and hoped for the best.

CHAPTER 95

Dominique Badeaux sang like a bird. He told Darcy how he moved to America to build the best facial-recognition prototype and then sell the technology to law enforcement. But he was not good at enticing the investors on Sand Hill Road to throw money at him, and when Guero showed up in his life, it seemed like a blessing.

He soon realized that he had made a pact with the devil, but by then it was too late. He had money coming in, he'd hired a whole team back in France, and the code was improving on a daily basis. So he turned a blind eye to what Guero was doing with the drones and just hoped that he could finish his vision before he was in too deep.

Darcy took the thumb drive with the interview and walked to CATCH to talk to Virago. Before giving it to her, he decided to bring up the topic nobody else cared about first.

He walked into the commander's office and sat down. "Just so you know, I want to pursue Nhu's investigation."

"You found her?" Virago asked.

"No. But Samantha Lee should arrive in a day or two, and I know she'll lead me to her."

Virago was quiet for a second. "I learned something about Jefe's case," she said, but didn't wait for him to ask. "Apparently, he was working with the feds, the SJPD, and the DA's office. But it was completely hush-hush."

Darcy forced himself to keep eye contact with her. He'd figured it would be best if she found out directly from the sheriff instead of from him. He was glad his brother-in-law had followed through with this quickly.

"Is that what Quinn was doing in all his escapades, working with them?"

She nodded. "Jefe was working a deal in exchange for delivering Guero as the center of a humongous enterprise. He covers his tracks way too well, so they needed Jefe."

"But why the secrecy?" Darcy had heard of cases where agencies put up Chinese walls, but he didn't know why this one merited it.

"Someone has a mole. Since SJPD and the DA were working on this, they couldn't risk it coming out until they figure out who it was."

Darcy thought about the tunnel where Jefe got killed. "That's how Nene was able to get a shank into superior court."

"Someone let him in with it or handed it over after he got there," Virago said. "And they were right to be careful. As soon as Big Chon caught wind that Jefe was talking, he had him killed."

"Any leads on the mole?" he asked.

"They're not sharing. They've been working on this case with Jefe for over a year. There're a lot of pissed-off bigwigs right now."

"Was Jefe getting a deal for killing Ochoa?"

She smiled. "You'll never believe this. The idiot was too dumb to understand the rules of the game. He maintained his innocence and kept pointing the finger at Guero." Her eyes crinkled with crow's feet. "Which now we know was true, but since Jefe ordered the hit, he was going to go down for it too. If he'd disclosed it from the beginning, they might have made it part of his deal."

Darcy shook his head. "It doesn't matter anymore I guess."

"The next step is to figure out whether Guero sent the order, or whether it came from Big Chon. Guero was making a lot of money for them, so either one had a huge incentive to silence Jefe."

Darcy changed subjects and went on to tell her about his conversation with Dominique Badeaux and the drones.

"Did GSU know that Guero was the sole investor in this drone company?" he asked.

"I don't think anybody knew."

"The burglary spikes that Jon found, I bet he was using the drones for the home invasions and then repurposed them to find Chavo."

"Find Chavo?" Virago leaned over her desk, framing the keyboard with her elbows.

"Dominique Badeaux just told me that Guero took the drones before they were ready because he was adamant about finding Chavo."

"Did he say why?" she asked.

"Guero told him that he was trying to find him so he could let him know about a funeral."

"His own maybe." Virago massaged the bridge of her nose. "Do you think he's telling the truth?

"I think Guero made that up and he chose to believe it. I think Badeaux was pretty scared of Guero." After a second Darcy asked, "What do you make of all this?"

Virago looked out of her office toward the whiteboard. Darcy did too. It was still as empty as it had been the last time he was there.

"I think we need to find Guero more than ever."

CHAPTER 96

The Airbnb was not the best command center replacement. They had to run extension cords from all of the nearby outlets so they could have the eleven monitors plugged in at the same time. Once they were up and running, Oscar watched each display to see if any of the drones had gotten lucky, but there was nothing more than random faces flipping on the screen.

He pulled the burner out of his pocket and called Matón. "Yo, give me some news."

"I got all my boys running around three different neighborhoods, but nothing so far."

"Get more guys." The silence at the other end wasn't reassuring. "I wasn't asking."

"You got it, boss. I'll report in an hour."

Oscar asked Spider for the car keys. He put on his hoodie and said, "You call me the second they find him, even if it is a low-percentage match, you got me?"

"Copy that."

He wasn't sure where he should go but had to be out of there, do something. He had to be closer to where Chavo was, even if it was only in his mind. Fremont was too far. It would take him forever to reach San Jose if the worm was spotted.

He had driven south for almost twenty minutes when he realized where he was heading. He parked across the street

387

from the church and killed the engine. Oscar looked at the white building with the large cross and almost chuckled. He wasn't religious. He had nothing to confess, he was going to hell, and nothing he could ever say to a priest would change that. Still, he found himself getting out of the car and crossing the street.

He opened the heavy wooden doors, and the coolness from inside bathed him in a soothing calm. There were only three people, spread across a few pews, praying. He passed the stoup holding the holy water without wetting his fingers. As he approached the podium, the image of Christ on the cross became bigger, looking down on him.

Father Gonzales was exiting a confession booth. *How timely*, Oscar thought. The priest waited for him. Oscar felt the urge to turn around and leave but didn't. He made it all the way to the front pew and sat down. The priest did the same.

"How's the shoulder?"

"Better. You did a good job, Father."

"You got lucky. You should've gone to the hospital."

He didn't reply. Both knew it was a moot point. The silence grew uncomfortable and Oscar got up.

"You want confession?"

"I'm good."

The priest stood, and Oscar shook his hand and walked away.

On the last row there was a man. At first Oscar didn't recognize him, but then he realized it was Berto. He looked as if he'd aged twenty years in just a couple of days. He sat next to him, but neither said anything for a few moments.

"I can't get the image of that woman out of my head," Berto said. "I'm sorry this happened to someone you loved."

Oscar wasn't sure how to respond, so he didn't say anything.

"When Serena died in the car crash, I thought I would never be able to get over the pain. She was my first born. And I know you loved her. Now... This woman. You don't deserve to have to go through this loss twice."

It took a second for Oscar to understand what Berto was saying. Then it clicked.

"Wait, Berto, you think I was in love with Carol?" he asked.

"You weren't?" Berto twisted his torso to look at him.

"No, old man. Carol was my mother."

CHAPTER 97

Sorensen kept watching the house, sitting in his newly rented car parked across the street. He'd been tempted to give up the search and go back home but stayed because even though he hated to admit it, since it'd been Quinn's hunch all along, he had a feeling there might be something to the story of Carol's baby.

So there he was, slurping the melted ice from what had been a 20 oz Dr Pepper a couple of hours ago while he waited for someone to show up. He'd done enough stakeouts to know that it was all about waiting. He'd already crossed off his list thirteen addresses. There were seven more to go. He'd been sure that the last one, lucky thirteen, was going to be the one, but it wasn't. He tried the phone number one more time, just to do something. It went straight to voice mail, like the previous five times he'd called it.

Finally, a dark-gray Cube appeared from the north side of the street and pulled into the driveway. A couple in their early thirties jumped out.

"Damn. Another miss," he said out loud.

He sighed and got out of the car, only because his ass hurt and he could use the stretch.

The male opened the trunk and started pulling out grocery bags. The female let a toddler out of the kid's chair. Sorensen waited until they were by the door and sprinted toward them before they went inside. The mother told the kid to go to his room, and both adults stood on the landing. Neither invited him in, even though he'd already introduced himself as law enforcement.

"How can we help you?" the man asked.

"Can I ask how long you've lived here?"

"My aunt got this house over twenty-five years ago. I inherited it when she passed away last year."

Yep, dead end.

"Did she ever talk about the family who lived here before?" This was a waste of time, but he may as well cover all the basis. "Maybe left a forwarding address?"

"That was a lifetime ago..." the woman said. "What did you say this was about?"

"I understand the family who lived here before adopted a little boy. We're trying to find him. His mother was murdered."

"Oh my god. I'm so sorry." The woman looked behind her, checking that her son wasn't within earshot.

"When we moved in, we found a few toys in the attic. It was strange, because my aunt didn't have children. Maybe they were leftovers from that family."

"Do you still have them?"

He shook his head. "We donated everything to Goodwill."

"Can you think of anything else?"

The couple remained silent for a few seconds, both looking at the tips of their shoes. Then the man said, "Wait one second," and disappeared inside the house.

The woman seemed surprised but stayed put, finding her manicured nails incredibly fascinating. Sorensen thought about making small talk, but he didn't feel chatty either.

A few minutes later the man came back with a folder. He was leafing through it.

"Here are some papers that my aunt had. I remember going through them when we moved in and..." He flipped a few pages until he found what he wanted. "Here." He pulled a single sheet with a handwritten address on it. "This may be where the previous owners went. We don't know anyone who's ever moved to California."

CHAPTER 98

Darcy agreed with Virago that the SJPD needed to find Guero. They had the whole department devoted to that. But he still thought that Chavo was the key to unfolding this mess. He knew he wasn't going to get any resources moved from Guero to Chavo even if he shared his theory with the commander, because he had yet to find any evidence to corroborate it.

Jon was still at the drone warehouse, and he had nothing more to discuss with the commander, so he decided to go back to his own office at the SO. Just as he was setting his laptop on the desk, Sorensen called him.

"Are you enjoying the sunny weather by your pool?" his partner asked.

"Yes, it's gorgeous out," Darcy said, looking at the beige walls that badly needed a repaint. The bullpen had no windows.

"You should be working like the rest of us."

"How's Seattle?" he asked, feeling a little homesick.

"Rainy."

Darcy laughed. "Anything interesting from the Emerald City?"

"Where to start?"

"Are you driving? It's hard to hear."

"Fine. I'll roll the windows up."

"I thought you said it was raining."

"I like the fresh smell."

The background noise was gone. Darcy heard the sound of a can opening and Sorensen smacking his lips.

His partner shared the conversation with Carol's mom and the priest, and told him about the black book of babies given away, and the conversation with the young couple. "Can you run the address? I'll try to catch the next flight back."

Darcy started entering it in the system but stopped when Sorensen said, "I think Quinn got suspended."

"What?"

Darcy couldn't believe Virago hadn't told him. He got up and walked to the kitchen to make a new pot of coffee.

"Well, I don't know exactly," Sorensen continued, "but Virago called him this morning and told him to haul his ass back home. I thought Quinn was going to have an aneurism. He was yelling and screaming on the phone, then got in the car and took off."

"Did he say anything before he left?"

"No. The asshole left me behind without an explanation. Or a car."

Darcy realized that he was leaning on the kitchen counter, still waiting on the coffee that had already brewed. He took the whole pot and a ceramic cup from the cupboard and headed toward one of the empty interview rooms.

"Why did you stay?"

"I wanted the day to try to find the family."

Darcy looked into his cup and then took a sip. It seemed that neither of them had the full picture. He told him what he knew about Jefe getting out of the life and Quinn's involvement in that case.

"Whoa. That makes sense, though," Sorensen said. "I didn't get much from Quinn's conversation, but I heard something about getting his orders from someone much higher than her."

"Ouch. I'm sure she didn't appreciate that."

"Didn't go so well. Knowing her, she'll never forgive him for not telling her. Trust is the one thing she values over everything."

Darcy poured a new cup. The coffee was hot, and he blew the steam away. "At the end he wasn't dirty, he was just working on a secret case."

"I guess I'm glad. One is enough." The silence felt heavy. "Was Quinn really sleeping with Carol?"

"The emails speak for themselves," Darcy said.

"And he didn't really help the Diablos?" Sorensen asked.

"Jefe would have been killed way earlier if that had been the case."

Sorensen slurped. "It's hard to believe that they were sleeping together and the sergeant never knew she was tampering with the cases."

Darcy heard a faint honk and wondered if it had been directed at Sorensen. "Love makes you blind I guess."

"Remember that depression I told you about?" Sorensen asked. "I put some feelers out. One of my old buddies knew a department shrink who likes to drink and talk, so he went for a visit with a nice bottle of tequila. The story goes that soon after his divorce, Quinn went into a downward spiral. Fast and furious down the rabbit hole. I think that's when he took the leave of absence. Apparently someone—it might have been Carol—found him about to eat his Glock."

"Shit," Darcy said. "This sounds very complicated. Carol's dating Quinn and working with Guero?"

"Maybe that's why he killed her," Sorensen said. "What if she got a conscience? Or Quinn started sniffing around and she got scared? She tells Guero she's getting out, and he kills her."

"Have you forgotten that crime scene?" Darcy still had the imprint burnt in his brain.

"Don't know, buddy, but I'm about to return the car, so I'll talk to you when I get back. Run that address for me, okay?"

CHAPTER 99

Oscar returned Berto's stare. He was just as surprised to hear that Berto thought he was in love with his mother as Berto probably was that Carol was not his girlfriend. He leaned back in the pew and looked straight up to the Jesus on the cross.

"Serena is the only woman I've been in love with."

And thinking that she kept his secret about Carol, even from her parents, made Oscar love her even more.

"So your mother didn't die in the fire?" Berto said.

"I thought that for twenty-six years." Oscar shifted in his seat. The wood of the pew made his butt stiff.

"All that time and you didn't know."

Oscar nodded. He knew how Berto felt. It was surreal.

"How did you find out?"

"Remember when I was in jail for killing Ochoa behind my club?"

"The one Jefe went in for."

He nodded. "I was arrested for it first."

"I remember. Your third strike." Berto shook his head. "We were so worried about you. Serena was going out of her mind."

Oscar thought about his last time behind bars. He was a third striker. He was going in for good—life in prison without the possibility of parole.

"Anyway, one day, while I'm waiting for the DA to finalize the indictment, Serena comes to visit out of the blue. Man, I was so happy to see her. She looked nervous, fidgety. At first I thought it was because she hated coming to see me in jail. I remember thinking that the last time I was in, she told me she would leave me if I ever got pinched again. So seeing her so distressed, I was sure she was going to break up with me."

"She loved you so much."

"I know. After she shared the latest gossip from the hood, she told me she received a weird call from a woman." Oscar shook his head, remembering how his girlfriend kept looking over her shoulder, as if she feared someone could overhear them. "She told me the woman said she was my mother. I went all white. I literally felt the blood drain from my body." He shut his eyes. "I stared at Serena for a very long time. She got even more nervous and told me that she was sorry, that she didn't mean to upset me. Poor thing."

"She became so withdrawn around that time," Berto said. "We thought it was because you were inside."

Oscar nodded. "She told me the woman said she knew I was in custody and to tell me that she was my mother and she would help me get out of jail."

Berto gasped.

"Exactly how I felt. Then I laughed. First of all, my mother was dead, and second, nobody makes a stupid-ass phone call like that. After I stopped laughing, I told Serena to brush it off, that it was a prank or the police was trying to set me up. She gave me one of those smiles she always gave me when she thought I was wrong, but she didn't argue."

Oscar closed his eyes. He missed his woman with all his heart.

Berto smiled and then shook his head. His eyes shined, and Oscar realized they were full of tears.

"A couple days later Serena comes back and says the woman had called again, still insisting that she was my mom and could get me off. My fucking mother, can you believe that? At that point I think, 'Hell, why not? If it's a police setup, so be it. I got nothing to lose.' So I tell Serena to tell the crazy bitch to get me out already."

Berto wiped his eyes but continued listening.

"I was surprised when Serena showed up the next day. She used to come every three or four, but there we were, talking over those sticky plastic green tables in the jail visitation room. She told me that she'd given the woman my message, and she said that she needed to know who I wanted framed instead. Just for giggles I tell her 'Frame Jefe.' I killed Ochoa because of him, so why not?"

"Oh no," Berto said.

"Yeah..." Oscar massaged his shoulder. "I was sure it was a big joke, so I didn't think much about it. The next thing I know they're dismissing my charges. I couldn't believe it at first. Hell, I even made up some story in my mind that Nhu's statement had worked out, that it had nothing to do with that woman. Serena picked me up, and she looked more scared than I've ever seen her before. She tells me that they arrested Jefe. I froze. I'd killed Ochoa to show my loyalty to Jefe, and now he was in jail because of me. I had set up the whole thing with Nhu to create probable cause for another possible killer, but now... This was not going to go well. I had fucked up big-time. No wonder Serena was freaking out. Hell, I was freaking out."

Berto laughed a nervous laugh.

Oscar remembered distinctly the feeling of dread in his gut. He knew the first thing Jefe was going to do behind bars was to draft a kite to get him green-lighted. Oscar's only way out was to find out who was going to do the hit and kill him first.

"What happened next?" Berto asked.

"While I'm hiding in one of those whore motels up on First Street, I'm thinking hard about what I'm gonna do. I tell Serena she needs to call this woman, find out who the hell she is and why she's doing this, but my girl tells me the woman always called from a blocked number. So we waited, hoping that she would get in touch."

CHAPTER 100

Darcy entered the address Sorensen had given him into the system. The house didn't exist anymore. The whole block had been turned into an open mall three years prior. He soon forgot all about it and called Gayler.

"Can you talk?"

"You got a huge break in the case and you need me to come and help you right away?"

It took him a second to understand what she was saying. "Yes, absolutely."

"You know it's Saturday, and I'm having some quality time with my family and friends. This is very inconvenient."

Her voice was louder than it needed to be. He assumed she was trying to make sure everybody heard her.

"You're really coming in?"

"Let me say good-bye. I'll call you as soon as I'm in the car."

They hung up and he waited. After what seemed like an eternity, he checked his watch. It'd been three minutes. How long did Gayler need to wrap up? Another minute passed, then two more. Finally, his phone rang.

"What's the story?" she asked.

He could hear music in the background.

"I talked to Sorensen. The SJPD still thinks that Guero killed Carol, probably because she decided to stop working with the Diablos."

Gayler didn't say anything, but the only noise was now the engine.

"Did you hear me?" Darcy asked.

"I heard you. I'm thinking."

The car decelerated. The blinker went on and then off.

"You think they're right?" she asked after a few more seconds.

He took in a deep breath, then got up and paced the empty interview room. "Guero could have felt betrayed and decided to kill her, sure. I guess nobody gets out of the life alive, right? But why kill her in such a sadistic way?"

"He's vicious enough. And gangsters kill for nothing. Trust me on that."

Darcy remembered Joker's crime scene photo. His guts looked like goulash.

"But where do we go with Chavo? It makes no sense that we have him and his crew at Berto's and that he handed Guero's gun to Robbie at the school if it's Guero who killed Carol."

"I'm almost there. Come down to the front desk to let me in."

Darcy placed the cell on the desk and pulled out the paper place mat they were using at brunch. He looked at the names on it—Chavo, Carol, Matthews—then wrote "Quinn."

He ran down the stairs and went to the main entrance to meet Gayler. Her skin was blushed.

"You got some sun?" Darcy said.

"The curse of being ghost white. We burn, never tan."

They walked up the stairs, and Darcy showed her the place mat.

Tapping on Chavo's name, he said, "I've been thinking about this since brunch. What if Bullet sent Chavo a kite from Pelican Bay to end the Gang Suppression Unit? They'd been hurting the Kingsnakes bad."

CHAPTER 101

O scar thought about the evening he was released and the grimy hotel room where they were hiding with the dirty sheets. He wasn't quite sure if the stains came from bodily fluids or were discolored spots from overwashing. He remembered chuckling, realizing how much he'd changed. He'd spend many days sleeping on the streets, and now filthy sheets grossed him out.

Serena sat really close to him. She stroked the top of his hand with her thumb. He wasn't talking. He was thinking.

He had to come up with a plan. They had to leave the Bay Area, or even California, if he wanted to survive the retaliation that would come from Pelican Bay. Jefe was sure to get Big Chon to mandate something brutal.

Serena's phone rang. The number was blocked. She handed it to him.

"Oscar?"

His first reaction was to hang up. But he didn't. He swallowed twice. The saliva felt like phlegm and got stuck in his throat. Was this a setup? A bad joke? He knew it wasn't. He was free because of her.

"Why did you get me out?" he asked.

She didn't answer for a long time.

"I found out you're my son. I couldn't let you go to prison with a third strike."

"My mother's dead."

He heard muted sobs on the other end. He felt nothing.

"Would you mind if we met in person?" she asked after she composed herself. Her voice sounded weak but not teary. "I have so much to tell you."

Serena was leaning on him, listening to the conversation. He looked at her and she nodded, then shrugged.

"You've put me in a very bad spot with Los Diablos," he said.

"I'm sorry. That was not my intention."

He considered her request. "Okay. Meet me at the motel on the corner of First and Archer Street. Room 106. And lady, you better come alone, and you better not be playing any games."

"I'll be there in one hour."

He stared at the dead phone. His world had done a 180 in less than twenty-four hours.

He looked at Serena. Her cheeks were blushed. He kissed her. She kissed him back. Her mouth opened and he played with her tongue, then pulled her closer. He inhaled and took in her scent. She smelled like roses. They kissed harder. She put both arms around his neck. He picked her up and sat her on his lap. He nibbled on her neck while he cupped her full breasts.

He stood and led her to the bathroom. He turned on the shower and undressed her, kissing her body, awakening a hunger for her he'd tried to kill in jail, thinking he would never touch her again. When she was naked, he took his own clothes off and they walked into the steaming shower. The water pressure seemed to be the only thing worth a damn in that hotel.

405

An hour later there was a knock on the door. Serena's hair was still wet. He'd put on a clean white T-shirt that showed his biceps and the "VI" tattooed along his left tricep.

He moved the blinds an inch and peeked out the window but couldn't see anything more than the small frame of a person wearing a baseball cap and a large parka.

Oscar opened the door and had to grab the doorknob for support. There was no doubt this woman was his mother.

She hesitated for a second but then launched forward and hugged him. She was very small, even smaller than Serena, but the strength of her hug warmed his entire body. She started crying. He felt his throat closing up on him, but he fought it.

A second later Serena came from behind and embraced both of them. Then he broke down and cried for the first time since he was twelve.

They remained like that for minutes. When they couldn't hold on to each other anymore, they sat. Oscar on the bed with Serena. The woman pulled a small metal chair opposite to them and massaged her hands.

"I was fifteen when I got pregnant with you." Her cap had been pulled up when she hugged him. She removed it. She had long shiny hair, pulled back in a loose braid. "I was raped."

Oscar's gut started burning, a fireball rising to his chest. He crossed his arms, creating some distance between them. Was she telling the truth, or was she looking for pity? Serena inched closer to him. He started sweating where their skins touched.

"When I found out I was pregnant, I didn't know what to do. I kept it secret for a long time. I didn't show for a while." She looked down. "I eventually told my mother. She told my father, and they sent me away to my aunt's so I wouldn't disgrace the family name."

She looked up, probably sensing he was gauging her. He was.

"Anyway, a couple months later I gave birth to a baby boy, who, they told me, died just a few minutes after birth."

A tear slid down her cheek. Another quickly followed. She wiped both away with her hand.

Serena jumped off the bed and hugged the woman. They both started sobbing. Oscar felt uncomfortable and wanted them to stop.

"What happened next?"

His voice sounded harsher than he'd intended. He stood and walked to the other side of the room and paced along the length of the bed. He didn't know why he was feeling so enraged. This woman hadn't done anything but bring him into the world. And yet somehow he blamed her for abandoning him. He looked down at her and saw, from the corner of his eye, Serena's admonishing scowl.

"Go on," his girlfriend said with a much softer tone than his.

The woman told them how she only found out that Oscar had survived when her mom told her at her dad's funeral. From that moment forward her entire free time had been spent looking for him.

Oscar wondered how different their lives would have been if he hadn't been taken away. He thought about the newspaper article his grandpa showed him when he started asking about his parents.

"I grew up thinking that both of my parents died in a house fire, so my grandparents raised me. Until Nano died when I was seven. Then Nana when I was twelve."

Carol met his eyes and nodded. "I'm sorry. Were they good to you?"

Oscar nodded.

Serena walked to him and took his hand. "Come," she whispered, and led him back to the bed.

He sat, but when Carol extended her hand to take his, he crossed his arms. He was feeling too many things inside. The physical contact with his mother would make everything even more confusing.

Carol leaned against the chair and hugged herself. "I've been looking for you for so long. I'm so sorry I haven't been there for you." She pulled on her sleeves, until both hands were hidden.

"How did you find me?"

She took in a long breath and then let it out. "I got the evidence for the Ochoa murder and found some blood on the gun that didn't belong to the victim. The blood type was AB negative. Only 0.2% of the Hispanic population have it. I'm AB negative. Since I discovered that my son was alive, I've been secretly running tests with all the suspects and victims that are a match with age and race."

He checked the web of his hand, where the small scab was already peeling. He didn't remember the pinching when he shot Ochoa. He nodded for her to go on, but he could imagine the rest of the story.

"I compared your DNA to mine and got a mitochondrial match." Their eyes met. "I had to act quickly. You were a third striker, and if I was going to do something to help you, I had to do it right away. The evidence against you was pretty solid, but I saw the report about the witness who came forward saying that she'd seen someone else, so that gave me the idea. That's when I contacted Serena."

Oscar's girlfriend smiled at the woman, letting her know that she had done the right thing.

"I know this is a lot to take in," Carol said. "I would like us to meet again. But I totally understand if you don't want to."

Oscar remembered not answering then. He didn't know what he wanted. He shook his head, pushing the thoughts away. That was when he noticed he'd gone down memory lane.

Oscar looked at Berto and shared most of what he'd just silently relived.

"What happened then?" Berto asked.

The first few weeks after he got out, he was too worried about one of Jefe's homies coming after him. He had slept with one eye open for days. Then he got a kite from Big Chon saying that all was good with Jefe and that Oscar better take the enterprise to the next level. They all counted on him to make them richer.

And that he did.

He didn't feel like sharing that with Berto. Instead he said, "I told myself I didn't need to see the woman ever again. But you know how Serena was. Once she got an idea in her head, there was no way to get her to let go. She convinced me to meet Carol again. Then the whole logistical problem came up. She worked for the crime lab, she'd tampered with evidence, and I was not only a known felon but also a gangster."

"That's when Serena came to ask me if she could use the restaurant," Berto said.

"Exactly."

"I never knew."

An octogenarian woman with a pronounced hunchback walked by them. Oscar thought about Berto's restaurant and the few early meetings with Carol and Serena. Then Serena died in the crash, and after that it was just Carol and him.

"Did you ever meet your father?" Berto asked.

"I killed the bastard." Before he could get into the details, his phone vibrated. He checked the caller ID.

He got up, hugged the old man. "Take care of yourself."

Oscar walked out of the church as he tapped the green button.

"We got Chavo," Spider said.

CHAPTER 102

G ayler nodded, taking in what Darcy was saying.
"If Chavo got the order from Bullet, he would've been
following Carol, not Guero."

She followed Darcy into the interview room he'd been
squatting at.

Darcy closed the door and paced. "Chavo goes into Berto's,
finds both, and in a moment of brilliance decides to kill Carol
and frame Guero, diverting the heat from the Snakes to the
Diablos."

"How's Matthews?" she asked.

"I think he'll make it, but he's still in critical condition. He
never saw his assailant. And I'm still waiting on the cell tower
records to see if I can match Chavo's."

His phone rang. He checked the number but didn't recognize it. He almost let it go to voice mail but then decided to
pick up.

"This is Marjorie Mullins, from the DOT. You have an active BOLO on a Toyota Corolla, correct?" The voice sounded
frail and old-school.

"You found it?" Darcy asked looking at Gayler while he
fought a nascent feeling of hope.

"One of our cameras just spotted such a car."

"Where?"

"Crossing Fuller Street, going south on Almaden Expressway."

Darcy set the phone on the table and mapped the coordinates.

Mullins coughed into the phone, as if trying to get his attention. "I can let you know if other cameras catch it."

"Yes please," Darcy said. "Can you text me the streets as he's spotted?"

There was a long pause. "I'm sorry, Detective, I don't have one of those fancy phones."

Gayler looked at him and smiled. He gritted his teeth. *Really?*

"Mrs. Mullins, do you have email on your computer terminal?"

"Yes, of course."

She sounded more offended than Darcy would have expected.

"Can you email me the information of any additional sightings?"

"Certainly. Would one email at the end of my shift suffice?"

Darcy suppressed a sigh. Gayler was smirking, enjoying the exchange way too much.

"Would it be a huge inconvenience if you send it to me as he's spotted? We really need to find this person."

"I can do that. In fact, a new one just popped up. He's still on Almaden Expressway, heading south. He crossed Curtner Avenue."

Darcy gave Mullins his email and hung up. "Get your stuff, we need to go." He led the way out of the bullpen.

"Where?"

Gayler got up and trotted behind him to catch up.

"I know where Chavo's going next."

"Where?" She repeated.

"If I'm right, he needs to finish what he's started. He's going south," Darcy gloated. "You know who lives South?" He asked, tapping on Quinn's name on the place mat.

"You think he's going after the Sergeant today?"

"Better be there if he does."

They went to the garage, and Gayler directed Darcy toward her car. He was going to have to get another vehicle for work. They got into her beat-up Volvo, and he searched for Quinn's address.

"You really think Chavo's stupid enough to go to Quinn's home?" She asked and turned the ignition on. The car whined, but then started.

"I have no idea, but we have no better place to start."

"We should call him. He may not appreciate us dropping by unannounced."

Darcy thought about his conversation with Sorensen. "I'd rather show up."

Her eyebrows disappeared under her bangs.

"Let's just say Quinn's day hasn't been the best. Trust me, if I tell him we're coming, first he'll laugh, and then he'll leave, and we won't be able to protect him."

They exited the garage and Gayler turned the headlights on. It would be dark soon.

CHAPTER 103

The drone had spotted Chavo getting out of a mobile home close to Lewis Road and into a car. The beauty of the drone software Dominique had designed was that because the cameras caught both the face and the street, Spider was able to tell Oscar that Chavo got into an old brownish Toyota Corolla.

The drone already had the target, but Oscar had enough to get the street crew engaged. He called Matón.

"I want all your guys to sweep the area around Lewis's Mobile Park. Start there and open the grid five miles."

Oscar provided the description of the car and reiterated that he wanted Chavo alive.

"You got it. I'll call as soon as we have something."

"How many guys do you have now?"

"Seventeen."

He wanted to get more, but now wasn't the time. He hung up and passed a car going way too slow on the left lane. He was several miles north from where Chavo was spotted and was eager to get closer.

A patrol car came out of a residential street. He passed it and then checked the rearview mirror. The uniform pulled into the lane next to him, still a few cars behind. Oscar signaled to get into the left lane and then one more over to take the turn. The patrol car shifted to the middle lane, then passed him, going straight. He took the left when the green arrow lit up, then took the first right and another right to get back onto North Capitol Avenue. He let the grip on the wheel loosen, feeling the blood rushing back to his fingers.

He checked his phone, resting on the passenger seat, and wished Pascual were with him. He fought the urge to call him. He wanted his homie there when things got bad, but he knew he couldn't drag him deeper into his mess.

Dr. Dre's "Bang Bang" ringtone filled the car. He smiled, thinking he'd willed Pascual to call.

"What's up?" Oscar asked.

"We spotted the shit stick jumping on Almaden Expressway." It was Matón. "I got two guys with eyes on him."

"Send your best four and have everybody else head south but not get close. Make sure they're not made."

"Already on it."

"Don't spook him." Oscar squeezed the steering wheel again. "Once I catch up with him, I want everyone gone."

He could hear the wind from the open windows coming from Matón's phone.

"Was that clear, or you need hearing aids?" Oscar asked.

"You don't want backup?"

"You find him. I'll take care of the rest."

"Yes, boss," Matón said.

They stopped talking, but both remained on the line so Oscar could get live updates in case Chavo changed course. Oscar decided to chance it and headed toward the highway. Chavo had too great a lead on him.

CHAPTER 104

There'd been no emails from Mrs. Mullins since they'd hung up. Darcy kept checking his phone, as if that would force the messages to pop up.

"The last sighting was still in South San Jose," Gayler said. "If you really think he's going to Gilroy, we need to jump on the highway if you want to get there first. It'll take us forever if we keep to the streets."

He saw the big green sign announcing the ramp onto Highway 85.

"Lynch..."

"Take it."

She accelerated to get ahead of the car next to her and took the exit. She merged onto Highway 85 South. He wondered if they should use the spinners but decided that was overkill. He didn't even know Chavo was in that car—it was just a hunch. Finally, Highway 85 merged into 101 South, a straight shot to Gilroy.

"You really think Chavo will go at Quinn in his home?"

"I have no idea. But my gut tells me he has a hit on Quinn. I think it's a matter of when. Quinn's taking some time off from what I hear. So unless he's gone fishing somewhere, he's most likely going to be at home."

"But how would Chavo know that?"

"How did he know where to find Carol or Matthews?"

She didn't respond. She passed a truck that was going over the speed limit and rushed in between cars until they reached the north end of the town.

"He lives on Miller Avenue," Darcy said, and gave her directions.

Once they got there, he pointed to a rambler toward the middle of the block. The houses were close together, almost hiding behind a line of old oak trees. They drove up and down the street, checking for Chavo's Corolla, but there was no sign of the car.

"Looks like we beat him," Gayler said.

"If he's coming."

Darcy suddenly felt stupid being there.

"Who's the defeatist now?"

Gayler punched Darcy's shoulder. It lifted his mood a smidge.

She parked about three houses north of Quinn's, and they walked under the trees. It was already dark outside. She was about to knock on the door when he stopped her.

"We should do a walk-through first."

Gayler headed toward the back. There was no fence surrounding the house. Darcy watched the street and waited for her to return. He didn't see anything out of the ordinary and still no Corolla. After a few minutes he checked his watch. Gayler was not back, and four minutes was more than enough time to check the perimeter of the house. He waited another two, then called her number. There was no answer.

CHAPTER 105

After a while of driving with no updates, Matón broke the silence to let Oscar know that Chavo had merged onto Highway 85. Oscar accelerated to close the three miles ahead until he could take the same exit. When he finally did, he rushed through, passing several wheels belonging to his guys. After another few minutes he finally spotted the beat-up Corolla.

He accelerated once more and caught up with it, soon passing it. He checked the driver. It was Chavo. He remained ahead for about half a mile, then slowed down to be able to follow him from behind.

"I got him," he told Matón.

"Calling the dogs off."

Oscar was about to hang up when Matón added, "You want me to stay with you just in case you need tag teaming?"

He thought about the offer. If it'd been Pascual, he would have gone for it, but it wasn't.

"I'm good. Tell Pascual I said everybody gets an extra G for the work today."

Matón thanked him and hung up. Oscar felt the wind coming through the open windows and smelled the burnt oil as the car sped behind the Corolla.

Chavo merged onto Highway 101. Oscar wished the worm would get off the highway already. It made him especially uncomfortable that he didn't know where they were headed, and he kind of wished he'd taken Matón's offer.

He reached for his Beretta and set it on the passenger seat. He wasn't going to shoot Chavo while driving. He wanted to have a conversation before he made him cry like the little bitch he was.

CHAPTER 106

Darcy tried Gayler's phone two more times, but it went directly to voice mail. He cursed under his breath, pulled his Glock out of the holster, and followed her steps. The space between the two houses was a few feet wide, and he almost tripped on the weeds growing along the wall. He peeked into the windows as he walked by, but the only thing he saw was his own reflection.

The path finally opened up into a small backyard. Gayler was nowhere in sight. There was a grill and one wicker chair. He kept his body close to the wall and continued walking, until he was less than a foot from the back door. The screen was open. He stood still and listened. There was no music. There were no voices. He heard crickets and tried to tune them out. Where did Gayler go? Why wasn't she answering his calls?

He leaned over to look inside. There was only a dim light coming from the opposite corner of the room. His eye adjusted, and he saw two people. Quinn was sitting, Gayler was standing. He walked in, and Quinn moved the Sig Sauer from his temple to point at Darcy's chest.

Darcy raised his Glock above his head. "What are you doing, Quinn?" he asked.

The kitchen behind Gayler was dark. To her left there was a hallway. Darcy figured it led to the front door. It didn't seem that there was anybody else in the house.

"Why are you here?" Quinn asked back.

"Chavo's after you."

Darcy slowly lowered his Glock but didn't place it in the holster.

"That's what Gayler keeps telling me." Quinn looked at her and pointed the gun back at his temple. "Not bad. Maybe he can do it for me."

"Why do you want to kill yourself?"

Quinn laughed an empty and hollow laugh. It was one of the saddest sounds Darcy had ever heard.

The recliner where he was sitting was faded, and the armrests were shiny from use. There was a low coffee table, most likely from IKEA. The only things on it were an empty bottle of Johnnie Walker Black Label and a tumbler with an inch of liquid still in it.

"Why do you think people want to kill themselves?"

Darcy had a million answers, but none seemed appropriate. He looked at Gayler. She didn't have anything either.

"Come on, Quinn, put the gun down," Darcy said.

He wished he knew the man better so he could try to appeal to anything that was meaningful to the sergeant.

"Go fuck yourself and get the hell out of my house."

"You know we can't do that."

Darcy kept his gun pointing to the ground but started looking around. The living room was sparse. If the furniture had been trendy, Darcy would've pegged Quinn for a minimalist, but it wasn't. The pieces were outdated and didn't match. There was one picture on the wall, the frame slightly tilted to the right. It was hard to make out, but it looked like the Golden Gate Bridge. There was a sofa underneath that looked slept in.

Darcy started walking from the back door deeper into the living room.

"I've seen what you can do when you get close to a subject holding a gun. You stay there, or I'll pull the trigger."

"That was a kid. I would never try that with you," Darcy said.

"Sure. Whatever. Just don't get any closer."

Darcy nodded and looked at Gayler. She was also a bit too far to immobilize Quinn in one move.

"I've had my run-ins with Virago, and I can tell you that she may seem like a hothead, but in the end she's fair and she cares about her people," Darcy said to Quinn.

Quinn snorted. It wasn't a laugh. It was more like the sound of doom.

"Quinn, I'm serious. All you did was to not disclose that you were having a relationship with Carol. Virago's upset about that, but that's no reason to suspend you."

"You think I give a shit about that?" Quinn asked, the Sig still pointing to his temple.

Darcy watched for signs that Quinn's arm was getting tired, but there weren't any. It was steady, the barrel making an indentation on his skin.

Quinn locked eyes with Darcy. "Virago told me to take a few days off. I told her to stuff her CATCH joke up her ass. I never wanted to leave the Gang Suppression Unit. We were a solid team, and she had to come in and mess things up. I wanted nothing to do with you losers. We had Jefe in line to make a huge case and take down the entire Diablos organization. And now all that is gone."

He waved the gun for a second, and Darcy felt his body tense up but tried not to show it.

"Then do this for Carol. Help us find who did this to her and then tell Virago you want out."

Quinn snorted. "Carol." He stared at Darcy. "That woman made a fool of me. I was in love with someone who lied to me for years. She used me so she could misdirect the cases against the Diablos, and I never knew. She had me wrapped around her finger, playing me the whole time, while I thought we were a team, leaving our skins behind to put the bad guys away."

That wasn't how Darcy expected mentioning Carol to go. He should have known better.

"How the hell do you think I can face any of my GSU colleagues after this?" Quinn said. "How could I even look at myself in the mirror?"

CHAPTER 107

Oscar saw Chavo exit Highway 101 and drive into a residential area. He had no idea where they were headed, but it didn't matter. He would follow him straight to hell.

He watched his enemy get out of the car and walk a few yards. He appeared to be looking for the right place. Eventually, he crossed the front lawn of a house. He peered into a window, then went back to the door and tried the knob. It wasn't locked, and he went inside.

Oscar ran after him, his eyes still adjusting to the darkness. He tried the door, and it opened as easily as it had for Chavo. He secured his grip on the Beretta and walked in. His sneakers were soft against the carpet, making his approach as stealthy as it could be.

The hallway was dark, narrow, and bare. He could hear voices, but the sounds were muffled by the overwhelming beating of his own heart.

When he reached the end, he had to stop and steady himself. He could taste the bile coming from his knotted stomach. He forced himself to swallow before he peeked inside.

What he saw once he stepped into the living room made him wonder if he'd drunk something bad and was hallucinating.

CHAPTER 108

Darcy was not a 100 percent sure that Quinn would end it there, with two cops by his side. But he was also not sure he wouldn't. He was about to open his mouth when a figure coming from the hallway startled him. He recognized him right away.

"What the—?" Quinn said.

"Gustavo Buenavente."

Darcy moved the Glock from pointing to the floor to pointing at Chavo's chest. From the corner of his eye he saw Gayler do the same. For a second he felt vindicated for being right. Chavo was here, in Quinn's home.

The gangster continued to approach them, until he was inside the room. He took two steps to the right, his back now protected by the wall. He had one gun in each hand. He looked from Gayler to Darcy and settled on Quinn right before he busted out laughing. He sounded like an injured hyena, and it irked Darcy even more than seeing Quinn with the gun at his temple.

"Put your hands above your head," Gayler said.

"You're responsible for the murder of Montes and the shooting of DDA Matthews." Darcy turned his body sideways toward Chavo and placed his weight on the balls of his feet, ready to fire.

"I just can't believe this shit," Chavo said between chuckles.

Another man emerged from the hallway.

Guero.

Chavo saw him too and took a few steps away from him. Guero's entrance had caught him by surprise, but he was quick to recover, and he immediately pointed one of his guns at him, keeping the other on Quinn.

CHAPTER 109

Once Oscar stepped inside the living room, he realized he wasn't seeing things. There was a man in a recliner, and it only took a second to recognize him. Sergeant Quinn. Oscar'd had too many encounters with him to forget his face. But his brain was trying to work out why Chavo was there, why the sergeant was pointing a gun to his own head, and who the hell the other two people were.

He studied the room. The two unknowns stood forming a ninety-degree angle with the recliner. They were armed and ready. And it was obvious they were cops. There was something about how they stood, how they looked at you, and there was something about how they smelled. It was the adrenaline spewing from their pores.

Chavo was a few feet to his right, just too far for Oscar to be able to grab him. He fought the urge to jump and snap his neck in two. But he knew he would be dead before he touched him. He took a quick step to his left and pointed his Beretta at his enemy.

"What you doin' here?" Oscar asked Chavo.

"I came to off this *puto*," the snake said, waving the gun that was pointing at Quinn. "You know how it is. I got the order from Bullet, so I gotta follow through."

Oscar's question had been mostly rhetorical. He was trying to buy some time to figure out what to do next. He hadn't risked everything to go away empty-handed. Or dead. But there were too many people in this room. He was fast with a gun, but he knew he would not be able to take out the three cops before he got to Chavo.

He'd envisioned taking his time. Making the worm squirm with pain, beg for mercy. Maybe even beg for his life. He'd fantasized about pulling out his fingernails, breaking his limbs, cutting out his tongue.

Chavo was his. Even if Oscar didn't get time to make Chavo suffer like he'd made his mother, at least he would make sure the *joto* didn't walk another day on earth.

But how?

CHAPTER 110

D arcy had expected to see Quinn side with them against the gangsters. But he hadn't. His gun still pressed hard against his head.

Gayler shot a quick glance at Darcy and pointed her gun at Guero, while Darcy kept aiming at Chavo.

"Don't do it, old man. I want to claim the job." Chavo waved the gun he had on Quinn, while the one on Guero didn't move.

Darcy stole a peek at Quinn, but the sergeant didn't look back. He had an amused expression on his face, but the situation wasn't enticing him enough to forget the suicide act. Darcy focused on the two gangsters, acutely aware that his lost eye dramatically impaired his range of vision. He took two steps back so he could keep both gangsters in sight.

"Why are you here?" Chavo asked Guero.

"I'm going to kill you."

Chavo laughed again. "Good luck with that, *puto.*"

Guero tensed, which made him even taller.

"You after me because I had a little fun with your *chola* at Berto's?" Chavo taunted him.

Oscar took a step closer to him, his fingers fanned around the Beretta's grip.

"If you wanted me, why did you kill her?" Guero asked.

"I wasn't after you." Chavo's smirk was unnerving. "I went to the restaurant to kill her. I was surprised to see you there."

Darcy watched Guero. He was taken aback, as if a huge weight had just landed on him.

"You had a green light on my mother?" As soon as Guero said that, he looked over to Quinn. "You were after the Gang Suppression Unit," he said.

Darcy took a second to process what Guero had said, and it seemed that Chavo was doing exactly the same thing.

"*Puto*, that woman was your mother?"

Chavo seemed even more amused with himself.

"Are you fucking kidding me?" Quinn's voice cracked.

"How many people are you going after?" Gayler asked.

Chavo turned slightly toward her. "You think I'm stupid or som'thing?"

"You know you're only getting out of here one of two ways: in a bag or in handcuffs," Darcy managed to say, even though his head was still spinning.

Chavo focused on him. His eyes were shining. Darcy didn't know if it was drugs or amusement.

"I'm gonna tell you how this whole thing's gonna go," Chavo said. "I'm gonna finish the job I came to do and put a bullet in the sergeant before he offs himself. Then, before anybody has time to react, I'm gonna kill Guero. Right as that bullet is entering his heart, I'm going to shoot you, and finally I'll get the lady over there."

Darcy didn't have a good comeback. He quickly checked with Gayler and turned to see if Quinn had finally stopped being a dick and decided to join them against the gangsters. But no such luck. The sergeant was still too full of himself to do anything but keep the gun on his temple.

A rush of fury filled Darcy's chest. He wanted to scream at him to stop being an ass and help them out. There was a very high probability that none of them would make it out alive. He'd hoped Quinn at least cared about that.

He bit his tongue rather than yell at the sergeant, knowing it would only make Chavo feel stronger. Darcy needed to devise a realistic way to save as many people as possible before the night was over.

A blinding light filled the room, followed by the deafening sound of a high-caliber firearm going off. Darcy squinted and blinked a few times until his eye adjusted to the darkness again. His ears were ringing. He saw the two men still standing and Gayler a few feet away. He then turned and saw Quinn's body slumped over the side of the old chair. A good portion of his head was gone, blood with brain matter sprayed over half the living room.

Gayler was still pointing her Glock at Guero. Chavo moved the gun from Quinn to Darcy, still holding the other one on the rival gangster.

"Both of you put your guns down," Darcy yelled.

No one spoke. Gayler took a step toward them. Darcy did the same. As he got closer, Chavo shifted the weight on his feet. Guero didn't move at all.

"Chavo, stop this shit. You can't kill us both before Guero gets you. You're not getting out of here alive if you shoot."

"I never miss," Chavo said.

"But you only have two guns and there are three—"

The sound of another shot deafened Darcy, followed by two more.

He felt a bullet pierce his skin. He dropped on one knee as he fired his weapon until the magazine was empty. From the corner of his eye he saw Gayler kneel, and he hoped she hadn't been hit. He felt relieved when he heard her reload.

He didn't bother. Chavo was on the floor. Guero was leaning against the wall, his T-shirt soaking with sticky blood.

The gun fell from his grip before he slumped down beside his nemesis.

CHAPTER 111

A week later

The hearse made its way out of the mortuary with two coffins inside. Hundreds of patrol cars from at least five agencies followed with their spinners on, but no sirens. Everybody was wearing their dress blues, a black band over each badge.

After the Mass the bagpipes played on the way to the graveyard. The sun was bright and the grass smelled freshly cut. The sea of tombstones spread out to the horizon.

For the final salute the officers brought their hands to the brims of their hats, then slowly moved them down to their side. The priest nodded, and the coffins were lowered into the ground. The only civilians were Quinn's ex-wife, his two adult sons, and Carol's mother.

Darcy didn't go to the wake right away. He knew the Old Wagon Saloon would be bursting with people honoring Carol and Quinn for hours. Nobody would miss him for a while.

After changing into regular clothes, he stopped at the morgue. He knew Madison was working.

"Doctor," he said when he stepped into the autopsy room. "I hope you're going to meet us at the Old Wagon."

"Good afternoon, Detective." The ME's eyes never left the body on his table. "I will. I just wanted to finish this before heading over."

"I understand. See you there," Darcy said, and walked toward the door. Before leaving, he turned and added, "Madison, thank you."

The ME met Darcy's eyes and nodded but didn't speak.

Darcy left to make his second stop. While he walked to the crime lab, he thought about Madison. He hadn't been sure at all that the ME would play ball.

After the shoot-out, Darcy and Gayler made a pact. The story they told Madison when he arrived was that when they got there, Chavo had already shot Quinn. There were no other witnesses who could corroborate or deny the story, and it was as plausible as anything else coming from a gangster with a hit list.

Darcy knew Madison was a superb doctor and he would know better within a second of looking at Quinn's body. So he held his breath, standing by Gayler while the ME did his initial assessment. When the doctor finally stood, he looked at both detectives and pulled his gloves off. Darcy thought he was going to pass out from lack of oxygen.

"I imagine the sergeant was taken by surprise," he had said. "I will do the full autopsy as soon as the body gets to the morgue. I don't expect either of you would be joining me."

The ME had tilted his head and left without another word.

Darcy exhaled and Gayler patted him on the shoulder. The autopsy report followed along the same lines.

Whether the doctor did it out of respect for Quinn or because the case was already closed and there was no reason to mar the sergeant's stellar career, Darcy would never know. He was happy that the ME had ruled it a homicide, and that made things right for Quinn and his family.

A few days after the shootings, Virago had called Darcy into her office. When he arrived, Jon, Sorensen, and Rachel were already there. A minute after Lou showed up and closed the door. Nobody asked about Burundi, and he didn't share any stories.

Virago got straight to the point. "I have briefed Lou on all our findings about Carol."

"I have reviewed every case since Jefe's, and I found no anomalies," Rachel said.

"Are you saying that you don't think she was colluding with the Diablos?" Sorensen said. He looked at Jon, probably thinking about the stats that the intern had pulled together.

"The decline in Diablos-related cases could have been caused by many factors that this department doesn't have the resources to pursue," Lou said out of turn.

Darcy looked at Sorensen. It wasn't for Lou to make that determination.

"You're going to drop it? Am I hearing this right?" Sorensen's voice was too loud for the small office.

Lou opened his mouth, but Virago held up her hand.

"Detective, the crime lab has done their due diligence. Bringing Carol's actions to light would cause every single defense attorney to have cause for opening cases that are closed. Not only would this cost millions, but the publicity would damage the reputation of one of the best crime labs in the country."

"Maybe it should," Sorensen said, and looked at Darcy to see if he would back him up.

Darcy was torn. Opening all those cases would be a nightmare, and the outcome would most likely be the same. But on the other hand, Carol had broken the law, and unless they investigated, they would never be completely sure she only fixed her son's case.

Jon looked down at his hands. He wasn't there to provide his opinion. He was there because he was in on the secret, and whatever decision they made they all had to agree with it.

The argument went on for a while. It got heated, and for a moment Darcy thought Lou and Sorensen would come to blows. But they didn't, and after much discussion Sorensen gave up, and they came out of there with another pact.

Since there was no record of Carol having a baby, or any evidence of her collaborating with the Diablos after the Ochoa case, there was no reason to share this information with anyone outside of the very few who knew about it already. And even if the rechecked evidence corroborated that Jefe didn't kill Ochoa, he was the one who gave the green light for Guero to do it. But since they were both dead, they closed the cases and all hoped that the Gang Suppression Unit would devise another plan to take the Diablos down.

When everybody left Virago's office, Darcy stayed. He told her about Gayler knowing the truth about Carol. The commander almost kicked him out of her office, and he was sure she would have fired him if he'd been reporting to her. But he wasn't, so all she could do was to ask him to make sure the Milpitas detective was in on the pact.

Darcy wasn't worried about Gayler, but he went to see her. Even before he brought up the subject, she said, "Secrets are only secrets when everybody keeps them."

He nodded and then told her about the other pact that involved the rest of CATCH, which she needed to get in on. She acquiesced, and Darcy invited her to the wake at the Old Wagon because he wanted Gayler to meet the rest of the team.

***

The crime lab reception was empty. Darcy knew Mary was at the bar with everyone else. He called Rachel to come and let him in. She appeared a minute later.

"I'm sorry I'm keeping you from the wake," she said, letting him in.

"It'll go on forever. There's no rush."

She led him to her office. Once they were there, she closed the door behind him and said, "I would have never imagined that Carol would..."

"At least Carol wasn't helping the Diablos get away with crime. She just did it once, and it was her long-lost son."

"She did it once, though," Rachel said.

"Hard call."

"We're officers of the law. It's not hard. It's actually very easy. We don't get to pick and choose who gets to go to jail."

Rachel's arthritic hands rested on her lap. She looked so sad.

Darcy knew she was right. Of course she was. But...

"I'm sorry," he said. "I know you were friends."

Rachel swiveled her chair toward him. For the first time they were at eye level.

"I've known Carol for many years. I never knew. I thought I was good at reading people, and for all this time I've been working with a dirty lab technician who could have compromised thousands of cases."

"But she didn't. She only did the one that saved her son from a life in prison."

"That he deserved."

"That he deserved," Darcy agreed.

He was surprised that she didn't show more sympathy for a woman who had thought her son died after birth and found him years later, when his life had already been set. At the same time he felt hypocritical for feeling pity for Carol while being so determined to prosecute Samantha Lee for aiding Nhu Tran evade court.

Rachel took the headphones out of her lab coat pocket and stuffed them in her purse.

"We could have had defense attorneys question every case she's ever worked on, potentially leading to a bunch of criminals being let back onto the streets."

Darcy stood. He didn't want to tower over Rachel, so he took a few steps toward the door while she finished getting ready.

"But it won't," he said. "We made an agreement, and this is the end of it. You need to let it go."

Rachel looked up at him and very slowly shook her head. "I don't know if that makes us any better than her." She put on her jacket and grabbed her purse. "You're driving."

Darcy jingled his keys.

Neither said much on the ride to San Pedro Square. The Cobra was loud, but Rachel seemed to enjoy the air tossing her hair. Darcy parked across the street on the second floor, and they both walked together into the bar. It was incredibly crowded, and they had to push their way through different groups of people to find their colleagues.

It looked like there were hundreds of officers and lab coats who'd come to give their respects to Quinn and Carol. They both deserved it. At that moment Darcy realized he wasn't sorry about the pacts they had made to keep their names honorable.

The alcohol was flowing freely, and there were already a few people who'd had too much to drink.

"I was wondering if you were going to make it," Sorensen said when he saw Darcy. "Rachel, I'm glad you came too."

"Wouldn't miss it," she said, and took the chilled glass of Chardonnay from Darcy's hand.

Sorensen ordered another round and led the newcomers to where they were sitting. As soon as they reached them, Sorensen asked, "So, Commander, is Lynch going to be our new addition to the task force, since Quinn won't be vetoing him anymore?"

"Detective!" Virago said, her voice matching the disgust she felt for his lack of manners.

But Darcy detected a trace of resentment. He met her eyes. They were black and, at least this time, she didn't have mascara smeared around them. She didn't blink. He looked away. She was still mad at him for telling Gayler. He wondered if it would pass, like the other times she'd been mad at him, or if this would scar their relationship forever.

"I call it as I see it," Sorensen said, ignoring their silent exchange.

"Let's raise a glass for Quinn and Carol," Rachel said.

They all did. When no one added anything more, Sorensen said, "Bottoms up."

Darcy felt the alcohol burn as it went down. He turned to look around at the crowd and spotted his brother-in-law. Damon motioned for him to meet him at the back patio. Darcy excused himself and was relieved to be breathing fresh air.

"This may not be the right moment to bring it up, but I want you to consider leading the homicide unit at the SO," the sheriff said.

Darcy was glad they were walking side by side. His expression of disbelief would have amused his brother-in-law a bit too much, and he wasn't in the mood to grant him that.

"That's insane. I'm far from qualified."

"Have you met Howard?" Damon said.

Darcy laughed, then brushed his hair.

"Think about it. Tell me on Monday."

His brother-in-law extended his hand. Darcy shook it, and the man walked away.

"You okay? You look white as a ghost." It was Gayler. She'd got into the restaurant through the patio's gate. "It's not the wound, right? That was only superficial."

"Yeah, that was nothing."

Darcy touched his side. The bullet had only grazed his skin. It'd been true what Chavo said, that he never missed, but at least he hadn't been as good as he claimed.

"I still relive that night every time I close my eyes," Gayler said.

He did too.

"I can't believe we made it out alive."

"Guero went there to avenge his mother. In a way I'm glad he got it." Her aviator glasses had a smear on the right lens.

"Let me get you a drink and introduce you to the crew."

She nodded and they walked in.

Darcy thought about the two open spots Virago had in CATCH. Maybe he could help fill at least one, killing two birds with one stone.

THE END

440

ABOUT THE AUTHOR

ELIN BARNES, a native Spaniard, moved to America to become a pilot. When her eyesight prevented her from flying passenger aircrafts, she obtained a BA in Philosophy, worked for a criminal appeals lawyer, and earned an MA in International Commerce. Finally settling in Silicon Valley, she's worked for companies such as, AT&T, T-Mobile, Google, Microsoft, TiVo, Samsung, and Apple. Her love for technology and the great weather keep her in the Bay Area with her dog Shelby.

Connect with me online:

http://www.elinbarnes.com

https://wwwfacebook.com/ElinBarnesAuthor/

http://www.goodreads.com/author/show/7390354.Elin Barnes

If you enjoyed reading Blood Allegiance, I would appreciate it if you recommend it to others, so they can enjoy it too:

Lend it - This book is lending-enabled, so you can share it with a friend.

Recommend it - Please help other readers find this book by recommending it to friends, readers' groups, and discussion boards.

Review it - Please tell other readers why you liked this book by reviewing it.

ACKNOWLDEGEMENTS

Anthony Kilmer—Thank you for teaching me so much about the San Jose Norteños and Sureños gangs. Thank you for the ride-alongs and for always being available to answer my many questions.

Bruce Wiley—Thank you for taking me under your wing. Thank you for spending so much time teaching me about how the Crime Lab and the CSIs work and so many other things about the SJPD and the Santa Clara Prosecutor's Office. I took some literary liberties in the story regarding CSI, and I apologize for that. Thank you for making all the arrangements so I could go to the CSI convention in Reno. I learned a lot there and got great ideas for future books. Thank you for reading the first version of this book and for working out the issues with it and for coming up with different possible options to make it more realistic. Thank you for never giving up on me. Thank you for your friendship and for introducing me to Irish Whiskey and everybody at West Coast Cigars. It is always a pleasure to hang out with everyone there!

Chris Sweeney—Thank you for all the information about Task Forces: how they are formed, how they are structured, and how they operate. This was incredibly important for this book and for the series, and I really appreciated your knowledge and insights. Thank you for taking me on a ride along and for sharing many of your experiences in law enforcement and as a best-selling author.

Christina—Thank you for the feedback on the earlier stages of the book, which helped me make it better.

Daniel Ichige Hideaki—Thank you for brainstorming different scenarios about motives and actions for my characters. Thank you for all the insight into your work and your experiences, and for always answering my questions. Thank you for being a speaker at our Sisters in Crime NorCal event.

Daniel Pfiefer—Thank you for taking me on a ride along and for providing so much information about the San Jose gangs. Thank you for taking me into gang territory and for letting me ask you millions of questions.

David Miranda—Thank you for providing me feedback in earlier versions of the book, which helped me make it better.

Eli Jackson—Thank you for taking the time to review my fight scenes. It was unreal how much more vivid they became after I incorporated your suggestions. Thank you also for teaching us so many great moves at the SWAT Academy 2016.

G. F.—Thank you so much for giving me a ride in your Shelby Cobra. It was an incredible experience and it made me able to write about Darcy's car in a much more realistic way. Also, thank you teaching me things about the Cobras that I probably would have never thought about (like how you are supposed to get in and out!).

G. W. and brother—Thank you for coming up with that long list of gang monikers, so I could make the names in my book much more realistic. Also, thank you for all the information about the Department of Corrections.

Gunilla Medina—Thank you so much for reading my book, thank you for all the insights that made it better. Also, thank you for being so encouraging, even though you got to read a fairly early (and raw) version!

Jack Zowin, Frances and Michael—Thank you for reading a draft of my book and for always being so supportive. Also, thank you for inviting me to join you for dinner so many times to enjoy Frances' awesome home cooking!

Jake H—Thank you for helping me with all of the car stuff (I so needed it!) and for setting up the Cobra ride.

Jarrod Valdez—Thank you for the ride-along and for inviting me to the courthouse so I could see a direct and cross examination in real life. Thank you for all the knowledge you shared with me and for your valuable experiences and insights.

Jemmy—Thank you for reading my book, for being so supportive and for always helping me to make it better.

Jim Lee—Thank you for taking the time to teach me so much about drones. Thank you for sharing what could be done and what would be science fiction. I did take some literary liberties, but I hope I still made it realistic enough.

John Marfia—The list to thank you for is endless. Thank you for always helping me with my research craziness. Thank you for introducing me to all the key people to interview and learn from and thank you for setting me up on the most amazing ride-alongs. Thank you for always answering my never-ending questions, even at crazy hours (I'll try to keep in mind that you work days now). And thank you for connecting me to your amazing wife Jodi, who always supports me and encourages me to write more.

Judge D. P.—Thank you so much for all the information you shared on how trials, juries and the judicial system operate. Thank you for providing a sanity check on how some judicial proceedings work and thank you for letting me visit your courtroom and your chambers so I could see what they really look like in Santa Clara.

Kelly Jacklin—Thank you for your feedback on my draft, for the insight into drones and all your other feedback on writing.

Killer Retreat—Thank you, Aline, Christine, Helen and Mary. I cannot tell you how much your support, your feedback, your help with brainstorming characters and plots, and your knowledge about writing fiction and the English language has helped me with this book. I learn so much from all of you and I can't thank you enough for your friendship, encouragement, and support through the entire process that is writing a book and in life! I wish you all incredible success with your own novels.

Marcus Trower—Thank you for the rounds and rounds of copyediting you do. I know it feels like it never ends, but I don't know what I would do without your help! Thank you for keeping my English straight and for not giving up on me when I can't get the dialogue grammar rules straight!

Jaime Levine—I still cringe when I remember how many things you marked-up in my first version. Your feedback on the story, the characters, motivations, pace, etc, etc was immensely valuable and the story is a lot stronger and I am a much better writer after working with you. Thank you!

Mark Nelson—You read my very rough, rough stuff. I don't know how you do it! Thank you for meeting me weekend after weekend at the coffee shop to write, for making me continue, and for giving me ideas and encouragement when I'm about to give up! My books would not be the same without your endless help.

Matt Croucher—Thank you for taking me on multiple ride-alongs and thank you for giving me the idea about this book. I think it worked out much better than the one I originally had. Thank you also for giving me so much insight into the gang culture.

Mike Ceballos—Thank for the many ride-alongs. Thank you for giving me the intro to the CA gangs, for taking me to see tagging and for explaining how the territories, the culture, and the hierarchy work.

Mike White—Thank you for all the intel on gangs. Thank you for reading the sections of the book where law enforcement interacts with gangs and helping me make them more realistic. Thank you teaching me how gangs talk and how they think, what motivates them and why they do what they do. Thank you for answering all of my questions, the billions of them, and for giving me so many ideas. Thank you so much for helping me with my research in ways I would have never been able to do without your help.

Mom—Thank you for being the best mom in the world. Thank you for keeping me sane, for reading every word I write (multiple times) and for always encouraging me to keep going. Thank you for the million brainstorming sessions, for giving me great ideas, for catching things that don't work or flow with the story and for helping me come up with better ones. Thank you for being with me every step of the way. I certainly could not do this without you!

Patrick Smith—Thank you for the amazing tag line. These are always the hardest to do for me and you came up with a brilliant one in a second! You are awesome!

S. P. and W. L.—Thank you for the great ride along. It was incredibly helpful to see how two officers work together. Thank you for letting me talk to the gangster. The insight I got into the life by interviewing someone who had belong to a gang and had been shot in the head for trying to get out was absolutely invaluable.

Sisters in Crime—Thank you for being such an amazing organization. Your support and encouragement are endless. I am honored to be part of this family.

SWAT Academy 2016—The incredible experience that you provided to all of us is beyond words. Every activity and every class kept playing in my head, especially as I reviewed the book, realizing what things I had to change and what things were okay to keep. I learned so much in those three days. Thank you!

Ted Smits—Thank you for reading my draft and for always being honest with the good and the bad. Thank you for believing in me.

ThrillerFest—Eight years running and I hope there will be many more. Pretty much everything I know about writing I learned it at ThrillerFest! I would not be here if it wasn't for the ITW Organization and the Thrillerfest Conference. Thank you!

XXXXX—Thanks to all of you who preferred to remain anonymous. Thank you for all the time you spent with me, helping me understand your world. Thank you for the contacts you provided and thank you for answering all of my questions. This book would definitely not be the same without all of you.

56248828R00275

Made in the USA
San Bernardino, CA
10 November 2017